"It's good to see you, Lo," I whis...

As if a spell has been broken, Lo pulls away, his eyes ...
a fraction in frustration as he struggles to remember. "So you're
Nerissa? Bertha told me that we were friends."

"Friends," I repeat, hearing my own voice break slightly on the word.

"We went to school together, right? Dover?"

I swallow hot bile at his nervous recitation. Even prepared, his
reaction comes as a shock. I don't even want to look at Bertha or
Grayer, or even Echlios. I don't want to see the expressions on their
faces. Instead I smile through trembling cheeks and watery eyes.
"Yes. We met at Dover. You don't remember me at all?"

The look in his eyes is tortured, as if he's struggling to place me in
his head. "There's a part of me that feels like it does know you,"
he says, gesturing to his chest. "But I can't remember it here." His
fingers jerk to his head and then flutter to his sides in a defeated
motion. "I'm sorry."

Praise for Amalie Howard and *Waterfell*, book 1 of The Aquarathi

"Howard has crafted a page-turning blend of magical realism
and fantasy.... Plot shifts, surprises, and a love affair not yet fully
realized sets readers up for the second in the fascinating trilogy."
—*Booklist*

"A fantastical surf-and-turf romance."
—*Kirkus Reviews*

"Exhilarating, romantic, and totally unique,
Waterfell is an absolute page-turner!"
—Kristi Cook, *New York Times* bestselling author
of the Winterhaven series

Books by Amalie Howard
available from Harlequin TEEN

The Aquarathi

(in reading order)

WATERFELL
OCEANBORN

OCEANBORN

AMALIE HOWARD

HARLEQUIN®TEEN

Recycling programs
for this product may
not exist in your area.

ISBN-13: 978-0-373-21125-8

OCEANBORN

Copyright © 2014 by Amalie Howard

Printed in U.S.A.

For my brothers, Gian Kris and Givan Kyle, who are the true ninjas.

Roll on, thou deep and dark blue Ocean—roll!
Ten thousand fleets sweep over thee in vain;
Man marks the earth with ruin—his control
Stops with the shore.

—Lord Byron

1

Glory and Pain

We are savage. We are proud. We are the dark rulers of the sea.

Deep in the ocean near the earth's core, I survey the Aquarathi people—a firestorm of color—as the four courts pay homage to their new queen. Closest to me, the Gold Court stands quietly proud. The Sapphire Court is flamboyant in their tribute. The Emerald Court, more demure. But the Ruby Court, I watch with silent, cautious eyes. Months before, they supported a rival queen in her bid against the High Court, and she almost won.

Almost.

The great hall of Waterfell is deep and cavernous, with cobbled golden stalactites and stalagmites spanning its entire length to meet in the middle like majestic columns. In the human world, I learned about the marble pillars of the ancient Greeks. Ours remind me of the pictures I saw of theirs, only the ones around me are far older and more forbidding. The floor glitters with all manner of earthly minerals, reflecting off our bodies like prisms.

Today we celebrate my coronation as heir to the High

Court. In Aquarathi society, it's a pivotal milestone, one made even more momentous by the fact that my father—the last king—is dead. If he were alive, years from now he would be the one to transfer the proverbial baton to me. The endorsement from one ruler to another is a vital piece of our tradition. An Aquarathi coronation isn't the same as humans might expect from what they know of royalty in the media, but power is passed from the old monarch to the new one in a ritual that's just as significant.

Aivana, which translates into the human language as *beautiful flower,* refers to an ancient Aquarathi practice. Like Sanctum, it is a gift born to those of royal blood. In our world, when kings or queens die, they can bequeath their power, should they so choose, to a next of kin. Aivana is not only a transfer of Aquarathi energy from one ruler to the next; it's a transfer of trust—a blessing of sorts from the old to the new.

In a parallel world, my father would be alive and standing at my side. I can picture his face, silvery blue and radiant with pride. Everyone would watch with bated breath as he touched his nose to mine and bent his forehead to rest directly upon my brow. We would both glow so brightly that the light would extinguish all colors save ours. Together, we would bestow Sanctum—an ancient Aquarathi practice used by royals to strengthen our people—to everyone in the room, reminding them of our strength *and* our love. Eventually his bioluminescence would fade, merging into mine and signaling the rise of a new ruler.

But my father isn't here, and there's no one to pass along a crown to make this any easier or to make the Aquarathi immediately accept me. I am alone. And I am already a queen. My coronation is but an afterthought. My people watch me in expectant silence, crowding into the great hall of Water-fell like silent luminescent candles flickering in a body of water. A shiver winds through me as I study their faces—my fledgling rule has already raised questions *and* a near-royal coup. I've had to earn their approval. I still have to.

I wish I were back in La Jolla.

The thought is errant. And cowardly. I am Aquarathi, not human. And I belong here. I *know* that. But the truth is, I miss being human—playing hockey and surfing, lunches in the quad, hanging out with my best friend, Jenna. *Being* human. But I'm not just a girl. I'm part of an alien marine species living on this planet, and my place is in the ocean, not landside.

I almost smile, remembering snippets of a conversation I had with Jenna during one of our sunny lunches in the Dover Prep courtyard, a couple weeks after I'd revealed what I was to her.

"So, do you live in a giant underwater castle? You know, like Ariel?"

I snorted soda through my nose at the Disney reference. "Um, no. There are no underwater castles in the ocean, Jenna, and I definitely don't sit on rocks grooming my hair in the sunlight waiting to be rescued by Prince Eric…even though he is kind of dreamy."

Jenna grinned. "Well, now that you've gone and dashed all my childhood ideals, enlighten me."

"Disney version or Jeopardy *version?"*

"Jeopardy."

"We live in underwater caves. We hunt, we sleep, we reproduce and we work. As a species, think of us as a cross between whales, dolphins and wolves. No castles, no tea parties, just the occasional sushi brunch. We're just like any other sea creature living in pods… pretty boring really."

"Don't you have an economic or political structure?"

"An economy of what? Trading in plankton? Our political structure is divided into four courts, as you know, with one high court. Unlike most humans," I said with a grin, *"we are a very simple species."*

"I don't get it. I mean, you're so evolved. Intelligent."

"Why? Intelligence is measured in different ways, not necessarily according to human standards or human categories. For us, it's about self-awareness. We exist within the parameters of our world, within our social and cultural structures, living as one with the environment. We don't belong up here, involved in politics and MTV and wireless Internet. A killer whale doesn't just get up and say, 'I want to play some video games and maybe try using a fork,' and neither would any Aquarathi. It doesn't make us any less intelligent."

"Yes, but you can transform to be like us. Human."

"Not all of us. Most Aquarathi can only exist in human form if they're in close proximity to me. It's not our natural state."

She stared at me as if I were an imbecile missing the big picture. *"Still, for argument's sake, think of what you could do if you did—I mean you could be a part of the government instead of working policy change from the sidelines. You could make sure we don't do anything to jeopardize your species. You could play an active part. I mean, more than you already do in secret, and you wouldn't have to hide."*

"If the humans knew about us, it would lead to worse things, Jenna."

She was so passionate, and what she said was partially true. We could make ourselves known. But what would stop us from seizing control and overpowering the humans if they didn't like our ways? It would be easy, with all of our abilities. After all, that was what Ehmora wanted. She wanted to control people so that this planet wouldn't face the same brutal end that Sana, our home planet, faced at the hands of the hominids there.

But that wasn't what my father wanted. And it's not what I want. There are always going to be those who think we are a stronger and smarter species—those like Ehmora who would view humans as less than. Those are the few who won't be happy coexisting. Eventually the humans would grow to fear us and we'd end up in the same place that Sana did—in an interspecies war. No, it's better that we live in secret, affecting change from the sidelines, as we have done for millennia.

And now it's my turn to take the reins.

My eyes flick to the restless Ruby Court. Those Aquarathi have been the slowest to accept my rule over the past few weeks, especially after the death of their leader. But I beat Ehmora on the sands of battle, and their allegiance has been sworn, if not truly won. I'm still working on that. Some of them still support what Ehmora was fighting for, and they're the dangerous ones…stirring seeds of malcontent.

I take a breath and close my eyes. On cue, the crown of bones on my brow pushes forward like a fan of finely webbed coral. I center myself, feeling my core connect with the heart of Waterfell—and the beating hearts of all the Aquarathi within it—until we are one and the same. I am a daughter of the old kings and a mother of the new. Every living creature in this room is tied to me. I exhale, and the whispered breath ripples across the hall from body to body, heart to heart. I open my eyes—the glow in the room is almost blinding, a tumultuous kaleidoscope like the northern lights in Earth's sky.

Echlios, my Handler and captain of my royal guard, moves forward to stand beside me, his body rigid. I can see the approval flashing in his bright silver eyes. He nods and arches his long neck, his dark red scales glittering, as he bares it to me in a gesture of submission. Golden-green lights shimmer down the length of my body, mirroring the deep ruby of his, and I click fiercely in my native tongue to my people, calling water-to-water and blood-to-blood.

My water is yours as yours is mine, I tell them, whispering the oaths I would have sworn to my father. Power ripples along my spine, making my golden colors flare so brightly that every finned head dips in deferent succession—gold to green to blue, and finally to red in a wave of reluctant molten crimson.

I must rule by strength now. Not just by love.

Trust is a luxury, and the time for compassion in Waterfell has come and gone. Ehmora planted dark seeds of doubt and confusion. If I don't control my people, all of the humans will be at risk. And everything my father fought and died for will be for nothing. I can never let that happen, even more so now that I am bonded to a hybrid—a half-human, half-Aquarathi prince.

I arch my neck, my tail curling through the water…and freeze as a violent wave of pain crashes into me like a rogue tsunami, destroying everything in its path. Lo's name reverberates like a hammer in my brain as if the sharp thought of him has summoned his consciousness to me in full force. My lights flutter and die. I can feel the startled pulses and the clicks of the courts, but I can't focus on them.

All I know is Lo's pain…a deep, shattering, all-consuming pain, as if a thousand blades are carving my body at once. The navy swirls on my flanks—Lo's marks—deepen like ink, sinking into me with scorching pressure. Everything disappears and I feel only the pull of the bond…and the one on the other side of the bond…calling to me.

And in that moment, I know. The threat isn't here.

It's *there*.

In seconds, Echlios is glued to my side, the rest of his guards surrounding us in a protective circle. "My lady, what is it?"

"Lo," I gasp. "Something's wrong. He's hurt."

"I'll go."

"No," I insist, nearly doubling over. "The coronation—"

"Can wait."

I shake my head, feeling my ties to the Aquarathi start to fade. I swallow. "This is too important."

Echlios nods, but I can see the uncertainty flicker across his face. Because of the bond with Lo, I am vulnerable, and if Lo is hurt, I can be, too. Echlios's mate, Soren, joins us, her eyes flashing gold fire. As my Handler, she is so in tune with me that she has felt the fear I'm now trying desperately to conceal.

Her voice is gentle, as is the pale green tail fin circling me in a protective manner. "Breathe, Nerissa. Try deep calming breaths. It will help with the pain. Echlios will go. It is his duty to protect you…*and* the prince regent."

I do as she says, letting the salt water enter through my gills and breathing out the sharp, pulsing pain until it becomes a dull throb. Nodding weakly to Echlios, I watch as Soren dismisses the courts that have come to pay their respects to the new queen. I don't know what they're saying, but I have to imagine that seeing their new ruler in an incapacitated state on the first day of her coronation has to be cause for concern. Still, that anxiety pales in comparison to the urge I feel to take off in a sprint for the mainland in response to the pull of the bond.

"I need a minute," I pulse to Soren as another wave of dizziness overcomes me.

"Go. I'll convene the High Council," she says to me and then frowns, her eyes narrowing in concern. "Not too far, Nerissa."

I nod and make my way out of the throne room and into the tunnels beyond. There are two silent black forms behind me—Nova and Nell—twins and two of my royal guard that I'm aching to get rid of. They're young but fierce—Echlios thought our closeness in age would make me less uncomfortable with having permanent shadows glued to my every move. I didn't mind, until now.

"Stay here," I click to the twins at the tunnel's exit. "I'm going to be right over there."

I swim away from Waterfell with a few short, powerful strokes, but stay within watching distance of the two guards. Their forms are indistinct, cloudy shapes, which means they can still see me and that's all that matters. I close my eyes and stay perfectly still, clearing my mind of everything but the feel of the water against my skin and the soft muted sounds of ocean life around me. I let the sea do what it does best—heal.

For a heartbeat, floating in a sea of space and nothing, it's easy to imagine that I live in a world where everything is different. That my parents are alive and together. That my father is here to watch my coronation with pride. That the one who has my heart isn't a million miles away…and that he hasn't been hurt, or worse.

Lo…the prince regent. My mate.

We are bonded for life, bound by an unbreakable tie. We

belong to each other in a way that only lovers can know. My gaze falls on the bands of navy shimmering through my golden-green scales—the marks of our bonding—and green bioluminescent lights tingle along my sides in automatic response. Fighting another wave of panic, I try to push the thought of him—and the thought of his blue-black eyes, so like the shadowy darkness of the ocean surrounding me—from my mind, but it's like trying to separate my skin from my body. Every breath I inhale, he inhales with me. As if in response, the tug from before becomes more insistent, less painful now but still sharp. I can only hope that Echlios finds him safe.

Drifting deeper into the deep blue coldness, I don't resist as the current drags my body with insistent force. I'm not afraid. I can handle the ocean at its worst, control it even, but I let it take me, enjoying the feel of not having to be strong for just a moment. I don't care that I've lost sight of my two guards or that the dim lights of Waterfell have faded. There's nothing around me but pitch-black murky gloom. I'm the deadliest predator out here, so it's not like I have anything to fear—especially with Ehmora dead and her allies in hiding. Those Echlios hunted down either swore fealty to me or were executed.

Inexorably, my thoughts return to Lo, the son of the very one who tried to usurp my throne. Ehmora's son. Sure, he killed her—for me—but our relationship is still delicate at best, and even at the core, a lifelong genetic bond wouldn't be the only thing that would hold me to him. At first, being with Lo was an act of defiance and desperation on my part. I wanted to be close to someone, to forget for a while what I was and pretend to be a human girl. But that one moment cost me so much. I bonded myself to the son of my enemy.

"Planning to drift to China?"

The unexpected voice jerks me out of my thoughts. Speio, the son of Soren and Echlios, is both my oldest friend in the world and, without a doubt, the biggest thorn in my side. I eye him, watching the tense way he's swimming toward me. His body is slender and pale gold like his mother's, with luminous green fins spanning his entire length. While the look in his eyes isn't exactly aggressive, the slow sideways motion of his body is. "Do you have any idea how far out you are?"

"No," I say truthfully. "I lost track."

Speio bares his teeth in borderline disrespect. "Everyone's on high alert because of what happened. The least you can do is stay with your guards."

"Since when do you care, Speio?"

Speio's resentment toward me was no secret while we lived on land—after all, he was landlocked after Dvija and coming of age. Which, in his own words, was a punishment worse than death. His baser instincts made him stupidly trust Ehmora and basically hand-deliver me to her on a platter. While I forgave him for his temporary lunacy, trust is a harder thing to regain.

"I care if you get hurt. Or if Lo is hurt."

I stare at him sharply. "What do you know about Lo?"

"I know more than you think," he says. I'm too drained to rise to the bait, so instead I start the swim back to Waterfell, the water in my body guiding me there. Speio follows. "You sure you don't want to know?"

"Know what, Speio?"

"I followed my father to La Jolla and I talked to Cara."

Cara? My archnemesis whom he hooked up with before we left California?

"That's weird. I thought you were done with the humans and you couldn't wait to come back home," I say.

Speio shoots me an exasperated stare. "Doesn't mean I don't want to keep myself in the loop, especially with the threat of hybrids running around."

This time he has my attention. "What did you say?"

"You heard me. Hybrids," he says. "What did you think, Riss? That they were just going to go away now that you've returned to your rightful place hidden in the deep? Ehmora's minions still want to take over the world. All you've done by getting rid of one of their leaders is slow them down."

I frown. "But Echlios says we haven't seen any hybrids in weeks. And what does Cara have to do with any of that? She's human. She doesn't even know what we are."

"That doesn't mean more of them don't exist," Speio says. "We have to be careful. And Cara's been hanging out with Lo this summer." I try to ignore the stab of jealousy those words cause in the pit of my stomach, but it's a losing battle. I can picture Cara's toned form in a swimsuit and imagine exactly what *hanging out* with Lo means. Speio grins, obviously enjoying my discomfort.

I swipe a clawed forearm at him. "You are the worst friend in the world, you know that? So, what did Cara say? And what did you tell her, by the way? That you were just dropping in from the other side of the world?"

"Um, Lo's bonded to you, Riss. It's not like he's going to go chasing after someone else," he says with a knowing look at my suddenly savage tone. "Calm down. Cara just thinks I was visiting from Los Angeles. Plus, Lo has been a perfectly well-behaved boy, if you must know. No hook-ups, not even with Cara," he clarifies with a very human-looking eye roll. "He's been surfing and working at the Marine Center all summer."

Even though I'm telling myself that I wasn't worried about what Lo was doing, I can't help the immediate relief that sweeps through me. I told him he had to find himself, and I didn't put any rules around what that should be. Any normal boy would have taken that as permission to play the field and have fun. Then again, Lo isn't any normal boy.

"Anyway…" Speio continues. Something flashes in his eyes before it's hidden. I gesture at him to continue. "Cara mentioned that Lo's been getting sick."

"*Sick?* What kind of sick?"

"Kevin at the center said that he passed out a couple times over the past few weeks. He told them it was dehydration, but last week he passed out again in front of a bunch of people on the beach. They called 911."

"Did they take him to a hospital?" I ask quickly, even though I know that it would have been all over the news and would have filtered to us in a heartbeat. I can see the head-lines now—Alien Species Discovered. They Walk Among Us! San Diego would be the next Roswell, New Mexico.

"No, Jenna was there. She told the paramedics that he's a diabetic and had low blood sugar. Don't ask me how that girl proved it, but she did. Anyway, Cara said that Lo went home with Jenna. That was last week."

"But I didn't feel anything those other times," I say. "Via the bond, I mean."

"That's what happened this morning?"

"Yes. It was bad, Speio, like I was being gutted from nose to tail. It was so strong I could barely handle it. It felt…wrong."

Speio leans his body into mine in a comforting gesture.

"He'll be okay, Riss," he says slowly with an uncertain look at me. "Look, I know things between us haven't been great, and I know that's my fault. I know you don't trust me. But I care about you, and I care about Lo."

"You hate Lo."

"I don't hate Lo," Speio says as we swim past a row of unfamiliar underwater mountains. I must have drifted farther than I'd expected. "I thought that he was hiding something, and he was. But now, well, he's a part of you...so that means he's a part of us." Speio stops, considering his words. "And if something happens to him, that's going to be bad for everyone here, right?"

"Nothing bad's going to happen to Lo," I say swiftly, just as I feel the pull of home. We're nearly back.

"No, you're right," he says. "Riss?"

"What?"

"I want you know that I'm here no matter what. I mean, I know you don't trust me and you have every right not to, but if we have to go back for Lo, then I'll go back with you, okay?"

"What about finding your mate here in Waterfell?" I ask. "It's what you've always wanted."

Speio shrugs, another humanlike gesture that almost makes me smile. "It's what I thought I wanted because I couldn't have it when we lived on the mainland. But turns out, just because we're home doesn't mean that I'm going to bond with someone. Plus, I miss skateboarding. And surfing. And our friends. And believe it or not, a part of me wishes that I could finish my senior year at Dover." He stares at me, his eyes vulnerable. "Too human?"

"Not at all," I admit, floored by his candid admissions. "I feel like that, too. I miss Jenna and Sawyer. I even miss

Cara sometimes." Cara...said archnemesis who'd had her eye on Lo and had been determined to banish me to hell when she realized that we were a couple. She even hooked up with Speio to get back at me. I grin. "But only on very special occasions."

Speio eyes Nova and Nell, who don't know whether to be annoyed at my disappearing act or relieved that I've returned before they got flayed alive by Echlios for letting me out of their sight in the first place. "You looked really good up there today, Riss," he says so softly that I can hardly hear him. "Like a real queen. Your father would have been proud."

"Thanks," I say, startled.

But Speio is already swimming away. It's more words than we've spoken in months, and I realize that I've missed him. I think back to what he said about Lo and frown. Dehydration is a common affliction for our species, particularly because of the combination of water and salt in our bodies. But Lo is a hybrid, which means that he should be able to tolerate it better than we can. Or maybe it's the reverse.

The way Echlios explained it, Lo is the best of both worlds—an Aquarathi with transmuted human DNA that allows him to live comfortably on land or in the sea. He is the product of accelerated evolution based on the laws of natural selection...accelerated because his mother and her cronies induced those genetic characteristics. We faced and fought others that looked like hideous mutations, hybrids that Ehmora, my mother and the brilliant genetic-scientist ex-headmaster of Dover Prep had concocted. As far as we know, Lo is the only perfect hybrid in existence. But maybe he isn't perfect. Maybe he's flawed in some terminal, human way.

The furious outward rush of breath leaves me weak. Lo can't be sick. He can't be. He's meant to be with me. All of a sudden, those countless arguments I had with myself about leaving him behind become meaningless. The only thing I can think about is Lo and figuring out what's wrong with him…figuring out how I can save him. Because I did this. It's my fault. The guilt is nearly suffocating. Maybe if I hadn't been so selfish about keeping us apart, things would be different. He would be happy and healthy, here with me where he belongs. Instead I'm going to lose him.

"Soren," I pulse, entering the core of the High Court. The Aquarathi in the chamber clear out, their heads bowed. I can sense the underlying tension, and a certainty that something isn't quite right floods my body. I try not to let the fear invade my head, but it does, like insidious ink. "Any news?" I ask her. "Is Echlios back?"

"Yes, there's news, and no, Echlios is not back," she says slowly. I can feel her sadness in the water rushing around in her body. I can see it in the shimmer of her melting green eyes.

"What is it? Is Lo okay?"

"Nerissa…"

Heaven help me, I already know what she's going to say. I want to shake her, to smash my head into her side. I want to scream my fear and shed it from the inside of my skin. Instead I pull on a composed mask and deaden the emotion running rampant within me. "Just *say* it, Soren. Tell me. I can handle it, I promise."

But I can't handle it at all, not when her lips shape the words that make my bones thin to air and my heart crumble into unrecognizable fragments. "It's not good. He's dying."

2

Impossible Choices

The faces of the six members of the Aquarathi High Council could be hewn from calcified rock. The lower-court kings and queens have already been briefed on the situation—I can see their varying reactions in the tilt of their heads and the rigid stance of their bodies. Their royal guards, including mine, the ever-present Nova and Nell, line the rear of the hall in a silent, ominous row.

Soren calls the meeting to order—she's acting in Echlios's stead since he's still landside. I swallow hard and bury my grief deep. I greet each of the High Council in turn, all of them baring their necks to me in respectful deference—Queen Miral and her consort, Hevan, from the Gold Court, Queen Castia from Emerald, King Verren and Queen Aylis from Sapphire, and lastly, Keil, the new king of the Ruby Court.

I watch him surreptitiously as he takes his place in the circle. Keil, Ehmora's cousin, is young but ambitious. He's probably the only other Aquarathi on this council who's around the same age as me. As if reading my thoughts, he winks at me and I blink, startled at the familiarity. I remember training with him when we were young, and have several memories of him being rebellious and funny, but it's not like we've seen each other a lot since then, nor is he someone I would consider an ally. The other royals are all far older—and likely more worldly in the ways of ruling—than either of us.

I clear my throat—my job is to reassure and to calm, to keep my internal fears compartmentalized. And the last thing I want to do now is to appear weak. "Before we start, what is the update on the oil spill off Hawaii? Has it been mitigated?"

Hevan, Gold Court consort, nods. "Yes, my queen. Most of it has been isolated with booms and removed with skimmer equipment. We have done what we can to assist with more rapid biodegradation from below the surface."

"Any more information on what caused it?"

Hevan hesitates, looking to his queen for guidance. Miral nods. "Someone hacked the ship's computer, forcing it to capsize. We're still working on it."

I have my guesses as to who could forcibly cause an ocean tanker to capsize and have the means to do so—Cano, it seems, will do anything to prove that he's still around. If we trace it back to him, maybe we can finally hunt him down and learn where he's been hiding. "Keep me informed the minute you hear anything. Any news from our friends at NOAA on the proposed initiatives to mark up the bills on marine debris at the recent House Committee meeting?"

"Yes, the bill was successfully amended, and funding allocated."

"Excellent. And the senate hearing on the offshore-industrial-waste issue?"

"Still on track for next month."

"Good."

I inhale deeply to counter my sudden inability to breathe, forcing the simmering dread out of my mind. Time to address the real reason the High Council had been convened. "As you've been recently informed, my...the regent has fallen ill. Echlios has been dispatched to further assess the situation. There's no cause for alarm."

"No cause for alarm," Castia from the Emerald Court huffs. "You are bonded to the creature. We saw you collapse from whatever it was you felt during the coronation! You cannot underestimate the bond, even one as...unique as yours." It's clear from her tone that *unique* was far from her intended word choice. "If he is in fatal danger, then you are in danger. And *we* are in danger."

"The *prince regent* is safe for the moment," Soren interjects in a firm, respectful tone. "As is your queen."

"Safe?" Castia hisses. "Look at her. She can barely focus despite the pretense."

"If the regent is dying, then you should go to him," King Verren says with a disgusted look at Castia.

"I cannot leave Waterfell," I say despite the lurch in my stomach at his words. I eye the Sapphire Court king, who has always been a strong ally.

"You invite destruction," Castia says under her breath.

Soren bristles beside me, but I shoot her a warning glance. Tensions are skyrocketing already, it seems. "Explain what you mean, Castia," I say carefully.

"What about these hybrid abominations that Ehmora created?" She spits out the name in distaste.

"Most of them have been eliminated, Castia. You know that. Echlios made sure of it. We haven't had any sightings of them in weeks."

"And the human, Cano? What of him?"

I sigh. "We're still looking for him."

"So he's still at large?"

"What is your point, Castia?"

Her eyes glitter like jade stones. "My point, my queen, is this—how do we know that this human isn't working with your…prince regent? How do we know that this half-human *hybrid* son of Ehmora's won't lead him right to us? That this isn't all some intricate ploy to infiltrate Waterfell…to expose us?"

I lift my chin and hold her challenging stare. "Lo is bonded to me. His loyalty is to me, and to Waterfell. He would never betray us to Cano."

"Your duty is to your people, not a hybrid."

King Verren and Queen Aylis share an anxious glance at Castia's provocative words. He moves forward. "I think what Castia is trying to say and failing to do so is that even if he does not intend to be disloyal, the prince regent is vulnerable." He looks at me with an almost apologetic expression, as if supporting Castia's claims is the last thing he wants to do. "Which means that you, too, are vulnerable. What if Cano attacked him to get to you?"

"Attacked him? How?" I ask.

"The bond is enduring, and if yours is anything like ours," Aylis murmurs, "you will feel every bit of his suffering as if it is your own, my queen. If the prince *is* dying, then you, too, are compromised."

"You are the only one who can give him the strength to survive the journey back here, and bring him back safely," Verren says. "You must go."

"But how can I?" I whisper, my heart aching as if it's being torn into two—love and duty clashing like titans—

even as Verren's soft words make a fragile, if unrealistic, hope bloom in my chest. As much as every cell inside me wants to go to Lo, how can I abandon Waterfell and expose my people with the threat of Cano still looming? But how can I forsake Lo, either? I swallow hard. "You suggest the impossible, Verren," I say softly. "If I go, our people are at risk. If I don't go, he dies. How can I possibly choose?"

"Your place is here," Castia snarls. "That creature is not oceanborn."

"Mind your words, Castia," Verren snarls back.

A wave of nausea makes my vision swim for a second. I steady myself and ignore the concerned glance that Soren sends in my direction. Following the attack during the coronation, I've been experiencing ongoing tremors—nothing like the first, but painful just the same. My claws curl into fists to quell their sudden shaking.

"We need you to continue to be a strong queen," Verren continues with a knowing glance, and then adds quickly, "As you have been. And you can be that only with the regent at your side. Alive and well."

I glance at Miral, queen of the Gold Court, who until now has been silent. She, too, has been one of my stronger supporters over the last few weeks. "Miral? What is your say on this?"

"I agree that this Cano is a threat. My reports have been unreliable, but he still poses a risk to us. If our existence is to remain a secret, then we must find and deal with the threat. While I agree that your prince is loyal and he has more than proven himself, he is still exposed, especially to this man. As are you." She exchanges a look with the Sapphire Court royals. "And Aylis is right. We cannot know how his illness will affect you."

"Keil?" I turn to the Ruby Court king.

"I think you should stay. Let Echlios handle the boy. If you leave now, the Aquarathi will view your absence once more as a conscious decision to choose this hybrid over them." He flicks his tail indolently. "It is, after all, reminiscent of your past behavior." As much as his blunt words sting, I know he's right. My duty as queen is to the Aquarathi people. I open my mouth to say as much, but Keil isn't finished. "That said, Cano is a threat, the prince is dying, you will be weakened and we will be defenseless if we don't do anything, so I propose four months."

"Four months for what?" I say, surprised.

"Four months to finish what you started landside," he says coolly. "Lure Cano out of hiding, remove the threat, save your prince, return to Waterfell. Uphold your oaths to defend our people."

The suggestive note in his tone makes me bristle, but I ignore it. "Just like that? And what if four months isn't enough?"

Keil's answer is as diplomatic as the conciliatory smile he sends my way. "Let's cross that bridge should we come to it, shall we? For now, you may choose a proxy to act in your stead."

"And the Aquarathi?"

"We will make sure our courts understand what is at stake," he says, his gaze sweeping the chamber. "Are we in agreement?"

The High Council had argued for hours after Keil's bombshell suggestion. While the Gold and Sapphire Courts were in agreement to protect the prince regent, Castia was of the mind that the laws of the wild should apply—

meaning Lo would live out his days and die like any other sick Aquarathi, regardless of the effect it had on me or my ability to lead. In the end, after impassioned debate on all sides, they had all reluctantly agreed to Keil's proposal. To his dismay, I left Miral in charge, and we had four months to join Echlios and "fix" the problem. If we didn't return to Waterfell in that time frame, I'd likely be forced to abdicate despite Keil's generous—and calculated—words about crossing that bridge if we came to it.

After I got over the initial shock of the High Council's decision, it was a foregone conclusion that we would return to La Jolla in short order. Hybrid or not, Lo was one of us and we couldn't abandon him. Especially not if an attack on him made me—and Waterfell—vulnerable to exposure.

And so, in much the same way as we left La Jolla, we arrive in the dead of night to join Echlios in our old house on the beach with a plan to get ourselves back into the routine of being human…not an easy task given the new weight sitting on our shoulders. We aren't here to learn or to acclimatize to humans. We're here to save one of us.

San Diego is the same as when we left it a few months ago…warm, sunny and clear blue skies stretching for miles. I didn't realize how much I'd miss the sky—the unending canvas of it, stretching out from the arms of the horizon, or the white tendrils of clouds drifting past and tinged in sunlight. Waterfell is beautiful in a different way, but nothing there can mimic the simple beauty of daylight.

Soren extends a glimmer outward and confirms that the beach is deserted. Shifting into human form feels strange, as if my body has forgotten how to do it, but of course it's just muscle memory. My bones crack and dissolve inside me, condensing and reshaping into the form of delicate human bones. Oddly, it hurts a little this time and I'm enveloped by a suffocating sensation as if I'm being stretched infinitely and then reformed into something far too tight. I try to relax into it and not force the shift—forcing means broken or excruciatingly misshaped bones. Breathing deeply, I focus on the ridged planes of my face softening and reshaping into smooth contours of cheek and brow. Human skin stretches over the shimmering gold-green tissue as I wave a slender forearm in front of me. My eyes are the last things to change, the protective coating slipping over the large, brilliant irises of my species. The hazel-hued shield mimics the appearance of human eyes.

Soren is already halfway up the beach, her nude form camouflaged by a glimmer. Even though the beach is deserted, anyone watching would see only sand. I glance at Speio, who is just completing his transformation. I catch him right at the moment when his face is halfway between beast and human. I'm shocked by how grotesque he appears as the fangs in his gaping mouth shift into human teeth and the puckered scaly hide of his face burns a mottled green. For a second he reminds me of the hybrid we killed, and a sour feeling fills my stomach. Lo is a hybrid, too.

"What's wrong?" Speio asks, shift complete, looking every inch like a tall, boyish seventeen-year-old with a shock of white-blond messy hair falling over one eye. His chest is lean and muscled, much the same as his Aquarathi one, but that's where my scrutiny stops. As much as I love Speio and have seen him naked countless times, I have to draw the line somewhere.

"Nothing," I say averting my eyes. "You just looked… weird."

He shoots me a confused look. "You've seen me change a gazillion times."

I shrug and wrap my arms around myself, the slick fuzzy feeling of my new skin slightly off-putting. "Seriously, it was nothing. I'm worked up about Lo and whether he's getting ill because of his, you know, hybrid genes."

"Could be," Speio says with a forced grin. "Or could be anything. Maybe it's a royal bonding thing we don't know about. It's going to be fine, Riss. Echlios will figure it out."

But I can see in Speio's eyes that he, too, thinks it's because Lo is a hybrid. It's the only explanation. Aquarathi don't get sick—it's the reason we were able to come to another planet and survive, thrive even—our immune systems are incredibly strong. So it stands to reason that Lo is sick because of his integrated human DNA...which means we have no idea in hell of how to help him.

Fighting my defeatist attitude, I enter my old room from the patio entrance off the pool deck and grab the robe hanging on the hook near the door. Echlios had the housekeepers come in to ready everything for our arrival, and the room looks exactly as I left it—my little mini pieces of Waterfell and home away from home. Glittering sea-glass ceiling, stained glass windows, walls painted in shimmering shades of blue...and one solemn auburn-haired best friend.

"Jenna," I gasp, and throw myself into her arms. "What are you doing here? Did you talk to Echlios? Have you seen Lo? What happened?"

Jenna nods, hugging me even more tightly to her after my rapid-fire questions. She doesn't answer immediately but pulls me over to the side of the bed and pats the spot next to her. I sit.

"Guess you didn't think you'd be back to visit me so

soon," she says, her mouth twisting in a half smile. "Wish it was under better circumstances."

"Soren says Echlios is with him at his house," I blurt out. "She wants me to wait to talk to Echlios, but it feels like I'm going burst out of my skin." I gesture at my human body. "Something doesn't feel the same. Like I'm going to explode into nothing."

"That's just panic, Riss. It's okay. Lo is fine," she says gently. "At least he seems fine on the surface, except for the passing out. That started in the last few weeks. I mean... he was fine. Surfing, working, hanging out. Then all of a sudden, he wasn't around. Sawyer tried calling him, and he was just holed up in his house. We thought he had the flu or something." She pauses, her eyes shifting and becoming shadowed. "But then we found out about the memory loss."

"The *what?*" I say in a shocked whisper. This is beyond bad. There's no awful human-brain condition I've learned about that doesn't start with some kind of degenerative memory loss—Alzheimer's. Huntington's. Dementia.

"After he collapsed on the beach a week ago, he had no memory of how he'd gotten there. I thought it was just a concussion from surfing or something, you know, so I didn't think much of it." She stops, watching me carefully. "We can talk tomorrow if that's better."

"No," I say. "Please, Jenna. I want to talk now."

Jenna takes my slack-fingered hand into hers and squeezes reassuringly. The light touch makes me want to snatch my hand away, because I know whatever she's on the verge of saying is going to be bad. I take a deep breath. "Lo asked Sawyer about his mother. About Ehmora."

"What do you mean? As in what exactly?"

"He asked him whether he's seen her around lately."

I can't help it. My jaw drops open. Ehmora is dead. *Lo* killed her three months ago. "What did Sawyer say?"

"He asked him why, and then Lo told him that she'd gone on some business trip and he hadn't seen her since. It was weird, Sawyer said, like totally out of the blue. Then he dropped the subject and they started talking about surfing as if he'd never even brought it up in the first place."

"Sawyer doesn't know about Ehmora, does he, Jenna?" I ask. Jenna would never give away what we are, not even to her boyfriend of three years, but I have to ask, anyway.

"Of course not. He just told me about it, and that's when things started to click into place. I did some research on his symptoms—dehydration, disorientation, unconsciousness and memory loss—but none of the existing diseases seem to match them. And it's not like we can take him to a hospital. They'd drag him to an underground, classified bunker in the blink of an eye."

"That was quick thinking, by the way," I say, remembering that she somehow convinced the paramedics that Lo didn't need to be admitted. "The thing with the diabetic stuff."

"It's amazing they even believed me," Jenna says. "It sounded so outlandish when I said it, but Lo was awake and nodding, so maybe they believed him."

"It was a glimmer," I murmur softly, nodding. It's something small, but Lo using a glimmer gives me hope, because at least he still knows what he is. And because he's a hybrid, holding on to his human form is far easier for him than it is us, so there's no immediate risk of exposure. I suppress a small sigh of relief.

"A what?"

"Something that we can do," I say. "Remember when

you asked me about mind control last spring?" Jenna's blue eyes almost bug out of her head, but she's known my secret long enough to know that I'd never use it to hurt her. "We can…suggest things to people. Not Speio or Soren so much, but me. And now Lo."

"Because he's with you, a queen?"

"Yes, and because he's the son of a queen."

"Oh."

I study Jenna, surprised by how much I missed her in three months. She's become far more than just a best friend. She's family. And because I trusted her with our secret, she's now a part of us.

"You cut your hair," I say, only just noticing the layered strands resting on her shoulders and the new sheared fringe across her brow.

"The bangs were a bad idea." She brushes them back with one hand. "But at least it'll grow. It was way shorter than this at first. I looked like one of those weird dolls with the button eyes. I must have been having separation issues when you left, because I literally chopped it off one afternoon."

"It looks good."

"It looks like crap, but thanks for the vote of support," she says with a smile. "You look the same."

"I mimic, remember? I can make myself have a short, spiky Mohawk if I want to," I say, shrugging. "Figured I look like this already, why change? Don't traumatize the humans any more than I have to and all that."

"That'd be interesting. Maybe I should have done that." She flips her hair self-consciously. "Sawyer hates it."

I roll my eyes. "That boy would be in love with you if you were bald, so don't even try to tell me that. I've never seen anyone so crazy about anybody else, ever."

"I have," Jenna says, and then bites her lip, her face flushing as the brief lightheartedness between us disappears in an instant. She clears her throat and grabs my hand. "Lo was a mess this whole summer, you know. Without you. Every time I saw him, I could tell what being apart from you was doing to him. Cara tried to move in, and he shut that down so quickly I think she's still recovering from the shock."

"Don't make me feel worse than I already do."

"Why did you tell him to stay, Riss? It's obvious that you two are meant to be together, even outside all of your bondage stuff."

"Bond-*ing*."

"Whatever. He loves you. You love him. I don't understand why you did what you did. And frankly, maybe he's sick because he has a broken heart."

"Seriously?" If the situation weren't so *not* funny, I would have laughed. "You sound like Sawyer. Humans don't get sick and die over a broken heart. That's ridiculous. They die from diseases."

"It *was* Sawyer's idea," Jenna admits. "And there are plenty of cases throughout history where people have gotten ill from the stress of emotional trauma. There's even an official condition called stress cardiomyopathy, caused by a temporary weakness of the heart from intense emotional issues."

"Easy on the big words."

"Let me make it simple for you. It's like your girlfriend telling you that she doesn't want to be with you even though she loves you but isn't quite sure how you're going to fit in her future and whether you have a place there. How's that?"

"Ouch. Harsh," I say, and pause, cringing. "And I didn't say that. I told him we needed space to figure things out."

"Same diff."

"So, even if it were true, are you saying this is *my* fault?" I've already thought it myself, but hearing another person say it out loud is something else entirely.

Jenna takes a deep breath. "Riss, I'm your best friend, and you know we've always told each other the truth even when it hurts. I'm telling you now. You made a mistake telling him to stay here. And maybe it's the human side of him that's making him sick, but we humans are more fragile than you could ever imagine. Our emotional responses can have catastrophic effects on our physical health. When Sawyer and I broke up sophomore year, I got really sick, remember? For some inexplicable reason, my immune system decided to go on vacation. I have no proof, but the brain/body connection is a powerful thing. Don't underestimate it." I try to stand, but she grasps my shoulders, forcing me to remain where I'm sitting beside her on the bed. Her eyes are clear and compassionate, as if she can see the guilt consuming me in waves. "I'm not judging you or blaming you. I'm just glad you're here now, that's all."

In truth, Jenna's words are like whips, but they're whips that I've already flayed myself with a dozen times over. I know I shouldn't have made him stay here, but I thought it was the right thing to do...to give him the space to figure out who he was in relation to me and vice versa. Only maybe in teenage hindsight, it was a stupid decision—and according to Sawyer and Jenna, I'd only succeeded in breaking his heart.

"Riss," Jenna says, her voice nearly inaudible. "There's one more thing. It's the reason Echlios wants to talk to you first before you see Lo."

"What's that?" I ask. Jenna's mouth twists as if she's about to say something that is as horrible as the look on her face. "Spit it out. Whatever you're going to say can't be worse than what you've already said. Truth, remember?"

"Okay," she agrees slowly. She blurts it out in a rush. "You should know that Lo asked Echlios two days ago who you were."

Turns out truth is overrated.

3
Confusion

I'm a nervous wreck. Not because I'm seeing Lo for the first time in months, but because there's a huge chance he won't even recognize me. I think that's why Echlios wanted to prepare me before I saw him. There's also a good chance that Lo *may* recognize me if I'm right in front of him, but I don't want to give myself false hope.

"Are you okay?" Echlios asks, as he pulls into Lo's driveway.

"Fine."

"That's six 'fines' since we left the house."

"What do you want me to say, Echlios? That I'm terrified? That I'm scared out of my mind that the boy I've bonded with won't know who I am? That I'm going to lose him? That without him, it feels like I won't be able to hold myself together? That without him, I'm dissolving?" I say in a dead, emotionless voice. "Let's just leave it at 'fine,' okay?"

Echlios's jaw drops open. "I didn't…realize."

I swallow thickly. It's completely incongruous, really, the whole situation. I'm the one who was hung up on the whole bonding thing. Lo and I bonded. But something inside me couldn't quite sit with the idea that I was tricked, and instead of accepting what was completely natural and consensual on both sides, I pushed it away. And now there's a very real possibility that the boy I love doesn't even know who I am.

"It's okay. Let's just get it over with," I say, forcing a bravado that I don't feel into my voice.

Grayer, Lo's valet-slash-butler, opens the door. His face is as stoic as I remember, but something like pity flashes in his eyes for a second, making me want to scrape that dead expression off his face with my nails. I don't want his pity, or anyone's for that matter, because it means that I've already lost.

"Where is he?" I blurt out, earning a censorious glance from Echlios. But I don't care. I want to see Lo for myself before reading other people's expressions and having to accept their hidden compassion.

"He's over here," a blonde, hefty-looking woman says from down the hall.

"Hi, Bertha."

Bertha, Lo's housekeeper, is as Amazonian-looking as ever, but she manages a small smile in my direction before enfolding me into an unexpected bear hug. Her affection throws me for a minute, but Lo is the closest thing she has to a son and I know that she knows how Lo feels—*felt*— about me. I return the hug a little more fiercely than I'd intended, stunned by my sudden surge of emotion.

"How is he?" I ask.

"We have our good days and our bad days. He's having a good day today. He surfed early this morning and seems to be in bright spirits. Come." She gestures for me to follow her into the sunroom that overlooks the ocean and the entire La Jolla coastline down to the beach below.

Echlios and Grayer follow like silent shadows. I don't want to let my eyes linger on the beach beyond the wall-to-wall glass windows…and the exact spot where Lo and I were together…but I do, anyway.

And then I turn in slow motion to the boy getting up from the couch. My heart climbs its way into my throat and stays there, choking me with silent, vicious pain. He looks the same—the salt-bleached sandy hair that's now curling into his collar, the bronzed sunburned cheekbones, and the wide, smiling mouth. Those dark, bottomless blue eyes reach into the most hidden parts of me and claim ownership. They're full of polite interest, but there's no recognition in them at all. I can't breathe, far less speak.

"Lo, you have a special visitor," Bertha says gently, her face stricken, mirroring my own response, still stuck in my chest. "This is Nerissa."

His eyes narrow at the sound of my name, but nothing clicks in them that suggests he recognizes it. Lo glances at Bertha and she nods. He looks confused for a second but then smiles widely and sticks his hand out. "Hi, Nerissa."

The sound of his warm voice wrapping around my name is my undoing. That hasn't changed—not the way he and only he says my name, like it's a sensual act instead of a mere word. Even if he doesn't know me, some part of him still does. It has to. I can't help myself—I step closer, ignoring his outstretched palm, and wrap my arms around the nape of his neck. I breathe in the smell of salt on his skin and press my temple against the soft stubble on the underside of his jaw. His body tenses, but I feel his arms slip around my waist in a tentative hug. I hug tighter, tears smarting behind my eyelids at how intimately familiar his human body feels against mine.

"It's good to see you, Lo," I whisper against his neck.

As if a spell has been broken, Lo pulls away, his eyes narrowing a fraction in frustration as he struggles to remember. "So you're Nerissa? Bertha told me that we were friends."

"Friends," I repeat, hearing my own voice break slightly on the word.

"We went to school together, right? Dover?"

I swallow hot bile at his nervous recitation. Even prepared, his reaction comes as a shock. I don't even want to look at Bertha or Grayer, or even Echlios. I don't want to see the expressions on their faces. Instead I smile through trembling cheeks and watery eyes. "Yes. We met at Dover. You don't remember me at all?"

The look in his eyes is tortured, as if he's struggling to place me in his head. "There's a part of me that feels like it does know you," he says, gesturing to his chest. "But I can't remember it here." His fingers jerk to his head and then flutter to his sides in a defeated motion. "I'm sorry."

"It's okay," I tell him in a choked voice. "You'll remember."

"I had some kind of seizure while driving and now I have a concussion—" Lo points to his skull "—hence the amnesia. I'm sorry I don't remember much," he says to me, and then forces a grin, one that still makes my knees turn into rubber. "I'd like to think yours is a face I wouldn't forget, but I guess the silver lining is that we get to know each other and be friends again."

But obviously, he *has* forgotten—not just meeting me, but me, period. "I'd like that," I say, unable to voice the truth that we are so much more than friends. I avoid Echlios's eyes. "You seem to be taking it well, your memory loss."

Lo shrugs, his mouth twisting in that casual, cute way

of his, as if he's trying to put on a brave front. "I'm hoping the doctors will fix it eventually. I just have to do the therapy and hope that it comes back. Freaking out doesn't help anyone."

It sounds so much like something he'd say that it's hard to think that parts of him aren't all there, or that maybe he's pretending and this is some big prank. But I know it isn't. I see it in his eyes—in that assessing look people give you when they're meeting you for the first time. He doesn't remember me at all.

"I'm sorry."

Lo slides me a soft smile. "I guess I remember the big things. The little things will come back in time." He trails off in awkward silence but then grins brightly. "Hey, I'm parched. You want a drink? Bertha makes the best pink lemonade this side of the Pacific."

Dying a little inside, I nod, and he walks out of the room, followed by a silent Bertha. I sit weak-kneed on the couch that Lo vacated a few minutes before, my heart feeling as if it's being crushed beneath a hammer.... *I remember the big things.*

"Exactly how much does he remember?" I ask Echlios in an unsteady voice.

"He has many, if not all, of his long-term memories, but there are big gaps in his short-term memory. Our local contacts have confirmed that he is suffering from some kind of retrograde amnesia, but we can't quite place whether the concussion from the accident caused the amnesia or if it was a symptom of something else prior to the accident. Bertha said that he couldn't remember little things at the beginning of the summer, long before any of this happened.

"Don't worry. We're flying in a top-notch neurosurgeon from L.A. at the end of the week. One of ours," he adds.

Of course, one of ours. We are a water species, living for the most part in the shadows of the deep, but that doesn't mean we don't keep our fingers on the pulse of everything landside, from global policy to technology to politics to neurosurgeons. If it can help Lo, I'm all for it.

"You think the amnesia was already there before he passed out?" I ask. "From what?"

Echlios walks to the wall of windows, staring out at the ocean beyond. His face is creased, the lines on his forehead deep with tension. He takes a deep breath as if trying to find the right words. "Stress," he says after a while. "Emotional trauma."

Jenna's earlier words come back to haunt me...about people dying of broken hearts and being physically compromised by their intense emotions. "Emotional trauma," I repeat.

Echlios nods. "He *killed* his mother. We have no idea what kind of effect that can have on someone."

"She wanted to kill him," I argue weakly.

"Doesn't matter. It's still traumatic."

"Why?"

Echlios sighs. "Because he's part human. He can't turn it off as easily as we can. Humans aren't predators. It's not so simple for them." He stops and walks toward me, his voice gentling. "What's going on with Lo is an incredibly rare form of amnesia—dissociative amnesia—that occurs after intense emotional shock. At least, that's the initial diagnosis."

As much as I try, I can't seem get my mind around it. Maybe it's because I don't have any human DNA, or maybe our Aquarathi brains don't work that way. It's not a lack of empathy, necessarily, more of an adapt-to-survive way of thinking. Emotions just aren't that critical to us—sure, we have them deep down, as I'd discovered from my people when I fought Ehmora in the arena, but other physiological needs like hunger and thirst take precedence. It's a matter of survival in the wild. Humans let emotions affect them far too much and, obviously now in Lo's case, to the point of physical weakness.

At that moment, Lo reenters the room carrying two tall glasses of pink lemonade. "Here you go."

"Thanks," I say. It was easier with him out of the room. My senses are so acutely tuned in to him that now I feel claustrophobic, as if his very presence is suffocating me. On top of that, every drop of water in my body is reaching toward him…reaching for its other half. The sensation is dull and aching, as if my skin is separating from the flesh beneath it. I take a deep breath and a sip of my drink.

"So, will you be at Dover for our senior year?" Lo asks, resuming his position on the couch beside me.

"I don't think so. We're not here for long. School started a few weeks ago, right?"

"Yeah."

Our conversation seems normal on the surface, but underneath, it feels stilted and uncomfortable, as if we're two kids set up by overeager parents. I clear my throat awkwardly. "So I guess I'll see you around—"

The shrill sound of Lo's cell phone interrupts my sentence. "I have to take this, hang on," he says to me, and taps on the screen. "Hey, Cara, what's up?"

Lo walks to the other side of the room, but I can still hear his side of the conversation. My stomach free-falls to my feet. They're making plans to meet up at the Crab Shack. "No, I'm free," he says. "I can meet you in, like, half an hour. Seriously, I'm almost done here." I'm crumbling inside with every word...every little sound that leaves Lo's mouth, saying I'm nothing to him.

Sinking into the couch, I'm barely conscious of Echlios taking a seat next to me. I was wrong about us being emotionless. Maybe our emotions run far deeper than those of humans, because nothing should feel like this. Nothing should feel like my very bones are breaking into tiny little pieces inside me, turning into ash. This isn't survival now; it's something else entirely...something beyond my comprehension.

"Echlios—" I choke out. And he's there, grabbing my numb fingers in his and drawing me back from the edge of the abyss.

"Breathe," he pulses to me softly in our language.

"I need to go. It hurts too much to be this near him," I whisper.

Before Lo and I bonded, I wasn't able to feel him as an Aquarathi because of his hybrid genes, and the link that finally connected us feels like it's weakening by the second. Queen or not, I can feel him leaning away, and there's no way to stop it.

Or maybe there is.

I squeeze Echlios's hand, unsure of what I'm about to do but knowing that I must do it nonetheless. "Can you wait outside? Take Bertha with you. I know what I have to do."

"My queen, I must insist—" Echlios says, his eyes widening at my meaning.

"Echlios, please. I have to know. And this is the only way—surely you of all people know that."

"But a glimmer?" Echlios's eyebrows snap together so tightly I'm surprised that he can see anything beneath that ominous frown. "What if he latches on unconsciously? You're bonded now. That connection goes both ways." He shakes his head. "With the amnesia, it's just too dangerous."

"I'll deal with that if it happens, but from what I've seen, he won't notice it. He doesn't know *me*. Trust me, I'll be safe, I promise. I have to try, Echlios. Please."

Echlios watches me, his eyes like a brewing thunderstorm, but eventually he nods and gives in to my wishes. "Be careful, then. If you feel anything, you separate immediately, okay? I'll be right outside this door."

"I will," I promise, even though a part of me deep down *wants* Lo to feel my glimmer and take me into him. I want him to fight for me.

After Echlios leaves, I source the water in my body and prepare myself for hydroprojection, or as we call it, glimmering. I can connect with other Aquarathi as well as humans via the moisture in the air and in their bodies. It allows me to speak to them, understand their impulses or even control them by the power of suggestion, if necessary. Which I've only ever done once. And never to any of my friends.

So this is still new for me, which is why Echlios is on edge. If Lo's Aquarathi side unconsciously fastens to my glimmer for whatever reason, he could suck the energy right out of me through our bond...as in my entire Aquarathi life force. But I'm stronger than I've ever been, and I've no intention of letting that happen. It's a risk, but one I'll take.

Calling upon my water, I pull it toward my center until it's a heavy weight resting near the middle of my chest. Gently, I push it toward Lo, who is still talking to Cara. The sound of her name ripples through me like a tidal wave, and the glimmer dissipates in a wild rush, slamming back into me and making me breathless. I'm still gasping and trying to compose myself as Lo ends his call and walks back over to me.

"You all right?" he says, frowning.

"Fine," I manage, coughing. "Lemonade went down the wrong way."

"I'm sorry," he says, and then gestures to the phone in his pocket. "Sorry about taking that call, too. I didn't mean to be rude. That was just Cara, one of my friends."

I take a gulp of my drink, ignoring the sharp sting of jealousy, and will myself to focus on what I'm about to do. "So, do you still hang out with Sawyer and Jenna?"

Lo's eyes light up. "Sure. Sawyer's teaching me how to surf, and Jenna takes pictures of me looking like an idiot."

Teaching Lo how to surf? The Lo I know could school *Sawyer* on all the ins and outs of surfing. He's that brilliant on the wave.

"I doubt that," I say, surprised that the amnesia would affect his actual abilities.

"Well, I'm better than I used to be," he says with a modest grin. "Hours of practicing. I'm determined to surf at Trestles one day."

Choking back the immediate retort that he used to dominate at Trestles and every other expert break in San Diego, I remain silent. That's different, too, I notice. Lo used to be arrogant and cocky. Now he's all vanilla pudding and apple pie, like a Stepford version of himself. It's not bad...I just miss the undertone of funny-boy snark. It kept me on my toes, and the witty comebacks had made Lo *Lo*. Maybe it's selfish, but I have to know what's in his head and whether any of the Lo I know and love is still in there somewhere deep down. I have to do the glimmer—it's the only way to be sure.

"So, how was the Marine Center this summer?" I ask to get him talking. I see his surprised expression and add, "We worked there together last year."

"Wow, we really did know each other well," he says with a rueful smile. "Seriously, I feel like I can't stop apologizing to you for not remembering any of this."

"It'll come back."

"I hope so," he says in earnest.

As Lo launches into some of the new ocean-conservancy initiatives he was overseeing at the center, I clear my head of everything but water and pull myself together once more. The glimmer stretches outward like a shimmering golden net and then connects with his. The pull of him is so seductive, so visceral, that I almost lose hold of the glimmer. What I'm doing is not exactly Sanctum. Instead I'm just trying to see if my Aquarathi side recognizes its mate within him. If Lo were himself, he'd naturally be able to feel me doing this and enjoy it as much as I do, but it's obvious that he has no idea who I am...or what I am. For all intents and purposes, he's just another person.

Only he's not. He's my *mate.*

And even in glimmer form, the act of being inside him is as intimate as being *with* him—even more so. I can barely breathe. Every inch of my skin feels electrified from the contact between us. The bond is still there, and strong. A thrill of brief relief flutters through me—he hasn't forgotten me entirely, even if the human part of him has.

Lo is still talking and, slowly, I glimmer past the barrier of his thoughts, trying to see past the indistinct memories... to see anything that would give me a sliver of hope. But other than the instinctual recognition from the dormant glimmer within him, there's nothing. There's no indication that he knows me at all.

Water rushes in my ears and I snap back into myself with a jolt, realizing that Lo is shaking my shoulders.

"What?" I gasp.

"Nothing," he says. "You looked like you were in a trance or something. Are you okay?"

"Fine. I must be tired, jet-lagged."

"Oh, right, you flew a long ways."

I nod, unable to speak, watching as Lo stands awkwardly with an odd expression on his face. He hesitates and then blurts out the question on the tip of his tongue. "Did you feel anything strange just before?"

"Like what?" I ask.

"Never mind." He opens his mouth and closes it, and then laughs out loud at himself. "It was nothing. I felt a weird connection, like from my belly button, as if something was pushing me toward you." He pauses, still looking awkward. "And then there was this bizarre glow stretching between us. You didn't feel or see anything?"

I shake my head and swallow. "No."

"*Twilight Zone!*" He shrugs with an embarrassed grin. "Maybe your jet lag is contagious, or maybe Bertha put crack in the lemonade." The slight appearance of the old Lo takes me by surprise, and my pulse leaps. Maybe he's not all gone. "Anyway, thanks again for stopping by. We should hang out before school. Maybe this weekend? Surfing Sunday?"

"I'd like that." I stand, not wanting to prolong the agony by watching him leave to go meet Cara. "Thanks for… seeing me."

"Sure thing. Catch you later, Nerissa."

During the car ride home, I stay silent. But I can feel Echlios's heavy stare, and I know I'm going to have to tell him what I saw with the glimmer. It's not something I can keep to myself, not now when we have so much on the line. We pull into our driveway and I turn to face him.

"He doesn't know me."

Echlios frowns, sympathetic. "Did you see anything at all?"

"There's no tumor or dementia, or anything like that from what I could sense, but you're right about the amnesia. It's definitely there." I pause and assess what I felt. "No other kind of infection was present. But there was something else that caught my attention that didn't quite fit, like really heightened brain activity on the human side."

"What do you mean?"

"I mean I barely got a read from the Aquarathi side of him." I raise terrified eyes to Echlios. "It's like he doesn't know what he is. At all."

"You mean—"

I nod. "I think he thinks he's human."

4
Surf Your Heart Out

The warm sun on the patio is definitely something I've missed. Jenna waves from the middle of the pool and I smile back, lifting a hand and watching the greenish-gold lights flicker down my forearm in response to the sun's rays. There's nothing quite comparable to sunlight, not even in the warm, jeweled depths of Waterfell. And while I miss my home, I've missed being here, too. And I missed my best friend. I'll admit freely that Jenna is the only person keeping me from falling to bits.

What I discovered about Lo has kept me wide-awake every night. After all, how do you make sure that a hybrid Aquarathi human doesn't go off the deep end if and when he starts exhibiting alien qualities? Not even the High Council could have anticipated this. It's uncharted territory for us—not just because Lo is a hybrid, but because he's a hybrid who *thinks* he's a human—so all in all, the situation has potentially catastrophic consequences, simply because he puts our entire species at a greater risk of exposure.

For the moment, we agreed that Echlios would keep an eye on him at home, and I'd do the same at school, which means official reenrollment at Dover. That wasn't part of the original plan. Readjusting will be tricky. I went from girl to alien queen in the span of four short months, and now I have to revert to who I was before. On top of that, going back to high school means seeing the boyfriend who isn't really my boyfriend anymore on an excruciating daily basis. It's going to be unbearable.

I sigh and say as much to Jenna. She swims to the side of the pool and props her chin on her forearms on the edge. She stares at me with a thoughtful expression, studying the flickering lights underneath my skin.

"Can't you just mind-meld him into remembering you? You know, with that shimmer-glimmer thing you do?" she asks, nodding at my forearms.

"Not that easy," I say. The lights on my arm die a swift death at the turn of the conversation. "I tried, and there was nothing there—nothing of me, anyway. It's like any memory of us has been wiped out of his head completely."

I gulp past the lump of misery in my throat. Apparently everything I learned during my previous human initiation cycle doesn't apply to relationships. Turns out you can break someone's heart…so much so that he eliminates everything about you just so he can cope.

Jenna hauls herself out of the pool and grabs a towel from the side table. "I did a little research on what you told me. Dissociative amnesia is pretty common after trauma, but the memories do come back most of the time. You have to believe that."

"I don't have a year, Jenna. I have months, and then I have to make a decision to go back, with or without him. With him would be so much better. Without him means things I don't want to consider."

"What things?" Jenna says, her eyes narrowing.

I meet them honestly, my heart in mine. "You know our laws, Jenna. We can't take the risk that he'll expose us."

"Oh."

She doesn't say anything more but stares at the undulating surface of the pool, lost in thought. She loves Lo as a friend, but if the time comes and we decide to leave without him, she'll have no say in what happens to him. She knows that as well as I do. After a while, she turns to me again.

"Won't that…hurt you, too?"

"Yes."

Her face drains of color. Jenna doesn't know the intricate ins and outs of bonding, but I told her what Soren once told me. If Lo dies, a part of me will die, too. And I'll never be able to bond with anyone again. Those are the rules of what we are—we bond for life.

"Well, you're just going to have to make him fall in love with you again," Jenna says with a forced, overbright smile.

"We've bonded, Jenna. There's nothing beyond that."

"For Aquarathi," she points out. "Not humans. And Lo's part human, right? Look, you said it yourself. He already loves you because you're bonded. There's a part of him that recognizes itself in you and probably always will. You just have to make him see that. As much as the human brain can incapacitate itself, so it can rebuild itself. It's a two-way street." She pauses, her expression intense. "And maybe if you can do that, then you can get him to remember everything else. Damaged neurons self-repair."

"You know this how?"

"Told you. I did research," she says, taking a peach from the fruit basket on the table and biting into it. As always, I'm amazed at Jenna's base of knowledge. She's more than smart—she's practically a human encyclopedia. And what she doesn't know, she makes it her business to learn. Like, obviously, rare neurological conditions. "According to some studies, once you get the cells refiring, the rest is inevitable. The human brain is an amazing thing. It can actually rewire itself."

I snort and attempt a lame joke. "So you're saying I have to hot-wire him?"

"Baby steps, Riss." Jenna laughs. "Remember last year? I mean, you couldn't even flirt without popping a blood vessel and freaking out. Every time Lo made a move, you, like, ran the other way like a frightened bunny."

"Did not," I retort, flushing.

"Total bunny." Jenna grins, enjoying my discomfort. "Your scary sea-monster side was completely bunnified."

"My scary sea-monster side is going to make an appearance if you don't quit it," I threaten, baring perfectly human white teeth in her direction.

"Oooh, I'm so scurred!"

"You should be," I say, and remove the human eye film from my eyes, revealing the shimmery multicolored iris and pale gold sclera beneath.

"You think some gorgeous eyeballs are going to freak me out?" she says, sticking her tongue out and rolling her eyes. "Been there, done that."

I shake my head at her comical expression and we both start laughing. Six months ago when Jenna found out the truth about me, she could barely look at any of us without her blood rushing around inside her in terror, and now she's totally at ease with the whole alien-best-friend thing. Things could have turned out worse if she hadn't been okay with it. Way worse…as in goodbye-best-friend worse.

"So, what does Speio say about all this? Coming back to Dover? Pretending to be human?" Jenna asks.

She and Speio weren't exactly on the best of terms during the last year. He was averse to me revealing anything to Jenna, and even though she ended up saving our collective hides on more than one occasion, things between them never went back to the way they used to be. I do give him props, though, because before we left he apologized to Jenna.

"He's fine with it, actually," I tell her. "Volunteered to come this time around."

"I thought he wanted to be back there."

I snort out loud. "He did, and then he realized that females are the same, no matter the territory. They don't come running just because a male decides he's ready for a mate. Let's just say that Speio had a rude awakening."

Jenna's eyes widen with that little bit of gossip. "So no bonding?"

"Nope."

"Wow, payback's a bitch," Jenna says. "Although I still feel sorry for him. All we're looking for is love at the end of the day. Aliens need love, too. Maybe that's all he really wants."

"And alien booty."

"TMI!" Jenna screeches, covering her ears. "Oh no! Icky mental image! Thanks for that," she says, and tosses her towel at me. I can't help laughing at her grossed-out expression.

"Come on," I say. "It's not that bad. We coil around and—"

"Stop! My bleeding ears!"

We are laughing so hard by then that Jenna starts snorting through her nose, a snort that she futilely tries to stifle when Speio walks out of the living room toward us.

"What's so funny?" he asks.

"Nothing," she spurts through her teeth, clamping her lips together and turning a splotchy shade of red. "Girl stuff."

Speio rolls his eyes skyward and shoots me a withering glance. I keep my thoughts carefully guarded and my face blank, knowing that he'd flip out if he knew we were making fun at his expense. He's still a little sensitive about the whole not-bonding thing.

"Whatever," he says. "So, are you guys going to the meet? Sawyer just texted me to see if you were on your way."

"Crap," Jenna squeals, jumping up to grab her phone out of her bag. "Yikes. He's texted me, like, thirty-eight times." She shrugs into a pair of cutoff jean shorts and glares at me. "Move your ass, queen of the sea! We have to go."

I sink backward into the lounger. "Do I have to? I'm not sure I'm ready to mix and mingle."

"It'll be good for you," Jenna says, her head disappearing into a neon-colored tank. "Plus, Lo's going to be there." She throws a meaningful look in my direction. "He asked you to come today, remember?"

I offer a noncommittal shrug. I don't know why I'm so cagey about going. Maybe it's because I don't want anyone—particularly any of our old friends from school—seeing that Lo's amnesia is so bad that he can't remember his own girlfriend. I don't want to feel their pity, or worse.

Jenna reads me easily. "Better to get it over with now than on Monday when you have nowhere to go but a four-walled classroom. It'll be fine, Riss. I'll be there, and Sawyer, and Speio," she says with a glance at him.

"Are you going?" I ask Speio.

"Yes."

"Oh."

Speio reddens as if he's hiding something. "You have to go. You're signed up to surf," he blurts out. "Sawyer did it!"

"What?" I splutter. "I haven't surfed in months. I'm not up for a surf meet!"

"Maybe it's what you need," he says.

Jenna agrees with Speio, nodding emphatically. "Totally what you need. It was my idea, by the way, so don't be mad at Sawyer or Speio."

"What are you guys? Best friends now?" I say with a half-hearted glare. I'm not a fan of being tricked and pushed into things, but Jenna's probably right. If I'm out surfing, I'm hardly going to be thinking about what people are saying about me. Or focusing on Lo. Or on Cara being all over Lo. Or vice versa. That last thought makes my stomach flip-flop, and not in a good way.

"Fine. Let's go."

I grab a shorty wet suit and tuck my surfboard next to Speio's in the back of the Jeep before climbing in beside Jenna. It's only a fifteen-minute ride from La Jolla to Pacific Beach Drive where Speio says the competition is being held.

She eyes me. "Seriously, I don't know what you're getting so worked up about. You command the sea. This is your space. Be one with it."

"Calm down, Yoda."

I stare out the window, preoccupied—or forcing myself to look preoccupied—to avoid further conversation. As we near the location, I'm surprised at the amount of traffic and cars parked along the side of the road. I can just see the tops of a few dozen multicolored tents along the edge of the beach.

"Which meet is this again?" I ask, my suspicion growing by the minute at the throngs of people walking toward the beach.

"RUSH," Jenna says sheepishly.

"What?" I nearly choke. The RUSH Annual Surf Series is one of the biggest surf competitions in San Diego, and is sponsored by *the* coolest surf magazine on the planet. I ignore the sudden dip of my stomach. Not only will Lo be watching, but thousands of people will be there, including photographers. "How did we even get in for that? I didn't qualify to compete." I stare at her with a disbelieving frown.

"Slow your roll, princess," Jenna says. "Sawyer hooked it up."

"How?"

"Technically, it's only an exhibition heat. He showed them some footage of you from last year and he called in a favor. No biggie."

"You're killing me. Really."

Jenna grins, hopping out of the Jeep as soon as Speio comes to a spot in the narrowest parking spot possible. "What better way to start your senior year at Dover than with a splash? No pun intended."

"This is a Pro-Am competition," I say with overexaggerated emphasis. "As in *pro*. RUSH is more than a big deal. And the exhibition surfers at these events are professional surfers, not amateurs."

"Seriously, Nerissa Marin, can you stop being such a wuss and suck it up for half a second? You're a great surfer. Better than great, if you know what I mean," Jenna says, grabbing my board and shoving it toward me. I shoot her a dry look. "Go have fun. And show off a bit. What could go wrong?"

The question is so loaded that I nearly start laughing hysterically. Besides enticing giant ocean predators like great white sharks, which are attracted to Aquarathi pheromones—mine in particular—what could *possibly* go wrong other than the worst possible thing? Like mangled, chewed-up people everywhere.

Speio pats my arm, sensing my panic. "It's a new moon," he says quietly. "Full moon's already gone, so you should be fine. Just try to keep it together." Okay, correction... maybe it's not the worst thing, since our pheromones are at their peak during the full moon, but that doesn't mean it's not risky.

With a resigned sigh, I walk down to the crowded beach, where we meet up with Sawyer. He's at one of the tents, pinning his number onto his rash guard. His smile is infectious as he comes in for a warm hug.

"Hey, Riss! Glad you got here."

"Thanks for the heads-up," I tell him, punching him half-playfully in the arm.

"Any surfing down in Cape Town?" Sawyer says, his teeth white in his darkly tanned face. A move to South Africa was the cover story for why we left months ago. "Heard there's good swell there year-round."

"Nope, didn't surf at all," I say truthfully, grabbing a piece of wax off one of the nearby tables. "I'm going to be rusty. Hope you don't have too much riding on me not completely wiping out."

"It's only exhibition," he says, and nods out at the ocean, where the waves are breaking in perfect sets. "Epic out there. I had an early-morning heat and it wasn't near as clean as those. High tide. Offshore winds. Epic combo."

"If you say so."

I survey the teeming beach—only exhibition…with a gazillion people watching my every move. Waving good-bye to Sawyer, I head over to where Speio's standing and crouch down next to him on the sand, slowly rubbing wax onto the deck of my board with rhythmic, consistent strokes. I breathe in and slowly exhale with each circle, feeling my body calm and center.

"Hey," a voice says over my shoulder, making my skin leap like it's alive. Only one person has that effect on me. I look up, shading my eyes from the sun.

"Hi, Lo."

"You came," he says, crouching down beside me. "You're surfing?"

"Sawyer's idea," I say, trying not to let his proximity or the citrusy-vanilla smell of him affect me. It's a losing battle. Here, with the ocean so close, everything is amplified. For me, anyway. I haul a deep breath into my lungs, furiously scrubbing the square of wax onto the board and remembering Speio's words about keeping it together. Fat chance with Lo looking on every second.

"So, you any good?" Lo asks, and then answers his own question. "Well, you must be if you're surfing RUSH. Heard it's the epic of the epics."

"Yeah."

"You nervous?"

"Some."

"Well, I'll leave you to it," Lo says with an awkward smile. "See you around." I know my body language and monosyllabic answers are anything but welcoming, but I can't help it.

Keep it together, I remind myself. "See you."

"Good luck, but I'm sure you won't need it."

I don't allow myself to turn fully around, but my gaze follows him despite my better judgment. Bad move. I'm just in time to see a bikini-clad Cara throw herself into his arms. Lo catches her effortlessly, tossing her over his shoulder. She laughs at something he says and kisses him on the cheek. I duck my head, letting my hair cover my overheated face. The jealousy that spins through me is like acid, scorching every part of my insides without mercy. I gasp, nearly doubling over my board.

Speio is at my side in a second, his hand over mine stalling my movement with the wax. "You all right?"

"Fine."

"You sure?" he says, his face concerned. He looks over his shoulder, and understanding dawns in his eyes. "You know they're just friends, right?" he says. His hand tightens on mine. "You don't have to do this, Riss. Stay here, I mean."

I squeeze his fingers, forcing the ache into a dark corner of my brain. "I have to deal with it sooner or later. Jenna's right. Better out here than in a closed environment." A loud bullhorn has everyone breaking out in a wave of mad cheering as the announcers of the event broadcast the exhibition heat. "That's me. Don't worry, Speio. I'll be okay."

As I paddle out to the lineup with the five other surfers in my heat, I try to leave all my negativity back on the beach. Being extra careful, I duck-dive under the oncoming waves, letting the ocean flow over and into me, taking strength from its dark blue depths. This is my space...my world. It's where I belong. With every stroke, I feel stronger.

Out past the breakers, I straddle my board and float, facing the beach. People cover every possible inch of sand for miles. I know exactly where Lo is because I can feel the magnetic pull of him even as far away as I am, but I keep my eyes averted, searching instead for the red flag of Jenna's hair. Instead a distorted, misshapen face beneath a wide-brimmed hat catches my attention, and I blink, my stomach dipping in fear. But when I look back, the hulking figure is gone. Shaking my head to clear it, I spot Jenna, jumping up and down and waving madly. I wave back and drop down to grab the rails of my board.

The waves are breaking in perfect sets, with glassy blue faces and white-tipped crests. Sawyer's right—conditions couldn't be more perfect. Paddling effortlessly, I streak past one of the other surfers to grab the second wave in the set. I pop up and carve steeply down the face of the wave, marveling at my human body's muscle memory. Everything feels fluid, as if my bones are one with the wave.

Exhilarated, I trail my right hand across the wave's face and then crank my hips up and over so that the board shifts into a sharp cutback. I'm gliding over the foamy crest, nearly suspended in air for a breathless moment and then slipping back down onto the face. By the time the wave starts to run out of steam, I'm on fire, adrenaline rushing through my entire body.

The cheering from the beach is deafening as I pump a triumphant fist in the air and somersault off my board over the back of the wave. I surf several more waves, even doing a three-sixty spin and a back flip off the last one, before heading back to the beach.

But once I'm back and surrounded by unfamiliar faces, I remember the figure I spotted from the lineup. I summon Speio and tell him in a few short words what I might have seen.

His eyes widen as he scans the crowd. "Are you sure that's what you saw? A hybrid?"

"I don't know. Maybe it was a trick of the sunlight."

"I'll check it out."

A grinning Sawyer thumps me on the back, along with a giant throng of people yelling out all kinds of greetings, as Speio melts into the crowd.

"Feel better?" Jenna asks me with a knowing smile.

"Yeah."

"Good. You totally rocked it out there. No one," she says pointedly, "could keep their eyes off you." The lurch of happiness in my chest is squashed by the sudden warning look in her eyes at someone over my shoulder. "Speaking of..."

"Jenna, help me with these boards, will you?" Sawyer yells out. She throws me an apologetic look and shrugs, mouthing, *Sorry*. As she leaves, I turn around to face a very impressed Lo and his not-so impressed entourage of Cara and her cronies.

"You were brilliant," he breathes, extending his hand for a high five. I slap it with mine, wincing at the torture of the too-brief contact, and fight the urge to beat a hasty retreat up the beach behind Jenna.

"Thanks," I murmur, glancing at the others beside him. "Cara," I manage civilly.

In response, she drapes a possessive arm around Lo's waist. "Oh, hey, Nerissa, didn't know you were back."

Sure she didn't. Last semester, I found out that Cara had lived with a foster family before enrolling at Dover, where her uncle—Cano—was principal. In some small way, she, too, was an outsider trying to fit in. She and Lo became friends, probably because they connected over the whole foster-life similarities. Lo told me that she'd never felt she could confide in anyone until she met him, and he liked being able to help. Deep down, I know I shouldn't fault Cara. Of all people, I know what it's like to want to run away from who you are—I did that for the past few years, and my people paid the price. I just wish she wasn't so smug and obnoxious all the time, but then again, maybe that's a front, too.

"Yes," I say. "Back for the semester."

Cara's voice is an insidious purr. "I think you'll find that senior year is going to be a lot different from junior year. There've been a few interesting changes. I can help you work those out if you like."

Or maybe it isn't a front...maybe she's just Cara, plain and simple.

"Thanks for the heads-up," I say coolly, refusing to let my eyes follow the motion of her palm against Lo's rib cage. I fight an equally violent urge to smash her pretty face in with the sharp end of my board. Instead I look away with effort. "I think I can manage on my own."

"You do that," she says. "Lo, you coming? We're going to get floats."

"In a sec," he says to her. "I'll catch up."

Cara shoots me one of her oh-so-familiar death glares of impressive proportions and I wink back, taking small pleasure at the instant heat blooming in her cheeks. Despite knowing that sinking to her level won't solve anything, I can't help giving in to the desire to make her suffer just a tiny bit for the grope-fest she just flaunted in my face.

"So, how amazing were you out there?" Lo says, shaking his head in admiration.

I try valiantly not to blush, or in my case, go all bioluminescent at his sincere compliment. "Thanks. Would you
believe it if I told you that you used to surf pretty much exactly like that before?"

"There's no way I could surf like you." The warmth in
his voice is deep and velvety, doing things to me that leave
me breathless. And his eyes...I force my gaze away, looking for anything to stop those eyes from breaking me into
a million pieces.

I swallow and force a smile to my lips. "You did, and you
will. One day. It will all come back...all of it."

"I hope so."

His whisper is soft, wistful almost—I don't know why it
sounds like a promise, but something in it does. And for a
second, looking into those earnest, bottomless blue eyes, I
let myself hope, too.

5
Game On

It is dark and empty—a cavernous, echoless abyss. There's no light, only oily black depths beneath and beside me. I am but a speck at its epicenter. I scream, but the only thing that escapes my mouth is a mute bubble that floats away into the ever-deepening silence. I thrash, my arms and tail caught in the motionless void. It is futile.

I am trapped.

Something snakelike slithers down my arm, and then another and another, until my body is fraught with it. Glowing red eyes appear in the distance, drawing closer and closer, blackened tentacles bleeding outward and encircling me.

Ehmora.

"You're dead," I say. "We killed you."

"Did you?" The voice laughs, the sound like a volley of bullets. "Then why am I here?"

"You're a ghost. A nightmare. Nothing more."

"So it would seem...."

I jerk upward gasping, sweat dampening my neck and back. My entire body is shaking from the visceral dream. I can still feel her tentacles cutting into me like a fiery brand. Of its own volition, my gaze slides down to the vinelike navy tattoo winding around the tops of my shoulders and neck. I take a breath, banishing the remnants of fear. The tattoo is a mark of the bonding with Lo, nothing more. It's not alive. There are no tentacles. And Ehmora is dead.

Still, the implication of the dream is haunting. I felt so powerless and alone in the abyss, unable to move or act. The phantom Ehmora's last words were so utterly chilling... so *knowing*...that I can't help the shiver winding its way through me.

Attempting to exorcise my irrational fears, I step out to the patio and into the cool night air and lie back on a lounger to stare into the dark sky. It's a cloudy night, with no moon or stars visible above. The wind whistles through the tops of the palm trees along the edges of the property, growing louder by the second. The unpredictable shift is in response to me—I'm sure of it.

I've always had a tempestuous relationship with weather, and while I've learned to harness my emotions, sometimes it's impossible to keep it all in. For a heartbeat, instead of suppressing my feelings, I release my inner demons, watching as jagged lightning rips the sky into two. Sure enough, the first droplets of rain hit my face and bare legs. The ensuing storm is violent but brief, the angry purple sky fading as the clouds part to reveal a gilded sliver of moon. The release feels good as the rain intensifies into a pelting force and I relish the sting, letting it filter through me. Eventually the rain gentles to something more tender as my thoughts drift to Lo. The drops of water from above mix with the salty tears on my face, and I allow myself the luxury of crying for the first time in months.

A queen must show no weakness.

Curled into a ball with sobs racking my body, I don't even

notice the gentle stroking across my shoulder at first. But after a few seconds, I lean back into the person lying beside me on the lounger, hugging me from behind.

"It hurts too much," I choke out.

"It's okay, child." Soren's voice is soft, pulsing in our language. Her fingers are softer still, caressing my back in a soothing motion.

"I did it, Soren," I whisper brokenly. "I made it happen."

"No, my lady," she says. "You could not have predicted any of this. You did what you thought was best to keep him safe. To keep all of us safe."

"He should have been with me. In Waterfell. Not here. And not alone." My words are raw, shattered gasps, clawing their way out of my throat. "He couldn't have known what bonding would feel like, either. And I pushed him away, ripping us both apart when we should have been together. Thinking it would be better. For both of us. But it wasn't. It *wasn't*."

Soren turns me around gently to face her, her eyes flashing green fire. "Don't do this to yourself, Nerissa. It is what it is." She wipes the tear-rain combination from my face with her thumb. "Lo is seeing the neurosurgeon this week. We'll know more then on how we can help him."

"We don't know that we *can* help him," I say in a defeated voice. "His human DNA is doing things that we have no experience with."

"He's Aquarathi, too," Soren says. "Which means his capacity to heal is better than any human's."

I meet her eyes, hope blooming softly. "I hope you're right."

"See what the doctor says, and we'll go from there. Come on, let's get you back to bed. Big day of school tomorrow."

"Soren, did you talk to Speio? About what I saw on the beach?"

Soren nods, her face grim. "No traces of anything."

"Was he sure?"

She pulls me close in a warm embrace. "Don't worry. Echlios will make sure Speio didn't miss anything. Now, you need to get some rest."

Despite Soren's comforting words, I can't help feeling a sense of dread, like an invisible net is closing in, one that we can't see or avoid no matter how hard we try. I know what I saw earlier—it was one of Cano's creatures…watching…and wanting me to see it. Taunting me…Cano's way of saying I have no idea what's coming next. And the truth is, none of us do. Not even with Lo. At the end of the day, he's still a cross-species alien/human hybrid, and anything the neurosurgeon says will be speculation at best.

With a last look at the rapidly clearing skies, I allow Soren to walk me back to my room, where I fall into a fitful sleep.

"Come on, slowpoke!" Jenna shouts, slamming her locker shut. "English is this way. Forget how to navigate these hallowed halls already?"

I haven't exactly forgotten, but the sight of Cara all over Lo at the far end of the lockers is already making me sick to my stomach. It's not so much her flirting that's getting me… it's the look on Lo's face, as if he's enjoying every minute of it. Which, I remind myself, he's bound to…he's a boy.

I remember Jenna's words from yesterday evening when we'd driven back from the beach. *Fight fire with fire.*

Of course, it didn't help that she made me watch *Grease* for inspiration—girl-next-door tutorial on how to lure the quintessential bad boy—emphatically stating that there's nothing that black leather pants can't accomplish. Laughing, I told her she'd have to kill me before getting me anywhere near leather pants. But she has a point. He's not exactly going to notice me if I'm a mute wallflower.

Smoothing my hair and cringing inwardly, I take a deep breath, lick my lips and strut past them.

"Hey, Lo," I say in a breathy voice, blushing furiously at how ridiculous I must sound. But obviously he doesn't think so. Neither does Cara. They both stare at me—him with an appreciative smile, and her, not so much. But I'm not there to win Cara over. I'm there for Lo. "You heading to English?" I ask him, ignoring her scowl. "I wanted to ask you something about Sawyer."

"Yeah," Lo says, grabbing his books. "What's up?"

Elated, I ignore Jenna's raised eyebrows and congratulatory wink from the rear of the room as we walk into class together. I turn slightly and see Cara trailing behind us, her face a hilarious combination of thunder and puke. Sawyer waves, and Lo plunks down in a vacant seat next to him. I take the spot next to Jenna and stifle a grin as Cara is forced to grab one of the few open seats at the front of the class.

Nerissa, one. Cara, zero.

Mr. Donovan clears his throat and pushes his spectacles up on his nose, smiling widely. "Welcome, class, we have a few new faces this week." Everyone looks around in unison to check out the "new faces." So far, it looks like one new girl and a guy who I thought graduated last year. Guess not. Oh, and me, which would explain why everyone's staring at me as if I have a bull's-eye tattooed on my forehead. Technically, I'm not new but, well, tell everyone else that. Mr. Donovan continues. "This week, we are going to start with *The Importance of Being Earnest* by Oscar Wilde, which is one of my favorite plays."

Amid the groans from the class, I smile to myself…finally something new that I haven't read on my own. At least I can drown myself in that if things get rough—nothing like academics to take a girl's mind off unrequited love. I glance at Lo through my lashes. He's flipping through the pages of the play, his lower lip caught between his teeth. I can't help noticing how cute he looks, yet how different. Gone are the rebellious flip-flops from last year, which aren't part of the Dover Prep uniform, as well as his permanently sand-covered feet. Gone also are the days when he used to cut class just to go surfing. The old Lo would have been horrified to be in class on time or to be caught without an appropriately bored expression on his face. A part of me desperately misses that boy, but I know he's in there some-where…somewhere beneath the meticulously neat hair and immaculate uniform.

Mr. Donovan thumps his book on the desk, making me jump, and people swivel to the front of the class. "You are going to work in groups of four or five, and each group will be assigned a specific theme to discuss. As part of your mid-term, there will be a debate between each of the groups to prove or disprove the theme you have been assigned. This will count toward half of your final grade in this class, so please take it seriously. The group assignments are as follows."

The assignments are all alphabetical, so my silver lining is that Cara is an *A* last name and Lo is an *S*, but nothing prepares me for the pure venom that comes my way when Lo and I somehow end up in the same group. In this class there aren't many last names between Marin and Seavon. Jenna is also in our group, as well as two other boys. Sawyer is with Speio, so he doesn't look too miserable at having to split up from Jenna. The new girl—Rian Thorn—is with them.

Jenna catches my eyes and I can see her lips twitching as she nods at the theme that Donovan has just written up on the blackboard for our group. I almost snort—*The Double Life*. Someone definitely has a sense of humor, considering that there are two aliens pretending to be human in this group alone. Well, not that Lo knows that he's alien, but who's counting?

The rest of the morning passes in a bustle of activity, running from class to class, and getting myself reacquainted with the routine. After American Government, Advanced Math and French class, I trudge toward the cafeteria and toss my books and my food-laden tray down onto an empty table. Jenna, Speio, Sawyer and surprisingly Lo immediately join me. They look exactly how I feel. Wiped.

"Seriously," I say. "Is senior year supposed to be death in a backpack? It's only lunchtime, for crying out loud. How'd you guys survive weeks of this already?"

"Dover Prep prides itself on academic preparation for college-bound students," Jenna intones, mimicking the opening statements on the Dover Prep brochure.

"Guess they didn't include torture and cruel or unusual punishments," Sawyer quips.

"I didn't think it was too bad," Lo says, and we all turn to him in unison, our expressions identical.

"Who are you and what have you done with Lo?" Sawyer says, widening his eyes in mock shock. "Oh, right, he's on hiatus, which means new Lo loves schoolwork."

Lo reddens. "I don't love it. I just don't think it's that bad. Big difference."

"Well, the old you couldn't be bothered, that's all," Sawyer explains. "I mean, you haven't even asked me to cut school once. So it's weird seeing you, of all people, flipped around and all about the books."

"Sorry." Lo shrugs. "It's just that I don't know how I used to be, and it feels like I should be good in school because this stuff isn't too complicated to me. If I do it well, why not do it?" We all start laughing and Lo gets even redder, realizing that that, too, is something the old Lo would never say. "Look, I'm just trying to figure out who I was. Give me a break, will you?"

"Sorry, man, just playing around," Sawyer says, chucking him in the shoulder. "We all know who you are. You'll remember soon enough."

"I guess we haven't really seen you since school started," Jenna pipes up. "You've been over there." She nods across the room.

"Sorry, Cara's been helping out," Lo says a trifle defensively. "I didn't want to be mean." His eyes dart over to where said stony-faced helper is sitting with her entourage. "I think I've made her mad by even coming over here."

"The old Lo wouldn't have cared," I blurt out, earning a swift glance from Lo.

"The old Lo sounds like he was a dick."

"Hardly. He just saw through the bullshit. He knew how to read people."

"Like you?"

"Especially me," I say quietly. The memory of a different type of conversation, on a boat in the middle of the harbor, whispers through my mind. Lo had always been able to see right through me, even at my worst.

"Wow, you two want to take it down a notch, or what?"

Jenna interjects to diffuse the sudden tension hovering over the table. "Dick or not, you're still our friend."

Lo lounges back in his seat. "So, what else did I do? Or *not* do? Besides not caring about school, seeing through bullshit and being an amazing surfer, according to Nerissa."

The sound of my name on his lips makes my stomach feel all fluttery, but I stuff a huge bite of cheeseburger in my mouth so I don't have to talk. Sawyer does instead. "Well, she's right. You were pretty awesome, but you're getting there," he says. "We'll have you back surfing double over-heads in no time. Right, Riss?"

Lo's eyes meet mine. "Sure," I choke out, stuffing another bite into my mouth. "Sorry, hungry," I say by way of apology and stare at my tray, avoiding Jenna's amused look.

"So, since we're on the topic, can I ask you guys a weird question?" Lo says, his eyes making the rounds at the table. Jenna nods on behalf of everyone. "Did I...date Cara?" The dead silence is so thick you could cut it with a knife. Everyone around me stares at the tabletop. Surprised, Lo hurries to explain. "I mean, it's just that she's so possessive sometimes, and I feel as if she expects me to be a certain way, so..." He trails off, a helpless expression on his face.

"Do you like Cara?" Jenna asks carefully.

"She's all right," he says. "A little neurotic, but who isn't? And she's been supernice over the last few weeks."

"That's not an answer."

I try to act like the real answer to Jenna's question won't affect me, but it's a losing battle. The silence thickens to uncomfortable proportions, and I realize that I'm holding my breath. I exhale silently.

"I guess I do. Or did. I don't know. I mean, it feels like we're close."

"So, which is it?" The question isn't from Jenna. It's from me. I'm shocked that I've even said anything, but obviously I have, if Jenna's open-jawed expression is any indication.

"I don't know," Lo says. "Sorry, I didn't mean to make things weird." He laughs awkwardly. "Please tell me I didn't insert my foot in my mouth because I dated any of you?"

To everyone's surprise, Speio leans in, his face grave. "Well, I didn't want to have to tell you this way. But, well, we dated. We were in love. I'm heartbroken that you don't remember the glorious nights we shared."

Relieved at Speio's thoughtful intervention, I try not to burst out laughing at the convincing wounded expression on his face, but the look on Lo's face is priceless. His eyes are wide and he's staring from Speio to each of us in turn.

"Really?" Lo asks just as Sawyer muffles a snort.

Speio and Sawyer convulse into gales of laughter. "No, dude. Not really."

"Not that I would care either way," Lo says, grinning good-naturedly at their teasing. "I mean, you're a good-looking guy, and, well, I'm me. So naturally, I could see how you would be devastated."

"There's a spark of the old Lo." Speio grins. "But yeah, not devastated."

"Yeah, that would be Nerissa," Sawyer blurts out, and Jenna kicks him in the shins. His eyes widen in delayed realization of his gaffe and he gapes, panicked, from me to Lo, his mouth opening and shutting like a fish. A part of me hopes that Lo didn't hear, but of course, I don't have that kind of luck.

"What?" he says. "Why would she be— Oh."

"We dated briefly," I say in as normal a voice as I can manage, despite my quickened pulse.

Lo's eyes are liquid. "We dated?"

I'm saved from having to answer as a shrill voice interrupts us. "I'd hardly call throwing yourself at someone dating, but whatever. Nerissa never says no, if you know what I mean."

As much as I want to stuff Cara into a tiny box for her catty comment, I'm grateful for not having to answer Lo's husky, far-too-intimate question. Pushing back from the table, I grab my backpack and tray. I've had enough of this conversation, and I have no interest in rising to Cara's baited words. Jenna, however, has no such compunction.

"You wish that were true, Cara," Jenna says with an eye roll in Lo's direction as she, too, stands and gathers her things. Her eyes are glittering like an avenging angel's, leaping to my defense. "If you must know, Cara was the only one who couldn't help flinging herself at you. If you don't believe me, ask her what she went as last year to Junior Prom."

"Shut up, Jenna," Cara seethes.

But Jenna doesn't wait for Lo to ask. "You were Neptune, and she was your slutty little sea snake."

"I was an electric eel!" Cara screams shrilly.

"Eel, slutty sea snake. Same diff," Jenna tosses over her shoulder, nearly shoving her chair into Cara. She's about two inches shorter than Cara, but it doesn't make a difference as she steps up a hairbreadth from Cara's nose. "I'd be very careful if I were you," she says to her softly. "When Lo regains his memory—and he will—you're going to look quite the fool because you're *not* his girlfriend. So remember that when you're trying to rag on *my* friend. Nerissa may have the patience not to respond to your crap, but I don't, so back the hell off."

I swear that everyone's collective jaw is on the floor, mine included, as Cara swings on her heel and storms off.

"You coming?" Jenna asks me in a casual voice as if she didn't just flay my archnemesis alive in front of the entire cafeteria. "See you after school, hon," she says to Sawyer, and bends to kiss his cheek.

"You are so hot right now," he says.

"I know."

"Thanks, I think," I say to Jenna, following her into the hallway. I wave halfheartedly in the general vicinity of our table, not interested in seeing what anyone thinks of Jenna's outburst—particularly Lo. Or Speio, for that matter. "What happened to your speech about forgiveness last year, and taking the high road with Cara?"

Jenna grins. "No one but me calls my best friend a tramp and gets away with it." She sends me a sidelong glance. "Sorry, I couldn't help it. I know you don't like scenes, but with all the Lo stuff, I just kind of lost it."

I smile. "No, it's okay," I say. It was oddly satisfying to see Cara looking like she was throwing up in her mouth. "But you know there's going to be payback, right?"

"I'm not afraid of Cara," Jenna says, wiggling her eyebrows. "Plus, I can feed her to my very own sea monster as a snack if she gets out of line."

I snort out loud. "Remind me never to get on your bad side."

A toothy grin. "See? I don't have to have fins to be fearsome."

I nod vigorously. "No. You definitely don't. We'll make an honorary Aquarathi of you yet."

"I'm going to hold you to that."

6
Make Your Move

"Poisoned? What do you mean some kind of biological agent?" I'm nearly screaming the rapid-fire questions at Echlios. "And how would someone even get close enough to *poison* Lo? Was it Cano?"

"All we know is that it's some kind of biotoxin," Echlios says. "And we don't know that it was Cano, although he is a strong possibility."

I know it's him—every instinct inside me says it's him. Cano is still on the loose, and out there...trying to destabilize us. He's the only one who would attack Lo with something like this, something this diabolic. He was the one to help Ehmora with her hybrids and to combine the DNA strands in the first place—and he's the only one who would know about Lo. From what we've all learned last year, he is not to be underestimated, notwithstanding the fact that he's a brilliant biologist. This has his signature all over it.

My body is shaking so hard it feels like my teeth are going to shatter inside my mouth. I can feel the dull knuckle of bones already protruding from my brow, see the freckle of fins appearing and disappearing down my cheek like a wave of reptilian skin in the mirror across the hall. I'm as weak at controlling the transformation impulse as I am at controlling the chaos in my head. My breath comes in shortened, desperate bursts, and I grab the edge of the wooden table in my fists. It crumbles to splinters at my touch.

"My queen…Nerissa, please calm down," Echlios says, his eyes anxious.

"Don't tell me to calm down," I rage, my clothing popping as razor-sharp fins emerge along the length of my spine, ripping through my cotton shirt like butter. "You're telling me that someone deliberately poisoned Lo. *How?*" Soren's fingers reach across to mine, her calming energy sweeping across our human skins and sinking into me. Accepting her gesture, I breathe slow and deep. "How, Echlios?" I ask less forcefully this time.

"Injected or ingested, we presume," Echlios says, resuming his seated position. I follow his lead and focus on keeping my breathing even. "But we have no way to be sure. We got lucky. The tests were inconclusive at first. The memory loss was just that—retrograde dissociative amnesia from the shock of what happened with his mother. But then Dr. Watson saw something and ordered more tests, this time checking for specific blood and neural toxicity. He saw some kind of odd discoloration in a group of cells near the memory center. He'd had a hunch that the memory loss didn't seem fully consistent with dissociative amnesia—it appeared as if it were being aggravated by something else. A marine biotoxin of some sort."

"What is that?" Speio asks softly. "Something from the sea?"

"It's an organic toxin that occurs organically in nature from certain types of oceanic algae blooms, like the red tide," Echlios says. Speio and I exchange a glance. We've both surfed at night during the red tide in San Diego, when the phytoplankton bloom makes the water turn a psychedelic blue.

"We've never gotten sick from that," Speio blurts out. "Or any of our friends."

"That's because our Aquarathi immune systems aren't affected by this toxin, but even so, the tide isn't necessarily caused by toxic algae. Some blooms are toxic, some aren't."

"So humans can get sick from it?" I ask.

"Sometimes. In rare cases, mammals and humans get infected from eating contaminated shellfish. In its natural form, it's called domoic acid, and the normal side effects range from nausea to coma to death," Echlios explains. The blood drains from my face. "However, in Lo's case, it appears that it has been chemically altered, which is how we knew that he has been poisoned."

"Altered? Why?"

"Because his Aquarathi DNA would find a way to combat the infection. They've somehow made it more resistant and human-centric at the same time. Meaning that it only targets the human cells and that it can't be detected by his Aquarathi immune system."

"That's just perfect," I mutter. "Trust Cano to come up with a marine toxin to weaken the hybrids he engineered in the first place to be sea creatures like us. It just seems *wrong*." I can't help shuddering.

"He's clever," Echlios says. "It's the perfect fail-safe."

Echlios is right. If something had gone wrong during their species-grafting experimentation, they would have needed something immediate to weaken the hybrids. Since human DNA is weaker than ours, it makes sense that they would have targeted the human cells. But I'd bet anything that Cano wanted to make the toxin as lethal as possible, not to use just as a fail-safe but as a weapon.

Snapping out my smart phone, I quickly run a search for *domoic acid poisoning*. According to the first website, it's also called *amnesic shellfish poisoning*. I scan the immediate symptoms—vomiting, nausea, cramps—but I'm more interested in the neurological symptoms farther down, like dizziness, disorientation, short-term memory loss and seizures... the ones that could lead to comas and death. And then my gaze spans down farther and my breath hitches in my throat.

There is no cure.

The rush of fear nearly makes me double over, but I can't afford to let it derail me. Nobody creates a poison without creating its remedy, especially for someone as valuable as Lo. Not even Cano would be that foolish...at least I hope he wouldn't. With a fortifying breath, I process all of the information from Echlios and the website as clinically as I can, but I can't seem to get my mind around one thing. I glance at Echlios, pocketing my phone.

"Even if it were Cano or Ehmora's people, Lo was—*is*— her son, and the perfect hybrid specimen. Why would they want to hurt him?"

Echlios spreads his palms to the sky. "If it means getting you out of Waterfell, I can see that being an option. Ehmora viewed him as an expendable bargaining chip. Why wouldn't they continue to do so? Bringing you here disrupts the courts and could create chaos."

"Wait a second," I muse. The vision of my dream, of Ehmora telling me she isn't dead, hovers over me like a wet, dark cloud. Even from the grave, we can't escape her influence. "You think Lo was poisoned to draw me back here?"

"It's possible. In Waterfell, you are safe. It's impenetrable."
Echlios shakes his head. "Here, it's open and we are vulnerable in human form. They knew you'd have no choice
but to come back for him once you felt him deteriorating."

"Deteriorating? You mean from the amnesia?"

Echlios stares at me. "No. From his failing body."

Of course. Lo's dying. As if I could forget.

Soren clears her throat, the soft pulsing sound reminding me to breathe, despite the fact that my body has gone
completely immobile after Echlios's quiet words. "We also
believe they—both Neriah and Cano—have been watching him, and that they still have ties to the school. Spies,"
she says.

The mention of my mother's name makes my stomach
twist into ugly knots. It's been hard not to think about her,
but I've taught myself to be numb if and when I ever do.
After her being instrumental in my father's murder, her betrayal had become unforgivable when she and her lover—
Ehmora—decided to kill me for my throne.

"That's not possible," I say. But of course it is. Just because we killed Ehmora and chased my mother and Cano
inland doesn't mean that they'd give up on Ehmora's plans.
If either of them is still alive, we are at risk...as they've obviously proven with Lo. Castia, the Emerald Court queen,
was partially right. They wanted me back here.

"There's more," Soren continues, glancing at her son.
"We suspect that there is a spy in school who's feeding Cano
information. Keeping tabs on you and on Lo."

"Like who? The acting headmaster?"

"No. Echlios glimmered her weeks before we arrived,"
Soren says. "Could be a teacher. The school nurse. Other
students."

"Can't we just leave?" Speio asks. "Take Lo with us to Waterfell and figure it out there?"

Echlios shakes his head. "That was my plan until Nerissa saw something when she glimmered him last week. He doesn't seem to know what he is, so—"

"So we can't take the risk of him freaking out a hundred thousand leagues under the sea," Speio finishes, wide-eyed.

"Or trying to return to human form," Echlios says grimly.

"It's not just that," Soren interjects. "How do we even get him to remember who or what he is? If this is part of a greater scheme to weaken the Aquarathi, that needs to happen sooner rather than later. The longer we stay here, the more we are at risk." She glances at me. "The more our queen is at risk."

"And Waterfell," I add.

"There is another alternative. Castia—" Echlios begins, but I cut him off with a furious glare, already preempting what he's going to say. The very thought of what Castia suggested about letting Lo die alone makes me sick to my stomach.

"That's not an option," I say. "We can't abandon him. That's a death sentence and you know it. The High Council has given us a chance and time to do something. We have to try. For him, and for Waterfell." *And for me.*

Echlios nods, bowing his head, and for a second I think I see what looks like relief flash across his face. A cold feeling slithers through me.... I left Lo behind before the last time we left for Waterfell. Did he think I'd do it now?

"We stay together," I say firmly. "We have just under four months to find Cano, figure out what he's plotting and find a cure." I break off abruptly and stare at Echlios, recalling what I read on my phone not two minutes before. "Please tell me there is something that can save him, Echlios."

"I believe there is. Cano is far too meticulous not to have reengineered a natural toxin without also creating its counter remedy." Echlios pauses. "And if Lo were to die, they would have no leverage, which leads me to believe that the effects of this toxin can be reversed or at least stopped."

"And Lo's memory loss?"

Echlios's face is compassionate. "That's a bit more complicated. The biotoxin inhibits the brain from healing itself. He could be trying to repair those neurons as we speak and yet be completely limited by the toxin's effects."

Speio's voice is small. "Will he be able to remember who he is?"

"Probably not without help," Echlios says. "If we don't counter the chemical effects, and soon, I'm afraid the memory loss could become permanent. But let's not get ahead of ourselves," he adds gently, seeing my stricken expression. "For all we know, Lo could start remembering things tomorrow. We Aquarathi are nothing if not strong. We fight even when we are down—it's the core of who we are. And that is true, too, at a base, cellular level."

I try not to put too much faith in Echlios's words, but a part of me fervently hopes that Lo's Aquarathi side will step up and defend itself. I can't imagine any part of myself not fighting to survive. It's in our nature. Hybrid or not, he's Aquarathi through and through, and he's bonded to me. That has to count for something.

The small bloom of hope blossoms into something bigger, and takes root deep in my abdomen.

I have to make him remember who he is.

★ ★ ★

Slamming my locker shut, I make my way out to the parking lot. Jenna has hockey practice and I'm left to my own devices. She's the mastermind, not me, but I have a plan and one that I hope is going to work. The first step is to get Lo out of Cara's clutches. Shaking my head as I exit the school, I can't help comparing the incongruous parallels of the whole situation. Cara Andrews is like the human part of Lo fighting for dominion, and I'm his Aquarathi side, determined to reclaim what is mine. I'm not in the least bit threatened by Cara, but I am worried that Lo will *want* to gravitate toward his human side and to the familiar. In the grand scheme of things, I'm someone new to him.

That has to change, starting with evening shifts at the Marine Center. It wasn't easy to get my old job back, but thankfully the manager, Kevin, hasn't lost *his* memory and remembers my involvement last year. Plus, a sizable donation from the Marin family fund for the oceanic conservation drive didn't hurt matters. As a result, I've been able to secure a few hours during the week after school.

Hefting my backpack into the rear of the Jeep, I climb in and surreptitiously peek at Lo and Cara in the rearview mirror, standing next to her car.

"So you can't come over to study?" Cara is saying to Lo in the parking lot, her arm wrapped around his. Seriously, it's like she can't stop touching him every infernal second.

"Sorry," Lo says with an easy grin. "Some of us have to work. Can you give me a ride over there? Caught a ride with Sawyer this morning after our surf lesson, so no car."

And that's my cue.

Putting the Jeep into reverse, I swing out and pull alongside. Cara's face immediately tightens. "I can give you a ride," I say to Lo. "I'm heading over there myself."

"Since when?" Cara says.

"Since I work there," I say sweetly.

"How did you—" she begins, and then snaps her mouth shut, eyeing me with a suspicious frown. "I thought you said they didn't have any open slots," she says to Lo. The flirtatious tone has gone into accusatory mode. Obviously she tried to get a job there to spend more time with Lo.

"They didn't," he says, shrugging.

I smile widely. "What can I say? I'm special. Come on, Lo. We're going to be late. Get in."

Resisting the urge to peel out of the parking lot and leave black tire marks in my wake, I drive more sedately, keeping my exhilaration contained. I don't even know why I'm keeping score, because it's so childish, but I do, anyway. Nerissa two, Cara zero.

My exhilaration wanes into acute awareness of Lo sitting in the passenger seat, and all of the unsaid things from the other day in the cafeteria lying between us. Neither one of us says anything, but the silence is comfortable instead of awkward.

"Hey, what song is this?" Lo says, twisting the volume button on the car stereo.

I fumble for my phone on the middle console and chuck it at him. "It's just a playlist I'm working on. That one's called 'As the Rush Comes' by Motorcycle."

"I like it. Very mellow," he says, stroking the face of the phone with his thumb and scrolling through the playlist. "I know some of these. You have good taste."

I laugh. "You know some of those because they're yours. You and I started this playlist."

With a raised eyebrow, he selects the next song. The opening chords of Blackmill's "The Drift" comes on. "This is one of my favorites. I love the piano instrumental with the backbeat. It's tight."

"Yep," I say. "You got me into them. Here, hand that over for a second. Bet you don't know these guys, but this one is all you." With a quick swipe, I select the last song I added to the playlist. I don't add that I've listened to the chorus of the song at least a hundred times while torturing myself about what he's been doing all summer with Cara.

"Who is it?" he says after a few bars, his foot tapping against the floor.

"Morgan Page's 'The Longest Road,' Deadmau5 remix."

"Catchy."

"Great lyrics," I add.

"I can see that," he says quietly. His gaze flutters on me for a second and then drifts away when mine flicks to his. I don't know if he's agreeing with me or appreciating that they mean something to me. He looks as if he has more to say, but then he bites his lip and releases a slow sigh. He stares out the window for a moment before shifting in his seat to face me. "Sorry about the other day at school," he blurts out. "I didn't realize we were a couple. I mean, it makes sense. When you were at my house, I felt something. It was so strong, like this weird pull toward you. Sorry, it wasn't weird…" He trails off with a stammer. "I am totally screwing up what I want to say."

"I know what you mean, Lo."

"I wish I could remember. I don't know how I could forget you or us, that's all," he says, shooting me a look that makes my heart flip-flop. "Sawyer told me that it was love at first sight," he adds with a laugh, "and then he told me the truth…that I had to work hard to even get you to go out with me."

"Hardly," I protest, but I can't hide the blush that heats my neck, nor the fact that it threatens to go supernova at his next words.

"I'm sure it was worth it," he says quietly.

At a stop sign, I turn to smile tremulously at him, my heart beating a hundred miles a minute. "It was for both of us. You helped me figure out a lot of things about myself. We're pretty similar, you and me."

"Seems like it," he says with a thoughtful glance, studying the playlist on the phone's screen. "You know, I was surprised that people didn't tell me about you. I asked because I found a prom photo earlier this summer." His teeth flash white for a second. "One of me dressed in some seaweed with this totally hot girl."

I know the one he's talking about—it was one of the few photos we took together at Jenna's house right before Junior Prom. "We were Neptune and Salacia. Roman gods of the ocean."

"I figured it was some kind of theme," he says with a somber smile. "I think Bertha thought it would be better if I didn't know. It's not like you were still around, so she told me you were someone I'd gone with. Maybe she thought it would be too painful if I couldn't remember. I mean, there I was staring at this girl with this expression…like she was everything to me and I couldn't even remember her name. I think Bertha felt sorry for me." He trails off to stare out the window, his voice going so quiet that I have to strain to hear him. "I wish someone had told me, because maybe I could have tried harder. Maybe I could have done something differently, made myself remember somehow." He shrugs, watching me, his tone wistful. "Because now here you are, and all I want is to be that guy in that photo."

Lo's eyes are intense and it's all I can do not to start crying then and there. "That guy is still in there, Lo," I say. "And that girl will always be here, waiting for you. You just have to take it one day at a time."

Everything inside me tenses up when he reaches over and slides his palm over the back of my hand on the gearshift, holding it there for the rest of the ride. I'm afraid to even look at him, so I swallow hard and keep my eyes on the road, barely conscious of anything but the warm seal of his skin on mine. We listen to the rest of the playlist in silence until I pull in to the Marine Center parking lot.

"I'm sorry," he says, drawing his hand away. "I didn't mean to overstep—"

"You didn't. This is new to me, too. One day at a time. Deal?"

"Deal," Lo says, then hops out of the Jeep with an overbright grin as if to make up for the earlier turn in the conversation. "Thanks for the ride. So this is going to be like old times, right?"

The question takes me aback for a second before I realize that he's joking. "You can't even remember last week," I toss back. "What do you know about old times?"

"I guess you'll have to show me."

I take a breath to calm my racing pulse and manage a half-teasing smile. "I don't think you're quite ready for that, but I'll let you know when."

"Promise?"

The evocative meaning in that single word makes my bones dissolve into nothing. Which explains why you couldn't knock the smile off my face as we walk into the Marine Center.

"Hey, Riss!" Kevin shouts, jumping over the counter to sweep me into a huge bear hug. "So glad you're back. Place just hasn't been the same without you. Where's your partner in crime?"

"Jenna? Don't worry, I'll get her back here to do her share. She's at a hockey game."

"No hockey for you this year?"

"I'm focusing on other things," I say. Yeah, like finding a cure for my boyfriend's imminent doom. I smile brightly. "But hey, at least Lo's been here holding down the fort."

Kevin grins, chucking Lo in the shoulder. "Well, if he could only remember his name, it'd be awesome," he teases.

"That joke never gets old," Lo says good-naturedly. "So, what do you have for us today? Beach cleanup?"

Consulting a clipboard on the desk, Kevin purses his lips. "Actually, someone just called in from La Jolla Shores saying that they thought they saw a bunch of garbage bags caught in the kelp beds. You guys want to check it out? Just radio back if you need help. Standard swipe and dump, shouldn't take the two of you too long."

"We'll take care of it," I say.

"Riss, you remember where the boat is, right?" Kevin asks, tossing me a set of keys attached to a bright yellow foam oval. "It's good to have you back."

"Great to be back." I find that I mean it. I've missed the Marine Center and doing my part to protect the world's oceans. It is where I live, after all, and although we aren't allowed to interfere in the day-to-day politics of people who share the planet with us, marine conservancy is an area where we can get more actively involved.

Lo and I get changed in the respective bathrooms and meet out on the beach near the shed where all the gear is stored.

"We probably won't need these if those bags are just floating, but do you remember how to scuba?" I ask him, tugging on one of the air tanks and tossing it into the back of the dune buggy.

"I do," he says, grabbing a hold of another tank. "It's weird that I remember clearly how to do something like diving, and yet other things like surfing I can't seem to get my mind around. I know I've done it before. I mean, I can feel that my body knows how to do it, but then something in my brain doesn't click and it becomes impossible...if that makes any sense."

"It does," I say. "Don't worry, it'll come back. You just have to give yourself time to get there." I toss him a long-handled net. "Now let's go save some fish from death by plastic, and get that memory muscle working."

Steering the speedboat out toward the middle of the bay, I close my eyes for a beat. The air is slightly cooler mixed in with the mist of the sea, and every cell in my body is responding to the call of the water. The ocean is a bit choppy, so we're tossing up a lot more wake than usual, but I don't mind one bit. I'd be out in a hurricane, if I could. Out here in the middle of the ocean with the sun on my face and the smell of salt in the air, it's the closest thing to paradise this side of Waterfell.

"This is incredible!" Lo shouts. "Kevin never goes this fast."

"Kevin's a wuss," I tell him, grinning. "Want to have a go? Come on, grab the wheel." I'm not prepared for him to step behind me, encircling me with his entire body and *then* placing his hands on the wheel on either side of mine.

"Like this?" His voice is husky in my ear.

I clear my suddenly dry throat, my voice breathless. "That's fine." It's hard to concentrate with him standing so close that I can feel every twitch of his body, each intake of breath. And after his soft touch in the car, all I want to do is to melt backward into him…fit each curve of his body into every curve of mine and be whole again. "So, when's the last time you were out on the boat?" I ask in a shaky voice.

Lo shakes his head. "Not since the last time with you."

"*What* did you just say?"

Lo steps backward, making every inch of my skin feel bereft. He screws his face into a deep frown as if struggling with his words and the force of the memory hidden behind them. "I don't know. I mean, I know I said with you, but now I don't remember doing it. I'm sorry." He shrugs, help-less. His face is tortured. "At least I think it was with you. It was. It wasn't anyone else. Maybe being with you now is helping me remember things."

"Maybe," I say carefully, even though my heart is fairly leaping with joy. Lo just remembered *me*…or the thought of us, but that's better than nothing. I bring the boat to a smooth stop just outside the kelp beds, and pull off my T-shirt. Grab-bing a pair of fins and a facemask, I sit on the side of the boat. "You coming?"

But Lo has gone perfectly still, staring at my skin beneath the straps of my bathing suit. Self-conscious, I hunch my shoulders until I realize that he's staring at the navy tattoos curling around from my neck. He pulls off his shirt and dips his shoulder to show me his back. It's only been a few months, but the sight of Lo's bare body takes my breath away—the sleek curve of his chest, the defined stomach and the smooth golden skin. He jabs at his back while I try to keep my pulse from leaping clear out of my chest. "See? Mine are the same, only green and gold."

My eyes rove over the tattoos that are mirror images of the ones curling along my neck and back. I fight a visceral urge to throw myself into his arms and force him to remember us. "We got them at the same time," I say.

"We must have been serious. Tattoos are a big commitment."

"Bigger than you can imagine." I, of course, have no way of telling him that these are way more permanent than permanent ink. Bonding markings can never be removed, nor are they truly tattoos. "And we were serious," I tell him honestly. "But you guessed that already."

His face is pained. "I'm sorry. I wish I could rem—"

"A boy I used to know told me that there's a silver lining," I interrupt him, wanting nothing more than to erase the sudden sadness from his eyes. "After all, how many couples you know get to go on repeat first dates?"

"Are you asking me out?" Lo says, a slow smile stretching across his face.

"What if I am?"

"Then I'd say yes."

7
Stop, Drop and Roll

The "date" with Lo could not have gone any worse. First of all, we went to the Crab Shack—notorious local high-school weekend hangout spot—which meant that every high schooler with a pulse was there. Put it this way: trying to have a romantic first date? Not easy. Trying to have a romantic first date with hundreds of curious eyes peering at you and judging your every eyelash movement? Impossible.

On top of that, one of Cara's minions was a waitress there, so I couldn't eat anything. Who wants spit in their calamari? Not me. So Lo and I'd ended up staring at each other in stifled silence and sipping lukewarm iced teas, while trying to ignore everyone around us who made no effort whatsoever to mind their own business. Awkward? Just a tad.

"So, I take it that it didn't go well," Jenna stage-whispers into my locker.

I shoot her a glare. "Stop pretending it isn't all over the local Dover wire," I say. "And everyone didn't have front-row tickets to the Nerissa-Lo failed-date extravaganza. Why weren't you there, anyway?"

"Sorry, I was grounded all weekend."

"What for?"

"For using foul language on school property," she says. "Catty Cara ratted me out. Luckily, my stellar academic record kept me from being suspended, but Mom still wanted to teach me a lesson. Go figure." She winks at me and yells down the hallway where Cara is standing near the girls' bathroom. "What a bitch, right?"

"Jenna! You really are going to get suspended," I warn.

"You must have heard me wrong," she says with a dramatic hand to the chest. "I said beyotch. Big difference. Whatever, if Cara wants to go to the rodeo and antagonize the bull, she's gonna get the horns." Jenna makes a pair of horns with the index and little fingers of one hand and smacks it on her forehead.

"You're so tough," I say with a grin. "Like are you back on the 'roids or what?"

"Is it that obvious?" Jenna jokes back, twirling an invisible mustache.

"You are hopeless."

"Yeah, well, good thing you love me, even with my steroid stash," she says, and leans a shoulder against the nearby locker. "So, was it really *that* bad? The date?"

I close my locker, books in hand. "Worse than bad. Catty Cara showed up and basically fake-choked on a French fry. Guess who had to drive her to the emergency room?"

Jenna's eyes widen. "That sneaky little b—"

"Pretty much," I agree, walking toward Advanced Math, which thankfully Cara is *not* in. "So yes, Lo took her because she was 'terrified'—her word, not mine—and that was that. End of date. Nerissa two, Cara one."

"We are going to have to take her down," Jenna says, shaking her head.

"It's not worth it."

"Hold the phone. What did you just say?"

I laugh at her expression. "It's not worth getting into a petty high-school war over. I have way worse things to worry about, including my people and what's going to happen with Lo. Plus, I don't want Lo to resent me because I've hurt his friend," I say.

Jenna grins, shakes her head in mock surprise. "Whoa. Queendom *changed* you."

"Thanks," I say drily. "Guess I grew up."

Jenna directs me to sit in the back of class. Today is obviously going to be a passing-notes kind of day, not a pay-attention kind of day. I'd honestly prefer to lose myself in some advanced precalculus, but I roll with the flow.

Jenna writes in her notebook, sliding it with an elbow toward me. *So, what'd you wear? Did you at least look hot?*

I roll my eyes and shrug. Hot for me means jeans and a T-shirt. That's about as dressed up as I like to get, but I'd switched it up, opting for a filmy sundress and sandals. *Dress,* I write back.

Jenna shoots me an appraising, impressed look. *Nice. And Lo?*

Black jeans, vintage Dead T-shirt. Hot. I can't resist writing the last word. He had looked entirely too hot, almost like the old Lo. I say almost, because he wore actual shoes instead of flip-flops or going barefoot as old Lo had done on more than one occasion. He'd told me that he liked the feel of the earth beneath his toes.

"So, chemistry?" Jenna whispers, and then taps at the notebook. I glance down. She'd written *DEETS!!!!!!* in big, bold letters.

I pause, studying the tip of my pencil. How can I explain such explosive chemistry that I felt every single drop of water surging to the forefront of my human skin, frantic to connect with his? And I felt it from him, too. If I learned one thing during our quasi date, it was that his body sure remembered mine. Just thinking about that makes a hot rush flood my cheeks.

Jenna pokes me in the arm, her mouth open and eyes, wicked. "*That* good?"

"Better."

We both jump at Mr. Devane's deep voice. "Ms. Marin and Ms. Pearce, if we could have your attention as well, please."

"Sorry," we both mutter, and obediently turn our stares to the front of the class.

Thank God Lo isn't in this class, because I would probably ignite the two of us if he were. I take a few quiet breaths to calm my racing heart and the water rushing around inside my body like a hurricane tide. Function derivatives and tangents take the edge off, but I'm barely a slow simmer by the time class is over.

There's only one thing that can clear my head in short order. I drag Jenna to a deserted corner of the building, casting out a quick glimmer to make sure no one is within hearing distance. I keep it there and hold it steady. Last thing I need is for anyone to inadvertently hear this conversation.

"What's wrong?" Jenna says. "We're going to be late for English and you know how Donovan is about tardiness."

"I have something to tell you. It's important."

"What?" she says.

In a few short sentences, I briefly explain the poisoning scenario with Lo, watching as her eyes widen to giant blue orbs with the information. Sure enough, the simmer in my body reduces to nothing but a cold kind of calm. Nothing like imminent death to take your mind off making out.

"But who?" she whispers after I'm done.

"We don't know. Soren says there're still spies in the school. Watching our every move."

Jenna's eyes dart down the empty hallway. "Now?"

"I did a glimmer. We're alone."

"But you would know, right?" Jenna says slowly as if she's deep in thought. "I mean, any Aquarathi have to reveal themselves to you. You're the only queen, now that Ehmora's gone."

I shake my head. "Not if they're hybrids. Lo, as Ehmora's direct descendant, could sense them, but…" I trail off.

"He doesn't know what he is," Jenna says. "Which means that even if he did sense something, he wouldn't know what it meant. So they basically knew exactly what they were doing by setting this all in motion."

"Pretty much."

"Wow, that's Machiavellian. So what do we do?"

"We keep our eyes and ears open. We check everyone out—new people, old people. The works. And we keep our guard up."

"What about Lo and the poison? Is it going to get worse?" Jenna asks, leaning in, her voice nearly inaudible, as a group of girls approach us from the far end of the hallway. I shake my head—the girls are already on the edge of my glimmer. But Jenna presses her hand on my arm, her fingers cold against my warm human skin. Her thoughts are as clear as a bell in my head. *What aren't you telling me?*

We communicated like this before once when I was in Aquarathi form. The oncoming horde of girls stops at a row of nearby lockers. Twisting slightly to move my arm out of sight, I press Jenna's hand between my skin and the wall behind us. Then I shift, just the part of me where her fingers are touching. At the hardened sensation of my scales beneath her fingertips, alarm flashes in her eyes, but she doesn't pull away. Instead she splays her fingers against my Aquarathi hide.

I manipulate the waters in my body to translate the sounds of my words to the waters in hers, like a vibration conduit of sorts. I'm careful, controlling the frequency of the sound waves as best as I can because the last time I did this, I pretty much exploded her eardrums.

I swallow, hauling a breath into my lungs. I pulse lightly to Jenna, *If we don't find a way to reverse the effects, he's going to die.*

What do you mean he's going to die? she says, shocked. *They wouldn't kill him, would they? He's one of theirs.*

They would. To get to me.

So, what's the plan? We have nothing, Jenna says, her breath erratic. *We don't even know where your mother and Cano are.*

Calm down, I pulse gently. I'm tempted to use Sanctum on Jenna—a form of emotional control used by the royals of my people. Speio once told me that it worked on humans. But Jenna would kill me if I did anything like that without her consent. I opt for words instead. *I can find my mother.*

How?

As queen, I can summon her to me.

Jenna's eyes are bugging out of her head. *And why would you do something like that? The last time you saw her, she tried to kill you. Remember? Plus, you kind of killed her girlfriend. Not like she'll be in a forgiving mood. That's suicide.*

I shrug. *I have no other option. I can't let Lo die. I'll trade. Me for him.*

But she wants you dead!

I don't think she does. I think she wants to punish me.

I can feel every emotion from Jenna, including her absolute rejection of the idea of me contacting my mother. She's terrified for me. *What does Echlios say?*

But before I can respond, a loud, scornful voice interrupts us. "Seriously, get a room and save the entire school the barf-fest of watching you two make out."

Jenna's palm peels away from my skin and I shimmer back into full human, slightly disoriented at the sudden shift.

"Eyes," Jenna hisses at me, and I realize I must have let go of the thin film that covers my Aquarathi eyes. I blink and slide them into place.

"You would think that, Cara," Jenna says in just as scathing a tone. "Because your mind is in the gutter."

"Hey, if the shoe fits." She stares at us, her mouth twitching. Her expression makes me uneasy.

"What do you want?"

"Not what *I* want," she drawls, "what Principal Andrews wants."

"Principal *who?*" Jenna says.

Cara grins. "Didn't you hear the news? My father's been transferred back here. Looks like they want to keep it in the family. He was appointed acting headmaster this morning."

"What about Mrs. Clarke? I thought she was acting headmaster," I say, frowning. I'd forgotten that Cara even had a dad, considering that she lived with Cano, her mother's brother, all of last year. According to the gossip mill, her father was always on the road and only saw his daughter once a year.

"Guess she wasn't the right fit for the job, so while they're looking for a permanent candidate, you're going to have to deal with Principal Andrews," Cara says in an annoying musical tone. "Anyway, chop-chop. Wouldn't want to be late for detention."

I glance at the clock on the opposite wall and gasp. We missed almost half of the class, and neither of us heard the bell.

"Donovan sent me to get you. I, of course, felt no desire to save either of your loser selves, so I told him I couldn't find you. And, well, now you're kind of wanted in the office for ditching class," she says gleefully.

"You are evil, Cara, you know that?" Jenna says, tugging on my arm. "Come on, let's go before she gets another taste of me."

"You wouldn't," Cara says, but she backs up a couple steps all the same.

Jenna folds her arms across her chest. "You think you can hide because your dad is now the school principal? Didn't work with Cano, won't work now. Don't push me, Cara, because you won't like what you get. I'm sure you wouldn't want Lo seeing that pretty face all banged up from a rogue hockey ball during practice."

"You'll be expelled in a second," Cara breathes.

Jenna shrugs. "Hey, accidents happen. And it's a risk I'm willing to take."

The fuzziness in my head finally clears and I follow Jenna's lead, walking toward the office and leaving a gaping, irate Cara behind us.

"You okay?" Jenna asks me. "You seem out of it."

"Fine." I rub my arm where we'd been touching. "I didn't want to hurt you like the last time, so it took a lot of energy to make sure I didn't. It's nothing, don't worry."

We wait in silence in the office before we are ushered in

together by the frazzled receptionist. Jenna and I sit in the empty seats across from the large desk and the man on the other side of it. Principal Andrews looks like a male version of Cara with thick chestnut-colored curls and icy blue eyes. I wonder if he's as competitive and calculating as she is. If he got this job, he probably is. It's really kind of ironic, actually, that Cara is now living with her biological father. It's even more ironic that he, of all people, is the new principal of Dover. Control issues must run in the family.

Principal Andrews's voice is as icy as his eyes. "Ms. Marin and Ms. Pearce, you've both been marked absent from English. As you know, we take skipping classes very seriously at Dover." He leans back in his chair, steepling his fingers on the edge of the desk. "As the new headmaster, I have to make sure that students attend class, and to punish those who think it's appropriate to flaunt the rules."

"Sir—" Jenna begins, and is cut off by a frosty glare.

"You will speak when addressed, Ms. Pearce." He studies us in turn, his pale gaze lingering on me. "I've read your files. Seems you've both caused this administration enough trouble—cutting class, harassing other students. I'll be putting an end to that. Do you have anything to say for yourselves?"

Jenna opens and closes her mouth. I lean forward. "Did you get that information in our written files or from another, less reliable source?" I ask coolly. "Because I wouldn't put any faith in your daughter's word, especially on your first day in office." Jenna turns to stare at me, eyes popping, and Principal Andrews looks like he's about to choke, his face turning a dark shade of purple.

"How dare you?" he sputters. "I'll have you expelled."

"For what?" I ask. "For speaking the truth? Mr. Andrews, my family has been on this school board for centuries, longer than you have. What makes you think you can have me expelled? I've done nothing wrong. I was late for class because of a family emergency, and was being consoled by my friend, who is now sitting here through no fault of her own." I lean back in my chair and steeple my own fingers. "I suggest you take a look at those files again. You will see that we both have A averages and are exemplary students. However, if you want to take this up with the school board..."

"Are you threatening me?"

"Merely suggesting, Mr. Andrews."

His face turns violently purple now. "Why, you impertinent—"

I cut him off with a wave of my hand as iridescent lights shimmer along my palms. Time slows and stops entirely. I can sense the whirring of a fly's wings on the far wall... hear the silent, liquid exhale of Jenna's breath. Every inch of me is alive, connected to the water in the air. I glimmer forward without a second thought and slip into the principal's brain.

What I'm doing isn't exactly mind control, more like mind suggestion. The weaker the mind, the easier it is to suggest. Very few humans can withstand the power of suggestion from an Aquarathi—far less an Aquarathi queen—which is why any kind of human manipulation is against our laws.

Then again, I *am* the law, and laws sometimes need to be bent.

I do know that the laws are in place for a reason. I can make any Aquarathi forget his entire life or make him do things in half a breath, and as I've seen before, my glimmers can crush a human mind into nothing simply by manipulating the pain sensors. Until Ehmora, my father's law has always been to share the planet and defend it, if we must. But day-to-day influence over humans is strictly forbidden... unless we are in danger.

This isn't one of those times, but I can't stand to see Cara get her way, or drag Jenna into this. I'm not making Mr. Andrews do anything untoward. I'm just helping him to see past his daughter's petty childishness. I release the glimmer—the entire process has taken less than ten seconds.

Mr. Andrews slouches back into his chair, a glazed look coming over his eyes before he sits up and examines the files on his desk. "Sorry. Where was I?" he says, tapping the edges of the manila folders.

"I was explaining that I have a family emergency, which is why we were late," I say helpfully. Jenna's mouth is open and she's staring at me with such an incredulous look I have to bite my lip from snorting out loud.

"Ah yes," he agrees in an affable voice. "Well, considering that you both have such stellar records, I'll give you a pass on this one. Next time, please come to the office first, Ms. Marin."

"Yes, of course, sir," I say.

He glances at the expensive watch on his wrist. "There are about five more minutes left of class. I'll let Mr. Donovan know that you were both excused. Thank you, ladies."

Jenna keeps it together until we are out of the office and outside on the deserted quad before turning on me, hands on her hips, and demanding an explanation. "What the hell did you just do, Nerissa Marin?"

"What?" I say with a guilty look.

"No one goes from complete detonation to have-a-nice-day mellow in less than a minute," she says, her eyebrows snapping together. "Seriously, I blinked, expecting the worst, and then he let us go. What'd you do? Spill it."

"I didn't do anything," I say. "Much."

Her eyes widen. "You totally mind-melded him, didn't you?"

"Seriously, Jenna, you need to get your mind out of *Star Trek*. I did not mind-meld the principal. I simply suggested that he reconsider his choices. There's a big difference."

"Reconsider his choices—" Jenna splutters and shakes her head, her eyes wide and accusing, as if I've somehow exploited my otherworldly abilities to nefarious ends. "I thought Speio said you don't do mind control." Her forehead furrows as she tries to remember the conversation from so many months ago. "Wait a second…he said that *you* could."

I take a frustrated breath. "Look, I'm not about to let Cara take her vicious lies to her father and affect your future at Dover. I couldn't care less about me, because it doesn't matter, but you are an entirely different story. You've already put everything on the line for me…your future, your life. I'm not about to let some immature drama queen get her daddy to put black marks on your perfect high-school record. So I helped him change his mind." I mimic her position, slamming my hands on my hips. "And if you have a problem with that, then too bad."

"Jeez, don't freak out," Jenna says, throwing her hands into the air. "It just took me by surprise. Thanks, I think."

"You're welcome."

We sit on the grass in the empty courtyard and enjoy the remaining minutes of privacy before the bell rings for break. I take an apple out of my backpack and bite into it, letting the sun warm my face. Jenna lies back beside me, her head on her bag.

"Can I ask you a question?" she says, hesitant, propping herself up on one elbow.

"Can I stop you?" I say with an eye roll.

"No," she says mildly. "Have you ever done that to me? The mind suggestion thing?"

I meet her eyes and hold her gaze. "No."

"Will you?"

"Not if you don't want me to," I say quietly.

"I don't. Have you done it to anyone I know?" she persists. God, she's annoying when she wants to be, but I know that if I don't answer, she's not going to back down.

"Kevin."

"Our *boss*, Kevin? From the Marine Center? What? When?"

"When I needed the boat in the middle of the night last year," I say. "And I didn't do anything other than to suggest that he hadn't seen me. Satisfied?"

She nods and reassumes her position, staring at the puffy white clouds floating above us. "So you can glimmer anyone you want?" she asks after a minute. "How come you can't just glimmer Cara into permanently shutting her trap? That would be all kinds of awesome."

"Because it's not technically allowed." I see her frown. "We aren't allowed to influence human will for our own gain. It kind of has to be approved in advance by the High Council in Waterfell, unless it's a life-or-death situation."

"But you just did, with Mr. Andrews."

"For you. Worth the risk, and *totally* life-or-death situation."

"Oh." Jenna chews on her lip and turns her head to me,

barely cracking a smile at my lame joke. "Thanks...for looking out for me, I mean."

"I've always got your back, Jenna. Just like you've always
got mine."

She flushes and looks away, as if embarrassed by the compliment. At that moment, the bell rings, announcing the
end of class. It doesn't take long before our sliver of courtyard heaven is no longer vacant. Jenna waves Sawyer over,
but before he reaches us, Lo in tow, she leans toward me,
her eyes shaded.

"So, are you going to do it?" she whispers. "What we
were talking about before? Summoning your mother?"

"Yes."

"Are you sure that's the right thing to do?"

"I don't know."

I sigh, watching one of the white clouds morph into an
ominous gargoyle shape above me. Maybe it's my imagi-
nation or maybe the silhouette is a total coincidence, but I
can't shake the sudden shiver that makes gooseflesh erupt
all over my skin.

8

A Kiss Is Just a Kiss

"Absolutely not! I will not have you knowingly put yourself at risk."

"Echlios," I say softly. "I'd rather have you by my side than the alternative." I squeeze his shoulder, meeting his furious gaze with an unbending one of my own. "You are my adviser and I trust your judgment. But I am your queen, and you must trust me that this is the right thing to do. We have three months left. Time is ticking, and Lo's memory loss is becoming more permanent by the second, which means the more we delay, the less chance we have of him remembering who he is. Summoning her is the only way to find them...to get them to come to us. We need to get on the offensive, not be on the defensive all the time."

"I cannot agree. It's too risky."

"It's all we have." I can sense him vacillating between his protective instincts and knowing that it's a valid option. "I'll meet her in a public place, with you and Soren there. If she refuses to cooperate, the silver lining is that you'll be able to track her when she leaves."

"You're going to let her leave?" Speio blurts out.

"I'm not going to kill her, if that's what you're suggesting."

"But...that's the law. She's an exile."

"We're not in Waterfell, Speio." I swallow hard, aware of the sudden ugly feeling swimming in the pit of my stomach. It was easy to fight Ehmora—an enemy of my father's court and a traitor. It would not be so easy to fight the woman who had brought me into this world, regardless of her disloyalties. "Look, I want to find Cano, deal with him and figure out how to fix Lo. If we kill her, we can't do any of those things. Right, Echlios?"

"Agreed," Echlios says after a while. The tension leaves my body on a slow, relieved exhale. Despite my earlier bravado, I wouldn't want to face my mother alone and without Echlios's blessing. "But we do it my way. I will send for more of the guard."

"Echlios, soon," I urge. "We can't afford to wait."

"Yes, my queen."

I walk out to the patio. The sky is a pale blue color without a swatch of white marring its perfection. Sitting on the edge of the pool, I dangle my legs in the warm salt water, watching the sun shimmer across its surface. I can't believe it's already been a few weeks since we've been back. On the one hand, it feels like we never left and that the entire summer never even happened. But then I think about Lo, and everything comes back in a wild, uncontrolled rush. I left him here at the mercy of Cano and my mother. Cano's end game still isn't clear—he hurt Lo, probably to get to me and to destabilize the Waterfell courts with my absence. But to what gain? Is he trying to align with Ehmora's old court? Build more hybrids? Expose Waterfell?

"Hey, Riss." Speio crouches down beside me, his white-blond hair falling into his face, one eye screwed shut against the sunlight. "There's a pool party at Jack's for his birthday. You want to go?"

I lie back on my elbows and shake my head. Jack Ryan is a loud, outgoing boy from our advanced math class, and he runs with some of Cara's crowd. "Think I'm just going to stay here."

"Jenna isn't going?" Speio asks.

"She has an away game. The hockey team left yesterday."

Speio cocks his head. "How come you didn't want to play? I mean, you loved field hockey. It's not like they don't need the extra help, especially since Sarah Winters had to quit." Apparently it had been a Dover-wide scandal at the start of the year. Our goalie Sarah's parents got divorced over the summer—her father had an affair with her tutor— and she kind of lost the plot, big-time. She almost dropped out of school, but her grandparents forced her to come back. Needless to say, being down a goalie wasn't doing much to boost team spirit.

"I don't have time for field hockey, Speio. You know that. It's already been a month. We're here for Lo, and that's it. Either way, we're gone in three months." I stare at him. "You go, though. It'll be fun."

"You sure? Echlios sort of said that I had to stay with you. But I guess I want to go."

"Oh," I say, squinting, wondering why he's gone such a dark shade of red. "Right. So, who are you going to see at this party that's putting you all into a tizzy?"

"No one."

"Doesn't sound like no one to me," I tease.

If possible, Speio flushes even redder. "Yes, well, I'm friends with Jack, and, um, Rian's going to be there."

"Who?"

"New girl, remember? She's in my English group. She's... new," Speio says in a choked voice. "Anyway, she asked me if I was going and I said yes, so I guess I'm going."

"So I guess you're going," I say, watching as tiny blue lights burst in pinprick fireworks along his arms. "Wow, *that* bad?" I vaguely remember the new girl from class—a slim, quiet-looking brunette—but at the time, I was too caught up in other things to notice any other details about her. Although it seems that Speio certainly did.

"What? No. I mean, she's a nice girl. That's all. And she has no friends here. She's from New York, staying with her relatives while her parents are building wells in Indonesia for a year." He shoots me a sidelong glance. "She seems nice."

"You said that," I say, grinning at his discomfort. "As long as Echlios cleared her, I'm fine with you doing your thing."

"I'm not *doing* anything."

"Wow. You must really like her," I say. "Well, here's some free advice that a good friend of mine once gave me—humans can fall for us hard, so be careful."

Speio purses his lips. "Who said that?"

"You did, dummy. Last year, remember? When I was asking you about Dvija? Coming of age and bonding?"

"It's not like that," he says, standing abruptly. "So, you sure?"

"Yes," I say. "Don't do anything I wouldn't do," I sing-song as he walks around the corner. I can't see him, but I can feel his answer pulsing back to me along the wind. I laugh to myself—it would be funny if I could translate that particular Aquarathi swearword into its English equivalent.

Leaning back on the cool concrete tiles, I close my eyes. A whole afternoon to myself...what more could I ask for?

I finished all my homework, already read *The Importance of Being Earnest* as well as the three other books on the curriculum, and I wrote out a detailed proposal for my ocean-cleanup drive coming up in a few weeks. I'd busied myself just so I wouldn't have to think about anything else, namely my mother. Now that the idea about summoning her is in my head, I can't stop thinking about it. And waiting on Echlios to coordinate an army of protection is killing me, but I promised him that I would wait.

My cell phone buzzes on the table, and my heart does a little flip-flop at the name on the screen. It's Lo.

I OWE U A DATE. YOU AROUND?

SURE, I text back. He's as good a distraction as any. WHERE TO?

SCRIPPS. PICK U UP 1 HOUR.

Scripps is a local beach break that's perfect for beginners. It's also way less crowded than La Jolla Shores with good wave quality. Typically more congested in the summer months, it shouldn't be too bad this time of the year, which means less chance of a repeat entourage from our date at the Crab Shack. Already clad in a bathing suit, I don't need to get ready, but vanity forces me inside to do a quick check.

My human eyes look more green than hazel today, but it's probably because of my purple-colored T-shirt. I drag a brush through my salt-tousled dark blond hair, then swipe on some lip gloss and deliberate changing into another swimsuit. Not that the one I'm wearing isn't appropriate, but it's more on the sturdier side as opposed to the sexier side of things. I know I'm working on winning Lo over, but there's a fine line between sexy and stupid. I shrug and decide to leave it on. The last thing I need surfing is for a string bikini to come undone or to ride up midwave. Talk about awkward. I replace my faded cutoffs with a pair of nylon boardies and head out back to grab my shortboard.

"Hey, Soren," I say, poking my head into the living room. "I'm going to Scripps for a bit, okay? Speio's at Jack Ryan's house. I'm meeting Lo."

Her eyes narrow a fraction, but then she nods. "Nerissa, be careful. No risks."

"Of course. I think we're just surfing." A loud car horn interrupts me. "That's Lo. I'll be back in a couple hours."

Tucking my board under one arm, I give my face one last check in the mirror before heading outside. I stack the board into the back of Lo's black truck next to his eight-foot longboard and climb into the passenger seat. The last time I was in this car, I was squished between Lo on one side and Jenna and Sawyer on the other. Let's just say that there was no room between our bodies whatsoever. The thought of it makes me flush, even though there's more than enough room between us now.

"Hey," I say, breathless, which has nothing to do with the fact that he's shirtless, and shoeless, too, I notice. His hair looks like it's been combed with his fingers, and a pair of silver-rimmed aviator sunglasses are perched atop his nose. He's the epitome of surfer-boy hotness, and even if he's forgotten how to surf, he's got the look down pat.

"Hey," Lo says, his teeth flashing white in his tanned face. I'm kind of glad that I can't see his eyes with the complete sensory overload happening. "Figured we could start that whole getting-to-know-each-other thing. I'm glad you were around. Wasn't sure if you were going to Jack's party or not."

"Didn't really feel up to it," I say, buckling my seat belt. "How come you didn't go? I'd have thought that was your scene."

"More like Cara's scene," he says. "But she's at an away game this weekend, so I wasn't feeling it, either." He glances at me. I try to ignore the ensuing twinge at Cara's name and the fact that she's at a game playing in my place as center striker. Lo frowns. "Didn't you used to play hockey? I mean, that's what I heard. Someone said that you were cocaptain last year, and even though you guys lost the finals, you were single-handedly responsible for getting them there."

"I wouldn't say that," I say. "Team effort, you know. And I needed a break from hockey this year. I do miss it, but I need to focus on stuff at the Marine Center while I'm here."

Lo shoots me a look. "While you're here? You planning to leave any time soon? You just got back."

"No, not planning to leave," I amend quickly. "It's just that my guardian's job is unpredictable, so we go where the work is. We're back because he has unfinished business here, so when that wraps up, we leave again."

"Back to South Africa?" he asks. It occurs to me that Lo has been asking questions about me, and the thought makes me smile inwardly. But then I'm distracted as he pulls hand over hand on the steering wheel to make a left turn. I studiously ignore the way his right biceps tightens and the lean golden mass of muscle beneath his arm running all the way down to the waistband of his pants.

"Yes," I manage, trying to control my body's response.

"Well, I hope you stay."

"I hope we do, too."

We find a parking spot on a side street and make our way down to the beach. As I expected, the beach isn't too crowded, even for a Saturday. Most beachgoers tend to stay near the lifeguards on La Jolla Shores. Lo spreads a blanket on the sand and starts to stretch, bending over to touch his toes and twisting his body to the side. I look away, counting the seconds between the waves and focusing on the number of incoming sets. They're three to four feet high, so nothing big, but they'll still be fun.

"You're not stretching?" Lo asks.

"I'm good."

"Sawyer says you need to stretch before getting on the board," he says. "Here, try this." Before I can move, Lo is standing behind me, his palms sliding up my rib cage and pushing my arms to the sky. "Now bend to the side," he says into my ear, one arm plastered against mine and his left palm like a brand across my ribs. I bend, my body on fire from the light touch. He switches hands, pushing me to the right. I can feel gooseflesh erupting beneath his fingers. "You cold?"

"No," I choke out. "Come on, let's go." I rip out of his grasp, nearly tumbling over as I grab my board and secure the leash to my ankle. I don't even bother to see if it's waxed—just want to put some space between us so I can breathe.

Lo jumps in next to me, skimming across the white water with his board, and we paddle out together. His board is a little more difficult to handle in the breaking waves because of its size, but he keeps pace with me easily. The water is still balmy from summer, not that it makes any difference to me, and I love the silky, salty feel of it against my skin.

Once we're past the breakers, I sit astride my board and eye Lo, who has done the same.

"Let's see what you got," I tell him.

"Right now? What about you?"

"You saw what I've got the other day at RUSH. Now it's your turn. Come on, paddle, paddle, paddle!"

"You're going to laugh. I'm really bad."

"I'm sure you're not," I say. "You used to school me, put it that way."

"If you say so," he says dubiously.

"I do. Now go."

I watch as he flips around to lie facedown on his board and begins paddling furiously to catch an oncoming wave. He misses it as it shoots beneath him, building and then breaking a few feet out. After a second, he resumes paddling to catch the wave coming behind the one he lost and pops up deftly onto the deck of the board just as the top lip curls over. And then he's gone, whisked away along the face of the wave, his arms pinwheeling in midair.

"Woo-hoo!" I yell before paddling for a wave of my own and riding it in toward Lo. "That was great! You're a natural," I tell him. "Even if you don't remember, the feeling that you have when you're on a board doesn't go away. That's in here." I jab in the general vicinity of my chest.

"Thanks. Normally I never get up on my first wave," he says, his face glowing. "Must be your vibes."

We ride a few more waves, catching some and losing some, until we're both breathing hard from all the effort. On the last wave, which we decide to take together, I detach my leash and ride my board as close as possible to Lo's before hopping up onto the wide deck of his long board. Tandem-surfing, we're facing each other as the board barrels across the front of the wave. Mesmerized by the delighted look in those deep blue eyes, I slip my hand around Lo's side, my fingers slick against his wet skin, and pull him closer. My left foot is wedged in between his legs, and my right leg on the outside of his left. Every inch of my skin is attuned to every inch of his, and it's as if time stops for a second with the wind rushing in our ears and our hearts beating in unison.

The moment is perfect for a short time until I'm distracted by a hulking figure at the end of the pier—the same one I saw at the surf meet. I lose my balance just as the board wobbles and flips out from under us, tossing us both into the crashing surf. I dive off one side as Lo falls backward on the other, and I put my hands up to cover my head from the board. Lo's not so lucky as a heavy thump is followed by a yelp of pain. The edge of the flying board has caught him square on the temple, and a thin trickle of blood makes its way down his hairline.

"Oh my God, Lo," I shout, standing in the chest-high water, and hop my way over the breaking surf to where he's standing, blinking and touching his head as if he's oblivious of where he is. "Are you all right?"

"A little woozy."

"Come on," I say, throwing his arm over my shoulder and glancing back at the pier. There's no one there. I'm seeing things. Again. "Let's get you out of here."

"I'm fine," he protests weakly. But as we get to the shoreline, I feel his body go slack like a deadweight against my side as he crumples to the sand. His eyes are closed, but I can feel a faint pulse. Grabbing his limp form, I half drag, half carry him back to the blanket. By the time I get us there, he doesn't even seem to be breathing. I glance around in a panic—there's no one even close enough to get help.

Jenna and I took a CPR class sophomore year, and I'm racking my brain to remember all the details. With a deep breath, I place my hands fingertips together and palms flat against Lo's chest, ignoring the immediate tingle that seeps from his skin into mine. Completing the thirty compressions is easy. It's the next part I'm worried about…especially my body's desperate reaction to any intimate contact with its long-lost mate.

With a sigh, I lean forward to hold Lo's nose closed with one hand. His skin, though damp, is warm. Gently tugging on Lo's chin to open his airway, I lean forward. I lick my lips and lower my head to his, only to find that the breath I'd taken is almost gone. The closer I get to Lo's pale, parted lips, the shallower the breaths I breathe in. Being this close to Lo is torture, especially after the uncertainty of the past few days and being apart the past few months. All I can think about is the look in his eyes while we were on the wave together, and my stomach becomes riddled with knots. Touching him then ignited it all and more. And now, even worse, having to put my lips on his…

Oh, get over it, I growl to myself. *It's not like you're really kissing him or anything. You're saving his life.*

With a deep breath, I touch my lips to his, slowly blowing in a stream of air and watching his chest rise slightly in response. But it's the only part of him that moves. I repeat the breath and then thirty more chest compressions.

"Wake up, Lo! Wake up," I mutter fiercely.

This time, I press my lips so hard against his mouth that my teeth nearly graze his. I close my eyes, willing him to awaken. But before I can breathe out, I feel his lips soften imperceptibly against me, fitting into the softer curves of my mouth. My eyes snap open only to become caught in the melting—and fascinated—blue depths of Lo's. He's awake. All I can think is, thank God he's half Aquarathi, or things could have turned out quite differently. Deep, even breaths fan against my face, bringing me to swift reality. I jerk away, putting inches of space between us, every part of me frozen. Lo's eyes are glittery and intense, not with recollection of any kind, but longing. I don't care—I'd rather he look at me with anything but the cold lack of recognition I'd seen there the last few weeks.

We stay like that for what seems an eternity—staring at each other in explosive silence—before Lo lifts his head off the sand, his hand sliding up my arm and splaying across my back to draw me back down to him. His lips press featherlight against mine, brushing gently from one corner to the next, before crushing into them more deeply. He tastes like salt, and I can't get enough as his mouth slants open over mine, nibbling across my lower lip and pulling it between his teeth.

In a smooth motion for someone who has just been clocked in the head with a surfboard, Lo flips me over to my back, propping himself up on one elbow beside me, his head descending once more to mine. I sigh, turning into the insistent pressure of his lips, letting Lo kiss me until I'm senseless. I give in to every part of it—the sensual slide of his mouth, the feel of every inch of his legs, the hard press of his hips—until we draw apart, breathing heavily. Lo's face is flushed, his eyes storm-tossed. And all I can think about is what kissing like this led to the last time we'd been on a beach much the same as this one. I swallow thickly, banishing the torturous image, and reach up to brush a lock of hair away from Lo's temple.

"It's electric," he rasps. "The chemistry between us."

I can only nod and lick my bruised lips.

His eyes flick toward my mouth, becoming even darker. "When I'm with you, I feel like everything is brighter, more alive. I don't know why. I don't know how. I just do. But it's so confusing to have my brain telling me one thing and my body saying another." He leans forward to graze a kiss along the slopes of my cheekbones and then up to my eyelids. My fingers flutter against his cheekbones, down the stubbly blond fuzz of his jaw. "But every part of this feels so right."

"It is right," I whisper. *You belong to me.*

But of course I can't say that, so instead I say it with my body, twining my wandering fingers into the wet hair at the nape of his neck and dragging his face down to mine. Within seconds, I silence the doubt creeping into my mind with the single-minded focus of satisfying my body's insistent demands.

9

The Challenge

I am literally weak-kneed from the look that Lo has just slanted in my direction from across the room in study hall—a look that is obviously just as effective as his kissing skills. My body feels like it's dissipating...literally *evaporating* into mist. After what had happened yesterday, Lo seems more determined than ever to remember our relationship, and not just because things got a little weird afterward. It wasn't his fault—reality just sort of kicked in. Reality, and the fact that he was making out with a girl he barely knew.

I duck my head, stabbing the end of my pencil into my teeth and trying to concentrate on the penciled notes on my desk. Echlios's most recent reports contained news of growing unrest in Waterfell. Castia attempted to usurp the Aquarathi queen I'd left in charge. And I'm willing to bet anything that Keil and the Ruby Court had something to do with it. Unseating a queen who isn't exactly seated on her throne is the best time to start a coup. I'm still weighing the pros and cons of heading back to Waterfell to set things straight. I don't need everything falling apart there, too. But maybe that was Cano's plan all along.

A sharp poke in my side distracts me.

"So, after you made out on the beach, what happened?" Jenna whispers. "Don't leave me hanging. I can't believe I had to hang up last night in the middle of that bit of juicy. It was torture."

"Not much," I say with an embarrassed flush. "We stopped in at his place for Grayer to have a look at him, just to make sure he wasn't concussed." I pause and glance at her, leaning in. "Did you know that Grayer is a doctor? He seriously has an M.D. and everything."

Jenna rolls her eyes. "Doctor, valet, butler. What's next? Black-belt ninja?"

"Probably," I say, stifling a snort. "Guess Ehmora wanted to be prepared that her son would be properly guarded when she wasn't around."

Jenna pokes me again. "Stop avoiding the subject. So, you go home with him, get checked out and then what?"

"Then he takes me home."

"That's it? He takes you home. And nothing else happens. He doesn't even say anything? Doesn't try to round the bases? Nothing?"

I shrug. "Honestly, after the haze of it all, I think Lo was confused. I mean, he liked making out fine," I say, another furious blush coloring my cheeks. "It was when he started thinking about it and his brain couldn't seem to make the connection with his body that things started getting weird. He said…" I trail off in embarrassment.

"Don't stop there. I'm your best friend, remember? It's my solemn duty to share your suffering."

I glare at her. "You are having way too much fun with this. Do you know what it's like to throw yourself at a guy, have him respond and then basically treat you like you're a stranger?"

"Welcome to most teenage girls' average Saturday night." Jenna's nodding sagely, and I snap my teeth in frustration.

"Like you would know. You and Sawyer have been married since you were five."

"I'm sorry," Jenna says, looking contrite. "Okay, I'm serious now. What did Lo say?"

I feel myself flushing more deeply. "He said that maybe he hit his head harder than he thought."

"What?" she breathes. Her blue eyes are wide and serious now with growing indignation. "Are you kidding me?"

"Nope."

"What a douche."

Shrugging, I eye the clock and place the notebook I'd been using in my backpack. "Can't say I blame him. Maybe he did hit his head hard."

"So hard that it made his tongue crash into yours?"

My startled giggle at her dry comment is drowned out by the sound of the bell signaling the end of class. Guess she has a point. Jenna pats me on the shoulder and grabs her backpack.

"Looks like we're going to have to change our strategy," she says.

"Change our strategy how?"

"Duh. *Make* him remember you."

I glare at her. "I don't think I can throw myself at him any more than I already have. It's demeaning. I am a queen now, in case you forgot, and that sort of groveling is way beneath me." I'm only half joking.

"Time to pull out the girl hidden under all those scales, Nerissa Marin," Jenna shoots back. "You want Lo? You have to win his heart. You know that the chemistry's there. His body remembers you. Now you just have to make his brain catch up."

"Easier said than done," I mutter sourly, slamming my backpack into my locker and grabbing my English books. I wave my copy of *The Importance of Being Earnest* in her face. "You know, the double-life thing seems almost easy in this book."

Jenna stares at me so hard I can almost feel her mind ticking over. "That's brilliant! That's it."

"What's it?"

"You should totally create an alter ego of yourself. You know, someone kind of smexy, like a Nerissa Marin black-sheep sister. We can call her Reese. Kind of inspires confidence like the name Ernest, don't you think?" she says with a wink, quoting one of the lines from the book.

"That'll never work."

"But it'll be fun." Jenna grins. "Just remember...*Reese.* Now come on, we have to present our group's position in front of the class today."

In class, Professor Donovan is all smiles as he pulls his chair to the side of the class. The group presentation will count for a large part of our overall grade, and he's excited to see what we've come up with. Speio's group goes first. They've been tasked to discuss the theme of marriage in the play and how the different characters perceive it.

"It's business," Speio suggests to the class. "People in the time period of this work get married because it's the social thing to do, not because it's something that they want. It's marriage based on what you earn, what your social standing is and your birth pedigree."

Rian steps forward to chime in, her voice soft. "In addition, there's much discussion in the play about whether the subject of marriage is a pleasant or unpleasant one. The view of it ranges from trivial to cynical based on the opinions of the characters."

As I watch her, my interest perks. She's the one Speio got all bent out of shape over for the party last weekend. Not conventional-looking by San Diego Barbie standards, she has long, glossy dark hair surrounding a heart-shaped, delicate face. Her eyes are a deep green color. Although her features seem soft, something about her strikes me as very intense. It's not like Speio to go for the quiet, passionate type, so I'm intrigued. I glance over at Cara making goo-goo eyes at Lo and roll my eyes. Then again, anyone would be a step up from that.

The sound of clapping interrupts my thoughts. "Questions, class?" Mr. Donovan says.

Lo raises his hand. "What if the marriage is based on a lie? I mean, Jack lied about who he was, and so did Algernon. Doesn't that change the meaning of it?"

"Good question. Sawyer, you want to address it?" Donovan asks with an approving nod.

Sawyer looks like a deer in headlights as he attempts to answer, but his voice fades into the background as Lo's question draws me into a forgotten memory. My father's politically arranged union to my mother had been based on a lie. She had chosen someone else—Ehmora—before they could consummate their bond, and my father had ended up being duped by two of the most calculating liars on the planet. All they had ever done was scheme for control of the Waterfell High Court throne, and my father paid the price with his life. And my mother was still scheming for it.

I center my attention to the front of the classroom, where

the groups are switching out. Cara takes her place with her group. "Our group theme is morality and hypocrisy," she says with an evil sidelong glance at me. Great. Undoubtedly I'm going to be the brunt of Cara's entire presentation. Cara continues, "Hypocrisy comes out of pretending to be someone that you're not, or when you're pretending to have certain virtues when you obviously don't."

Jenna nudges me, whispering, "Reese should have no virtue whatsoever."

"Be quiet," I whisper back with a grin. "Cara's going to pitch a fit if we steal any of her spotlight."

We both turn back to Cara, who drones on. "In the play, Jack pretends to be his imaginary brother, Ernest, to escape his social and moral duty. This contributes to his hypocrisy. Algernon, on the other hand, pretends to have a sick relative whom he visits, which is a little more virtuous, but still deceptive."

"Her brain may explode with all those big words," Jenna whispers to me, and I stifle a snort just as the laser of Cara's pale eyes falls on us and she stops midsentence as if someone asked a question.

"Ms. Pearce and Ms. Marin, do you have something to add?" Mr. Donovan asks, following Cara's silent glare.

"We were agreeing that the best thing about hypocrisy," Jenna says, "is that it always come to light. You can't hide the truth of what you are underneath, even if you're desperately trying to get people to see you a certain way. They will always see you for what you are. A sham." She raises an eyebrow in silent challenge and then adds, "For the two Ernests, I mean."

Cara's face turns a splotchy shade of pink, but unfortunately for her Mr. Donovan sees it as a valid point and not as any perceived slight to Cara's character. "Excellent point, Ms. Pearce. The truth does come to light in the end. Carry on," he tells the group.

Another boy steps up to continue the presentation. Jenna slides her hand out in a parallel high-five motion and I slide mine across the top of her palm. *Nerissa three, Cara one,* she mouths. I forgot I'd even been counting.

We are the last group in the class to go. Lo has prepared his piece on introducing the double life with complete poise—a far cry from his performance in school the year before, where he didn't care squat about any classes. Jenna and I exchange amused looks. We'll save that little teacher's-pet tidbit for later.

I clear my throat. "As Lo has explained, this is one of the play's core metaphors. What Jack has created in his fake brother is an intricate deception that allows him to escape who he is. Eventually his fictional life catches up with him and becomes tied in to his reality, so the whole double life comes together, forcing both Jack and Algernon to come clean."

Cara's hand shoots up. Of course it would. "Yes, Ms. Andrews?" Mr. Donovan says.

"I don't get it."

"You don't get what?"

"Why create a fictional reality? Maybe Jack should just realize that he's never going to be earnest. He's a complete hypocrite."

"Maybe he wants to be earnest because he's fallen in love," I shoot back.

"He's still a hypocrite."

Childishly, I meet venom with venom. "He gets the girl, doesn't he?"

Professor Donovan's eyebrows are nearly fused together. He can guess that there's a little more going on than a heated discussion of the play's metaphors and themes. Oblivious of his dawning understanding, Cara bares her teeth in a knowing sneer. "Only because Jack is a total man-whore."

"That is enough," Mr. Donovan says in a firm voice. "Are we both talking about the play here? Or do you need to take *your* discussion to the principal's office?"

"The play, sir," we both mumble.

Jenna finishes up our group's presentation just as the bell rings, but inside I'm still seething. Not that everyone got Cara's insinuation, but she pretty much called me a whore in front of the entire class. Somehow she found out about Lo and me, and what happened. The smug, knowing look on her face says as much. My fingers curl into fists and I half step toward her before I feel a gentle but restraining pressure on my arm.

"Don't," Jenna whispers. "It's not worth getting suspended over."

"But—"

"Nobody got it. Trust me. And you said it yourself, she's not worth it."

"She knows—"

Jenna stares at me. "She knows what? That maybe you made out with Lo this weekend? Trust me, that's killing her more than anything else right now. Let it go, Riss."

I nod, slamming my books into a pile. I don't know what I'm angrier about—the fact that Cara's nasty dig at me has somehow gotten under my skin, or Lo's unexpected coolness toward me. He's held me at a courteous arm's length all day, even though I feel him studying me when he thinks I'm not looking, as if he's trying to work everything out in his head. A part of me doesn't blame him. He's confused, and desperately trying to remember who he is…and who we are to each other. Jenna's right. This is neither the time nor the place to lose control. I need a swim. A swim far, far away.

"Where're you going?" Speio yells out, just as I swing into my Jeep and rev the engine.

"Away."

Speio's face furrows with worry, but I can't even stick around to explain. Trying to be calm and tread water over the past few days while feeling like a vicious riptide is taking me out to uncharted waters has been nothing short of draining. I feel like I'm being held together by the whisper of a glimmer. And if it breaks, I'll be lost.

Breezing past Kevin at the Marine Center and yelling out that I'm taking the boat, I don't even bother to change. I kick my shoes off at the bottom of the pier, let my toes sink into the sand and haul breath by cleansing breath into my lungs. And then I'm in the boat, speeding out to sea with spray on my face and freedom like salt on my tongue. For the first time that I can remember, I don't want to be on land. I want to be down there—in the deep water, where I belong.

Where everything makes sense, even with the rivalry between the courts. At least there I am wholly me…not some creature pretending to be human and forced into a double life I've nearly grown out of. Now I understand why the Aquarathi aren't meant to live with humans more than necessary. They drain us. I can't play the catty games with Cara. I can't try to be a flirt to make Lo fall in love with me. I can't win. Not this time.

The boat veers past San Clemente Island. Out here, the water is so blue it's nearly black. I have to force myself not to think that it's the exact color of Lo's eyes. I close mine, not even sure what I'm running away from. There's no way I can leave him behind while I return to Waterfell. Releasing the throttle on the boat, I drop anchor and let it sway gently in the wide rolling waves of the open sea.

The breadth of the ocean is unbroken, the deeper blue of the water nearly merging into the lighter blue of the sky in the distance. I hold my breath, turning my face to the sun. Golden shimmers of air dance across the top of the glasslike surface of the sea, and for a second not a drop of wind stirs. I am suspended between my worlds—the ever-reaching deep below me and the endless stretching sky above.

Where do I belong?

A shimmery glitter catches my eye as a school of dolphins breaks the surface, swimming nearer as if drawn to me. They circle the boat like playful children, their sounds happy and light. Leaning over the side of the boat, I let my hand drift through the rippling waves lapping against the side. Several dolphins pass below me, bouncing upward barely enough to let the slick rubber of their skins graze the human fuzz of mine. A trickle of golden light ignites at the electric tingle of their bodies, firing along the length of my palms. The water inside me surges to the surface in desperate response.

There's only one place I can be at peace.

Bands of dewy green light shimmer along my bare arms as I strip off my clothing and somersault into the ocean, letting my body sink as it begins the transformation from girl to monster. The dolphins scatter, their shrieks turning fretful as I go from friend to foe. Bones crack and lengthen, pushing outward through soft skin as fiery green lights explode like fireworks along my entire span. I am something immense erupting from something insignificant. Hardened golden scales shimmer over fragile human tissue as a ridge of fins emerges from my spine, fanning into sharp, iridescent existence to the barbed tip of my tail. Fingers curl into talons and feet extend into claws as a crown of coral thorns sprouts in a fierce semicircle on my forehead—my glorious crown of bones—the final mark of what I am.

No longer a girl, I am every inch an Aquarathi queen.

The ocean ripples beneath me, holding me close as I cleave through it, swimming down and down until there is nothing but a streak of green in a river of black. Within seconds, I am surrounded. My change has called them to me—the predators of the deep—circling just out of sight, large and terrifying, but none more monstrous than me. I pulse outward, barely a soft warning hiss, but one that makes them scatter as quickly as the dolphins did up top.

With single-minded purpose, I swim the several thousand miles to my kingdom in a few hours, until I'm surrounded by a different kind of creature, ones more like myself and loyal to me. My Queen's Guard.

"Convene the High Council and the courts. Everyone," I click to them. They obey in swift silence.

Entering Waterfell, I swim deep into the fortress, the jeweled walls firing off the light of my body. Aquarathi disperse from the great hall, pulsing softly in my wake at my unexpected return. But I'm not concerned with them—not yet, anyway. Instead I brave the darkest part of Waterfell, my father's burial chamber.

"Father," I call out. He guided me before when I faced Ehmora in a head-to-head battle to the death. Perhaps he will now, too. "I need you."

For a second, the water around me floods hotter, pulsing

with something ethereal, something of the spirit, maybe. And then I feel him. I can feel his gentle smile, the fronds of his tail pulling me close. The sound of *daughter* echoes along the water and sinks into me with delicate strength.

"I don't know what to do. I feel so lost."

Trust yourself.

I clutch my father's headstone, the rock warm beneath my nails. "How? I can't choose between him and my people. How can I? It's an impossible choice. And he's nearly lost to me already. I'm so torn, Father."

My father's voice is faint. *Look to your heart.*

"My heart says to save him."

Then trust it.

"But what about the Aquarathi? What about Waterfell? My duty?"

I can feel the water around me getting cooler. My father's essence is retreating, heading back to its rest once more. *Your duty is to be a worthy queen.*

The water settles into its previous state, not a single eddy marring its perfect, ghostly silence.

I exit the chamber, nodding to the guards stationed there, and the rest of the Queen's Guard falls into line behind me.

One of them swims forward, extending his neck toward me, as is our custom. His waters have already made him known to me—water calls to water—but I appreciate the loyal gesture nonetheless. *Doras. Gold Court. Head Guard.* I acknowledge him with a nod as he faces me.

"Doras," I say. "What is it?"

"The courts are waiting, as you have commanded. In the great hall."

"Good."

The lower courts—Gold, Ruby, Emerald and Sapphire—

are amassed on either side of the hall, bowing with extended necks as I pass them. I take my place on the giant dais at the end of the room, stepping onto a throne made of ebony volcanic glass. Razor-sharp spindles extend from its base, making me look quite fearsome on it, I imagine.

"I am your queen, am I not?" I say into the space. Already, I can feel their bodies responding to the sheathed fury in mine. "And yet I've been advised by my Handlers of dissent and questions about my loyalty. I am loyal to the Aquarathi. Yes, I have bonded to one who is not only Aquarathi, but also human. A hybrid." I survey Keil, standing arrogantly in front of the Ruby Court, his eyes calculating. "The son of Ehmora of the Ruby Court, no less. *Your* old queen," I say to them. "And yet you would hold me accountable for something that she has machinated and continues to maneuver from the grave. Now your *king* is dying because of her."

"That's because he's not Aquarathi," a small voice says. The entire room falls into suspended silence.

"Who speaks?" I ask, but no one answers. I close my eyes and glimmer outward through the slow-beating hearts of my people to find the one who spoke. I shimmer through the Ruby Court first, expecting the insurgent to be one of theirs. But I move past them to the Emerald Court before I find him. Broad-shouldered, he is but a child—barely my age—but he has passed through Dvija already and is an adult in our eyes. I went through our coming-of-age transition just before my seventeenth birthday. I fall back into myself with a sigh.

"Speak, then, Carden of the Emerald Court."

The entire Emerald Court ripples anxiously around him, but Castia's stance at the forefront is fiercely proud. She never would have voiced those words herself. I can feel the approval seething through the Ruby Court. One insubordinate court I can handle, but not if it grows into a full-scale mutiny across many courts. Before the boy can answer, a small, turquoise-finned female swims to his side—his mother, I presume—and drags him out of sight.

I let him go. He's Castia's pawn, nothing more. My gaze spans the cavern, falling on Soren and Echlios near the entrance. They would have known the minute I changed to Aquarathi form. I incline my neck to them slightly, acknowledging their presence. I take a breath. This is no time to be weak, to show leniency. I must be ruthless.

"I am your queen, and you are oath-bound to me."

"One who brings death to Waterfell," Castia challenges, and a wave of unease makes its way across the hall. "Our warriors found two of your hybrid abominations skulking in our waters. We dismembered them."

Shock silences me for a second—hybrids this far from La Jolla? And how would they have even been able to find Waterfell? Only a true Aquarathi could have led them here, which means there's a traitor in our midst. I bare my teeth at Castia and turn to Miral. "Why wasn't I told of this? They needed to be interrogated."

"My queen, the Council—"

"You weren't here," Castia interrupts silkily and glances at Keil, something unspoken passing between them before she addresses everyone else. "Can you not see for yourselves? Our queen would have kept the scum alive. She would have welcomed the spawn as she did the regent—"

"Enough!" My roar shakes the cavern walls, my fury causing even Keil to flinch. "My duty is to the regent, just as much as it is to the Aquarathi within these walls. The High

Council has given me a time frame in which to rectify the situation." I signal to the two guards standing at the side, waiting as they escort Castia to the front. Her glittering eyes are unrepentant. "I left Miral in charge, and yet you take it upon yourself to challenge my authority? I am your queen, by birth and blood, and yes, I am bonded to a hybrid, but my word is law. You will be imprisoned for treason, Castia of the Emerald Court, and punished for your crimes."

The shocked murmurs in the hall fade into hushed silence as Castia is led away. To her credit, she doesn't say a word, her fiery gaze boring into mine until the last second. She must hate me—and Lo—with every fiber of her being. Regardless of his ties to Ehmora, Lo is not one of us, and some of the Aquarathi are afraid, understandably so. Because of him, they will always question me as queen, more so because I am bonded to him. Perhaps that was Ehmora's plan all along—she couldn't undermine my birth, but with Lo, she could undermine our people's trust. Naturally, if she were alive, she would have stepped in to calm their fears.

I meet the king of the Ruby Court's eyes, and Keil inclines his head slightly as if to say, *Well played.* I ignore him. I'll bet anything that Keil's been the one whispering in Castia's ear to challenge Miral, even though I can't prove it, and she just took the fall for him.

"Let's go," I say to Echlios and Soren. "We have a prince to save." My face is grim. "And, Echlios, either those hybrids were very lucky or they had help from someone on the inside." His gaze hardens as he takes my meaning. I nod. "There's a traitor in Waterfell."

10
Water and Blood

Hours later and back on land, I'm lying in my room with Jenna. I have no idea if my actions will create peace or more chaos in Waterfell, but based on Echlios's reports, I couldn't remain blind to what Castia was doing, or Keil, for that matter, regardless of the loyalties it would cost me. On top of that, the existence of a possible Aquarathi spy working with Cano makes things a thousand times more deadly, because we have no idea what he's planning...or who the traitor is. Time is running out, and if we don't figure out a way to save Lo, there may not be a throne—or a home—to go back to.

"Okay," Jenna tells me with a wink. "Mission Memory Reboot, operational. Too bad you can't just hypnotize Lo—that'd be the easy way," she adds with a laugh. Lying on my bed, she counts off her fingers. "Surfing, check. Crab Shack, check. Next stop, got to stir up those deep blue memories with some...scuba!"

"Scuba?" I repeat dumbly.

"How hard can that be?" She studies me up and down, turning over to prop her chin atop her hands. "Romantic undersea paradise, no one around to bother you, just two ocean gods frolicking in the deep. Could work. Just be... not the old you."

"What does that even mean?" I say. "I haven't changed."

"Be likable," she says in an affected voice, flinging one hand in the air dramatically. "Flirty. Engage him. Find your inner goddess. Think *The Bachelor*."

"The what?"

She huffs at me and rolls her eyes. "The TV show with the guy who has to pick his wife from a bunch of girls. They all compete? Where have you been? Under a rock?"

"As a matter of fact, I have been. That sounds archaic."

"Survival of the fittest, my dear," she shouts, jumping out of bed and standing beside me. She grabs my shoulders and turns me to face the floor-length mirror behind the door. "Come on, let those animal instincts of yours take over. You're an ocean predator, top of the aquatic food chain. Now act like it!"

I stare at her and shake my head, meeting her laughing blue eyes in the reflection. "You would make such a bad-ass Aquarathi—you have no idea." It's not the first time I've thought that.

Jenna's arms slip around me in a hug from behind, her chin resting on my shoulder. I clasp my arms over hers. In the mirror, we look like two ordinary girls—one with wild, reddish-blond hair and the other, a deep auburn. We could be sisters. But it's so far from the truth, it's not funny.

"What are you thinking?" Jenna says softly.

My mouth twists in a half smile. "That in another world, we could be related. See? We're the same height. We're both redheads. We're twins."

"You are so not a redhead." Jenna snorts and studies our

reflections. "You're a blonde with a smidge of ginger. I've got blue eyes, and yours are hazel. But yeah, we totally could be fraternal twins."

"My eyes look greenish-blue if I wear purple."

Jenna grins. "Which ones? Your fake human eyes, or the crazy psychedelic alien ones? Come on, let's see them!"

Giving in to her demands, I slip back the protective film, and my eyes' multihued, jewel-toned colors become almost blinding. Jenna's heartbeat quickens against my back, but she doesn't pull her arms away from around me.

"So cool," she whispers.

"Guess we're not even a related species," I say, slipping the human eye cover into place.

"We're still sisters," she says, and squeezes her arms. "Just in here. In our hearts."

"I really missed you," I tell her, leaning my temple against hers. "When I was back there."

"I missed you, too, more than you know. What's it like?" Jenna asks, spinning away to fall on the bed and stare up at the multicolored sea-glass coating the ceiling. "Waterfell? Does it really look like this?"

I glance around my room, watching the sun sparkle through the stained glass windows and stream down in patterned hues over the blue walls. It's pretty close as far as replicas go, but nothing could ever match the real thing.

I nod, a catch in my throat. "A little," I say. "Just all underwater. There are huge caverns connecting the different areas, bigger than you can imagine. In some of them, you can't even see the tops. In others, you can't see the bottom. There are stalactites everywhere, some as slim as needles, and others as wide as your giant sequoia trees." My voice drifts into near silence, but Jenna is hanging on to every word. "Everything is in constant movement, shifting and shimmering with each swirl of the currents. One day it looks one way, the next it's entirely different.

"People think it's freezing cold, but there are some parts that are as warm as hot springs, deep down near the planet's core. Those are some of my favorite spots. If I close my eyes, I can almost imagine lying out there on the sand with the sun roasting my body."

"Hydrothermal vents," Jenna breathes, nodding. "That would make sense...shifting tectonic plates. I read up about it after you told me where you were from last spring," she adds at my look. Shaking my head, I'm amazed at her thirst for knowledge—she's like a sponge, sucking up all kinds of bits and bytes. She stares at me with wide eyes. "I read that it can get up to five hundred degrees near the vents. That's hot."

"It mixes with the colder water," I tell her. "Don't worry, we can take it. Alien proteins and all. But the temps are not half as bad as the pressure. Imagine ten thousand tons lying on top of you. *That's* enough to liquefy human bones."

"But not you," Jenna says.

"Not us," I agree. "Our scales are an extra layer of exoskeleton above our tissue, and in Aquarathi form we have a similar high internal pressure."

Jenna studies me, shaking her head. "You know, even though I've known about the real you for months, it's still inconceivable. I just can't imagine you—my best friend—becoming this other creature and living a thousand miles beneath the surface. It's insane." She takes a steadying breath. "So, besides you guys, what other things live down there?"

"Mostly muddy bacteria," I say, grinning at the look on her face. "Crustaceans and tubeworms. Some other bioluminescent fish like eels, octopi and jellyfish. Cute sea pigs. Had a couple of them for pets growing up. Further up, there're nastier things like goblin sharks, anglers and viperfish. Oh, and frilled sharks. Vicious little things," I say with a shudder.

Contrary to what's known about frilled sharks, they aren't solitary creatures, and they often attack in pods. Though only about six feet long with over three hundred rows of razor-sharp teeth, they are fierce and deadly. My father once ran into a dozen of the beasts, and he bore the sharp marks of their bites on his underbelly until his death. I wouldn't wish them on my worst enemy.

"Tell me more about Waterfell," Jenna says, interrupting my thoughts. "What's your room there like? You live in sea mounts, right? Underwater mountains?"

"Let me guess. You researched?" I ask her, and then I grin, ready to blow her mind with something that the Internet sites won't tell her. "You're right, most of Waterfell is located within connected seamounts, kind of like a submerged archipelago. Think Hawaii, only underwater. But my favorite place of all down there is my glass cave."

"Your what?" Jenna says wide-eyed.

"It's my special place. Only Speio knows about it," I say. "I found it one day when we were exploring. Thousands of years ago, a submerged volcano erupted and exploded upward. Do you know anything about pillow lava?" I ask her.

Jenna nods. Of course she does. "When magma erupts underwater, the coldness of the water makes a hard crust form around the lava, so it looks like little pillows."

"Sometimes I think you're the one with the alien brain," I joke. "Right. So imagine an underwater volcano erupting into an enormous mound of pillow lava. I don't know if it was the composition of the surrounding sand or the minerals there or gases or what, but for some reason, the pillow kept growing and the lava melted the sand into some kind of volcanic glass. The gases reacted with the heat and expanded." I pause for dramatic effect. "So basically, the whole inside of it is hollow, like an obsidian cave."

"That sounds amazing," she blurts out, and then frowns. "Wait. Isn't that dangerous? What if it explodes while you're in there?"

"The volcano is inactive," I say. "The walls are like the inside of a marble, perfectly formed with rivers of red running through the black. I wish you could see it."

"Me, too."

I sprawl on the bed next to her, folding my palms underneath my head. "Maybe one day."

"That would be awesome. Maybe we could borrow James Cameron's submarine," Jenna offers brightly. "You know he went there last year, right? The Mariana Trench."

"I remember. You have no idea how close he came to being a snack. It was a very close vote by the Aquarathi High Council. We kept an eye on him the whole time."

I laugh and stare at my Waterfell ceiling, but then my humor fades. If I don't do something about Lo, neither of us will have a home to go back to. I glance at Jenna out of the corner of one eye. "So, back to your *Bachelor* theory, what exactly do I have to do to jump-start Lo's memory? Besides being utterly charming and unforgettable?"

"That's pretty much all you can do," Jenna says. "From your end, anyway. I still think you have a chance to work the human side of him. Any news from Echlios on a cure?"

"They're still working on it. In the meantime, Lo has to undergo weekly psychotherapy sessions to help recover the buried memories." I take a breath, watching Jenna carefully. I'm not sure I should tell her any more than necessary, but she has more than earned her place in my life. "Echlios thinks they may have a lead to Cano, but I think it's a long shot. I still think our best option is for me to summon my mother, but Echlios and Soren think it's too dangerous."

"Why?"

I shrug. "They don't know if she's compromised her own cells with the DNA research she and Ehmora were working on. After all, Ehmora can't have been the only one to have hybrid offspring."

"You think there are more of them?"

"It's only a guess," I tell her. "Remember that other hybrid? The messed-up ugly-looking one that you Tasered on the beach? I think there are more of those, but ones like Lo…not entirely sure. I think I saw one at the RUSH competition and then again at Scripps."

"Because…" Jenna prods.

I hesitate, not sure what I'm basing my guess on. "I don't have any real proof. Just the way Ehmora was willing to let Lo die last year. If he were the only hybrid, she would have cared more to save him. He was…disposable."

Jenna rolls over and props her head up on one hand. "But we're talking about a crazy ex-queen with world domination on her mind—her son isn't going to factor into that if he's become a liability or your supporter. He was disposable because he wasn't loyal to her anymore. He was loyal to *you*."

"I guess that makes sense."

Jenna's phone buzzes loudly, making us both jump. She slides it from her pocket to read the text and sighs dramatically. "Crap. I'm so sorry to bug out right now, but I have to go. Mom needs me for some dinner party she's having for her work people, and I promised I'd help out." She leaps up, grabbing her denim jacket and her backpack off the armchair in the corner of the room. "But seriously, on the Lo thing, scuba is the way to go. With no one around, it'll be perfect—just you and him. Remember, Riss, he already knows you deep down. Don't let go of that. Anyway, I'm really sorry I have to bail on you. I didn't realize it was so late."

"No, go," I tell her.

"Okay. I'll call you later. See you at school tomorrow."

After Jenna leaves, I decide to go for a swim to clear my head. The sun has nearly descended into the horizon with shades of purplish twilight dappling the evening sky. I pulse softly to Soren, letting her know what I'm doing, and walk past the pool down to the beach. The sand is soft and crumbly between my toes, the wind a whisper against my cheeks. I walk down to the water's edge and sit on the damp sand, letting the waves curl over my feet. Breathing deeply, I soak up the water and the salt like a sponge, feeling it spread through my insides in a velvet rush.

The beach isn't deserted, but I'm not planning to go full morph or anything. I just need space to think—to figure out this thing with Lo. Plus, I'm not alone. I can feel Soren's eyes on me from the house. She still doesn't trust when I'm alone that I'm not going to run off and do something stupid. Truth is, it's not like I haven't thought about it. That's my nature. Jump first and think later, but if I've learned anything from last year, it's that my people come first. My responsibility is to them. And even though my heart may say one thing, I have to listen to what my mind says, too. Emotion must be tempered by logic, or so Echlios says.

Lo is your people, a voice whispers in my head.

I shrug it away. Jenna's right. The only way I can help Lo right now is to try to jump-start his human memories. If the biotoxin is inhibiting the Aquarathi side of him from healing his human side, then I have to think outside the box. At least until Echlios finds Cano, which could be weeks away. I sigh and lean back on my elbows, watching the fading light glint off the tops of the waves. It would be so easy to summon my mother to me. She'd know where Cano is and we wouldn't waste any more precious time. But I promised Echlios.

The sound of laughter behind me draws my attention. A couple is walking their dog along the upper part of the beach, a large black Doberman. Without warning, the dog rips off its leash and barrels in my direction, teeth bared and spit flying from the corners of its mouth.

"Prince, get back here! Prince, *no!*" the woman shrieks.

The dog pays her no attention. He has sensed a threat, and as dogs do, is running head over heels to confront it. In this case, me. I sit up just as the dog jerks to a stop a few feet away from me, growling ferociously and barking his head off. I study it—all the dog wants to do is protect his masters, defend them from me. I almost smile.

A guttural sound escapes my throat—half growl, half command—and the dog's ears flatten atop his head. He stops barking immediately, as if confused. I am a far bigger threat than he anticipated. Prince bares his teeth, reconsidering his options. I have to admire his gumption. I growl again and flare my eyes. Cowering on the sand, he whines just as his owners reach us, panting with exertion. The woman who shouted out earlier looks at her dog, still crouched on the sand, and her face goes from fear to anger.

"Prince, you okay, boy?" she says, and glares at me. "What did you do to my dog?"

"I didn't touch your dog," I say, bristling at her accusatory tone. "He was about to attack me, if you didn't notice. I haven't moved from where I was sitting and minding my own business."

Indecision plays across her face. She knows what she saw, but she also knows what she's seeing right now—her fierce dog crying and whining as if it's scared out of its mind.

"Sorry," the man behind her says, bending to grab a hold of the abandoned leash. "We don't know what came over him. He's a bit unpredictable, which is why we only walk him at night when the beach is empty for the most part. Do you have a dog? Maybe he smelled something on you."

"No," I say. "I don't have a dog."

The man clears his throat uncomfortably. "Well, sorry about that. Prince is only a year old. He's…temperamental."

I force a smile, relaxing my face. "It's okay. It happens. He was doing his job, trying to protect you. He's just loyal."

"We're not exactly in any danger from you," he says with a pointed look. I imagine how he must view me—a slender, completely unthreatening girl sitting on the beach. "I guess we're not quite finished with obedience school."

"Maybe he sensed something else," I murmur. I stretch out my hand toward Prince. I make a slight sound that only he can hear, watching the fear slip from his chocolate-brown eyes. He creeps forward until his cold, wet nose touches my fingertips and then curls his entire sleek head into my palm. I stroke his glossy, short fur, feeling barely audible growls of pleasure emanating from his body. He's happy but still scared, fascinated yet terrified.

"We should go," the woman says to her partner. "It's

late." Her body is rigid, her face a mask, but I can tell that she, too, is as nervous as her dog is. The man obediently tugs on the leash, but Prince makes no move to leave the comfort of my hand.

"Go," I whisper to him gently.

As they walk down the beach, the woman turns once to look at me, and then whips back around, recoiling as our gazes collide in the darkness. Sometimes—just like animals—certain humans can feel things about us. Not often, but there are a few who can sense that we're not quite who we seem to be. That we're something *more*.

I stare at my fingers, recalling the sensation of Prince's fur. Dogs and Aquarathi don't really mix, but I've always liked them even if they're petrified of me. Prince was fierce and loyal, defending his owners with every fiber of his being, regardless of the risk.

Loyalty.

I owe Lo the same. Don't I?

Pushing aside the immediate twinge of guilt for disobeying Echlios's wishes, I stand and walk to the water's edge where the tide has receded. Nearly invisible in the darkness with only the lights reflecting from the homes along the shoreline, I gather my strength from the ocean, feeling it rush into me with a force far unlike the gentler sensation earlier. I am the queen of the sea.

Clouds roll in as thunder cracks in the distance, and I sense someone running toward me from the house. I breathe out slowly. I knew she would try to stop me. Soren is so in tune with me that she would have felt what I was doing the second I started amassing my strength.

"My lady, no," Soren shouts. "You don't know what she's capable of."

"I know," I say in a calm voice. "It is my duty to protect my people. And Lo is bound to me. Neither of us can afford to wait for Echlios any longer."

"What if she's not bound to you?"

"Then she won't hear my summons and she won't come. And we will have lost nothing." I turn around, my body trembling. "We can't not try, Soren. Call Echlios, if you must, but I am doing this tonight."

Soren's face is worried, but she knows better than to argue with me in my frame of mind. She turns to nod at Speio, who is now standing a few feet behind us. "Go," she tells him. "I'll stay with her."

Shedding my clothing in the darkness, I dive into the ocean and strike out until I get beyond the breakers. I swim fast and hard, diving deep enough so that my light won't be seen from the surface. The energy coils into my center, bursting outward as I shift into Aquarathi form, wincing at the push of sharp bones against my thickening skin. I probably could have summoned her in human form, but I want the summons to be felt, no matter where she's hiding. And my full power is in Aquarathi form.

I close my eyes and picture my mother's faces—both human and Aquarathi—the soft curve of cheekbones, the golden eyes, the ridge of her brow, the lustrous purple fins shimmering over her buttery flanks. I see her as she is and as she was. I see every part of her. I hold the image and then I slam it into me, into the very core of my being... commanding her to come to me. The force of it blasts outward into the water in a golden spherical ripple until it disappears from my sight.

It is done.

Making my way wearily back to where Soren is waiting,

I nearly collapse into her arms at the edge of the beach. She wraps a towel around me. I'm shivering so hard it feels like my teeth are going to shatter inside my mouth.

"Do you think she'll come?" I manage after a few seconds.

"I'm not sure," Soren says. "She may not be bound to you, but if she is, she will have no choice but to respond. None of us would have the strength to ignore your call."

"What happens now?"

"We wait."

I pull on my discarded shorts and T-shirt, and sit on the sand. Soren lowers herself beside me. I'm grateful for her company. I wonder if my mother will come and whether she's still a part of the Gold Court. Even if she's on the other side of the world, she'll have to find me. But I suspect that she and Cano aren't too far away. How could they be? They lured me here by making Lo sick. A tiny part of me hopes that Soren's right…that maybe she won't come. But if that happens, then we have nothing to go on to help Lo. I lean into Soren, feeling her soft touches on my hair, and close my eyes.

"Well, well," a velvety voice says. "Isn't this cozy?"

I wake from slumber and swipe at the drool from my cheek with my forearm. I must have passed out. Blinking the sleep from my eyes, I focus in the darkness to see my mother completing her transformation from Aquarathi to human and stepping out of the waves. She is nude, but still as beautiful as I remember. The last time I saw her, her head had been shaved—no doubt to prove some point when she and her lover had flayed off her crown and sent it to me as a message. Now dark blond hair like mine hangs in deep gold strands across her shoulders and breasts.

"Neriah," Soren says, grasping my arm and pulling me up.

My mother eyes us, an odd emotion flashing in those honey-colored eyes for a second before disappearing. Her face hardens. "I see you're still trying to take my place as a mother, Soren. Pity you never had your own daughter to smother."

Soren doesn't rise to the bait, remaining silent instead. There's no love lost between the two of them. Soren was the one to discover that my mother had bonded with Ehmora—queen of the Ruby Court—before she could consummate the union with my father. She bore the brunt of my mother's rage for years. Still, I can feel her body clenching beside me.

"She's been far more of a mother than you ever were," I say in an even voice, throwing my discarded towel to my mother. It falls to her feet. She stares at me, an odd expression glimmering in her eyes, before raising an arched eyebrow.

"What do you want?" she snaps.

"What did Cano do to Lo?" I ask.

She smiles coldly. "Nothing that can't be undone."

"Why?"

"You know why, Nerissa."

I shake my head. "For what? To bring me here? You can't kill me. You could never be queen of Waterfell. You're a traitor and everyone knows it. Whatever you're planning won't work."

"We'll see," my mother says cryptically. "Are we done?"

I step forward so that we're nose to nose. Her eyes burn

into mine, so many things racing across them that I can barely keep track. I keep my own emotions in close check. "You will tell me where Cano is. And you will tell me how to fix Lo."

"Oh, will I?" she laughs. "I'll just hand over the serum because you want me to, is that it?"

I refuse to show the relief on my face at her words that there is a cure. "You came here at my summons. I am your queen. You will obey."

My mother's laugh transforms into something terrible, making my stomach feel like it's suspended in midair. "Nerissa, queen or not, you mistake that you are *my* queen. Or why I came. Of course I felt your summons—you are powerful and we will always be forever linked, but I am not bound to obey you."

The world falls out from beneath my feet as she turns her back on me and walks toward the ocean. I step forward to stop her, but Soren's gentle fingers on my arms restrain me. I opt for words instead. "Where is Cano?"

A smile tossed over her shoulder. "Closer than you think."

"Why did you even come if you didn't have to?"

"Because, my darling, I wanted to see the queen you have become."

"And?" I say.

She stops, silent for several seconds. "You are as formidable as I imagined."

Her softly uttered words make the breath catch in my throat, but I can't allow myself to feel anything but indifference toward her. "Why are you doing this?"

"I tried to tell you months ago, Nerissa. This is bigger than you or me, or Waterfell. The hybrids are the future. Lo is the future."

"So Cano's breaking him?"

"No, my love," she says, her face shimmering with burnished golden scales. "He's breaking you."

11

Braving a Glimmer

Seeing my mother opened up a well of emotions I'd thought closed. And her obscure parting words left a cold river of dread in the pit of my stomach. Was she trying to prove a point about bonding by attacking me through Lo? What did she mean when she said that Cano was *breaking* me? Breaking my spirit? My willpower?

My head is drowning beneath the weight of a thousand questions. And then there's the fact that she has zero allegiance to me. When I came of age, all the Aquarathi in my kingdom were bound to me as their queen. Only she wasn't, which means Soren was right—the only way my mother could cut ties with me is if she, too, has somehow been genetically altered, just like Ehmora. Maybe I wasn't so far off when I told Jenna my suspicions about the existence of other hybrids like Lo. Or I could just be paranoid.

I sigh. It's hard *not* to be paranoid after my mother's cryptic words. On top of that, the fact that she and Cano are so close is driving me crazy. I had to hold myself back from diving into the water and following my mother the minute she left. But of course, it would have served little purpose. She's far too smart for that. So I let her go, and I didn't follow.

I pull the brush through the gold snarls of my hair and secure it with an elastic band before tugging on my Dover Prep uniform. The last thing on my mind right now is school, but of course, keeping an eye on Lo is still part of the plan, more so now after my mother's ambiguous words. The only silver lining out of that conversation was the confirmation that there is indeed a way to reverse what they did to Lo. I vow to find it even if it kills me...and before it kills Lo. That's the thing about toxins—they don't care who engineered them. Once they inhabit a host, their sole aim is to take over, to mutate, to rot.

With a deep, cleansing breath, I walk into the kitchen and toss a couple pieces of sashimi off the breakfast island into my mouth. Everything is eerily still. I chew slowly and swallow. The room isn't empty, but with the heavy silence, it could well be. Speio is staring into a half-eaten bowl of food, Echlios is eyeing me warily above the edge of his newspaper and Soren is busy at the sink scrubbing the bottom layer of Teflon out of a pot. They're all making a concerted effort not to antagonize the beast in their midst...in this case, me.

"What?" I say out loud, exasperated. "I'm not going to fly off the deep end or anything."

"Are you okay?" Echlios asks slowly, placing his paper to the side on the table.

"Why wouldn't I be?" I say. "I saw Neriah." I don't miss the exchange of looks at the use of my mother's name. I'm sure Soren already told them what happened, but I summarize, anyway. "She says there's a cure. She's not bound to me. They drew me here to destabilize Waterfell. And they're still moving forward with Ehmora's grand master plan to have the hybrids take over the earth." I pause, meeting Echlios's eyes. "And I'm sorry for calling out to her, even though you asked me not to. I couldn't wait anymore, without knowing whether Lo had a chance or not. Now that I know there's a cure, I'm not going to stop until I find it. Or Cano. He's going to pay for what he has done to Lo."

"Agreed," Echlios says softly. "You do not need to apologize to me, my queen."

"Yes, I do. I gave you my word and then I broke your trust."

"As you say," he murmurs, bowing his head.

"Any news on your end?" I ask.

"We're getting closer. Our contacts in the local police department are tracking a cell phone that we believe to be his. He's also been picked up on several security cameras near the school, so he's definitely in the area."

"What about Rancho Santa Fe?" I ask.

That was both his and Ehmora's previous neighborhood. I was surprised to discover, months before, that they had been neighbors. But once we realized how they were connected—Cano's brilliant bioengineering background, my mother's cross-species DNA research and Ehmora's genes—it all made sense. They *engineered* Lo, as well as many other imperfect specimens before him, one of which I had the horror of meeting in a head-on collision last spring. More beast than man, it was terrifying. I suppress a shiver at the memory—the thought of others like that one out there watching me is not a pleasant one.

"No. Both houses appear to be empty. Nothing on surveillance," Echlios says. "But we're close."

"Good. Because I have a plan."

"What's that?" Echlios and Soren ask at the same time. Even Speio looks up, his spoon paused halfway to his mouth. He's been awfully quiet the last few days. Normally he's on me like a shadow. I smile, remembering that Lo used to call him my warden. But now he seems preoccupied. My smile turns into a frown. The last time Speio was preoccupied, he fell prey to my mother's gilded promises of a better life and served me up on a silver platter to her. I make a mental note to talk to him later...see where his mind is.

Pondering the course of action with respect to my new plan, I answer Soren's question with a question of my own. "What's the latest update from the psychotherapist on Lo's status? Any progress?"

"Unchanged," Soren says. "He has gaps in his memory. He remembers certain things quite clearly, but for others, it's a completely blank slate. Including everything Aquarathi." Soren has been tasked with accompanying Lo to these sessions by my order. I don't trust not having eyes and ears on him at all times, on the off chance that he'll remember something important. Or that he will remember something and try to shift into a terrifying alien form in front of people. That could cause instant chaos.

"What's your thinking?" Echlios asks.

I shrug and exhale in a rush. "I think we should try hypnosis, and then a glimmer." Turns out that Jenna's idea of hypnotizing Lo is nothing short of brilliant.

Soren's gasp is muffled. "Too dangerous."

"We'll do it in a controlled environment." I glance at Echlios. "With guards. With all the necessary precautions."

"Why?" Echlios asks, exchanging another look with Soren, this one quelling. He's willing to listen, which is more than I hoped for. I can guess how risky this option will be, especially if it triggers something inside Lo—something that only he can control. If he can't get his mind around the physical expression of himself, the consequences could be bad…as in say-goodbye-to-your-sanity bad.

Shaking my head, I rush forward with my idea before I change my mind. "There's something missing," I say. "All along, I kept thinking that this whole thing was human related, but something just didn't seem to fit. Remember what you told me about Lo having dissociative memory disorder?"

Echlios nods, frowning. "Go on."

"Well, I know it's possible because he's part human, but what if the toxin part wasn't just to draw me back here? I mean, I'm not naive enough to think that they wouldn't want to strike at me where I'm most vulnerable, but they didn't have to inhibit Lo's memories to do that. They could have done almost anything to get me here." I know I'm rambling because I can see the confused expressions on each of their faces. I hasten to get the rest out before I lose my train of thought. "They could have hurt Jenna, but they *chose* Lo instead. It was baffling me as to why they would hurt the one thing they had going for them, even if Ehmora thought Lo disposable." I glance at them in turn. "So why?"

"You think there's something more?" Soren says.

I nod, mulling over the idea and feeling it take form. "Yes. I think they're hiding something. Something that Lo knows. Something big. Maybe the real reason Cano wanted me out here."

"Something that they don't want us to find out." That last statement is from Speio.

"Correct," I say. "And they want me here for whatever it is they're planning. But that whole biotoxin memory-loss thing isn't to hurt Lo—it's something they want to use against us...against *me*." I meet Echlios's eyes. "My mother talked about Cano breaking me. They want me to feel like everything is lost, to lose hope, so I don't see the bigger picture." I swallow hard. "Which is that Lo knows something. We have to find out what that is, and if hypnosis is what it takes, then that's what we have to do."

"It's too risky, Nerissa," Soren murmurs.

"Trust me, I know." I sigh. She's right. A lot of who we are depends on mental muscle—to hold our human form takes deep concentration and unshakable willpower. With the hybrids, it's a little different because they are both human and Aquarathi, but the same mental strength is required; otherwise they'd be shifting back and forth between forms at a thought. If we mess with the mind's ability to preserve different parts of itself, we open ourselves up to a world of volatility. "But we don't have a better choice."

"When do we do it?" Speio asks.

I glance at him. "Today, after school. The sooner the better." I turn to Soren, who still looks apprehensive. "This session will have to happen here or at the Marine Center, to be safe. We need a contained saltwater pool or tank in case he shifts. And we need guards, lots of them." If Lo morphs into Aquarathi form, he will be strong, especially because of his union with me. The connection between us is a two-way street, meaning that he can take as much strength as he needs from me just as I can from him. The bond transcends my royal blood. I can see the worry pooling in Soren's eyes...and fear for my safety. I embrace her before leaving for school, resting my forehead in the crook of her neck.

"It will be all right," I murmur against her human skin. "Lo won't hurt me. Don't worry."

She doesn't believe me, but squeezes tightly. "My water is yours."

In the car on the way to school with Speio, I stay mostly silent and stare out the window. Despite my brave words to Soren, the doubt remains with me like a noxious cloud. The truth is, Lo isn't the same boy. He's different now. Even when we made out on the beach—the passion was there, but that had never been something missing between us. We've always had a strong physical connection…an undeniable chemistry drawing us together.

I'd wanted to believe so badly that he remembered me that I overlooked what was so glaringly obvious. Physically, we are more than compatible and connected by a bond older than time, but emotionally, we are nothing more than strangers. The truth is hard to swallow. Perhaps that is why I want to try the hypnosis so badly—I want to reach him somehow. Go deeper past the human side of him…the part that's letting go of me.

"You okay?" Speio asks me in a quiet voice as we pull into the parking lot.

"Fine."

"I'm here if you need to talk," he says, fiddling with the car keys between nervous fingers and pocketing them.

"About what? Whether Lo will ever remember who I am?"

"Riss—"

I turn to face him, my voice stony to cover its trembling tenor. "What are you going to tell me, Speio? That we should give up? Go back to Waterfell? Forget Lo ever existed? That I'm stupid for believing some part of him still knows who I am? Who *he* is?"

"No, of course not."

I bite my lip hard, my eyes stinging as I try to stop my voice from shaking. "I already know all those things. I know there's a chance that he's lost to us forever, but I also have to believe there's a chance that he's not." My voice does break then, into a half sob. "Or I'll break."

"You're not going to break." Speio's hand flutters over to rest on my knee in the passenger seat. "Just hang on, Riss. He'll be all right, you'll see. How can he not?" he says.

"How do you know?"

"He has you."

My voice catches. "He doesn't even know who I am."

"Then make him remember." He chucks me under the chin with a grin. "And stop sniveling. Reminds me of the old you—all scared and pompous and totally lame—crying all the time about Dvija and bonding, and making moony eyes over some human boy."

I stare at him, but the twinkle in his eye almost makes me smile back. Almost. I swipe at the tears on my face. "I did nothing of the sort," I mutter, flushing.

Speio makes smooch faces with his hands, pretending he's air-kissing someone, and rolls his eyes. "You managed to get him then, and you weren't even half of who you are now. So he had to like something."

"He *wanted* me to like him," I remind Speio. "He was tasked with trying to make me fall for him, remember? Now it's the reverse. I feel like I have to do cartwheels in a gold-spangled bikini just to get his attention."

Speio shoots me a wicked sidelong glance. "You don't own any bikinis?"

"I'm not Cara," I snort, just as she catches my eye from the top of the school stairs. I envy the easy smile on her face and the attention of the boy who's leaning against the wall with one foot propped up behind him. Lo laughs at something she says and slings his backpack over his shoulder. His sandy hair is choppy, and even from this distance, I can tell that it's still damp from an early-morning surf session. My breath turns solid in my throat.

Speio follows my gaze, his expression sliding from teasing to sympathetic. "Cara's got nothing on you, Riss."

I drag my eyes away. "Speaking of your ex-girlfriend, what's she saying about the whole thing?"

"For the last time, she's not my ex," Speio groans. "She likes Lo. Always has. Always will. With you temporarily out of the picture, Cara wants what Cara wants." He grabs my shoulders. "Look, sometimes you have to make the effort to put yourself out there. It was easy for you last year. Lo wanted you to fall for him. It's just as simple for you to turn around and do the same. The humans want to be chased. They want the pursuit." Speio's eyes are fierce. "He belongs to you, Nerissa. Defend what's yours."

"And what makes you such an expert on human love?"

To my surprise, Speio blushes a deep shade of red before mumbling something about being late for class, nearly falling out of the Jeep in his haste to get out. Happy to steer the conversation away from me, I leap out and glue myself to his side, fascinated.

"So, your theory? It's based on personal experience?"

"No."

"Why so secretive? Thought we share everything."

"Nothing to share."

Just then, a voice yells out for us to wait up, and I have

the distinct sensation of every drop of water in Speio's body tensing up in response. He turns helpless eyes in my direction just as Rian Thorn catches up to us at the top of the stairs, her chest heaving with the exertion of running. Her hair is tousled and her eyes are bright. She puts a hand on Speio's arm, and I can feel the pressure of his heartbeat pushing against me through the water in the air. I swallow, closing off the open connection between us. I'd forgotten how that had felt—the excitement, the rush of first love, the weightlessness.

Oh.

"Did you get my text?" she asks Speio, kissing his cheek. "About tonight? I have a thing with my dad. But tomorrow, I'm free. Rain check?"

"Sure," Speio mumbles, his color heightened with embarrassment. I meet his eyes, and incline my head in subtle approval.

"Hi, Nerissa," Rian says, turning to me with an unaffected, bright smile.

"Hey."

I smile back and quicken my stride so I'm a few feet ahead of them. While I have no intention on letting up on Speio, I don't want to embarrass Rian. Glancing over my shoulder, I can see why she's caught his interest. Not just a pretty face—there's something intense in her eyes, along with a deep intelligence and sharp humor. I like her, too.

Inside, I head for my locker, walking past Cara, Lo and the rest of their group without making eye contact with anyone, despite the outward rush of breath at Lo's nearness. Every part of my body is reaching toward his with impossible force. I resist, chewing at the inside of my lip until I feel my salty blood coating my teeth.

"Wow, that looked intense," Jenna says, standing at the locker next to mine. Her hair is tied back into a high ponytail, making her look like an eighties rocker. She sees my look and shrugs. "Didn't have time to shower after practice this morning." She nods down the hallway. "So, new strategy? Is it working?"

"Is he looking?" I shoot back.

"Yes."

"Then it's working."

"Playing hard to get," she says. "I like it."

I slam my locker shut, grabbing my French books. "Speio's idea, believe it or not."

"Speaking of, I notice he's getting really close with the new girl. She seems nice, not pretentious like some people we know," she says with a pointed glance at the people near Lo. "Did she check out?" she asks in a low whisper. "What if she's a hybrid?"

I nod. I can understand why Jenna's suspicious. She knows exactly what is at stake. We have to be careful of everyone—new and old. We can't trust anyone, not even those we know as allies. Everything has changed. "Don't worry—she's not. Echlios has some special scent thing they developed off the old hybrids. My guard cleared her."

Her eyes shoot into her hairline. "Your guard?"

"Royal guard." I wave a nonchalant hand, cringing inwardly as we walk to our classroom. "You can't see them, but they're here. Watching."

"Wow."

"Comes with the territory," I say. "Especially with all the silent spies we can't see lurking around. They're here for my protection. Echlios insists on it."

Jenna's eyes grow as round as saucers as she peers down the hallway. "This is some serious *Princess Diaries* shit."

"You have no idea," I say with an exaggerated eye roll. "The Aquarathi Secret Service. Seriously, I have ASS watching my back."

Jenna giggles. "So, do these supersecret ninja guards look like us? I mean, like other kids?"

"Put it this way," I tell her, grabbing a vacant seat near the back of the classroom. "There are more of us in here than there are of you."

"But these are kids we've known for years," she nearly screeches, glancing around in a panic.

"We mimic, remember?"

This time Jenna's eyes nearly bug out of her head. "They're not *them?*"

Grinning, I poke her in the side. "God, when did you get so gullible? Seriously." I don't admit that we could indeed mimic existing humans should the need arise. Instead I giggle at her expression. "You should see your face!"

I glance around the classroom. Speio's sitting next to Rian near the front, and I wickedly push a small glimmer out, brushing it against the back of his neck. He spins to shoot a death glare in my direction and I wink, mimicking his smoochy faces from earlier. He turns away, his neck now the color of a maroon flag.

"You're loving the payback, aren't you?" Jenna says.

"So much."

"She's cute. Rian, I mean."

"Anything's an improvement over Cara."

"Ah, Cara," Jenna says, rolling her eyes. "She still slumming in your pudding?"

"Apparently my pudding is now fair game to anyone with

a spoon," I say drily. Jenna guffaws loudly, which turns into a suffocated bout of coughing. I thump her on the back helpfully, watching her eyes water as she tries to stifle her choked laughter.

"Don't do that again," she gasps, clutching her stomach. "Omigod, I can't stop."

"Glad you find my love life so hilarious."

Madame Dumois sweeps into the room and all eyes settle onto her tiny frame. Dumois may be small, but she commands her classroom like a seasoned general. The rules of her class are simple—disrupt at your own peril. I've always liked her no-nonsense approach, and the feeling is mutual. She adores me, considering that I'm fluent in French...and Spanish, German, Chinese and any other language spoken in the human world.

"I'm part French," I told Jenna once.

"What about Japanese? You speak that fluently."

"Part Japanese, too."

"Funny," she said with narrowed eyes. "You don't look Japanese."

The memory makes me smile. Now that Jenna knows the truth—she can guess how many languages I can actually speak without any invented family genealogy. It is yet another of our early Aquarathi learning requirements— know everything about the humans—languages, cultures, customs.

A commotion at the door has everyone's necks craning toward it, mine included. My breath hitches in my throat at the unexpected visitor. Lo's standing there with a mischievous smile on his face. I frown—he's not in this class.

"Oui?" Madame Dumois asks imperiously.

"I have a transfer note from Principal Andrews."

Madame Dumois consults a note on her desk. "Ah, Monsieur Seavon, *oui*. Welcome, *bienvenue*."

Jenna leans over, a conspiratorial look on her face. "Looks like your pudding's back in play. Your strategy is on fire!"

"Not mine," I whisper back, my frown deepening. "I don't have that kind of power."

With a start, I wonder at the sudden class switch and whether it does have anything to do with me. It would have been something the old Lo would have done just to irritate me, but the old Lo is well and truly buried somewhere underneath that new, preppy Banana Republic exterior. The new Lo would hardly care whether we are in the same classes—he's just here to learn, or so he says. Maybe the new Lo just likes French.

I force myself not to breathe as Lo squeezes past Jenna and me to a seat on the far side of the room, but a sudden bolt of pain tears through me, making me gasp. It feels as if someone is electrocuting the inside of my brain. Feeling my eyes water with the force of it, I grip the sides of my desk so tightly that the metal crumples like putty beneath my palm. Jenna's hand slides over mine and I release the desk with shaking fingers. Her eyes are wide as she studies the curved, finger-shaped marks.

"You all right?" she whispers.

I shake my head. "It's getting worse."

"What is?"

"The biotoxin," I manage. "It's spreading and poisoning everything that's Aquarathi in its path."

12

Monster

We've decided to do Lo's hypnotherapy session on a boat in the middle of the ocean. Irregular, I know, but what part of what I'm trying to do is *not* outside the realm of normal? Plus, all of the saltwater tanks at the Marine Center are occupied, and we can't risk not having somewhere for Lo to transform if that happens, which is a very real possibility. We even discussed doing it here at the house, but the risk of one of our neighbors seeing something is too high. And the truth is, if I'm going to incite the darkest depths of Lo, we have to be prepared for the worst. In this case, the worst means a hybrid that thinks it's human transforming into a giant, scaled monster and unleashing months of pent-up, restrained fury onto innocent people. Not ideal...so the farther away from civilization the better.

The beach in front of my house is deserted but for a few people fishing down at the water's edge and a handful of surfers out beyond the breakers. The descending sun casts a heavy orange glow along the sand, turning my shadow into an elongated black caricature. Studying it, I lean on the white gate separating the beach from the boundaries of my property, letting the slight taste of salt on the breeze fan over me. What we are about to do is more than danger-ous, but I can't think of any other way to reach Lo. I glance back at the silent faces standing in a semicircle behind me, grateful for each of them.

Apart from the usual suspects—Echlios, Soren, Speio and me—Echlios has also recruited six of my royal guard, including the ones who've been here in hiding protecting me. I know them instantly as their waters bow in defer-ence to mine, but it's a little strange to see them looking so *human* after so many months of seeing them in Aquarathi form. Two of the human faces I immediately recognize from school, the twins Nova and Nell, but the others have older and less familiar human bodies. In human form, Nova and Nell look as much alike as they do in Aquarathi form with their short, spiky silver hair and pitch-black eyes. Nell's left ear is peppered in silver hoops, while Nova sports wide black plugs in each of his earlobes.

They all stand beside Echlios, muscles tightly coiled, faces carved from stone. Any of them would die to defend me... even from my own mate. I hope desperately that it won't come to that, but if I am in any danger from Lo, I know that they will not hesitate in their duty. For the briefest of seconds, as I eye their stern stances, doubt slides along my spine like an ominous icy prickle. I shrug it away.

Lo won't hurt me. Not the Lo I know.

What if the Lo you know is gone?

The errant thought disappears like a wisp in the wind, leaving a nasty memory of its existence. If the Lo I know is gone, then we have nothing to lose. My people will protect me at any cost. A strange sensation tugs on the edge of my mind—not a glimmer exactly—but a presence...a familiar one. I turn toward it, catching the pale face peering from behind the screen in my room.

"I'll be right back," I click to Echlios. He frowns but doesn't stop me as I head toward the house. I close my sliding glass door behind me and draw the blinds.

"You can't be here, Jenna," I say softly, watching as she comes out from behind the screen.

"I have to be here," she counters in a quiet voice. "He's my friend, too."

"He's not human. He could hurt you." I wave a hand behind me. "And it's not just him. They would do anything to protect me, and you're…not one of us." I know my meaning is clear. They'd kill her if they had to.

Jenna's eyes flash blue fire as she slams her hands on her hips. "Well, they weren't here when Lo was sick all summer, were they? And I wasn't one of you then, was I? Where were they?" She eyes me. "Where were you?" she adds more quietly. "You can't shut me out, Nerissa. Not now."

I flinch at the veiled fury in her voice. I'm torn between letting her come along and having to deal with Echlios. He won't like potentially endangering a human, even if it is one who knows all our secrets. Plus, the others wouldn't understand. It's not like they know what Jenna has done for me. But still, the risk is too high.

"It's too—"

"Don't say it," Jenna says as if sensing my indecision. "Look, you're taking Lo out on a boat because you think it's safer, and that's smart. But he's not going to know any of you if worse comes to worst."

"He knows me," I say. "And Speio."

"Does he?"

"What are you saying, Jenna?"

"Lo knows me more than you right now. You need me, and I know that you can see that. Look, if anything happens, I'll hide. I'll stay out of danger so you don't have to worry about me." Jenna steps forward, eyes bright and lucid. "But you know I'm right, Riss. Lo trusts me. I'm a familiar face...the *only* familiar face that he's known all summer."

I hesitate. A part of me knows that involving her will mean putting her life in danger from others like me. Again. But I also agree that she has been a constant in Lo's life ever since he became sick. If things go badly, she could be the only real person he'll know. Sighing, I click for Soren, who appears immediately. Her green eyes widen as she looks from Jenna to me and back again.

"No," she says in a decisive voice. "Your guard will never allow it. *Echlios* will never allow it."

"The guard obeys my wishes, Soren. Including Echlios," I remind her. "Jenna has to come. What if we can't reach Lo? Jenna is the only person he still knows. She's a human failsafe. And she is the only human we trust. It makes sense."

Soren's mouth is a tight, uncompromising line. "No."

"Yes."

"The guard—"

"I'll deal with them."

"They won't trust her." Soren exhales a long breath. "They won't trust you."

"I'll make them."

Soren bows to the steel in my voice, her mouth tight, as I open the patio door and step outside. The sky has morphed into a fiery orange, but the wild beauty of it is eclipsed by the thunder on Echlios's face. His eyes—and the eyes of all the others—fall on Jenna's slight form behind me. Their bodies are bristling, their faces fierce. Nova's and Nell's eyes widen as they recognize Jenna. None of them know just how much she knows. And I'm about to tell them that I've broken one of our cardinal rules—trusting a human with our secret.

Staring at them all in turn, I force the ridge of bones and fins to push outward from my human brow, shimmering gold-and-green lights rippling down my shoulders and forearms. Even in my human form, my crown is fearsome to look at—corded, razor-sharp coral points interspersed with brilliant fronds fanning my forehead—a medieval monster of the deep. Burnished scales shimmer along my sharpened cheekbones as I halt my transformation in its tracks. The protective membrane that mimics human eyes flips back from my eyelids, and my Aquarathi eyes burn jeweled fire. They demand obedience. Each Aquarathi before me bows to stare at the ground.

"This is Jenna," I say in my language. My human lips shape the clicks and pulses. "She knows what we are. I have allowed this. She will accompany us. You will protect her as you would me. This is my command."

Nova's head lifts. "But, my queen, she is human. The law—"

"She saved my life," I say. "Twice."

"My lady," Echlios begins. I cut him off with a meaningful stare.

"She comes."

Despite my unbending words, I can still feel their worry, and their fear. They will obey me because I'm their queen, but I know they won't trust Jenna, not as I do, and her presence will be a distraction. I sigh. Only one thing will work to convince them, and that is to make them see the truth.

I push a glimmer outward to touch each of the guards

and connect them to me, framing my memory of the day I'd stupidly tried Sanctum with Speio in human form and paid the ultimate price. Jenna had found me, shriveled and on the brink of death. She'd brought me home to Echlios, despite not knowing what I was even though it'd been obvious that I was anything but human. In quick succession, I push my other memory into the glimmer—the one where Jenna had Taser-gunned an enemy hybrid spy of Ehmora's who had been about to kill me *and* Speio. She had saved us both from capture and certain death. I hide nothing from them.

"Now you see," I say, snapping the glimmer back into myself. "You will accord this *human* the respect she deserves."

"My lady," Soren calls from behind me. "He's here."

Nodding, I retract my crown, feeling the bones shift and dissolve back into their human shapes. The rest of my guard melts into the growing darkness along with Echlios until it's just Speio, Jenna and me. Soren has gone back into the house, presumably to get Lo. Speio clears his throat and I turn to meet my wide-eyed best friend.

"They're like silent ninjas, your guards. No wonder you said I couldn't see them at school. You weren't kidding, were you?" she says, an apprehensive look flitting across her face. "Seriously, who would have thought the Goth twins were one of you?"

"I know. Are you sure you're okay?" I ask her.

"What just happened?" she says slowly as if trying to find the right words. "I mean, at first they were all looking at me like I was the enemy when I came out, even Echlios. And now they're not..." She trails off, flushing uncomfortably. "What did you tell them when you spoke in your language?"

"I showed them what you did…how you saved me."

"Oh."

"Don't worry. No one's going to hurt you, Jenna. Not when you're with me." I smile tightly and squeeze her arm. "You sure you still want to come? You can still change your mind. I'd understand."

"No. I want to. He's my friend, too."

We both turn to greet Lo. The breath hitches in my throat as every drop of water in my body rises to meet his. My fingers tighten on Jenna's arm and she winces.

A slow grin eases its way across his face. "What is this? An intervention?" he jokes. Jenna's eyes widen.

"No," she blurts out. "We're just hanging out."

"I'm just kidding, relax," he says, grin widening. "Soren said Nerissa was going to join us today. She thought it would help with my session—to try something different."

I toss a reassuring smile at Jenna. It'd been surprisingly easy to convince Lo. Soren had suggested maybe recreating a date with me during their last therapy session to see if it would stimulate any memories. Lo had been skeptical at first, given that he barely remembered who I was, but apparently Soren had been quite persuasive in her argument. Coloring at the thought of Soren's intimate knowledge of my love life, I don't even want to know what she said to him.

"You guys know Dr. Aldon?" Lo says, nodding to the tall man dressed in blue slacks and a brown cashmere sweater. "He's a shrink, helping with the memory loss." Lo says all this as if it's matter-of-fact, but I can sense that it's not as easy for him as he's making it out to be.

"Cool," I say in a calm voice, ignoring the deep ache

his easy smile has opened up in my stomach. "Nice to see you, Dr. Aldon."

"And you." His dark eyes are appraising. He, of course, knows who I am. I meet his gaze with an unflinching one of my own.

Dr. Aldon and I have met several times before via Soren to discuss Lo's progress. He is one of the select few who are privileged to know of our existence. As is the Aquarathi way, we keep our finger on the pulse of human activity—in every field of study, in every area—monitoring developments that could affect our way of life. Dr. Aldon, like several other prominent human scientists and doctors before him, went through a rigorous approval and security process with Echlios and his men before he was allowed into the inner circle. Dr. Aldon understood the risks and knew that if he broke the circle in any way, he would pay the price with his life. Like the others, in return for his discretion and occasional services, he receives unlimited grant funds for his research.

Jenna is different because I made that decision on my own, and to the Aquarathi she is no one of consequence. Her knowledge of my true form and my species was a secret until now. Convincing my guards was easy—convincing all the other lower courts of Waterfell will be another matter entirely. I shiver to think of the consequences, but still, Jenna's unwavering loyalty to me, and to a species not her own, has to count for something.

"Shall we?" I say. "Jenna's going to come along with us, Lo, if that's okay with you." I want to put him at ease, but it's not like he'll have any choice in the matter.

Lo nods, with a half smile that makes rivers unwind in my stomach. "Sure, it's not like she doesn't know what's going on with me." I stifle a gulp. Right now Jenna knows far more about him than *he* does, not that he's aware of that, of course.

Piling into the waiting town car, we drive in silence toward the marina where Dr. Aldon's ninety-foot yacht is docked. Notwithstanding his good fortune with the Aquarathi, Dr. Aldon comes from old money, and this is just one of the fleet of private yachts his family owns. Suppressing a grin at the boat's name—*Sea Queen*—I climb aboard and am greeted by Aldon's welcoming crew. They leave the minute we are all ensconced on the yacht. Aldon prefers privacy in case anything goes wrong.

"Neat digs," Lo remarks, taking in the luxurious vanilla-colored leather seating and the plush carpeting inside the main cabin.

Aldon glances over his shoulder, waving a well-manicured hand. "There are five staterooms, laundry room, full kitchen, gym, mezzanine, entertainment center, the works. Make yourself at home."

Lo sprawls out on one of the chaises, grinning. "I could get used to this."

"Nerissa?" Aldon says. "Do you want to take her out?"

"Sure."

Navigating the tight marina is tough, but I manage to exit the slip without too much hassle. Out on the open ocean, the air is warm with a tinge of coldness brewing off the tops of the waves. Echlios and the rest of the guard aren't in sight, but I can sense them following in our wake beneath the surface. Glancing at Lo, seated between Dr. Aldon and Soren in the bow, I swallow hard. His sandy hair blows into his face, the wind whipping into his bronze cheeks. He looks so healthy and normal on the outside with no sign of the poison eating away at him on the inside. My fingers clutch the wheel so hard that the boat yanks right.

"My bad," I shout out as four heads swivel my way. "Sorry."

"What's up?" Jenna asks, climbing up to the bridge and propping herself on the white seat next to me. "You seem really distracted."

I stare at my best friend and let my rigid self-control ease for a second. "Worried."

"Why?"

"Never tried this before. Could go bad." I force a smile. "Can you imagine a rogue Aquarathi on the loose? The damage? The chaos?"

"That won't happen, Riss. You'll reach him. It'll work."

"How do you know?"

Jenna's blue eyes light up. "Because you're Nerissa and Lo, the queen and king of the sea. You're meant to be together. You've bonded—he's yours and you're his. And that's all there is to it. If anyone can do this, it's you, Riss."

Unexpected tears sting my eyelids. "Thanks."

I reach out to squeeze her hand just as the looming shape of an island creeps out of the horizon—San Nicolas, one of California's channel islands, and controlled by the U.S. Navy. We're almost to our destination. Steering the boat to the west of San Nicolas, I hold our speed steady at sixty knots just as the sun takes its final plunge to its rest.

"Where are we going?" Jenna says, peering out onto the horizon. "There's nothing out here."

"Exactly," I say, lowering the throttle. It's too deep to drop anchor, so I just turn off the engine and nod for Jenna to follow me down to the stern's open deck, where the others are already waiting. The huge yacht barely rocks on the almost flat ocean. "Remember, stay out of sight if things get out of hand. Do not intervene unless I call you, okay?"

"Okay."

We both watch as Aldon starts the hypnotherapy. My entire body tenses up. Jenna leans forward, her voice a whisper against my ear. "What's wrong?"

"Not that I know much about anything, but does hypnosis on humans actually work?" I should have researched it online myself, but looking it up would have made it more real than it already is. Jenna would know. She'd have made it her business to know everything about it inside out.

"Sometimes. For depression, reducing anxiety, things like that. For dissociative conditions like Lo's, it's a little more iffy." She pauses. "There's a lot of research behind the whole mind-body connection, and getting people into an altered state of consciousness to retrieve memories, but those memories may be false. What you're going to do is a little more involved than that."

What Jenna says is true. Lo's Aquarathi side won't be affected by clinical hypnosis, and if the human part of him goes into a temporary trancelike state, we hope that we can reach the *other* part of him.

Aldon nods for me to approach. "He's ready."

"Be careful," Jenna whispers to me. I squeeze her hand and swallow.

Aldon is escorted into the cabin by one of Echlios's men for his own safety. The rest of the guards form a semicircle around me. For a second I study the shimmery surface of the ocean stretching out behind us like a carpet of ebony glass. Not a whisper of wind disturbs its surface. It's so eerily quiet that a shiver races over my back.

The calm before the storm.

Taking Aldon's vacated seat, I stare at Lo. His face is relaxed, his mouth curved in a half smile. Silvery blond streaks of hair fall across his forehead and onto closed eyelids. My fingers ache to brush them away and I give in to the urge. The strands are like silk against my skin.

Lo's eyes flutter open, such an unearthly limpid shade of blue, and I lick dry lips before grasping his hands in mine. "Hi, Lo," I say.

"Hi, Riss."

"Do you trust me?"

"Yes."

My eyes meet Echlios's and then Soren's. Just because Lo is in such a serene, accessible state doesn't mean things can't go from calm to chaos in the blink of an eye. I take a slow, steadying breath as I close my eyes, summoning the water in my body. The glimmer forms almost immediately in my core, more powerful than anything I've ever created. I know it's in response to the bond between Lo and me, but it's also because of our proximity to the sea. And the fact that I'm a queen.

Instantly I feel the visceral response from the other Aquarathi around me. Gathering the glimmer, I push it toward Lo to connect with the water in his body. A raw memory of the time I stole his energy just before I fought his mother rips through me, but then we're connected and all I can feel is a surge that makes my back ramrod straight and every cell in my body come alive.

Lo's eyes are lucid, but his fingers grip mine harder than before, and I know he feels it, too—the bond between us, savage and pure. I swallow hard, watching the green-and-gold lights ripple along my arms. The navy swirls—Lo's bonding marks—writhe upon my skin, twining down my wrists to my fingers to meet the greenish-gold swirls coming alive on his.

Lo's eyes hold mine, something intense flowering in their depths. In response, a hot spiral unfurls in my stomach, desire making my blood rush and my pulse throb. The air turns electric, connected by the mad currents in our bodies. Every Aquarathi drop of water in him is responding fully to me. Lo pulls against me, sucking me into him, and unguarded, I let him. He hasn't forgotten. It's been so long since I've felt so whole. All I want to do is push myself deeper into him until I can't feel anything but us... intertwine my body with his and forget everything.

Focus.

The soft click is from Soren. Grateful for the needed encouragement, I exhale and strengthen against Lo's demands. Following the thread of the glimmer connecting us, I breach Lo's mind, past all the human defenses and into the dark alien part of him. The part I know. The glimmer thrums with instant recognition.

Lo?

Lo's human eyes widen as his fingers twitch against mine. *Nerissa?*

I almost collapse. There's only one person who can say my name the way he does, like it's a liquid, delicious shape. I shiver. *Where have you been?*

Here, he says. *Trapped. How are you doing this?*

I'm inside you, I say. *It was the only way I could reach you.*

Nerissa— The worry in his voice is evident. He, too, knows the risks of what I'm doing.

I know, Lo. I don't know how much time I have, so I blurt out my thoughts. *You've been poisoned. It's some kind of biotoxin that's inhibiting your Aquarathi side from healing your human DNA. You've had amnesia for months.* My voice breaks. *You don't know me. You don't remember us.*

That's impossible. I know you.

This Aquarathi part of you does. Not your human side.

What do I do? he asks.

You have to force yourself to remember to heal the broken pieces. Let me help you.

He frowns. *What if it doesn't work?*

It has to work.

Lo leans forward, sandy scales shimmering to life in a ripple along his cheeks, and brushes warm human lips against mine. It's a kiss magnified a thousandfold by the tidal wave of energy crashing between us. My breath stalls. *In case I haven't told you lately, I love you.*

Eyes stinging, I can only nod as he pulls away. *Let me in, Lo.*

He agrees, and without hesitation, I breach the human part of him—the part that won't understand what I am—the part that will see me only as a monster. But I have to try. I have to make him remember—and accept—all that he is. I open myself to him completely, mindful of Echlios's warning, showing him everything that happened in the past year...letting him see himself through my eyes, letting him feel everything through me...letting him see the Aquarathi.

Lo's fingers tighten like vises onto mine, the crack of bone sharp in the silence. One of the guards jerks forward, but he's immediately restrained by Echlios. The pain of my broken fingers is nothing compared to the agony tearing through Lo at the onslaught of memories, the toxin reacting like a mad virus against them...fighting against me, fighting against him.

"No!" Lo screams aloud, shoving away from me. "Get

away from me! All of you. You're a monster." He eyes me with wild, crazed eyes. The connection between us splinters to a thread as he staggers back, his palms in front of him as if warding off something horrific. Then he clutches at his body, screaming.

"Aldon!" I yell, holding on to the glimmer with everything I have. "Sedative!"

"It's too late. He's already shifting," Soren shouts, just as Lo swipes at Aldon's outstretched hand and breaks the syringe into pieces. The next blow is to Aldon's temple, knocking him out cold.

I focus on Lo. Sure enough, his human form is elongating and bulking outward, his skin hardening into burnished silvery-gold scales. The rear of the yacht sinks into the water at the weight. Lo's tail smashes into anchored stools along the stern's deck, ripping them from their anchors. Nova and Nell attempt to restrain him, but their human bodies go flying as the next casualties of Lo's strength. Three more of the guards follow suit. Tethered to me, he's stronger than all of them put together, but I can't let go. Not now.

Lo, I beg. *It's me, Nerissa.*

He flinches at my voice, tearing at his scalp with taloned half-human fingers. "I see you! You're all monsters," Lo screams gutturally. His skittish eyes meet his reflection in the open glass doors to the cabin. "I'm a—"

I approach him cautiously. *Lo. You have to control yourself. Trust me. You have to trust me.*

His gaze falls on me, his body quieting, and for a second I think I have him, just before a heavily muscled, scaled forearm smashes into my side. The pain rockets through me and I'm airborne, landing fifty feet away into the arms of the ocean with a splash, my body transforming to Aquarathi form almost instantly. The scene on the boat is like one out of the *Jaws* movie, with handrails hanging drunkenly off their hinges and pieces of furniture floating beside the boat.

But that isn't what makes the breath die a slow death in my throat.

It's the sight of a slim auburn-haired girl squaring off against a beast thirty times her size…and one that has just scented prey on the wind.

13
The Rules of the Game

"Jenna, no!" My terrified shriek makes every Aquarathi around me leap into motion, and then I'm whipping through the water toward the boat. When I resurface a few feet away from the busted stern, my heart lodges in my throat. It's like the finale scene out of a horror movie...the scene where someone gets ripped to bloody shreds.

Lo has Jenna cornered against the side, his body driven by a basic need to survive. Soren is standing motionless near him, still in human form, and the others along with Echlios are in the water, awaiting my command. I hesitate. If Soren attacks, Jenna will be in Lo's direct path. Frustrated, I grind my teeth. Why didn't she just stay hidden, as I'd told her? There's no part of Lo that's human right now, and all she is to him is a target. Jenna isn't just some casualty—she's my friend and I can't let her die, not even if it's a choice between the two of them.

I shift back into human form, treading water with my arms. "Jenna," I say in a careful voice. "Try to move away toward the water. Slowly."

She complies, but before she can even take one step, Lo

opens his fearsome jaws and screams, making her freeze in her tracks. The color drains from her face. Jenna has seen me in human form, but seeing an Aquarathi who wants to be seen and one whose sole purpose is to hunt are two totally different things. Bringing her here was a bad idea, even though it seemed like a convincing one at the time. I should have known that Lo's Aquarathi side would view her as foe, not friend.

"Lo," I say in my language, changing tactics and drawing his attention away from Jenna as I climb onto the lower deck. His slitted, jeweled eyes focus on me. I keep my voice carefully modulated. "It's okay. Just calm down. Jenna is your friend. We are all your friends."

Lo's neck arches, his eyes rolling back in his skull as if he's fighting the biotoxin inside his brain. I know what he's struggling against—the human side of him that's making him think he's crazy, that all of this isn't really happening. We're still connected by the glimmer, albeit thinly. I take a breath and push it forward despite my own waning strength.

"Lo, you know me. You know all of us. You understand what I'm saying to you now. This is all real."

"What am I?" he growls out, and then claws at his head. "So much pain."

"I know," I say, my voice still low. "We're going to fix it, I promise. But first, you need to shift back to human form, Lo."

He eyes me, but then his head swings back toward Jenna in desperate hunger. I swallow. I don't want to hurt Lo, but I'll do it if I have to. Lo's entire body tenses, his tail fin undulating like that of a rattlesnake on the verge of attacking. It's now or never. Gathering my strength, I slam the glimmer into him with brute force. It spreads outward and through him as I hold him in place. Wild, furious eyes meet mine. Lo fights my glimmer with everything inside him. The faint thought that my mother was right flits through my brain—he is strong, stronger than I'd ever thought. I squeeze harder, my glimmer overcoming his will, even as his pain flicks back toward me through the bond.

"My queen," an urgent voice says from behind me. Echlios's brow is furrowed with worry. "You're going to kill him."

Gasping, I relent slightly. It's a mistake. Acid-blue eyes fixate on me and blue lights flicker to life along Lo's deep gold body as if sensing a momentary advantage. I brace, but the weight of his glimmer slams into me like a freight train, and then he's draining me—doing exactly what Echlios had feared—taking every drop of energy that is his for the taking. And there's nothing I can do to stop him.

Suddenly Lo rips away, leaving me feeling as if a layer of my skin has been singed off. Sinking to my knees, I crumple against Echlios, gasping for breath. Echlios's fingers tighten against me before he leaps forward. Lo snarls and shrugs him off easily. Of course he does. He's full of my strength…my water. None of them will be any match for him, not now. Lo dispatches one of Echlios's men, disemboweling him with his barbed tail. Two others rush him, only to meet the same fate. The air is thick with the smell of fury and blood.

This is my fault. Stupidly, I opened myself up to him, thinking I'd be strong enough to withstand him. But I wasn't. The bond makes us strong, but it makes us weak, too—weak to each other. And I'm powerless against him.

Nell clutches a broken arm, her brother standing beside

her covered in his own blood. They both step forward, uncaring of their own well-being, loyal to the end.

"Stop," I say weakly, staring at the iridescent Aquarathi blood spilling across the deck. "Don't attack him. He's too strong." I pause, propping myself up against a bench that's still intact. "This is my doing, and I'm the only one who can stop him."

"My lady," Soren says. "You're not strong enough."

"I'll have to be."

"Then take my water." She's made the offer before, but never like this where taking it could mean her death. I lick dry lips and nod.

"Mine, too," Echlios says.

With a trembling breath, I prepare to do just that, but to my surprise, Jenna steps forward until she's within Lo's reach and the billowing courage seeps of out my sails. If Lo wants, he can snap her neck off her head in half a breath. I hold mine, transfixed, as Jenna spreads her palms slow and wide in a nonthreatening gesture. Astonishingly, she leans closer.

"Jenna—" I begin in warning but she ignores me.

"Lo," she says in a low voice. "It's Jenna. I know you know who I am. And I know you're still somewhere in there. You're strong. You have to control it." Her voice is hypnotic. "Find something that you know is true and hold on to it. You know what's real, and you know who you are. Don't let go of that one thing."

Lo's body goes preternaturally still as I exhale an incredulous breath. He's actually listening to her. Somehow she's reaching him. My eyes flick to Soren. She looks as I imagine I do, wide-eyed and disbelieving.

"Listen to my voice, Lo," Jenna is saying. "You know who you are. You *know*. Now change back, make yourself human again. Hold on to that one thing—the one part of what makes you, you. Only you know what that is, and let it bring you back."

Time slows for an endless minute, our heartbeats like distant echoes of thunder. And then I feel it before I see it, radiating back along his flanks. He's transforming. In seconds, the bulk of his body melts into the slender shape of human bones, scales shifting into skin, fins flowing into fingers, until he's a pale shivering form on the floor of the deck. Echlios moves forward, but I raise a hand as Jenna places a towel around Lo's hunched shoulders.

"You all right?" she asks him softly.

"Kind of a loaded question, don't you think?" he murmurs with a half smile. I breathe a sigh of relief at the nonchalant answer.

"I guess it is."

"There's so much…"

"Don't try to process all of it now," Jenna says. "Just breathe."

Lo stares down at his arm, frowning. "I remember it, but it feels like a dream, like none of it was real." His eyes shift to each of us in turn and then to the shambles of the stern. "But it was real, wasn't it? I… Them…" Lo grips Jenna's leg, and my heart jumps into my throat, but he only wants to ask her a question. "I did all this, didn't I?"

Jenna seems unsure of what to say, and then just nods. She moves to squat beside him. "It's going to be fine, Lo."

"How do you know?"

"Because I do." And that's when she jabs the tranquilizer needle that fell out of Dr. Aldon's hand into Lo's neck. He arches against her, but he's no match for the powerful sedative, not in human form. "Sleep now. You'll feel better, I promise."

She cradles him as he slumps against her, his eyes opening and closing with delayed blinks. "Okay, Jenna," he says drowsily.

With a glance at me, she brushes the hair out of his face. "Lo, when I asked you to hold on to something before, what did you think of?"

Those languid dark eyes meet mine just before they slip closed, his eyelashes fluttering across the tops of his cheeks. For a second, I think he's gone to sleep, but then Lo's lips shape a whispered answer.

"Her. I thought of her."

I glare at Jenna in the mirror of the girls' bathroom. "Seriously, you could have asked me first. I told you I was done with hockey."

She glares back just as fiercely, not backing down for an instant. "Look, I'm your friend and you're more stressed than I've ever seen you. You don't surf. You don't swim. You don't do anything to get all that negative energy out. You're going to explode, Riss. So yeah, I talked to Coach Fenton. You can play in the scrimmage after school."

"I don't have time for hockey. You know that," I say tiredly. I splash some water on my face and take a deep breath. I'm stressed because I'm worried. Bertha and Grayer told Echlios that Lo hasn't moved from his bed all week, except to sit at the water's edge for hours at a time, staring into space. Since what happened on the boat, he hasn't said a word to anyone about anything. His silence terrifies me.

Jenna sighs, meeting my eyes. "He hasn't talked to you?"

"No," I say. "Still out sick. No calls. Nothing. The only

reason I know he's alive is Grayer. On top of that, I can't find my phone. I think it's at the Marine Center, so I don't even know if he's texted me."

"He needs some space, Riss. He'll come around when he's ready."

I stare at her. "When's that? It's not like we have a ton of time."

"I know. But you can't break yourself into pieces in the meantime. Look, it's one game. I think you need to take your mind off everything, and hockey is the one thing you had that was yours...unrelated to the two of you."

We both jump as a toilet flushes behind us. I'd been so preoccupied that I hadn't been aware of another person inside the bathroom with us. Hastily thinking back over the conversation, I'm confident that neither of us has said anything too outlandish. Still, I'm hoping beyond hope that it isn't Cara. That would be the last straw. The stall door opens and I heave a sigh of relief.

"Hey, guys," Rian says with an embarrassed, apologetic look. "I wasn't eavesdropping or anything. Sounded kind of intense, so I was waiting for you guys to leave. But then, I didn't want to be late for class."

"No big deal," Jenna says, wiping her hands with a paper towel and busying herself searching for something in her backpack.

"Sorry," Rian says with a sympathetic smile at the neighboring sink. "Boy stuff?"

"Sort of."

I run my wet hands through my hair, twisting it up into a ponytail. Although I like Rian, I don't want to be rude, but it's not like this is any of her business despite overhearing our conversation. An awkward silence descends on the bathroom, with the three of us looking anywhere but each other. Jenna is still applying sixteen layers of lip gloss and Rian finishes rinsing her hands in silence. She clears her throat at the door, chewing on her lower lip as if she hasn't quite decided whether or not to say anything. She hesitates and shrugs with a wry twist of her mouth.

"I know it's none of my business," she says as if she read my mind, or my tight expression. "But for what it's worth, you should play today. Speio told me that you used to be really good. Maybe it'll…take the edge off. Just my unsolicited two cents. See you guys in class."

Jenna grins after Rian leaves, pocketing her gloss. "See? Even the new girl thinks you should play."

I shake my head. "Fine, I'll think about it. Your lips are really shiny, by the way. Like someone-could-get-blinded shiny."

Jenna puckers up. "That's just how I roll."

"Too bad you almost blew a lip-gloss bubble. I'm surprised your lips aren't stuck together."

"They kind of are," Jenna admits with a snort. "Give us a kiss."

"No way! Go kiss Sawyer." Giggling as she blots her lips with a tissue, I grab my discarded backpack and sling it over my shoulder. "Now come on before we get sent to the office for being late and I have to mind-meld Principal Andrews again."

Barely sliding into our seats in English just in time as Mr. Donovan shuts the door behind us, we're still grinning like a pair of idiots. Not wasting any time, he taps his copy of *The Importance of Being Earnest*. "Class, please open up to act two, part one. Sawyer, please begin the part of Algernon. Marcus, you take Jack."

Despite Jenna's droll expression, my lightheartedness is short-lived as my gaze lands on Lo's empty chair. Despair returns in full force. What I wouldn't give to be done with this whole double life and be back in Waterfell where I belong with Lo at my side, pretending that none of this ever happened. I wouldn't have to say goodbye to Jenna again, and things would be as they should. Seriously, this play is like a metaphor of my life. Monster invents fictional girl. Fictional girl falls for boy who has a fictional reality of his own. Pair admits to inventing fictional other lives. Fiction becomes reality. All bets are off.

Oh, and history repeats itself.

Staring down at the cover of my worn copy of the play, I think about Jack's sense of duty and obligation being his downfall. Maybe Jenna and Rian are right—a fun hockey game would take the edge off. Funnily enough, just the thought of it makes it feel like a weight as been lifted off my chest. Not completely, but just enough so that I can breathe.

I coast through the rest of class, getting more excited by the minute as the last bell gets closer. By the time I've stashed my books in my locker, my pregame adrenaline is skyrocketing. I forgot how it feels...how all your senses zing in anticipation of facing off against another team, of pitting your skills in an arena, of working as a team toward one single objective.

"So, you in?" Jenna says.

"I don't have a uniform with me."

Jenna's eyes light up like the fourth of July. "I've got extra."

"What about my lucky stick?"

"With skills like yours, you don't need a lucky stick, but I've got an extra stick that's lucky enough for the both of us."

In the girls' locker room, it's as if I never left. You'd think that the odd combination of sweaty gym socks and fruity conditioner would be off-putting, but it's soothingly familiar. I'd never realized just how grounding hockey had been for me. Tracing the old sticker with my name on my old locker, I realize that in an odd, unexpected way, I've come home. With a sad smile, I wonder whose locker it is now. It would have been reassigned for sure.

"Welcome back, Marin," a quiet voice behind me says through the open door. Coach Fenton looks the same as I remember—his smiling, no-nonsense face with kind blue eyes. I follow him outside.

"Thanks for letting me play, Coach."

"It's good to have you here. Thought you would have come back to us when you transferred back in, but I understand family commitments. We've missed your talent on the field."

"I've missed the team, too. Not so much the three-a-day practices on the weekend," I tease. "Or the early-morning runs."

"Well, suit up. I'll see you out there." He grins. "Let's see how rusty you've gotten without my three-a-days." He points at my locker. "Forgot how to open that, have you?"

"I thought it was someone else's."

"Nope. The girls wanted to keep it for you just in case you came back." He shrugs, crossing his arms over his chest and leaning against the doorjamb. He nods to someone behind him in the hallway. "Plus, no one else could open it. Thing gets stuck every time."

"You mean like this?" I double-punch the upper right corner and the locker pops open.

My jaw hits the floor. The locker is crammed full of

streamers, photos and welcome-back signs, in addition to my old uniform and my gear. *Jenna*. But before I can react, the whole room erupts in shouting and screaming as some of my old teammates throw themselves on top of me, including a delighted Jenna. I see Cara out of the corner of my eye, standing in the corner with a scowl on her face. Of course she couldn't just be happy that I was there.

"Did you plan this?" I ask Jenna amid the cheers, jerking my head toward my locker. "You knew I'd say yes?"

"Of course I did. It's hockey…kind of like giving crack to a baby."

"That's a messed-up visual, but thanks, I think."

Kate, the right forward, thumps me on the back. "Good to have you back, fearless leader."

"Great to be back," I say. "For this scrimmage, anyway."

Kate shakes her head. "Jenna hasn't been the same without her cocaptain. She kind of sucks as full captain, honestly."

"Hey!" Jenna chucks her in the shoulder, grinning. "All right, ladies, get your gear on. Let's show our old cocaptain exactly what she's been missing."

On the field, I tap my stick onto each of my cleats for good luck and troop out with the rest of the team. I wave to Speio, who is sitting in the stands next to Rian. They wave back, grinning and cheering with the rest of the crowd. Seeing Speio happy at one of my hockey games is a far cry from how against it he'd been last year. Must be the company. Rian's certainly had a good effect on him. He's far less moody and even smiles occasionally. I'm not complaining. I don't miss Sour-Patch Speio one bit.

"You ready?" Jenna shouts to me breathlessly.

"You bet."

Breaking from tradition, we're playing a mixed coed game with the boys' team for the pep rally. As usual, the boys' team is nowhere near as good as the girls' team, but with the mixed teams, it'll make for a good matchup. I was surprised that Coach Fenton agreed to let me play, considering that they're facing our school's nemesis—Bishop's— the following week, but I'm not complaining.

Jenna and Cara face off in a bully at the centerfield mark. I'm sure Cara's thrilled that she's playing against me and not with me. She's the captain for the opposing team, and even though Jenna picked me first, I know it'd be a cold day in hell before Cara voluntarily chose me to be on her team. Or vice versa.

I forget all about Cara as the whistle blows and the ball is in play. Complete athletic instinct and muscle memory take over as Jenna passes me the ball, and I race up the field toward the goal with it. I deftly swing my stick, passing it back to Kate—my old right-wing attack forward—before dropping back and to the right. It's our old bait and switch, and one that Kate obviously remembers as she passes me the ball with a devilish grin in a backward swipe from between her legs. The boy on the other team facing Kate is at a complete loss until he sees me veering up to the right, ball in play. Maneuvering it toward the goal past two junior defenders, I take the strike, watching as it pounds into the far left corner of the net.

"Goal!" the crowd cheers.

Jenna thumps me on the back, exhilarated. "Like riding a bike, right? How are you feeling?"

"Better than I have in weeks."

We smash sticks and it's all I can do not to hug her right there on the field. She's always known how to bring me back to my center, or how to read the signs of when I'm close to losing it…first as a human, and even now as an Aquarathi. If there's one thing I can be proud of during my cycle here on land, it's Jenna. She's as loyal a best friend as they come, and more than most. And she's saved my skin on more than one occasion. I don't know what I'd do without her.

"Let's show them what we've got," she yells to our team, high-fiving Gregg, a senior from the boys' team who is playing with us.

Nearing the end of the two thirty-five-minute regulation halves, the game is tied five-all, so we go into overtime. Technically, we don't have to play overtime since it's just a scrimmage, but the crowd is on its feet cheering wildly. This has turned into an exhibition match more than anything, with older players flaunting tricks and sick stick skills all over the field.

I show off some fancy footwork of my own, trapping the ball up onto my stick's curved face and into the air, only to have it snatched out from under my nose by Cara. Grinning, I chase her down the field, watching her expert handling of the ball. I forgot just how good she is. I hold back even though I know I can tackle her easily, and let her think she's got the advantage just before making my move.

At the last second, I dart to the right and then twist in a half circle in the reverse direction, putting me nearly nose to nose with Cara. We jostle for position with rough elbows and high-sticking until the umpire blows his whistle for a double foul. We square off in a bully near the midfield line.

"Why don't you go back to South Africa or whatever hole it was you crawled out of?" Cara growls.

"And miss seeing you break a sweat?" I toss back. "I think not."

"You think you're so tough, don't you?"

"If you say so."

"The truth is, you don't even belong here." She glares at me.

I eye her evenly, despite the hollow feeling spreading in my chest. "You would know."

"Know what?"

"About belonging." I lower my voice and lean in just as the umpire drops the ball between us. "After all, you're not even *from* here. Tell me, do you miss L.A.? Truth is, Cara, you're the biggest outsider of them all, aren't you?"

Her eyes narrow to such slits that I can barely see her pupils. Despite the twinge in my stomach at opening old wounds, Cara's unknowing jab touched a nerve that made me respond in kind. She had no idea that I knew about her not-so-perfect foster-child past, discovered during a misguided break-in to Cano's office last year. Still, I shouldn't have said what I did, even in the heat of anger. Not now, not after I've come so far. It isn't who I am.

"I'm sorry. I didn't—"

But despite my best intentions, I can't even finish the apology. An unfamiliar tug interrupts my words and jerks my attention toward the sidelines, but there's no one there. The pull intensifies sharply, making the hairs rise on my human skin and wrenching a pained gasp from my lips. Something wet and cloying stretches its way across my mind like a vise. The sensation is cold and alien. *Assessing.*

Then it moves with icy purpose, twisting down into my center with vicious hunger. It feels as if something— *someone*—is digging clawed talons into the center of my belly and eviscerating me. My stomach clenches against it with futile resistance, white-hot spots bursting like fireworks behind my eyes. I close them for a split second, and then the pain is gone as quickly as it came, as if it had never been there in the first place...as if I've imagined it all.

A hollow feeling spreads through me just as the whistle blows, and there's a mad flurry of movement around us. Disoriented, I face off against Cara, but the last thing I see coming toward my face is a snarling girl and the blunt end of a short stick.

And then all I see is darkness.

14
Sleight of Hand

The sharp scent of ammonia wafts into my nostrils, making me sit up and gag. I swipe at the smelling salts in front of my nose and wince at the pain shooting across my cheekbones.

"Be still for a minute," an indistinct voice says. Dark shadows flicker in front of my eyelids. My eyes flutter open and squint shut against the glare of the sun as Speio's worried face comes into view. My eyes flick to Jenna, kneeling at his side.

"Riss? What happened?" Speio whispers in my ear as images come flashing back—Cara's furious face and her stick swinging toward my head—neither enough to knock me out on my worst day. And yet she did. And what was that strange gutting sensation in the pit of my stomach? It was as if someone was taking the measure of me, of what I am.

Jenna frowns, leaning in. "Kate said she saw Cara clobber you in the face. That true?"

"I…don't know."

Truth is, I have no idea what happened. Even seeing that stick coming toward my face would have given me enough time to either dodge or deflect the strike, but I didn't. I was too distracted by the unexpected intrusion. My gaze flicks to the bleachers, but there's no one there now. The sensation was so utterly foreign that I can't even imagine what it might have been. Maybe it's something related to Lo, and what's happening with him. Although I can't imagine that it would be—I *know* Lo. My body can identify him in a breath. Maybe Soren or Echlios would have more of an idea.

Wincing at the dwindling sting on the bridge of my nose, I take a deep breath. Cara's strike was a lucky one. I didn't think she had it in her, but everyone has a breaking point. I'd obviously pushed her to hers. I look for her in the crowd of faces hovering above me. She looks as surprised as I do, but the emotion disappears from her face as soon as we make eye contact. A flush winds up her neck. She knows that if I say anything, she'll be suspended.

"It was an accident. I went down when she went up."

Jenna frowns. "That's not what Kate said."

I squeeze her hand. "Kate was wrong. I'm fine," I say, and push myself somewhat dazedly to my feet, grabbing Speio's arm. "Coach, just going to sit out the rest of the half."

Coach Fenton nods. "Payton, you're up," he shouts to a junior sitting on the bench. "Come on, the rest of you, back on the field. We have a game to finish."

Hobbling over to the bench with Speio, I watch the start of the game halfheartedly, my mind racing while Speio goes to get me some water. Within minutes, I see Echlios at the edge of the field, his brow furrowed. Nova and Nell are with him. They would all have felt that I was in some kind of jeopardy.

"Where's Lo? Is he safe?" I ask once Echlios reaches my side. Nova and Nell melt into the rest of the kids sitting in the bleachers behind us.

"Yes."

Relief floods through me. "So he's not hurt?"

"No," Echlios says.

"Did you feel it?" I ask. "What I felt?"

"Somewhat. It was hazy to all of us. We sensed your fear and pain more than anything. Are you all right?" Echlios asks. I shake my head slowly and he sits next to me. "We need to get you somewhere safe. This is too open, especially since we don't know what just happened."

He has a point. What I felt was foreign and invasive—it wasn't the touch of something friendly, even if it hadn't been overtly hostile. It was like nothing I've ever felt before—*nothing*—not us, not hybrids, not human. We can't afford to take any risks. I nod, watching as he walks over to Coach Fenton. They exchange a few words, and Echlios returns just as Jenna jogs over, calling for a time-out.

"How are you?" she says, eyes narrowing as Nova and Nell appear at my side.

"Fine. Heading home." I see her worried look. "Nothing major, I'll fill you in later. Don't worry. Just a precaution. Speio's going to stay here with you, just in case." Speio shoots me a look but knows better than to argue with Echlios standing right there.

"Okay." She doesn't look convinced but seems reassured by Speio's presence. "But you better call me."

"I will. Promise."

In the car, Echlios doesn't waste any time as he helps me into the passenger seat and climbs in on the other side. Nova and Nell get in the back in eerie silence. Their faces are expressionless, but I can feel their combined worry. Echlios's thumb brushes over the already fading bruise in the middle of my forehead for a second before he starts the engine.

"Tell me exactly what you felt and when," Echlios says. "Every detail. Don't leave anything out."

I explain the sensation to Echlios as best I can recall, watching his frown deepen with every word. "So, do you know what it is?"

"No," he admits. "No human can breach your Aquarathi defenses, and if it were an Aquarathi, you'd know it."

"That's what I thought. What about the hybrids?"

"I doubt there are any hybrids strong enough to do what you've just explained, even though you are not able to sense them." He pauses. "In fact, the only person strong enough to get into your mind is the prince regent."

"But you said it wasn't him."

"No. I said he was safe." Echlios lowers his voice. "My queen, we still do not know what the aftereffects of your… interaction with him could be. He is still not himself."

"It isn't him," I say. "I would know. I'd recognize him instantly."

"The hybrid part of him?" Nova says from the back.

A shudder ripples along my spine, but I shake my head in resolute confidence. I know Lo as intimately as I know myself. "All of him. If it were him, I'd feel it."

I twist to stare at Nova, eyeing him and his sister in turn. Their dark eyes are stony. I can't blame them for not trusting Lo. My choice of life partner has created unexpected aftershocks within the Aquarathi realm, even among my own guards. They know that Lo's loyalty is to me and not necessarily to our kind. He'll always be half human…half of what all Aquarathi mistrust the most. But I chose him and I trust him. That is all they—or any Aquarathi—need to accept.

"He is your prince," I say through my teeth. "Bound to us. To me."

Nell's voice is quiet, though she's ever respectful of my capricious emotions. "And the toxin? What if it's weakening… your bond?"

"Enough. He would never hurt me," I snap, anger racing through me at her choice of words—*your* bond.

"As you say," Nell murmurs, bowing her head.

The trip to our house takes less than ten minutes, and we drive the rest of it in silence. Echlios seems preoccupied, his fingers like steel clamps on the steering wheel. He is as confused by the turn of events as I am, and that scares me. Echlios knows everything about who we are. *Everything.* So maybe he's not far off to assume it's Lo. Maybe I'm the one who's being naive by believing that Lo can't hide things from me. He is a hybrid, after all, and one who has lied to me before.

But that was before you bonded, a voice argues. *He is bound to you now. No other.*

Then again, being bonded hasn't helped either of us since the negative effects of the biotoxin began. Maybe Nell was right. Since his attack, our bond has become weaker, making Lo forget his Aquarathi side—and me. What if Lo is changing into something else, something that none of us, including me, have anticipated?

I turn to look at Echlios as we pull into the driveway. "Where is he? The prince regent?"

"He is with Dr. Aldon."

"Are you sure?"

Echlios eyes narrow. "Why?"

I meet his eyes, and then Nell's. She nods just once, making the painful admission stick in my throat. Somehow what

I'm about to say feels disloyal. It feels like I'm giving up on Lo. On us. But the alternative is too scary to contemplate. It's my duty to assess any and all threats to the Aquarathi people. The truth is, we don't know what he is or what he can become, and my feelings for him aren't going to influence any of that. Nova's eyes are glittering in anticipation of my command.

Ruthlessly, I shove the words out with such force that my eyes water. "Go now. Find him."

Dr. Aldon's house in Rancho Santa Fe is deserted. So are his boat moorings down in the neighboring marina. After Lo's earlier transformation, the *Sea Queen* was sent in for repairs, but she isn't the only toy in Aldon's fleet. Her counterpart, an ostentatious yacht aptly named *Scylla,* is nowhere to be seen. It could be anywhere, but that is hardly a problem for me. Standing on the dock, surrounded by my royal guard, I stretch my glimmer out, feeling it immediately bolstered by the others. Breathless with the sheer force of it, I cast it outward until I sense the vessel—and the ephemeral essence of Lo—floating haphazardly in the middle of the ocean, a hundred nautical miles west of San Nicolas.

Shielding my emotions from my people, I feel the fear seize my stomach. The yacht is devoid of life, human or otherwise, but I can sense the blood…the metallic shimmer of Aldon's blood, the visceral sheen of Aquarathi blood. As I release the glimmer with a gasp, my eyes meet Echlios's, my heart in them.

His lips tighten into a white line. "Let's go."

We reconvene at my house, a line of swimmers entering the water and transforming into something otherworldly once out of sight of human eyes. We reach the abandoned silver craft in minutes, where the cloying smell of blood is even stronger. Huge great white sharks are circling it, drawn by the floating human bodies—the fractured remains of the crew. Despite my relief at none of them being Lo, I feel a moment of pity for those who have lost their lives. I scatter the sharks with an enraged click.

I swim closer, and transform into human form to pull myself up on the slatted wooden rails of the transom.

"My queen," Echlios begins in warning.

"There is no one alive on that boat, Echlios." I sigh, and wait on the edge. "But go first, if you must."

Following Echlios, we step into the spacious cabin. I gasp, clutching my fingers to my lips. There's no doubt that this was a carefully orchestrated massacre, and one left for us to find. A message of sorts. Wide swaths of crimson spatter the plush gunmetal carpeting. A suit-clad man sits at the far end of the gray sofa as if in repose. But the thin line of red along his ashen throat suggests otherwise.

Aldon is dead.

Unlike the rest of the crew, Aldon's body is carefully intact. The thick scent of blood is noxious. Upon closer inspection, Aldon's charcoal suit is drenched in his blood. Echlios moves aside the outer lapel, and my stomach freefalls to my feet. Violent clawed gashes stretch from shoulder to navel, the cloth and flesh shredded like crepe paper.

Echlios's voice makes me jump out of my skin. "Aldon knew his killer."

"How do you know?" I ask, my mouth dry. But if anyone would know, it's Echlios. He's a master of forensics.

"No struggle." He sniffs at the blood, making my stomach roil. "No distress. It was someone familiar."

Did Lo do this?

Echlios moves over to a spot behind the sofa, kneeling to touch something on the floor. "Arvus is dead."

Recognition is slow as a human form with white hair and a lined face comes to mind. His silvery Aquarathi body is more familiar. Arvus, one of the Aquarathi who was on the *Sea Queen*—one of my guard, obviously tasked with Lo's protection. Arvus was paired with a blue-scaled, equally seasoned Aquarathi. Kemari, a female. She'd be here, too, unless by some miracle, she escaped with Lo. But hope dies a swift death at Nell's shout.

"So is Kemari," Nell says from the far side of the bow.

"And the prince?" I say out loud. "Any sign of him?" Lo was definitely on this boat. I can sense a faint memory of him, one that is fading quickly.

"No, my queen," Echlios says.

Nova clears his throat, studying the remnants of Arvus. "They were all murdered by someone familiar. Quick and silent."

I wave a hand at the dismembered crew. "And the rest of them? The humans?"

"Quick, too. But not silent." Nova gestures to the bodies in the water. "Some tried to escape. They didn't make it far." He glances at me. "If the prince regent survived, you will be able to sense him via the bond, unless his human side is blocking you. Maybe you can try to summon him?"

What Nova is suggesting makes sense, but something is stopping me. A part of me almost doesn't want to know what happened, whether Lo has indeed lost his mind and killed all these people. "Echlios?"

"He was here. Perhaps he was taken." He pauses, and the dullness in his voice makes me shiver. "Perhaps not. Nova's suggestion is sound. You can try to summon him, but do not get your hopes up, my lady. We cannot be sure of anything."

It *can't* be Lo, not him. He wouldn't have done this—he's not capable of this kind of cold murder. I think of Ehmora, and a violent wave of trembling ricochets through me. How well do I truly know Lo...who he is deep down? He's Ehmora's progeny, genetically tied to a stone-cold, brutal killer.

"Lo's nothing like her," I hiss to myself. "You're wrong."

Desperate, I fall to my knees, pushing a glimmer out. I try to sense Lo, a fevered summons bursting out of me, calling to him. I brought my mother to me with a summons once. Via the bond, I should be able to do the same with Lo. But there's nothing but an echo of emptiness along the connection. In despair, I push so hard that a slow trickle of blood leaks from my nose as I reach out into the endless void. But I can't feel him. I drive deeper into the void, frantic, until my skin feels like it's separating from the flesh beneath it. My brain is buzzing, its edges blurry, and still, I push myself deeper into the beckoning darkness.

"Leave us," a foggy voice says, the sharp command drawing me beyond the reach of oblivion. Dimly aware of movement around me, I sway dizzily and fall into strong arms.

"Nerissa, enough," Echlios whispers gently, pulling my shoulders back against his body. "You're going to hurt yourself."

"I want the boat swept," I scream to the guard standing just outside the glass cabin door. "Every inch of it."

"They have already looked, my lady."

"Then look again." There's no way I can equate not being able to reach Lo with a betrayal this ugly. There has to be something, something that we've missed. "He didn't do this,

Echlios. Every drop of water inside me knows it. Please, just check again. We have to be sure. *I* have to be sure."

"As you say." Echlios studies my face for a long moment before pulsing my wishes to the guard. We wait in silence—in weightless hope—until there's a shout from the bow. Water rises like a surging tide from deep within.

"My queen, come quickly."

As I follow Echlios in breathless anticipation, my fear is palpable. Images of the time Ehmora sent me a piece of my mother in a box flash across my mind. I force myself to go to where Nell is crouched beside a shimmering drop of something smudged on one of the upper railings, near where she found Kemari's remains. It's so tiny that it's no wonder it was missed the first time around.

"What is it?" I ask. "Aquarathi blood?" *Please don't be Lo's,* I think to myself. *Please don't be his blood.*

Nell's eyes are wide. "Yes, but—"

"But what?"

Echlios crouches down beside her, his nostrils flaring and brow furrowing. "It's not from one of ours. It's not the prince's."

Relief floods me, making my knees almost buckle. "Hybrid?"

"I can't tell."

"Kemari must have got in a strike before it killed her," Nell says quietly. "A rogue exile, perhaps?"

Rogues are unpredictable, but still bound to me even though they've been banished from their courts and from Waterfell. Echlios wouldn't be able to recognize an exile. Neither would Nell, or any of the others. But I could. With a breath, I sink to the deck. "Let me."

I swipe the oily substance onto my human fingertip, rubbing it back and forth between forefinger and thumb so that the remaining essence breaks up into pungent molecules. A few minutes more, and it would have been too late. The drop would have dried up from the sun and disappeared. This tiny, near-evaporated smear is all we have to go on.

Electric green-and-yellow lights shimmer along my arms as I call forth my Aquarathi form. A shimmer of movement gleams across my face, replacing human skin with golden scales, as my crown of bones and luminescent fronds tears through my forehead. My jaw locks and elongates, rows of razor-sharp teeth protruding from wide greenish-yellow lips. The half transformation is gruesome, but I need all of my Aquarathi senses. I slip my human finger into my mouth, mindful of my fangs, letting the remnant of blood dissipate on my alien tongue.

A cold, familiar rush of sensation hits me like a tidal wave—the very same one I felt earlier on the hockey field: alien and unyielding. No rogue, after all. Something different. Dangerous. Steeling myself against the immediate panic, I try to separate the indistinct fragments of thoughts and images blooming in lightning-quick succession—*female, no court, no allegiance, royal, Lo, hybrids*—before I collapse into a heap and revert to full human form.

"My queen!" Echlios shouts. I clutch his arms so hard that he winces. "What did you see? Was it one of the hybrids?"

I nod. "They're strong, Echlios. They've been watching us—me. That feeling earlier? It was the same."

"Are you certain?"

"Yes."

"And the prince? Is he with them?"

I wrench away, a guttural sob bursting out of me. Nothing I'd seen suggested it wasn't Lo who had betrayed us, but

I can't let myself believe that. "It wasn't Lo, Echlios. I know it. He has no reason to hurt Aldon, or any of them. And there has to be a reason I couldn't even sense him before. Maybe he's hurt, or they're holding him prisoner. Maybe it's Cano," I blubber wildly, turning to face him. I can hear the shattered desperation in my own voice. Echlios's face is tortured. "Or my mother. They've taken him to keep him from me. To keep us from finding out what he's been hiding, because they know we're getting close. We were getting close, weren't we? Oh my God, Echlios, what if he did do this? What then?" The single sob explodes into a horrific cacophony of sound—heart-wrenching cries of pain erupting from my mouth as I slump backward. "What if he's with them?" I say in a half-broken whisper. "Like Castia said."

"We will find him, my queen. And then you will decide what needs to be done."

"How?"

"We will renew our efforts."

But Echlios's words offer little comfort. We haven't been able to find anything on Cano or my mother. And now Lo has disappeared without a trace, presumably to wherever they are with a powerful hybrid that owes me no allegiance. I have no idea whether Lo is still with me or not. All I know is that I have to find him before other people get hurt. The biotoxin may have weakened our bond, but the Lo I know and love wouldn't have done anything to hurt me like this. He wouldn't have left me like this. Not willingly. Despite the mistrust and fears of my guard, I have to believe that. I have to hold on to that with my last remaining shred of hope.

Lo loved me. He *loves* me.

Not just the Aquarathi side of him, but also his human

side. He'll remember who I am. He has to. When he changed into Aquarathi form, he told Jenna that he had come back to his human side by thinking of me. That has to mean something. Pushing to my feet, I inhale a harsh breath and reopen the connection into the infinite abyss between us, putting everything I've ever felt for Lo into the summons. I release the message into the fabric of time and space with nothing but frail human hope anchoring it back to me.

15
Friends and Frenemies

I'm slowly drifting, the surfboard following the gentle swell of the ocean. Beyond the breakers, the sea is calm and glasslike, waves building in flat, glossy swells before entering the foamy white surf zone. Golden sunshine filtering down from a cloudless blue sky bathes my salt-crusted body with deliciously hot rays. A stone's throw away, Lo beckons, a grin on his face. Shimmery navy scales flicker across his cheeks, making lights illuminate in instant response along my forearms. Even in human form, he is beautiful, majestic. Something warm pools responsively in my stomach, and winds its way up my neck and down my legs, until I'm breathless.

Chasing the beginnings of a perfect wave, Lo signals to me again, and this time, I follow. We crest the wave in synchronic exhilaration, Lo descending across its face and me skimming across its top before gliding down to meet him. He twists back to look at something behind me, his dark eyes exultant. I follow his gaze, and the breath stops in my throat as the wave beneath me surges to an impossible height. But it's not the wave that terrifies me—it's Ehmora's face stretching within it, her tentacled arms wide and reaching.

War is coming, *her fanged mouth screams before it swallows me whole.*

"Nerissa!" someone is yelling. "Wake up. You're thrashing around like a fish out of water." A bleary Speio swims into view as I drag myself out of the nightmare. "Bad dream?"

"Sort of," I mutter, my surroundings coming into sharp focus. An agonizing twinge rips through my shoulders. I stretch my cramped body. I fell asleep in a chair next to the pool—strange for me—and until I had the dream, it seems like I barely moved all night. A pinkish tinge is seeping across the blue-gray dawn sky. "What time is it?" I ask Speio.

"About five."

Yawning and pulling myself from the chair, I crawl to the edge of the pool and sink into the water, letting it soothe the ache of my sore muscles. Speio hesitates, waiting for permission before I wave a weary arm for him to join me. My body shivers in delight at the sensation of the salt water on my skin. I should have just fallen asleep in the pool. It's not like I would have drowned, and I'd be a damn sight less sore than I am now. I let my human body sink down to the bottom.

"Echlios told me about what happened on Aldon's yacht," Speio says in our language, his blond hair floating around him like a silvery-white cloud. "I liked Aldon. He was a good guy."

"He was," I murmur. "Arvus and Kemari, too."

"They had to be strong, whoever took them out. I mean, they were seasoned fighters, part of your father's King's Guard. You really think it's the hybrids?"

"Probably. No one else could attack so savagely." I don't bring up the blood we found. We discussed it enough after we returned home, and both Speio and Soren were there.

I know he's only trying to help, so I let him ramble on. I close my eyes and count backward in my head, trying to oust the tension still writhing beneath my skin.

"So, Echlios said they kidnapped Lo, or that's what they're going with, anyway." He shrugs as I open my eyes midcount. "Nova and Nell have other ideas."

I know exactly what kind of other ideas those two have. "Lo didn't do it."

Speio spreads his palms wide, making the water ripple. "I'm not saying he did, but you should know that there's dissent in the ranks."

I smile grimly, my shoulders drooping. "There's been dissent in the ranks since the day I claimed my crown with a hybrid at my side," I say. "They never accepted him then, and they don't accept him now. They'll only bend to me for so long. The last time I was in Waterfell, Castia tried to usurp Miral, who I left in charge. The discord will only spread unless I return to Waterfell. And if Lo *is* with this hybrid army, I won't be able to protect him, not from the Ruby Court or any of the courts."

"But you don't think he is."

"No."

"What are you going to do?"

"I don't know," I say with a sigh. "Find Lo. Find Cano. Destroy the hybrids. Go back to Waterfell. Lay down the law. Live happily ever after."

"Sounds like a monster plan," Speio says, grinning.

I shoot him a glance, but he's only trying to make light of a pretty crappy situation. I'm aware that my so-called plan is flimsy, but I don't want to admit that I have absolutely nothing. A near-sleepless night following savage disputes on how we should respond to the attack on Aldon and our people left me with a pounding headache. Nova and Nell voted to swim back to Waterfell and amass the armies of all the courts to make a stand against the hybrids. It was over-kill, I argued, considering that we didn't know Lo's position. In the end, they caved, albeit grudgingly, to my order. We find Lo first. If it turns out he's with them and against us, we will convene the High Council.

I let myself float to the center of the pool, surrounded on all sides by water. I stare at the sun, now rising in the distance, and sigh. In less than an hour we'll both have to get ready for school, on the off chance that Lo is there. It's so ridiculous that I even have to go there after everything that has happened. I argued hotly with Soren on the matter, but she was adamant that I keep up appearances while my guard tracked down the hybrids.

"This is stupid," I said. "I should be out there looking for Lo, not studying useless trivia that I already know."

"It's the safest place for you," Soren countered.

"I'm going with Echlios."

"You are not."

"I am your queen, Soren."

Her mouth curved into a rigid line. "And I am still your Handler, who is not about to let you, queen or not, have a royal tantrum to get your way. It is my duty to protect you, and I will do everything in my power to do so." Her lips tightened into a white-hot line of displeasure. "Even if it means restraining you."

"You wouldn't."

"Try me."

Obviously, I gave in. Queen or no queen, arguing with Soren always ended badly for me. I've only ever won once. Within the Aquarathi, trust and respect are both valued and prized. I lost Soren's trust once when I went against her wishes our freshman year and drove to a rave in Los Angeles with Cara. The cops raided it, but luckily we got off with a warning as neither of us had been drinking. Two other kids who went with us got arrested and summarily expelled from Dover. It took me months to earn back Soren's trust.

I sigh. Soren means well, but I hate feeling imprisoned, like I can't do anything to help. It's frustrating! I kick my legs underwater in a fit of pique.

"What's wrong?" Speio asks.

"One word," I grumble. "Soren."

A laugh. "Tell me about it. Seriously, she's only your Handler. Imagine her as your mother. What'd she make you do now?"

"Nothing," I snap. "That's the point."

"Hey, I'm stuck here, too, you know. You don't think I wanted to go follow leads and track down bad guys instead of having to learn about Victorian dandies and how to build a wooden clock?"

I stare at him, my anger fizzling. "Can we talk about something else for five minutes? Besides your mom or the hybrids or Cano's grand master plan to take over the world? Something normal. Something unrelated to an earth-shattering war between species."

"Like what?"

"How about you? And Rian."

Speio's expression is almost comical. His face turns the flaming red color of a sunset. "You want to talk about what?" he splutters.

"Rian. Your new bestie."

"She's not my bestie," Speio says with a scowl.

"You guys sure hang out a lot."

"There's nothing to talk about. I mean, I like her and she's great. And we get along. That's it. Can't a guy have any friends? Or any privacy?"

"Yes to the first, no to the second," I tease, grinning. "If I can't have any privacy, then you can't, either. So spill it. What's she like? Where's she from?"

Speio concedes defeat, but his eyes light up a little. "She moved from New York, but she says her family is of mixed Indian and Spanish descent."

That would explain her silky dark hair and caramel complexion. "Sounds exotic," I murmur. Speio shoots me an amused sidelong glance. "You know what I mean...for the humans."

"She's really smart," Speio continues. "She's into sociocultural anthropology, as she calls it, especially with her ethnic background. She told me that she spent a lot of her childhood in an area of the world where racial segregation was the norm, so she's interested in understanding the social complexities between people of different cultures."

"Sounds interesting."

"Yeah," Speio says, more animated now. "She wants to study how different living situations impact people of the same race, and whether they develop entirely different cultures. So she's planning to do an—" He breaks off, a frown on his face. "Sorry, I can't remember the word. Oh, wait, ethnography. It's a kind of research study that analyzes groups of people within a specific environment. Cool, right?" he asks, and I nod. "She's applied for early admission to Stanford."

"Impressive," I say, recognizing the prestigious name.

"She's driven," Speio agrees.

"What's her family like? Have you met any of them?"

"She's an only child, but her extended family is huge. Lots of aunts and uncles and cousins, all back in Queens."

"So why'd she come here?" I ask through a tired yawn, wishing I could sleep for six more hours. Speio is doing an awesome job of distracting me from my own arduous thoughts.

"Turns out that very few high schools even have anthropology programs." He glances at me. "That's why we're here, aren't we? To learn about humans? Well, I guess that some humans want to learn about themselves, too. Anyway, Dover happens to have anthropology in the curriculum, as you know."

I frown. "I haven't seen her in any of my classes."

"She's doing independent study with Professor Birch."

My frown deepens. "I didn't even know you could do independent study in high school. Seriously, have I been under a rock?"

"Told you," Speio says. "She's gifted. Plus, you didn't do it because you have to stay out of the limelight, remember?"

"Oh, right." I swim over to the side of the pool and heave myself out. "Sounds like she's a great influence on you. You're actually going to classes now. You're a whole new you. So, what are you going to name your little hybrid babies?"

"Eww, Riss. That's just gross," Speio says, blushing a furious shade of red. "Plus, we're just having fun."

Despite my inner twitch at the poorly timed hybrid joke, I can't help teasing him. "Thought you said you could never fall for a human?"

Speio joins me at the side of the pool, lifting his body out lithely. His answer is soft. "Not one like her. She's different. I can't explain it. It's like she *sees* people, you know.

She wants to know about them, and she's really interested. She doesn't ask questions for the sake of asking them. She actually cares about what you're going to say."

"What kind of questions?" I ask with a swift look.

"Jeez, relax. She's not going to dissect my alien insides or anything." His blush intensifies. "More like feeling questions, okay?"

"*Feeling* questions?" I snort.

"Let's just drop it," he says, and jumps to his feet. "Come on, or we're going to be late."

"How do you feel about that?" I ask, grinning. Instead of answering, Speio stabs a rude finger gesture in my direction before stalking inside. "Come on, Speio," I shout after him just as the door swings shut, "use your words."

Still smiling at the exchange, I shower and get dressed, but it isn't long before the lightheartedness disappears. That happens the minute I step into the living room, where Echlios is waiting with half of my royal guard. They're muttering among themselves over a map of California that's spread out over the dining room table. I catch the words *Cano* and *army* before the whispering abruptly stops, eyes centering in my direction. Echlios bows once, rolls up the papers and snaps a sharp command. I watch in irritated silence as they all melt from the room like shadows, following him without so much as another word.

"Seriously," I snap to no one in particular. "What are we, five? Is everything a secret? They can't even talk in front of me now?"

"We all know how that turned out earlier this year, don't we?" Soren says in a cheerful voice, placing a plate of artfully arranged sushi in front of me. "Eat. You have ten minutes before you have to leave."

"What's the point of being a queen if no one tells me anything?" I say through a mouthful of salmon. I know exactly what Soren's referring to—the fact that I snuck out on my own to Cano's house last year to try to track down my mother. Still, I'm not a china doll that they have to protect every infernal second. I've demonstrated that I can defend myself. I *fought* Ehmora on the sands of battle in Waterfell. Doesn't that count for something?

"Uh-oh," Speio says, walking into the room fresh from his own shower, dressed in his Dover uniform. A smile breaks across his face at my thundercloud expression. "Watch out, Queen Brat is on the warpath."

"You want to start with me, Speio?" I say in a silky voice. His grin widens. "Only if you use your words nicely."

"Speio, don't provoke her," Soren chastises. "Now, off, you two. I don't want to get any calls from the principal that you're tardy again." She turns to stop me just as Speio heads out the front door, laying a hand on my shoulder. "And, Nerissa, you must know that this is for your own good. Dover is the safest place for you."

I pull away from her. "How? I'm a sitting duck."

"Better a live duck than a dead one," she remarks mildly. "They drew you out here, remember that. If you run headlong into their snare, it's not going to help anyone. Lo, least of all."

The mention of Lo snaps the angry retort from my lips. At the compassionate expression in Soren's eyes, I struggle to find the right words. "Soren, do you think he's innocent? Lo? You don't believe what all the others believe, do you?"

"I don't think the prince regent would ever intentionally hurt you," she answers carefully. "However, I do think that the toxin is doing more damage than we expected, so he's not exactly himself. The evidence suggesting that he has changed is...overwhelming."

"What are you saying?"

"That you should be prepared for any outcome, no matter how painful. Now go. Scoot. Echlios will alert you the minute they find anything."

Despite the rock forming in the pit of my stomach at Soren's words, I do as she says and climb into the Jeep with Speio. The smirk on his face fades as he studies me. "It'll be fine, Riss. Just hang tight. My father will find Cano. And Lo."

I don't answer him and we drive in silence, until Speio turns onto an unfamiliar road to a nearby housing development. I raise an eyebrow, half hoping that we're going to do some reconnaissance on our own. But it's an idle hope at best. Speio will never do anything to go against Echlios, not now. He'd learned his lesson last year when my very own mother made him betray everyone he loved, including me.

"Where are we going?"

He shrugs apologetically. "Told Rian I'd give her a ride, if that's okay."

"Sure," I say, slumping back into the passenger seat.

Rian's house is a pretty, ranch-style house on Via Valverde, surrounded by lush green trees. She's waiting on the front step, a smile on her face. I look away as she and Speio embrace through the window. Looks like things are a little more serious than he'd have me believe. Not that I'm complaining—I'm liking this easygoing, happy Speio a lot more than the sour-faced, perpetually angry version of himself from last semester. I'm betting that Rian has a lot to do with that, and I'm not going to begrudge him a smidgen of happiness in the midst of all this Aquarathi drama. At least one of us gets to be happy.

"Hey, Nerissa," Rian says, climbing up on the back wheel and hopping into the backseat.

"Hey," I say. "You know you can call me Riss, right? Everyone else does."

"Sure, I will," she says, strapping on her seat belt. "You guys ready for the quiz?"

"Um, quiz?" I ask.

"Yeah, Donovan's essay quiz today on different themes in the play?"

I groan out loud. Of course I'm not ready. I haven't studied at all. "Nope. Guess we're going to have to wing it."

"What's this 'we' stuff?" Speio jokes. "I'll have you know I studied."

"What? When?"

"Rian and I studied after the game yesterday."

I glare at him. "After the game? You were supposed to stay with Jenna, remember? Give her a ride home?" I amend quickly, with a glance to the backseat.

"I did. She was fine."

"Speaking of the game, how are you feeling?" Rian asks. "Looked like you got whacked pretty bad. Guess you and Cara don't get along, do you?"

"What do you mean?"

"She kind of went right for you. At the whistle? Speio and I saw the whole thing." She pauses, frowning. "Speio mentioned that you two have history."

"He did, did he?" A flush winds its way up Speio's neck, but I'll save my wrath for later. No point embarrassing him in front of his almost-girlfriend, no matter how tempting that is. "We do, but what happened yesterday was an accident."

Rian grins. "That's good, then. She's not someone I'd want to intentionally tick off. Seems like she has the whole school in the palm of her hand."

"She kind of does." I twist back in my seat, opting for a different kind of payback to make Speio squirm. "So, Speio tells me you're applying to Stanford to study anthropology."

"That's the plan," Rian says with an unpretentious smile that makes her green eyes twinkle. "I'm trying to get him to apply locally, too. But he's resistant."

I smile back. "Yeah, Speio's never been interested in school. He's always been more interested in scraping by, doing the bare minimum."

"I'm right here, you know," Speio interjects. "And Nerissa knows that college is…on hold for right now. We don't know if my dad's going to be transferred out of the country any time soon."

"It can't hurt to apply, though, right?" Rian interjects.

"Maybe," he concedes. "No promises, though."

"Great! I happen to have some applications in my bag."

Grinning, I can see why Speio thinks Rian's a force of nature. Though she's small in stature, I would be wary of testing her mettle. She seems to have a will of steel, which is pretty much exactly what Speio needs in his life, even if it's for a short time. He needs a boost of confidence, of ambition, with someone pushing him to do something with his fake human life. Maybe it'll translate into his other life.

We pull into the school parking lot and join the masses heading up the stairs. In spite of myself, my eyes are drawn to the spot where Lo usually waits, but of course he isn't there. Neither is Cara for that matter. I frown, but my suspicions are allayed as a pink BMW convertible blaring music roars into the lot and screeches into an empty space. A shimmer of blond catches my eye in the front seat, and for the first time ever, I find myself wishing that it was Lo sitting there. My heart skips a beat as a tall, lanky boy exits the car, but it's only another senior.

Oh, get over it, I tell myself. *It's not like he's going to disappear from the scene of a gruesome crime out at sea and show up at school the next day.*

Making my way to my locker in a daze, I nearly crash into the person waiting for me there. "Oh, hey, Sawyer, didn't see you. What's wrong?" I ask, noticing he's a little pale under his tan. His gleaming smile is conspicuously absent.

"Have you heard from Jenna?"

The floor tilts beneath my feet and Sawyer's face swims out of focus for a breathless second. "What do you mean, Sawyer? You haven't heard from her? Since when? Speio said he dropped her home after the game."

"Yeah, she called me. We talked for half an hour before dinner, and then my phone died. I forgot to charge it. Then when I woke up this morning and I turned my phone on, I had a bunch of texts from her saying that she was at the marina, and she saw something weird that she was going to check out. Then she said something about seeing Lo and to call you if I didn't hear from her. This was last night, but I only just saw them. Did she text you?"

"No. I mean I don't know. I lost my phone. Wait, why was she at the marina? With *Lo?*"

"I don't know."

"And you haven't heard from her since?" I ask.

Sawyer shakes his head. "I tried to text her, call her, but nothing. Goes straight to voice mail. I called her house, too, and her mom told me that she said she was studying at your place."

My stomach starts doing a weird flip-flop thing. Sawyer's face is distraught, his voice laced with guilt. I smile reassuringly despite my thudding pulse. "It's not your fault, Sawyer. Jenna's always doing harebrained things, and you know neither of us can do anything to stop her. I'm sure she's fine. Do you mind if I take a look at the texts?"

"No." He hands me his phone.

I try not to let my emotions show as I thumb through the hurried texts from Jenna, saying what Sawyer had recapped. The last one is time-stamped at seven-thirty.

Cano. Imperial Beach.

One hour after we'd returned *Scylla* to its mooring in the marina. More than enough time for Jenna to get herself into a boatload of trouble. What was Cano doing at Imperial Beach? And worse, what was Jenna doing there? It's the closest city to the Mexican border. Is Cano in *Mexico?*

For the five hundredth time, I curse my lost cell phone. Jenna would have texted me for sure, I know. And she would have been way more specific than she'd been with Sawyer.

"What's going on?" a panting Nova says as he shoves his way past Sawyer. Of course, he would have been watching me. I really have to work on shielding my expressions from prying guards.

"Hey! Back off, bro," Sawyer growls, grabbing a hold of Nova's collar. "This is none of your business."

"No, it's okay, Sawyer," I say, distracted. "He's a friend."

Sawyer's eyes widen into brown orbs, but he releases the handful of Nova's uniform. "Since when are you friends with those guys?" With a confused look, I stare at Nova's pierced ears, black eyeliner and pissed-off look. Granted, I can see how this would be weird for Sawyer, considering that he's known me for four years and has never seen me talk to anyone like Nova.

"We have a class together," I say. "Just give me a minute."

"What's wrong?" Nova snaps as I pull him a couple steps away. My eyes narrow at his borderline disrespectful tone.

"Nothing," I say. "Jenna's sick and we have a group test today for English."

To his credit, Sawyer doesn't say anything at my lie even though I know he can hear what I'm saying. I don't even know why I didn't tell Nova the truth. Something about the way he and his sister have assumed Lo is one of the bad guys just rubs me the wrong way. I don't need their help. Or their judgment.

"You got that worked up over a test?" Nova mutters under his breath. "I felt it all the way across the quad."

"I'm an A student. I want to keep it that way. Now run along."

Nova's lip curls, but he does as I command, his dark eyes unreadable. He's still suspicious but nods abruptly and heads back the way he came. Near the end of the hallway, I see him whisper something to Nell, who turns to stare at me. I paste a bright smile on my face and wave.

"So, what was that about?" Sawyer whispers. "You really hang out with those guys?"

"Not really. Now come on. We need to find someone."

"Who?"

"The only person who can help us figure out what happened to Jenna," I say grimly, still clutching Sawyer's phone.

"Who's that?"

"Cara."

16
Hell Froze Over

"I can't let you do that." Speio eyes me, his arms crossed over his chest. He looks so much like his father that I want to laugh. We're standing in the deserted boys' bathroom near the rear soccer fields. It's always empty this time of the morning, but that doesn't make it any less disgusting.

"I've never been in here," I say, looking around and pinching my nose. "It's gross. And what is that god-awful smell?"

The sound of a toilet flushing at the far end breaks the silence, and a kid I don't recognize waddles out to wash his hands. He flushes a deep red, one that goes atomic when he sees me—a girl—standing between Speio and Sawyer.

"Sorry," he mutters, rushing past us and staring at the ground. "Someone had a cupcake and I'm lactose intolerant. No one ever comes in here, so…"

"That's okay, Marco," Sawyer says with a grin. "This is my secret spot, too."

I wrinkle my nose as Marco makes a hasty exit. "Do boys always have to be so disgusting?"

"Hey, better out than in," Sawyer says. "Then again, this

is a *boys'* bathroom, so if you want to come into the nest, you gotta be prepared." He eyes me curiously. "What do you guys do when you have to go?"

I glare at him. "We hold it."

"You know that's not good for you, right?"

Speio clears his throat, knowing as well as I do how much Sawyer tends to go off on a tangent once he gets fired up about something. In this case, bowel movements. I move closer to the entry door and stand against it just in case. "Sawyer, can you give us a sec?"

"Sure," he says, slipping outside. "I'll make sure no one comes in."

Nodding my thanks to Sawyer, I turn back to Speio. "Just cover for me today while I check it out." I resume the conversation I started with him in the bathroom before Marco made his untimely appearance. "That's all I'm asking. I'll be with Sawyer. You know the twins will go nuts if they see I'm not here."

"They'll know you're not here, Riss," Speio says. "They can sense it. You're forgetting what they are. They're not high-school kids—they're trained Aquarathi guards."

"I'll glimmer myself."

"All the way from Imperial Beach?" Speio shoots back.

I shrug. "I'll figure something out. Do you have my back or not?"

"Riss...I can't," he says, raking a hand through his hair in frustration. "You're asking the impossible. You're asking me to betray Echlios's trust. I can't risk putting your life in danger."

"Spey," I begin, unwilling to play my trump card but knowing I'll have to. "You kind of owe me one." Speio's eyebrows crash together, his fists clenching at his sides. I hate having to coerce him with guilt, but if it will get him to help me, then I'll do it. "You know I've never called in a favor, or blamed you for what happened, but I need your help, Speio. And you owe me for last year." I take a breath and lower my voice, mindful of Sawyer on the other side of the door. "For serving me up on a platter to Ehmora."

"Fine. I get it. No need to rehash old demons." Speio grabs the bridge of his nose between his thumb and forefinger. "Just give me a second."

"Look, I'm not asking you to lie to Echlios or Soren. Just give me today, just this morning to drive down there and see what Sawyer and I can find. Couple hours, tops. I'll get Sawyer to text you updates every thirty minutes. If you don't hear from me after an hour, you can call Echlios and alert the wonder twins."

"Why don't you want to tell Nova and Nell, anyway?"

I sigh. "I don't trust them. Not with Lo."

"Fine," Speio says. "Only until the end of the school day, Riss. I mean it. The minute that bell rings and you're not back here, I call Echlios."

"Deal." I throw my arms around his neck. "Thank you, Speio."

He clutches my shoulder as we exit the bathroom to where Sawyer is waiting. "Promise me one thing? That you'll be careful and you won't do anything rash? It's my ass on the line, too. If you find Jenna and she's in any danger, you have to call Echlios right away. I need your word, Riss."

"You got it."

"I'll make sure she doesn't do anything stupid, bro," Sawyer says, chiming in to the tail end of the conversation.

Speio's mouth curls into a resigned half smile. "It's not her I'm worried about," he says with a meaningful glance at me. He's worried about what we're going to find if we do manage to walk into some kind of hybrid nest with Sawyer of all people there. Sawyer's not going to be a given like Jenna, whom I protected with my life when my people discovered she knew our secret. They won't be so forgiving a second time. "Anyway, how are you guys even going to get out of school?"

"Got it covered," I say. I'd already called Bertha, Lo's guardian-slash-housekeeper, and she agreed to call the school to get us excused for a Marine Center extra-credit project. She'd gotten Lo and me out of enough scrapes from missing school the previous year, and I trusted her. Luckily, Lo has only been missing a day, and since he tends to go walkabout, Bertha wasn't too surprised by my cover request.

One down. One to go.

Cara. This one I'll have to do on my own, and it's going to be a hit or miss. I asked for her help once, and it blew up in my face. But this time, I really need it. Combing the streets of Imperial Beach will take hours, and I don't have that kind of time, not with Speio on the clock.

"Sawyer, I'll meet you out front in ten," I tell him. "Need to make a pit stop in study hall. You know what you have to do, right?"

He nods. "Yes."

Sneaking in through the back door of study hall, I take the only empty seat at Cara's table despite the barrage of hostile glances settling onto me like nettles. Honestly, it's like walking into a hornet's nest with all of them ready to defend *their* queen.

Cara's pale blue eyes meet mine. Surprise flickers in them for a minute before it's gone, and they're back to their icy, unfriendly state. "Are you lost, Marin?"

"Can I talk to you for a sec?" I whisper. "It's important."

"Here?"

"Outside," I say. "Five minutes, that's all I need." Her eyebrows rise toward her hairline at the urgency in my voice. She hesitates for a moment, as if deciding whether this is some kind of elaborate payback trick on my part for what happened at the game.

"Quiet over there," Professor Walker says with a glare in our direction.

We both stare at Cara's open textbook, awkward silence between us. Of course she's going to make me beg. Gulping down my rush of anger, I'll grovel if I have to. "Please, Cara. You know I wouldn't ask if this wasn't life and death."

Her eyes widen, but her voice is still disdainful. "Can't this wait? You know the rule. Walker only lets one of us go at a time."

"I took care of it."

Right on cue, there's a knock on the door and Sawyer pokes his blond head in. "Er, Professor Walker, I've got a note for Cara Andrews and Nerissa Marin to report to the office? Something about extra credit at the Marine Center?"

"Give it here," Walker says. He glances at the note and then stares at us over his wire-rimmed spectacles. "You heard him. Office. Now."

In the hallway, Sawyer has disappeared, presumably to the parking lot where he's waiting for us. Cara and I don't speak until we're near the row of lockers. Turning toward the entrance doors away from the direction of the office, she grabs my shoulder hard and drags me to the empty inner courtyard. "We're not going to the office, are we? I'm not taking another step until you tell me what's going on. What do you want, Nerissa? You want me to apologize for hitting you in the face? Is this what this is about? Your fragile ego? You want me to say I'm sorry? Because I'm not. You deserved what you got."

A surge of anger overtakes me at the unprovoked attack, but I know where Cara is coming from. We've had nothing but tumultuous history—it makes sense that she'd strike first and question later. I take a deep, calming breath. "No, it's not about that. You're right, I was wrong. I shouldn't have said what I did."

She frowns, taken aback. "So, what do you want? Is the Marine Center thing for real? Or is that another lie?"

"Yes, it's for real." I twinge at the white lie, but if it will get her to come, I'll risk it. I glance at my watch. Sawyer will already be waiting. But if I rush and say the wrong thing, Cara is just as likely to turn around and walk away. "It involves Lo," I blurt out. "He needs your help. Ten minutes, Cara, to hear me out. That's how long it takes to get to the center. If you want to come back, we'll bring you back, and I won't bother you again. I promise. Ten minutes, that's all I ask." I don't have to add that she owes me, too, especially as I lied for her on the field the day before, but the suggestion is there between the lines.

"Fine." She sounds bored, but I knew, if anything, she'd take the bait about Lo.

Sawyer's waiting in his truck as planned, and he guns the engine as soon as we get in. "Head to the Marine Center," I tell him. It's on the way to Imperial Beach anyway, and if she agrees to help, which I'm hoping against hope she will, we won't have lost any time. If not, well, there's always plan B, which has significantly more holes than plan A.

"So, what's going on with Lo?" Cara says, frowning. I twist around in my seat to face her. She's sitting in the rear row directly being Sawyer, and already looking like she's regretting her decision to trust me. I counter her question with one of my own.

"Have you heard from your uncle?"

Her frown deepens, suspicion glinting across her face. "Not since he took off without a word before the summer. Are you, like, obsessed with him or something?"

My mind is racing between truths and half-truths, trying to figure out what will work best to get Cara to cooperate. If worse comes to worst, I can glimmer her, but even that is an unpredictable last resort. Over the past few years, Cara has demonstrated on more than one occasion that she's got a strong enough will *not* to be open to the power of suggestion. That's what a glimmer does…it suggests. Contrary to what Jenna may sometimes assume, I can't control the minds of humans, only other Aquarathi. And I also have to be mindful of the fact that Sawyer is in the car, and that he, too, is in the dark about a lot of things. Namely who and what I really am.

"Not in the way you think." I opt for a minor truth. "You know that he was a molecular scientist, right? Worked with DNA and that sort of stuff?"

"Yeah, so he was a freak. So?"

"He actually was pretty brilliant at what he did." I don't know where the words come from, or why I want to make Cara feel better as to why her uncle disappeared into the blue without so much as a goodbye.

"If you say so," Cara says, studying her manicure. "I don't see what this has to do with me. What does he have to do with anything? Federal agents came to our house and seized all his research. It was in the news. Go get yourself a copy of the newspaper if you're so curious."

The truth is I know exactly who went to their house—an Aquarathi cleanup crew. Having that hybrid research lying around was a liability that had to be taken care of. Disguised as feds, they'd had a comically easy time performing a complete sweep of all Cano's known residences. However, it seems we missed one…in Imperial Beach.

"I'm trying to find him," I say.

"Why?"

"I'm doing an…independent study on genetics, and I wanted to see if you were still in touch with him."

Cara's eyes narrow, and, once more, I realize that I've underestimated her intelligence. My reasoning sounds lame even to my ears. Her eyes glint icily. "Either you tell me what's really up or I'm out of here. We used to be friends, remember? I can still tell when you're lying through your teeth. You guys can turn around and take me back right now."

"Wait a second." I take a deep breath. I'm about to go out on a really shaky, unstable limb with a girl I wouldn't trust with a ten-foot pole. Yet here I am, doing exactly that. I don't have much choice, not with Jenna MIA. "You have to promise not to say anything to anyone. I'm not kidding, Cara. This is FBI serious. You, too, Sawyer." He nods, keeping his eyes on the road.

"Got it," Cara says. "Lips sealed. Moving on."

"There's a warrant out for your uncle's arrest," I begin.

"Tell me something I don't know."

"He was working with Lo's family on a project, like some kind of supersecret DNA experiments. Lo's mother was funding it all. It was all under the radar because they didn't want it to be flagged by the California state laws that prohibit reproductive genetic cloning. There isn't much federal regulation on human biotechnologies, but what your uncle and Emma Seavon were working on had to do with more specific human–animal hybrid exploration."

"You mean like chimeras?" Cara interjects.

"What?"

"Mythical creature? Lion head, goat body, snake tail?"

"Sorry, I know what you mean. I just…"

"You didn't expect me to have a brain or eyes. I saw what was going on. I used to sneak into his lab all the time. He never spent any time with me, so I wanted to see what he was working on and what was so important that he'd disappear for entire weekends. That's what he used to call them. Chimeras." She turns to stare out of the passenger window, words flowing out of her mouth as if she can't stop them. After all, it's not something she could ever talk about with her entourage at Dover. It must have been eating her up inside for years. "I saw one once when I was a kid. It was hideous, like a monster, a half-human thing in a metal cage. All I can remember are the eyes…like slitted, glowing lizard eyes. They were so…knowing.

"I even asked him about it once." She smiles sadly. "About the one I saw. He was so enraged. He grounded me for weeks and threatened to send me back into foster care in L.A. I was so scared that he'd do exactly that that I convinced myself I'd imagined it. But I never forgot." She half smiles to herself. "That was the day I got into advocating for animals. They don't have a voice, so I became theirs."

That's another thing I didn't know about Cara, or maybe I did know but never really thought about it. She's always raising money at school for PETA and the SPCA.

Cara pauses, turning clouded eyes to me. "So, is that why he left? They found out about his research? The chimeras?"

"Yes," I say with a shiver. I don't even want to imagine the half-human, half-Aquarathi creature Cara had seen, but I can't help wondering whether it looked anything like the one that attacked me on the beach last semester.

"What about Lo?" Cara asks. "What does this have to do with him?"

I inhale another breath, formulating the pieces of the story in my head and taking a huge gamble on how much to tell her, as well as Sawyer, who is listening intently. "So you know that Lo has acute memory loss."

Cara nods. "Some kind of trauma thing after his mom died."

"Yes. The thing is, Lo's mother went missing shortly before your uncle did. When Lo realized she was dead, he was a mess. He wanted answers that he didn't get. And then I left, and everything went to shit." I pause for a beat, seeing hurt flash across her face. "Look, I know you care about Lo a lot, and thanks for being there for him over the summer. I don't think he would have made it without you."

"I didn't do it for you."

"I know, Cara. I know how you feel about him. And I wish things could be different, but Lo and I..." I trail off with a choked sob. *Are a pair,* I want to say, but the words refuse to come.

"I get it, Nerissa. And I know how he feels about you, but I'll always be his friend no matter what. So just tell me what I need to do or what you need to know."

"Thank you," I say quietly. "I think Lo went looking for your uncle. For maybe some...closure. And I think Jenna saw something and followed Lo wherever he went. And now they're both missing."

"Missing?" Cara says. "Have you tried calling or texting?"

"No answer."

Cara shrugs. "Lo takes off for days on end. It's just something he does. You know that. He'll come back."

"But Jenna doesn't. And she left some weird texts for Sawyer." He nods in the rearview mirror, confirming what I've said. "About Lo and your uncle."

"And you think Lo went looking for him?"

"I think there are a lot of people looking for your uncle, and I'm worried that something may have happened to Lo. I know Lo doesn't remember who I am, but everything inside me is telling me that something's wrong. And now with Jenna gone, too, it just doesn't feel right. Look, Cara, I know it's a lot to ask, but I need to know if you're in or out. Sawyer can take you back to school and we'll forget any of this ever happened."

She hesitates for the briefest of seconds. "Fine. I'm in. But this doesn't make us BFFs or anything. I'm doing this for Lo."

I almost grin at the snarky flash of the old Cara I used to know. "Deal."

"So, I guess we're not going to the Marine Center," Cara remarks as we drive past the entrance toward the freeway.

I show her Jenna's texts on Sawyer's phone, scrolling down to the last one with Cano's name and the note on Imperial Beach. "Do you remember anything about a house or a lab in this area? Anything at all?"

"My uncle has a lot of property all over California."

"So it doesn't ring a bell?" I ask. Cara shakes her head. My heart sinks—all this for nothing, and now she's a loose end that I'm going to have to figure out how to tie up. I slump back in my seat and try to come up with a new plan. We're already on Interstate 5 heading south. Other than driving around randomly or waiting for Jenna to turn on her phone so we can track her GPS, we have nothing. I hinged everything on Cara at least knowing *something* about her uncle's whereabouts.

Cara leans forward, tentative. "But I think I might have a way to find out."

"How?"

"Every single house my uncle owned was gutted and renovated. Not a lot of basements in California because of the fault line, so he built custom-fitted labs in each and every one of them. I bet we could pull the construction permits in Imperial Beach at the town office."

"Whoa," Sawyer says with a fist pump. "That's brilliant."

"That is brilliant," I agree, my brain firing with hope.

"I do have my moments," Cara says, thumbing through a website on her smart phone. "It should all be a matter of public record. We just need to get there by eleven a.m. That's the end of the morning counter hours. If my uncle is at his house, that's where Lo will be. Jenna, too."

"I could kiss you right now," I say.

"Let's not get ahead of ourselves," Cara retorts, but I can see the tiniest smile hovering on the corners of her mouth. "I really hope my uncle is there. I have a few things I need to say to him myself."

We get to Imperial Beach in thirty minutes flat, and head toward Imperial Beach Boulevard where the City Hall is located. Sawyer pulls into the building parking lot with five minutes to spare before the counter closes. We race in breathless, nearly colliding with each other at the last window.

"Look in the online records over there," a bored-looking clerk tells us. "Building-permit lookup by owner name. If you can't find it, come back this afternoon between three-thirty and five."

"Wait—" But before I can finish, she slams the window shut and pulls the blinds closed.

"Come on," Sawyer says. "She said over here." We hover together across a terminal as he starts to type in Cano's name in the search bar. "Wait, what's his last name again?"

"Cano is his last name," I say. "George is his first."

"His name is George?" Sawyer snorts. "That's so normal."

We watch with bated breath as Sawyer hits Enter after typing it in. The computer terminal ticks over for a few seconds before a message comes up on-screen: Your search returned no results. Please try another search.

"Try it again, Sawyer," I say. The same message comes up. I glance at Cara. "Any ideas?"

She purses her lips and leans over the keyboard. "Let's try the correct Albanian spelling for his first name. It's the Albanian version of George. Type in Jorgji. I saw it on one of his old diplomas at home."

Sawyer complies, but the search comes up the same. He shrugs. "Maybe he wouldn't use Cano if he was trying to hide something."

"Good point," I say. "The question is, what would he use?"

Cara's eyes light up. "Try Jorgji again, but instead of Cano, type in Agron. It's his middle name," she clarifies at my look, and rolls her eyes. "Years of teenage spying, what can I say?"

The counter ticks over and then brings up a screen full of results, all under a Mr. Agron. "There are at least ten of them as far as I can tell," Sawyer says, scrolling through the permit list. "Six P.O. boxes, and five separate properties." He clicks on one of the line items with a quarter-million-dollar permit price tag. Cano must have been doing some major renovations for one of his secret labs.

"There," I say, jabbing at a blue line of text on the pop-up window. "Click on Property Map. Let's see where they all are."

Oddly enough, the properties run in a straight line, nearly identical to the Mexican border, just on the edge of the state park. "Which one is it?" Sawyer says, glancing at his phone. "We have two hours before we have to head back, before Speio does what he's going to do at last bell."

"Wait? What's Speio going to do?" Cara says.

"Call my...guardian," I say. "Which means I'll be in a boatload of trouble if we're not back before then."

"You really don't like authority, do you?" Cara says, smirking.

"As I recall, neither do you," I shoot back. We share an unexpected grin.

"So, which one do you think it is?" Sawyer asks again, tapping his finger along the five dots on the map.

"Follow the money," I guess. "That's our best bet. Big permits mean big installations."

"What if we're wrong?" Sawyer says.

"Then we're wrong," I say. "It's all we've got." Sawyer's phone buzzes in his hand and he opens an incoming text. "Is it Jenna?" I ask.

"No, it's Speio checking in." He texts back a quick response and then taps on a blinking icon on his phone, his eyes going wide.

"What is it?" I ask.

"I think I know which house we should go to."

"How do you know?"

He raises shocked eyes to mine and stabs his phone in my face. "Because Jenna's GPS just came on."

17
Chimeras

The Spanish-style house with flashy terra-cotta trim on Seacoast Drive bordering the ocean is on a gorgeous piece of property, albeit deserted, as far as we can tell from our vantage point hunkered down in our car on the other side of the street. I shake my head. My family has a ton of money, but Cano must have obscene amounts hidden away to be able to afford so many million-dollar homes. This one is no exception, resting right at the feet of the ocean, with its manicured lawn and intricate brickwork...along with a multimillion-dollar lab beneath it, if the public records are any indication.

"Nice digs," I say to Cara, nodding at the house.

"Wish I'd known it existed," she says. "So you think Jenna's there?"

"That's what the GPS says," Sawyer says. "What's the plan?" He is still clutching his phone as if he's expecting it to ring any moment. I had to restrain him from calling Jenna immediately—if she happens to be in a precarious situation, we don't want to put her in any more danger by calling her. He finally relented and listened to reason, but I'm watching him like a hawk.

"We can't just go walking in," I say. "We don't know what's in there."

Cara frowns. "Why not? We're just seeing if Lo came to find him here. That's not a crime, is it?"

I deliberate explaining more to Cara, but I don't know how much to reveal. It's too risky for all of us. The less she knows the better. Then again, she knows about her uncle's experiments. I haul a hot breath into my lungs. "Cara, there's something else. The reason we can't go barging in there is that...your uncle may not be himself. It's too dangerous."

"What do you mean? Dangerous how?"

I don't have a gentle way to put it, so I just blurt it out. "If he's creating these chimeras, we don't know how many of them are in there. Or what we're going to find...." I trail off. "Or if he's even still...there."

"Don't be dramatic," Cara says. "This is California. My uncle may be crazy, but he's not *that* crazy. You're acting like he's got a chimera army hidden in there or something." She steps out of the car and stretches. "We'll be fine. Let's go see if Uncle George is home."

"Cara, wait!" But it's too late. She's already on the other side of the street and walking up the flagstone path.

"Shit, shit, shit," I mutter, watching as Cara rings the doorbell before peering into the side window.

"What do we do?" Sawyer says, wide-eyed.

"Nothing," I say. "We wait. Hopefully no one will be home, and we can find Jenna and get the hell out of Dodge."

Desperately willing Cara to turn around and come back

to the car, we watch as she rings the doorbell once more before twisting to shrug in our direction.

No answer, she mouths. I wave her over, but she ignores me, instead tugging on the handle. The door swings inward. I'm halfway out of my seat, mentally screaming at Cara not to go in there, but of course she pays me no attention and ducks her head into the opening.

"Cara," I stage-whisper. "No."

"It's okay," she says over her shoulder. "No one's home. Just going to have a peek." Before I can shout another warning, she disappears from view around the doorjamb, the door closing behind her with a click.

"Nothing like a little breaking and entering," Sawyer says, making me jump after several minutes of silence. I'm trying to figure out what to do—leave Cara and hope for the best, or follow her and risk all of us getting caught. Especially me. I heave out a breath. Knowing what we know about Cano, there's no way I can abandon Cara in there on her own.

"Technically, it's her uncle's house, but yeah, we could be in big trouble if someone calls the cops." I pocket my car keys and sigh. "Let's go get her."

Sawyer and I make our way to the house a lot less confidently than Cara did, hunched over and skulking. I can't help feeling we're being watched, although no one is around apart from the occasional car driving down the street. I'm probably just being paranoid. Maybe Cara's right—this is California in the middle of the day. It's not like a swarm of flying monkey-men are going to fly out of the bushes.

At the house, we peek in one of the side windows, but the interior is shrouded in extra-creepy darkness. Once more, Cara seems to be right. It does seem to be empty, but if

I've learned anything over the past few months, it's not to underestimate Cano. Sawyer moves to walk up the front stoop and I stop him. We have no idea what happened to Cara once she went inside and it's been radio silent for the five minutes that she's been in there.

"Wait," I whisper. "Maybe we should check if there's another entrance just in case."

We walk with quiet, careful steps, our bodies flattened along the back wall. Suddenly all the hairs on the back of my neck stand at nervous attention, and my pulse beats a shade faster. We're no longer alone.

"What the hell are you doing here?" a harsh voice whispers from behind us.

Sawyer and I turn in slow motion. *Jenna.* She looks no worse for wear, after obviously spending the night awake doing who knows what. Her hair is tangled, and her clothes are rumpled as if she slept in her car. Sawyer immediately swoops her up into a silent, frantic embrace, hugging her as if he never expected to see her again.

"Hey, babe," he says into her temple. I stare at him incredulously. That's it? *Hey, babe?* I can feel my face turning purple. Unlike Sawyer, I want to throttle her for putting me through the last few hours.

"What are *you* doing here, Jenna?" I nearly screech. "You scared the hell out of me with those texts. What were you thinking?"

"I saw Lo. People brought him here. I couldn't look the other way."

"You could have called me."

"On what? Seashells?" she whispers drily. "You lost your phone, remember?"

I eye her up and down. "You've been here all night?"

She nods. "They only just left. No sign of Cano, but there are some seriously scary-looking dudes going in and out of this house. They took Lo in there." She eyes me meaningfully over the top of Sawyer's head, mouthing the word *hybrids*.

Shit, and Cara's still inside. I don't even know how I'm going to explain that one to Jenna. "Is he still in there?"

"Didn't see him leave. I've been camped out on the beach behind those rocks all morning."

"I still don't get why Lo came all the way here for closure," Sawyer says.

Jenna's eyebrows shoot into her hairline and I shake my head. "I'll explain later. Right now we have to get in there and deal with two things. Lo and—" I exhale a loud breath "—Cara."

"Cara?" Jenna swivels toward me. "Did I hear you right, or did you just stutter?"

"Nope, you heard me right," I say. "Cara came with us. She was actually pretty helpful in finding this address, once we got past all the niceties of why I needed her help and why she should give it."

"What'd you tell her?" Jenna asks in a low voice.

I shrug. "Nothing she didn't already know."

"The truth," Sawyer interjects. "Which you guys should have told me earlier. What? Didn't I qualify to be in your little superspy club? A dude deserves to know that the principal of his school is a homicidal DNA-splicing maniac, and that his girlfriend is Nancy Drew with a death wish."

"Who's Nancy Drew?" I blurt out.

"She's a fictional...never mind," Jenna says. "Come on, this way. Let's go find Lo and Cara—which I still can't get over by the way—before those goons come back." We follow her around the side of the house to a sliding patio door that's also unlocked, but before she opens it, I lay a hand on her arm.

"Wait one second," I say, and close my eyes. Pulling the water toward my center, I form a glimmer and extend it outward like a net, letting it rest on the surfaces inside the house. The scent of something bitter and foreign permeates it, almost making me recoil backward. Now that I've learned to identify the hybrid essence, the feel of it is like a hundred reptiles slithering across my skin. It's thick and cloying, everywhere my glimmer touches. But there's something familiar, too, underneath it all. A hint of another essence I instantly recognize. Lo.

"Lo's definitely in there," I whisper, snapping the glimmer back into my body. "But he's weak. I can barely feel him."

"Anyone else?" Jenna says.

"Not that I could tell," I say. Sawyer's staring at me like I've grown two horns on my head, which I know I haven't. At least not right now. I roll my eyes. "Seriously, for a Zen surfer, haven't you ever heard of meditation before battle? Sharpening your senses?" Jenna smothers a giggle as Sawyer nods, surprisingly easy to convince.

We let ourselves into the house like silent ghosts. There's no sign of Cara or anyone else on the first floor. The coffeemaker light is still on in the kitchen, I notice, and there's a box of half-eaten pastries on the table. Jenna puts a hand to her lips and points to a wide set of stairs leading up, then gestures to herself. I shake my head. We all stick together. I'm not going to risk losing anyone else.

We take the stairs two at a time. All the rooms upstairs are open, with the exception of one at the far end. My heart stops as I turn the handle and crack open the door, only to see a girl's body lying draped across the bed.

"Is that *Cara?*" Jenna says at my ear, making my heart leap into my throat. "Is she—"

"She's asleep," I say. "Sawyer, you need to stay with her. If she wakes up, take her out to the car."

"But what about you two—" he begins, and then stops at the freezing look on Jenna's face. "Be careful, babe."

I bite back a snort, even though I'd probably quail before that look, too. "Basement," I tell Jenna on the way down. "Quickly. Someone knows we're here."

"Cano?"

"I don't know. There are too many scents, essences. It's confusing. Just keep your eyes open. We're here for Lo, and that's it. I'll go first. You follow."

The thick metal door leading to Cano's industrial lab is open, and we have no choice. It's the only room we haven't checked. We pad downstairs on silent footsteps, and I stop so quickly that Jenna crashes into my back. The room is a replica of the lab that had been in Cano's Sierra house in Rancho Santa Fe, all metal floors and tables with huge black electronic cables coiling along the floor like fat pythons. Flat-screened televisions dominate the walls. Some are on with various news channels; others display previous recordings of experiments. I force myself not to watch and hope Jenna does the same.

A row of indented cages of varying sizes frame the far end of the room. They aren't empty. Glowing red eyes peek out from one of them near the center, the creature making a high-pitched whining noise. A shadowy, hulking figure sits in another, while something that looks like a half jaguar, half monkey paces in the other. A thinner cage on the far right houses a flock of birdlike animals with bristly fur and shiny scales. They eye Jenna and me with vicious and calculating intelligence. I fight back a shiver.

"What the f—" Jenna breathes.

"Chimeras." I nod to the doors on the far right of the room. "Over there." I can feel Lo's pull, drawing me toward one of the doors, that same tug connecting to the core of my center. "He's in there."

I open the door and gasp, my heart shrinking to the size of a pea. Lo's sitting on a metal chair, his arms shackled to the armrests. Thin white tubes connected to long silver vials are plugged into the ragged flesh at his wrists. His shirt is torn and gaping open. Blood dampens his hairline, making his sandy hair seem almost black, and is congealed on his neck in clawlike lines. His bare feet are bloody and dirty, caked with an oily bluish fluid. And his eyes are wild. Unseeing.

I sink to my knees beside him. "Help me untie him, Jenna."

"Riss, he doesn't look good," she says slowly. "Maybe it's not safe. We don't know…if the Lo we know is still in there." Sure enough, as she nears the other side of the chair, Lo bares his teeth at her, navy-and-gold lights flickering like the Fourth of July along his bare forearms. The greenish-gold tattoos just visible beneath his open shirt writhe like snakes inking his skin.

"I don't care," I say desperately, working one hand free and trying to figure out how to remove the IVs without hurting him. "I can't just leave him like this. We have to help him."

"You can't help him," a voice behind us says. "At least not without this."

I whirl around, and my eyes narrow at the woman leaning casually against the doorway with a heavy metal syringe in one hand. My mother looks the same as she did when I summoned her, with long blond hair and shimmering Aquarathi eyes. Beautiful, cold and unreachable. And she has something I want, something I desperately need. I eye the syringe in her fingers—Lo's cure.

"Did you hurt Cara?" I say, dragging my eyes away and making my voice inflectionless.

"Just a mild concoction," she answers. "She'll be fine. I didn't expect to see her, of all people."

"Well, you know what they say about keeping your enemies close and all that. What are you doing with Lo? What are all these tubes for?"

"He is the perfect hybrid specimen. Cano wanted to replicate his DNA. Reproduce it."

I eye her. "Speaking of, where is Cano?"

"Out, I expect."

"So why the biotoxin? You could have just taken his blood."

Neriah walks into the room, every inch of her still imperious royalty. I stand my ground until we are inches apart before she sways past me with a faint smile at my standoff. She ignores Jenna, who is standing still against the far wall, and brushes a lazy hand across Lo's matted hair. "I told you. Weaken the human side, undermine the Aquarathi side. We wanted to test if your bond could be broken."

"Why? You put us together. It was Ehmora's elaborate trick that made us bond in the first place."

"You're wrong, my darling," she says. "That was my idea." She's so calm and condescending that all I want to do is rip her face to shreds, make her *feel* something for once.

A thread in her voice catches, making me look at her. "But things change. Players change, and plans change. Enemies and all that," she says cryptically, mocking my earlier words.

"Are you going to kill us?"

"If I have to." She rakes Jenna with a contemptuous glance. "I see you've brought your human pet." I bristle and she laughs, reading me easily. "The one thing about you, Nerissa, is that you are so predictable. You have to think outside of the box. Be fearless. Formidable."

"She *is* fearless," Jenna bursts out, and blanches as the weight of my mother's terrifying eyes falls on her.

"Ah, the mouse speaks."

"Don't speak to her like that," I growl. "Don't even look at her. She has more courage in her little finger than any of you traitors—" I spit the word like a barb "—have in your whole body." I take a breath. "Now give me that syringe before I take it from you. I don't need a Taser gun to take you down this time. That must have hurt." I offer a consolatory smile.

"There's the fire I was talking about," my mother crows. "Well, you'd better work fast because your young prince is running out of time."

I glance at Lo. He does look paler than when we first entered the room. "You're going to let him die?"

"Why do you care? You're stronger without him."

I shake my head, a maniacal laugh erupting from my mouth. "Is that what you think? That he makes me weak? Well, he doesn't. He makes me better—a better friend, a better leader, a better everything. You once told me that love doesn't matter. That's because you never understood it. You've never experienced it. This bond? It's nothing compared to what the humans *choose* to give each other every single day." I smile softly. "Don't you see? That's where you're wrong. I'd give up everything for him."

"Then that makes you a fool." My mother's face is a blank slate, giving away nothing as we stare at each other in frigid silence. "So you would choose him despite what he is? If you weren't bonded?"

"Yes." I swallow hard. I would choose Lo again, no matter the cost. "I would."

She eyes me, her eyes unfathomable. "So be it."

I hesitate, not understanding her words or the expression on her face. And then I feel it—the thread of a glimmer weaving its way toward me, winding its way through my blood like honey...like an old, cherished memory, familiar and beautiful. My father's glimmer.

Fight, Nerissa.

"Jenna, get out of the way and get down," I snarl. My body starts transforming before the glimmer can recede, my nails sharpening into claws at the ends of my human fingers, and my teeth to fangs. My mother bares razor-sharp incisors of her own and deflects my strike. Lunging toward me, she punches me in the face and I feel a hot trickle of blood wet my upper lip. Enraged, I swipe at her chest, feeling my nails dig into soft human flesh, and rake ruthlessly downward. Power swirls through me like a mad thing, uncontrollable and punishing. I hit her again, this time in the stomach, ripping through skin like paper. She gasps, staggering backward. Rage blinds me and the scent of blood fills my nostrils. I push forward, not losing any ground, and continue my assault with blow after blow to her shoulders and back until she's on the floor and I'm on top of her like a dark and ruthless avenging angel.

"Nerissa, stop!" Jenna's voice pierces through my haze of

fury, and my mother's bloodied, nearly pulverized human face swims into focus. Her bones are like putty beneath my hands.

Well done....

The echo disappears as quickly as it had come, and for a moment, I think I've imagined it. That, and the pride surrounding the words. I haul myself off her battered body and grab the syringe out of her hand. It was almost too easy to get it...almost as if she'd *wanted* me to get it. I shrug off the strange thoughts. Adrenaline is making me crazy. I raise the syringe and growl. It's empty.

"Where's the serum, Neriah?"

For a second, I think she isn't going to answer me, and then her lips part on a pained exhale. "F-fridge," she breathes, a bubble of blood foaming at the corner of her lips, and closes her eyes.

Jenna scoots over to the refrigerator and gnashes her teeth. "It's locked," she says. "What's the combination?"

I shake Neriah, but her eyes remain closed. I slap her on one cheek. "What's the number? Dammit, wake up." I spare a desperate glance toward Lo, who is now slumped over in the chair, held in place by the one hand still tied to the armrest. "What's the number? Neriah, what's the number? Mom, please." Her eyelashes flutter against her cheeks and her lips move, but no sound comes out of them. I take a breath, ready to plunge into her mind and extract the information forcibly.

Seven, four, one, six, three. Her glimmer is faint, but seeps into me as clear as a bell. I repeat the numbers to Jenna and the fridge pops open. Bottles clink and crash into each other as Jenna sweeps her hand inside. *Silver color. BT4.*

"That one," I tell Jenna. "The silver one on the left." She

tosses it to me, and I dunk the syringe into the plastic stopper. "Help me get him loose, and careful with those tubes. We have to get out of here."

Gently disengaging him and hoisting Lo's limp body over my shoulder, we make our way out of the shattered room, leaving my mother's prone body behind.

"What about her?" Jenna says.

"We Aquarathi heal up nicely," I say in a dead voice, despite the trembling unfurling in the pit of my belly. "She recovered from slicing off her own crown and sending it to me. She'll survive this, too. She always does."

We run past the beasts in the other room, ignoring the mad cacophony of shrieking, and pound up the stairs, Jenna shouting for Sawyer above the noise. He meets us in the living room with a woozy Cara slung over his own shoulder, and stares at me.

"What was all that banging? And all that screeching? It sounded like a zoo down there. Is that *Lo?*" He frowns. "You're strong for a girl. He's not a small dude."

"Time and place, Sawyer," I snap. "Get the car, and get Jenna and Cara back to La Jolla to Echlios now."

"Wait," Jenna pants. "What about you two?"

"We'll be right behind you. I just have to take care of one thing first."

Jenna turns toward me, her eyes wary. "You sure?"

"I've never been more sure of anything in my life. Now go."

Watching to make sure they drive off, I half carry, half drag Lo down to the water's edge, syringe still in hand, until we're waist-deep in the ocean. The noon sun is high in the sky, making lights glitter off the tops of the foamy waves. I can already feel the salt water rejuvenating my body, and can only hope it's doing the same for him. Lo is barely breathing now. Whatever they've done has taken a lot out of him. It's almost as if they've *drained* everything from him.

"Hold on," I say, and gently stick the needle into his neck, releasing the plunger. "Please work. Please work." Lo's body starts to convulse as the serum enters his bloodstream, halting the biotoxin in its tracks. I hope. I hold him to me with all my strength and whisper against his temple that he's going to be all right, even though I know he can't hear me.

A loud crash and a terrifying bellow make me look up at the house. A chair crashes through the patio door, followed by a huge, hulking figure. I squint in the bright light, but the thick curly hair and beefy stature are the same. Cano's back—we got out just in time. The blood in my veins turns to ice as the sun glints off something on his face. *Scales.* Now I know what Cano has been doing with Lo's blood.

I drag Lo's still-bucking body into deeper waters, but not before Cano sees us. A cry of hideous rage echoes across the sands as he charges toward the ocean. There's only one place we can go—out and down where Cano can't follow. But first Lo has to transform, and I'm not sure he's ready for that. I glance at Cano closing the distance between us rapidly. Then again, we don't have much choice.

"Lo, open your eyes." Drawing us out into the open ocean and kicking my legs to keep us afloat, I press my lips to his cold ones, willing him to see me, willing him to know me...to come back to me. Opening the conduit between us, I engage Sanctum, pushing my energy into his body and feeling him absorb it like a sponge. "I'm here. Listen to my voice. Find me."

Slanting my open mouth against his in a desperate kiss, I bite his lip harder than I intended. His lashes flutter open, and his navy eyes meet mine just before he crushes his mouth against me in an almost violent response. As much as I want to lose myself in the fierce sweetness of him, I wrench away.

"Are you okay?" I ask, breathless.

"I think so."

"Do you know who you are?" I ask, staring at him, unsure. "*What* you are?"

"Riss, what's going on? Of course I know who and what I am." He winces. "Why does my head feel like it got sledge-hammered by a bunch of drunken gremlins?"

"It kind of did, only not gremlins. Hybrids. There's one now." I clutch his shoulders. Cano is about thirty feet away and swimming strongly. "We have to go. Can you...shift?"

Lo looks over my shoulder, his eyes widening. "Is that *Cano?*"

"Yes. And he looks angry."

Lo and I swim out to where the water turns from green to deep blue, his strokes becoming stronger with each second. With a last look at Cano bobbing in the distance, we grasp hands, our bodies shifting simultaneously and lengthening into sharp bone and finned sinew.

Just before I submerge, my eyes fall on the house, barely a speck on the shoreline, drawn there by something... movement, maybe, in one of the windows. Deep down, I know it's her, watching me. The faint sensation of a glimmer curls around me like an echo of an echo. It's so tender, so heartbreakingly familiar. It's only at that moment that I realize that the glimmered voice I heard in the basement wasn't my father's.

She told me to fight.

And the pride was hers.

18
The Call of Land and Sea

We sink into the embrace of the deep like falling rock, far out of the reach of our pursuer. Watching Lo transform is like watching a movie reel of something fantastic, something so achingly beautiful that your mouth drops open and your breath feels full, like it's going to burst out of your chest. And for a moment it's as if your very heart stops—as if time itself stops—enough for you to savor this one moment forever.

My breath catches.

Even midtransformation, Lo is striking—all elongated curved muscles swathed in mesmerizing bands of gold and silver. Delicate forearms widen into muscular limbs, peach-fuzzed human skin shimmering across them into sand-colored scales. Lustrous navy fins rise like a reverse waterfall along his neck and spine as his bones push outward into something terrifying, yet spectacular.

It's like I'm seeing him for the first time, and he is beautiful.

His face is creased with deeply gold ridges running down an elegant snout, and his jeweled eyes—so intensely

melting—are staring right at me. If I'd had any doubt before that he'd know who I am, I don't anymore. The same
desperate longing I'm feeling is written all over his face.
Self-conscious, I slide my greedy gaze away.

"You are beautiful," he pulses to me in our language, a
gentle sound that winds through the watery space between
us, a caress in itself. I wasn't even aware that I'd transformed,
too, my body aligning with every twist, every contortion,
every ripple of his. A delicious shiver runs through me.

"I was thinking the same about you," I say.

Lo swims forward to wrap his neck around mine, and the
feel of him is better than anything I've imagined...or remembered. Twisting against him, I fit myself into the curves
of his new form until there's nothing but our heartbeats between us. We stay like that for a long moment, weightless
and unrestrained, our bodies glued as the will of the bond
between us takes over and our glimmers merge into one.

I love you. Lo's thoughts are as clear as a bell. *I never forgot that.*

I know, I say. *It was touch-and-go for a while, with that biotoxin. Can you remember what it felt like?*

Lo's tail slides along mine, making my stomach do a weird
little flip-flop. *It was fuzzy. A part of me knew who you were,
but I couldn't remember. It was like looking through a cloud of fog.*
He shrugs, his muscular body rippling along the length of
mine. *I'm just glad you got the serum when you did. Some memories were eaten away by the toxin. Like I can't remember our first
date. The details are kind of fuzzy, too.*

I think back to the fiasco of our first date and grin. *Yeah,
you can live without that one. Just imagine something incredibly romantic with both of us saying the most perfect things to each other.*

So no hot and steamy?

A shiver. *I'm not that kind of girl, but yeah, that came later.*

Where are we, anyway? Lo nuzzles my neck, my pulse leaping madly beneath it. I could stay in his embrace—human or Aquarathi—forever.

Somewhere near the Coronado Islands if I had to guess.

With a sigh, I pull away from Lo. Now that I've gotten him back, I don't want to let him go. I glance around, feeling the different temperature of the currents tugging at us on all sides, and my eyes widen. We're surrounded by all kinds of marine wildlife, including some frolicking sea lions—they've been drawn to us, drawn by our combined energies.

"Are you seeing this?" I pulse to him wide-eyed as the sea lions gambol giddily around us, flipping, spinning and rubbing their soft bodies against our hides. "I've never seen so many of them. They're like underwater puppies!"

Lo chuckles and does a somersault that makes the sea lions go nuts, chasing him around with enthusiastic barking and chirping.

"They like you," I say, grinning at Lo, who is now in a spiraling dive with six sea lion pups trailing behind him. I watch them for a few minutes before reality sets in, and if the changing tides are any indication, we've been out here long enough. "We should probably get back before Speio sends out the ASS," I click to Lo.

"The what?"

"The Aquarathi Secret Service."

"That's just wrong."

I bare my teeth in a grin. "I know, but I love sticking it to Speio."

Leaving the sea lions behind, we swim up the coast toward La Jolla together. The temptation to dive down and swim to Waterfell is compelling, but I'm not sure how either of us will be received there. I'm still the queen, but that doesn't mean I don't have my share of enemies waiting for me to make one bad move, which technically I've already done by getting myself bonded to a hybrid. So as much as I feel the appeal of my home, I have to ignore it. For now.

Reaching the break near the Scripps pier, we change back into human form and skirt around the breakers to avoid the long line of surfers. "Over here," I tell Lo, directing him over the Marine Center pier. I dive down to the base of one of the wooden pillars holding the pier up. A plastic bag weighted down with a flat rock sits at the bottom. Tugging on it, I remove two pairs of board shorts and a swimsuit top.

"Your shorts aren't going to fit me," Lo says.

"Would you rather walk up the beach naked?" I ask, glad that the deep water partially hides the hot blush rising up my neck at the thought. I don't know why the thought of him naked in our natural Aquarathi form—though sexy— isn't quite the same as seeing him without clothes in human form. Maybe it's because of their social conditioning— people don't tend to wander around nude.

"I may as well be naked," Lo mutters, taking the shorts.

"Relax, they're Speio's."

"Why didn't you just say so?"

"Wanted to see you squirm," I tease, and dart away out of his reach, sticking my tongue out at him. "Plus, aren't you always talking about getting into my shorts?"

"I'm going to toss both these shorts in a second if you keep doing that," Lo growls.

Despite his joking threat, we manage to slide on the clothes underwater without losing either of the shorts, and casually swim our way to shallower water before body-surfing into shore. Lo is taller than Speio and more muscular, so the shorts are riding up his legs with each step on the beach. I can't help noticing the sleek, sculpted bulge of muscle of his thighs and the curve of his butt through the clingy wet material.

"Want to take a photo?" Lo says over his shoulder. "It'll last longer."

"You wish," I say, blushing, and twist my hair up into a ponytail.

"Relax. The Lo Show is here to stay."

I smother a giggle. "And this is where I wish you were the other Lo. All J.Crew and proper. He was the perfect gentleman."

Lo whirls around to grab me around the waist, and my breath whooshes out of me in surprise. His voice is low and husky, causing me to tremble. "Did the old Lo do this?"

I don't have time to inhale before his mouth descends onto mine in an insanely hot human kiss that leaves my entire body feeling boneless. His tongue delves into my mouth as if it belongs there, sliding between the crease of my lips and out again, until I can only drag him closer to me, lost. By the time Lo releases my mouth, I am senseless. I can't even speak. The stormy look in his eyes says that he is just as shaken by the kiss as I am. I blink, slightly bemused. With kisses like that, he can put on the Lo Show all he wants.

"I can't wait to get you alone," he says against my hair, nearly making my knees buckle. My hands slip across the flat planes of his chest, down the bunched muscles of his stomach. His skin is warm to the touch, flexing responsively beneath my fingers. I slip them around his rear and drag his hips in closer.

"Hey!" a voice up the beach shouts. It's my boss, Kevin, from the Marine Center. Oh my God. Did he just see us making out on the beach? Blushing madly at Lo's knowing grin, I put some space between our overheated bodies, folding my arms across my chest.

"Hey, Kevin."

"When did you guys get here? I texted you, like, an hour ago."

"Sorry," I say. "Lost my phone. What's up?"

"I had three calls from the school looking for you and Cara Andrews. They said you were on some extra-credit project here, but I didn't have anything down in the log."

"What'd you tell them?"

He grins. "That I was aiding and abetting high-school ditchers?" He gestures to himself. "I may be old, but I'm not that old. Next time, give me a heads-up, okay? If Andrews is around, you two need to head back to school, stat."

"Thanks, Kev. I owe you."

He tosses me a set of keys. "Take the boat. You may want to get back in uniform." He grins. "And try to keep it PG, all right?"

I don't have to look in a mirror to know that I've just gone fifteen shades of red at Kevin's teasing, but Lo's soft response makes my flush go supernova. "Not if I can help it," he murmurs.

We take the boat to my house and tie it to the dock before we run hand in hand up to the house. I'm hoping to avoid Soren, but of course that is next to impossible. I swear I must have an ankle bracelet that goes off every time I try to sneak in somewhere. Sure enough, she's waiting poolside, her face expressionless.

"Is she angry?" Lo whispers to me as we walk toward her, her back ramrod straight.

"More than you can imagine," I tell him.

"Soren," I say brightly. "We're back from the Marine Cen—" She cuts me off with an eviscerating look that needs no words. "Sorry," I mutter, staring at the ground. My fingers are still caught tightly in Lo's. Remembering my mother's words, I lift my chin. I have nothing to feel bad about. Other than the tiny deception of sneaking off without telling anyone, that is.

We don't exchange any words, but Soren must have seen the brief glint of courage in my eye. "We called the school. You've been dismissed for the day. They're waiting for you inside," she says with the slightest incline of her neck. I bite back a smile. Impropriety doesn't come easily to Soren, but she must want to prove a point.

Standing in front of her, I bare my neck, meeting her shocked eyes before placing a soft kiss on her cheek. It's the highest display of respect—and apology—that I can offer her. "Thank you, Soren."

Lo and I walk, fingers threaded together, into the living room, where we are greeted with smiles, frowns and combinations of both. I glance around at the familiar faces and equally familiar expressions—impassive Echlios, trepidatious Speio, grinning Sawyer, triumphant Jenna, expressionless royal guard…and bewildered Cara. Well, she's certainly new to the equation.

The silence in the room grows heavy until I realize that they are waiting for me to speak. I clear my throat and release Lo's hand. "As you can see, Lo—" I don't use his Aquarathi title of regent for Cara's benefit "—is alive and well." I nod imperceptibly at Soren, who steps forward to graciously offer a tour of the house to Sawyer and Cara.

After they leave, the stoic expressions of my guard melt into varying stages of irritation and frustration. Nova and Nell eye Jenna with unveiled distaste, but she's handled more than her fair share of angry Aquarathi, and holds her own. I almost grin when she asks Nova and Nell whether they've had the house tour. The sour look on their faces intensifies something fierce.

"The prince regent is safe for the moment," I say in an imperious tone, drawing attention back to me. "But this battle is far from over. We discovered that Cano is still experimenting with human and Aquarathi DNA." I pause. "On himself."

"What?" Echlios says.

"He had scales," I say. "Lo and I both saw it. And he's strong. Unbelievably strong."

"How is that even possible?" Speio breathes. Echlios silences him with a look. There's a charged energy between him and Echlios, and I'm sure it's my fault.

I meet Echlios's gaze with a fierce one of my own. "You should know that I commanded Speio to obey me. He tried to dissuade me and I refused." Speio shoots me a grateful look, which I acknowledge with a wink before continuing. "It is possible because Cano is injecting himself with Lo's DNA, and because we are bonded, it is more powerful than ever."

"How did you find the cure?" Nova asks.

"I fought my mother for it."

"Is she dead?"

The coldness of the question hits me like a slap, but Neriah is a traitor and branded an exile. "No."

"You dare let a traitor live?" he says under his breath. Echlios steps forward, but I stall him with a raised palm.

Be formidable.

I turn burning eyes upon Nova, letting the crown of bones tear from my forehead. "You dare question my judgment?" The fires of a glimmer pool at my center like an explosive ball of flame, until it consumes me in its entirety. Raw power and fury whistle through me like twin dragons. Nova's eyes widen to round black orbs before he kneels before me, his neck outstretched. "I will forgive you this once because you are young, as am I, but do not believe I will forget this transgression. Mind your words."

"Yes, my queen."

"Now out," I command. "Take Nell with you." He scurries from the room with his sister in tow. I nod curtly to the rest of the guards, dismissing them, as well. By the time the room has cleared, only Echlios, Speio and Jenna remain. She, for her part, is watching me in astonished glee.

Speio brings his hands together in a long, slow clap, and leans back on the couch. "That was impressive. Remind me never to get on your bad side. Oh, wait, I've felt the force of the dark side myself."

I spare a glance at Jenna, who is now staring at me with unabashed pride. "You go, girl. That was badass." She eyes me up and down, shaking her head. "And in a bikini, no less."

"Thanks," I say.

Standing beside me, Lo doesn't say a word, but his shoulders brush against mine, leaving me in little doubt of what he's thinking...that he still can't wait to get me alone. Boys. So utterly single-minded. Then again, I wouldn't mind being alone with him, either. I suppress an instant shiver and focus my thoughts.

"So, what now?" I ask Echlios.

"Cano will be coming."

"With an army of hybrids at his back," I say. "I smelled them in the house. He has many. He wants to take down Waterfell and wage a war against the humans. If I had to guess, I'd say he has allies...like Ehmora."

"What about the Lady Neriah?" Echlios asks. I'm startled by the fact that he still calls her "lady," but I don't say anything.

"I don't think she's on his side," I say carefully. At his look, I explain in a few short sentences what had transpired in the basement room. I shake my head. "It was as if she wanted me to take it from her. She goaded me to fight." I frown, recalling the events in my mind, all the questions, and her song and dance. "She fought back, but I know she's far stronger than that. She *let* me beat her."

"Or maybe you just think that," Speio says softly.

"What do you mean?"

He stares at me. "I mean that you're strong, Riss. You have so much power rippling through you even now. Can't you feel it?"

Speio's right. My waters are brimming inside me like the sea at high tide. I glance at Echlios. "Is that normal?"

"Only a few Aquarathi have ever been able to pull power from the sea or the sky or from the water around them. It appears that you, too, can summon it at will." A vague memory flits across my brain—one of me commanding the skies and punishing myself with lightning bolts, when Echlios himself ended up saving me. He knew even then what I would become.

"And Lo?" I say.

"You can take power from him, too," Echlios says. "Aquarathi and hybrid."

"Hybrid?" I gasp.

"Yes. You are bonded. It appears that as with the traditional Aquarathi bond, his strengths—and weaknesses—are both yours, should you will it."

I frown, repeating the words slowly. "Strengths and weaknesses."

"You could survive inland, should you so choose. Dominion over both earth and sea," Echlios says, trailing off. I signal for him to continue. "However, this bond also includes human weaknesses like emotional frailty and self-doubt." His gaze is solemn. "That is what some of the Aquarathi are most afraid of—that your judgment will become skewed and not in their interests, because of—"

"My bond with Lo," I finish.

"Yes."

Lo moves to stand beside me, his hand tracing slow circles on the small of my back. I accept his touch gratefully. He's grown stronger, too, I realize. His energy is more palpable...unless I've never noticed that before. Or maybe we're feeding off each other. Either way, I'm thankful for his presence, especially after Echlios's last words on why my people may rise against me.

"You mean like Nova and Nell?" I ask bitterly.

"And others," Echlios says.

"If they think someone else will be a better king or queen, then let them come forth," I say. "Just because I was born into the Gold Court doesn't mean I wanted any of this. I fought Ehmora to protect the people. I stepped up and claimed my father's legacy." I slip cold fingers into Lo's. "My choice of a mate does not impact my ability to lead."

"But it does, Riss," Speio interrupts in a soft voice. I turn a shaken glare on him. As if reading my thoughts, he throws his palms into the air in a supplicating gesture. "Hear me out. Think of it from their point of view. You won back your throne on the sands of battle. They offered you their trust and a crown. Then they find out that you've bonded with a *hybrid*—an abomination in their eyes—and not one of the eligible suitors from any of the lower courts. No offense, Lo," he says with an apologetic look in Lo's direction.

"None taken," Lo says.

"That wasn't my fault." I hear Lo's swift indrawn breath at my rashly spoken words, but I'm too incensed to think clearly about what I'm saying. Or what it means.

"Doesn't matter. To them, it's a betrayal at the core. You chose him—a hybrid—over them."

"I didn't betray them. The bond chose him," I blurt out. Lo's fingers slip from mine and for a second, I wish I could take back what I've just said, but it's too late now. His presence, so comforting before, is now rigid and cold.

"You and I both know that isn't true," Jenna chimes in feelingly. "I was there, remember? In that room with your mother. She gave you the choice to let Lo go, and you chose not to. That wasn't the bond. That was you, Riss."

"She's right," Speio says. "But regardless of how it came to be, you are now one, despite him not being oceanborn. Because Lo isn't one of us. He is your regent, not theirs." Speio sighs, pressing on. "They don't trust him, which means they won't trust you. At some point, *you* will have to choose. Land or sea. From their vantage point, you can't have both. You can't defend both. They need a queen who is one hundred percent on their side."

"Is that what you think?" My voice breaks slightly. "That I don't have my people in mind every second? That Waterfell isn't my first priority?"

"It doesn't matter what I think, Riss. I will always have your back—you have to know that by now. It matters what they think. In the end, it's him or them." He takes a breath. "Why do you think Neriah was trying so hard to release you from the bond?"

"Speio, that's enough," Echlios says.

"Wait, what?" I whisper with a tortured glance at Lo, the floor dropping out from beneath my feet. "She was trying to do *what?*"

"Give you a fair chance," Speio says, braving Echlios's ire.

Echlios steps in, his voice measured. "I suspect that she, too, has spies in Waterfell. She is well aware of the cost to you, despite what she may have done in the past. Perhaps she wanted to make amends for…bringing you and the prince regent together."

All of my mother's cryptic questions come back to haunt me in hindsight—the ones asking me whether I'd choose Lo again if we weren't bonded, whether I'd risk everything for him. My response then had been impassioned and heartfelt, but now that push comes to shove, I find myself hesitating. Would I do the same if the cost were my people? Would I choose Lo? Could I give Lo up if that is the choice the Aquarathi require of me to remain their queen? Maybe this is what Echlios means about human weakness—my mind says one thing, but my heart is screaming another.

The sudden attack of conscience does nothing to change what I told my mother. Speio's right. Jenna's right. They are all right. A crown is nothing compared to what I would give up for Lo. He has my heart and my life—they're both his for the taking.

"My choice would be the same…my water is his," I say simply, searching for Lo's hand and grasping it tightly. He squeezes back, guardedly at first, and then more forcefully. "But I was born to lead my people, and I won't give up my throne, either. My father told me to be a worthy queen, and that is the only thing I can do."

"Good," Echlios says in fierce approval. "For now, we have a bigger threat than Waterfell politics. Cano needs to be contained. He must be dealt with swiftly and quietly. Anything more, and we risk certain exposure. We need to know how many hybrids he has created, and where he's hiding them all."

"How are we going to do that?" Speio asks.

"We hunt him down."

"Yeah, but *how?*"

I'm wondering the same thing when my gaze is drawn to Cara laughing loudly at some story Soren is recounting out on the patio. Without her help today, things could have turned out way differently. Maybe Lo would be dead. Jenna, too. Either way, I couldn't have done it without her. Nor what I'm about to do. I shake my head at the incongruity of it all. Who would have thought that she of all people would become the linchpin in this whole plan? Then again, stranger things have happened. I am an Aquarathi queen with a human for a best friend and a hybrid for a boyfriend. Stands to reason that my sworn high-school enemy would factor in somehow.

A slow smile spreads across my face. "I think I have an idea."

19
Clash of the Teen Titans

Every single eye lands on us with varying degrees of disbelief, and hallway chatter peters out to stunned silence. I can imagine what the Dover students must be seeing—you know that scene out of every high-school movie where the mean girls walk down the corridor dressed in careful artlessness wearing matching uniforms, and everyone stares at them and gets out of their way?

Well, it's not that.

It's the one where the queen of the mean girls walks down the hallway with the kids on the very bottom of her peon list, and everyone's head explodes.

"Keep walking," I say to Cara under my breath. "Over there. Outside courtyard."

"How did I get roped in to this?" Cara groans once we are at the far end of the courtyard under a large coral tree. She glances back at the school, where inquisitive faces dart away from windows. "No one's going to buy this, you know. There's too much…bad blood between us."

I force a smile to my face. "Just act natural."

Cara jams her hands on her hips and purses her lips, glaring from me to Lo, to Jenna and Sawyer. "You know, just because we went all *Abduction* down in Imperial Beach, it doesn't mean I'm on your side. I helped to find Lo. Period."

"Hey," Sawyer protests. "I'm way hotter than Taylor Lautner."

I glare back at her, biting back a grin at Sawyer's indignant expression and Jenna's immediate eye roll. "You don't care that your uncle might have gone off the deep end, creating more of those chimeras with unsanctioned experiments?" I ask.

"No," Cara says, and then sighs. "Yes, but I don't see why we have to pretend to be friends. It's our senior year and I'm…"

"Worried we may rub off on you?" Jenna says snarkily.

"Exactly," Cara shoots back.

"You know not everything is about being prom queen, Cara."

"Says she who could never be prom queen," Cara says with scathing contempt. I feel a short burst of dislike before I stifle it. God, she can be catty at the drop of a hat.

"Stop," I say to the both of them. "None of us may even be around to enjoy prom if we don't do something about Cano."

"It's not like he's *here*," Cara says sourly.

Jenna's face goes from irritated to pissed off. "Listen, dimwit. Where do you think he's going to go now that he knows we broke into his house? And didn't you hear Nerissa last night? He's doing genetic experiments on himself. How dangerous do you think that is?"

Cara's eyes widen to shocked orbs. My gaze flicks to Jenna, who reddens and looks away. Cara hadn't been inside for that part of the discussion, and Jenna knew it. "What?" Cara whispers.

"It's true," Lo says gently. "I saw him."

"Yeah, dude," Sawyer chimes in. "He's totally gone Dr. Moreau on us."

"Dr. Moreau?" Cara repeats.

"I'm sorry we didn't tell you earlier," I say, sighing at Sawyer's clueless and insensitive comparison. "I thought you already knew, but forgot you were outside when it came up. We can't prove anything, but after you guys left, we saw him. He looked...different."

"That doesn't mean he's experimenting on himself," Cara whispers, but I can see that she doesn't quite believe that. She knows exactly what her uncle is capable of.

"He ran down the beach faster than any human being could," I say.

"We could go to the police," Cara says. "Report it."

"We could, but we don't have any actual proof of what he's doing." I pause, not wanting to say that involving the police would cause more trouble than it was worth. "Plus, if word got out, it'd be a media circus."

"I..." Cara trails off miserably.

I take pity on her a little. "Look, you're already friends with Lo. Think of us as his...accessories." With a deep breath, I decide to tell her the truth...a partial truth. "The thing is, there are people at Dover looking for your uncle. We don't know who they are, and that's why we need to put up a front at school. I want to draw them out. If they are working under your uncle, someone may slip up, mention something."

"What about my dad?" she asks. "Can he help? He's the principal."

"No, Cara," I say. "You can't say anything. It could be anyone, even him." I hasten to explain. "I'm not saying it is your father, but you'd do anything to protect your family, wouldn't you? I would, and so we can't take the chance." I gesture to the five of us. "It stays here, in this circle."

Cara opens her mouth as if she wants to say something and then shuts it. She swallows hard. "So, then…why are you trusting me?"

"You didn't have to go with me to look for Lo and Jenna yesterday," I answer honestly. "You could have walked the other way and you didn't. You earned it. And you deserve to know what's going on with Cano, and put a stop to his animal experimentation for good."

"Hey, guys!" someone shouts from the top of the court-yard. Rian waves and heads down to join us.

"Speio, the circle thing goes for you, too," I warn him swiftly. "I mean it. No one outside of us five."

"What are you guys doing down here?" she says with a bright smile, blinking in surprise at Cara. "Oh, hey, Cara. Didn't see you there."

"Hey," Cara mumbles, and stares helplessly at me.

"We were talking about doing a charity fundraiser for the SPCA with Cara," I improvise madly. Cara stares at me with a bewildered expression, but then catches on as the words tumble out of me like dominoes. "And since we're all animal advocates, we kind of thought it'd be cool to do an event at the Marine Center." I make a mental note to check with Kevin.

"Right, fundraiser," Cara repeats.

"Yeah," Sawyer interjects. "For dolphins."

"And turtles," Lo adds helpfully.

"That's a terrific idea," Rian says, looping her arms

around Speio's waist. "Count me in. I can do the flyers—I'm really great with graphics."

And this is why lying never pays off. On top of drawing out Cano's spies at Dover, I now have to add planning a Save the Dolphins and Turtles event at the Marine Center to the list. As if I don't have enough to worry about with an insane, self-splicing, genetic scientist hot on my heels. Just awesome. With an inward groan, I nod brightly at Rian. "Of course."

As if sensing a window of opportunity, Cara waves and makes her escape from our clutches as quickly as she can.

"See you at lunch, bestie," I shout after her, grinning as Lo stifles a snort beside me. The look she tosses over her shoulder is just priceless.

"So, when is it?" Rian asks as we walk toward the building, retracing Cara's rapid dash exit. "The charity thing?"

"Next weekend," Jenna pipes up.

"Whoa, that's really short notice," Rian says. "That's not much time to get the word out."

"Yeah, Jenna," I say through clenched teeth. "Not enough time."

"It's the perfect time," she insists with a meaningful stare. "We want to draw a crowd, don't we? From all outlying areas, all the way down from Solana to Imperial Beach." I don't miss the emphasis on the last two words.

Oh. And this is why I have a brilliant best friend. Cano won't show up at the school or at my home. Too risky and too heavily guarded. But a public fundraising event is a whole other ball game. After we thwarted him in Imperial Beach, this will be a perfect opportunity for payback. He won't miss it.

"Yeah, it's next weekend," I confirm.

"Cool, I'll get to work," Rian says. She kisses Speio and takes off. "See you guys later. Have to go meet Birch." Oh, right, for her independent study. So she's a prodigy who knows everything there is to know about humans, a talented graphics artist and literally a force of nature. At least all that energy will be put to good use. "I'll send you a proof tonight," she says over her shoulder. "And I can help with getting some local sponsors, too."

"Sure," I say a bit dazedly.

"Got your hands full, mate?" Lo raises his eyebrows at Speio, who shrugs with a sheepish grin. "You know, if this were a sitcom, it'd be called *Five Minutes with Rian*."

"More like three minutes," Sawyer says with a guffaw.

"Eww," I shout, covering my ears. "TMI. And how would you know about Speio's three minutes, anyway?"

"Boy talk."

I shake my head at him. "Seriously, if there were a sitcom about you, it'd be called *Gossip Boy*."

Sawyer smiles smugly. "And it would be awesome."

"Come on," I say with a wry grin. "Let's get to class before Sawyer goes all XOXO on us."

The morning passes quickly as all my classes flow into each other with predicable promptness—history to calculus to French. The bell rings and we stumble to the next in rehearsed ranks. The only class the five of us have together is English, but we see each other in the hallway at the lockers between classes. Lo and I are the only two who have exactly the same schedule. He transferred to French earlier in the year to prove that he could. I frown, remembering the day he showed up, impressing Madame Dumois with his flawless accent. Jenna and I had thought it was to impress me, but maybe it wasn't. Maybe he was placed there.

"Lo," I whisper, braving Madame Dumois's explosive wrath. "Who transferred you into French?"

"No one," he says. "The office said there was a mistake on my schedule."

"And you didn't think to worry about it or question why you were suddenly enrolled in advanced French?"

"Why?" he answers in perfect French. "I'm fluent, and you're here. It was a win–win."

I literally have to force myself to look away from the magnetic traction of his eyes, and the sound of those sonorous French words falling from his lips like candy. I've never wanted to throw myself at someone more and ravage the French from his mouth. I drag my eyes away from those infernal lips.

"Monsieur Seavon," Madame Dumois says sharply. "You have something to say? The answer, perhaps?"

Lo's recovery is impeccable. He smiles and stands with a flourish with barely a glance at the paragraph in the textbook we're supposed to be reading. "*Oui,* madame. According to the text, DeMille's friends find him to be too impractical, especially after the death of his brother. The answer is B."

"Excellent," Madame Dumois says approvingly. Her eyes drop to me, and I breathe a sigh of relief as they keep going to the far side of the room, where they settle on a more alert Rian. "Mademoiselle," she says to her, "next question, *s'il vous plait.*"

Rian's answer fades into the background. I'm still worried by the fact that Lo's schedule was changed without any viable explanation. I mean, sure, a mistake could have happened, but assuming it was a mistake is a giant leap. Not making the right connections could be the difference between life and death. I shrug as Dumois's onyx stare flutters in my direction. I fix my eyes diligently on my French textbook. I'll have to figure it out later or risk getting thrown out of French class. Luckily there's only five more minutes before the bell rings.

"What was that all about?" Jenna asks me as we dump our books in our locker before heading to lunch to meet Sawyer. "In French? You looked distracted. See anything weird?" She glances around, searching for something...or someone. "Where'd Lo go? Wasn't he just here a second ago?"

"Bathroom," I say absently. "No, I didn't see anything. I was just wondering how come Lo got transferred. He said it was a mistake."

Jenna shrugs. "They make scheduling errors all the time. Last semester, they had me signed up for advanced chorus. Can you imagine me even holding a tune? Yeah, huge mistake."

In the cafeteria, Sawyer waves to us from an empty table as we get in line to get our food. Seeing him reminds me of another scheduling error that I'd forgotten. "Oh, right, didn't Sawyer get placed in aerobics in sophomore year or something like that?"

Jenna swings around with an exaggerated sigh. "Oh no. He signed up for that one all on his own. I swear to God if he didn't have Adonis abs and the cutest butt I've ever seen, he'd be history."

"You love him," I say with a grin. It's not that Sawyer's not smart. He pulls A's and B's. He just walks to his own beat, and he's more in touch with his feminine side than most boys, which in my eyes is a bonus. And he'd do anything for Jenna. "He's got a good heart and he loves you, and that's all that matters."

"You're right," Jenna says. "And when you're right, you're right."

As if his ears have been burning, the object of our conversation wanders over and hugs Jenna around her middle. "What's taking so long? What are you guys talking about?"

"The hottest guy on the planet," Jenna says with a wink.

"Who? RPattz?"

I snort into my tray. Unable to help myself, I nod with a deadpan expression. "Yeah, sure, we're talking about Robert Pattinson."

"He has cool hair," Sawyer says. As Jenna and I burst into laughter, he shakes his head, eyeing the two of us. "So, no on the hair?" We laugh even harder, so hard that my stomach hurts and tears are leaking from my eyes.

"Give the guy a break, will you?" Lo says, sneaking up behind me, his dark eyes twinkling. "It's not his fault he's a Twi-boy."

"A Twi-what?" Sawyer says, and suddenly wises up to our teasing. "Asshats. That's the last time RPattz and I save a table for you."

Still giggling, I grab my tray to follow them and see Cara sitting with her entourage at her usual table. She's watching us with a strange, half-wistful look on her face and a smile on her lips, but when she sees me looking, she turns away. Rome wasn't built in a day, but it's not like we have a ton of time to play happy families. And she's a key part of what we're trying to do. I head over to her table without a second thought.

"Hey," I say. "You got a sec?"

"Marin, you lost again?" Lila—a self-absorbed, pampered friend of Cara's—snickers. It's obviously a mockery of what Cara had said to me the day before in class.

"I'm talking to Cara, not you," I say. "And lost would imply that I'm where your brain is, so no, not lost."

Lila's face goes puce. "Did you just—"

Jenna materializes at my elbow. "Yep, she totally just called you brainless. Can you handle it? Now scoot, let the big girls talk. Unless of course Cara needs her minions for fetching? Come to think of it, I feel like some dessert. Why don't you be a dear and get us some?"

Lila shoves her chair back. "You're such a bitch, Jenna."

"And you're such a sycophant, Lila," Jenna mimics. "That's a fancy word for minion, by the way. And you should try not to use such big words. You could hurt yourself."

"Jenna," I warn under my breath. She's on fire at the moment. The last thing I want to do is piss Cara off, but when I glance at her, I swear I see a shimmer of amusement in her eyes at the standoff, an emotion that she's quick to mask. She's probably wanted to see someone put Lila in her place for years. "Jenna, just give me a minute, okay? I'll meet you back there." With an odd, blank look, Jenna turns without a word and heads over to our table.

Cara lounges back in her chair. "What do you want, Nerissa?"

"We need to talk." I ignore the collective gasp of the rest of the horde at her table hanging on to our every word.

Cara runs a bored hand through her hair. "Just because we're doing a charity event together doesn't mean I want to spend every waking minute with you."

"Oh, snap," a girl whispers.

Despite a wave of irritation, I understand what she's doing. She's trying to save face with her friends, and while it doesn't matter to me, I realize that it's important to her. "Sure, just let me know when's a good time."

"I'll do that," she says dismissively.

Walking back to my own table where Sawyer and the others are gathered, Jenna studies me furiously over her tray, jabbing food around on her plate like she wants to murder it. "Explain to me why you didn't give her a piece of your mind. Why'd you let her talk to you that way in front of everyone? For God's sake, you're a—"

"Jenna," I cut her off, but it's too late as Sawyer catches on. Lo and Speio pause enough to stop shoveling food into their mouths, and Rian watches the unfolding drama with curious eyes as dead silence settles over the table.

"She's a what?" Sawyer asks.

But Jenna can't answer because I've grabbed her arm and steered her out of the cafeteria to the girls' bathroom across the hall. After checking all the stalls, I bar the door with the garbage can and face off with Jenna. "What is with you? You were fine before in line and then you snapped at Lila like you were going to bite her head off."

"I just don't get it, the whole Cara thing." She stares at me, confusion written all over her face, and something else, too. "Why does she have to be involved? Because of Cano? We can find him without her. We can do the event thing and he'll be there, and it'll be over...." She trails off, staring at the floor.

I hold her shoulders and drag her chin up to face me. "Look at me, Jenna," I say gently. When she does, the misery in her eyes is palpable. "What's this all about?"

"It's nothing," she says, avoiding my stare. "Just having a bad day."

"Don't you lie to me, Jenna Pearce."

"How do you know I'm lying?"

"Because I'm an Aquarathi queen who can sense every emotion running around in you, just from the way your heart pumps blood through your veins and the sounds the water in your body makes. What do you have to say to that?"

"I'm not lying," she insists, although with slightly less bravado.

God, she's stubborn. "Don't make me mind-meld you," I threaten with a smile, remembering how freaked out she'd gotten when I'd done a little brain manipulation with Principal Andrews.

That gets her attention as her eyes snap to mine. "You wouldn't dare."

"I'd dare a lot of things, Jenna. You know that more than anyone," I say. "And if you're not going to tell me what's bugging you, then I'm going to go looking in your brain to find it, and I'm going to poke around and mess around with all your junk, and I'm not going to be responsible for what may happen, whether you suddenly start cross-dressing or talking with a funny accent."

"Okay, stop. I get it." She shakes her head. "You have issues, I hope you know that."

"I do."

Jenna takes a deep breath, as if she wants to get it all out in one go. "I just don't see the point of involving Cara. I mean, I know you needed her to find Cano's house in Imperial Beach, but I can't see why she's still part of everything… with you."

"With *me?*" I say slowly, and then understanding dawns at Jenna's wretched expression. She's jealous. Of Cara. The unflappable, supremely confident Jenna Pearce is worried about Cara Andrews? I want to laugh because it's crazy ridiculous that she could even think that, but I resort to words instead as the dejected look on her face intensifies. "Jenna, you have nothing to worry about with Cara. That girl has nothing on you, and how much you mean to me."

"She used to be your best friend," she says in a small voice.

"*Used to be,* those are the operative words. She's not anymore. And the fact that she's helping in a minute way to shake things up is so minimal that it's not even worth talking about. So get it out of your head right now, do you hear me?"

She sighs. "I'm sorry. It's stupid, I know. I just..."

"You have nothing to be sorry about, Jenna. You never have to hide anything from me, not anything like this. I'd be pretty messed up if your ex–best friend showed up out of the blue, too." I pull her in for a hug. "You're my best friend. Forever. You know things about me that no one—no human—will ever know. You know my secrets, my fears, my hopes...everything. You are the only one who knows it all. Do you understand that?"

"Yes," she sniffles. "I'm sorry I'm so lame."

"Would you stop with the apologizing? It's making me uncomfortable." I grin wickedly. "Almost like you've been mind-melded into this whiny, sniveling version of yourself." I open my eyes wide, holding her at arm's length to study her. "Seriously, *were* you mind-melded? Who are you and what have you done with Jenna Pearce?"

"You're so dumb." Jenna shoves me away, smiling, and wipes her eyes. "And I don't snivel."

"No, you don't," I agree. "So, we good?"

"Yeah."

"You won't throw Cara off a cliff when I'm not looking?"

"I can't promise miracles."

"I can roll with that," I say. "Now let's go finish lunch, because I'm starving, and I don't want to have to eat anyone during English. Joking!" I add hastily at her appalled face. I grin. "I am a humanitarian. Get it? Like a vegetarian?"

Jenna snorts, splashing some cold water on her face at the sink. "That's lame, even for you."

"Got you to smile, didn't I?" I say, handing her a paper towel. "And, Jenna?" She looks up, her face still splotchy and reddened from crying. "You're so much more than a friend to me—I hope you know that. You're not even my best friend."

"I'm not?"

"You're my family," I say quietly. "In this world, they say that blood is thicker than water, and that may be true, but in my world, water is king. I've said it before and I'll say it again. You're an Aquarathi at heart, and no one, not even Cara, can ever take that away from you."

Jenna manages a teary smile. "Will you teach me to mind-meld?"

"Baby steps, youngling. Baby steps."

20

A Queen's Word

Things couldn't be more perfect timing-wise on land. The planning for the Save the Dolphins and Turtles event has been moving along at a great pace. The combination of Rian's posters and great marketing skills with Cara's impressive social network has made the fundraiser go viral. We've had thousands of donations from all kinds of local organizations, as well as a couple of global ones. Kevin at the Marine Center said he hasn't seen this kind of activity, not since the attention surrounding Speio's green-jellyfish harem earlier in the year. Not that Kevin's complaining— the heightened awareness for marine-animal conservancy is phenomenal. He'll be able to do tremendous amounts with the raised funds.

Despite that being the only bit of color in an otherwise dismal landscape, my Queen's Guard have been working around the clock to beef up my security. They've been observing all of Cano's known residences, although there hasn't been any sign of him since Lo and I saw him at the beach. There's no movement at the Imperial Beach house, which means that he's either gone underground or moved his base of operations to yet another secret location. Either way, I can't shake the feeling of impending disaster, especially now that Cano is…no longer Cano.

According to sparse reports from Echlios's men, down in the ocean depths, it's an entirely different story. With rumors of Lo's return, the political climate in Waterfell has degenerated into a creature with an ugly life of its own. From the get-go it seems, Ehmora's old court—the Ruby Court led by Keil—has done everything possible to destabilize my position as their queen, and one by one, the other courts have shifted to their side. Speio was right. There's a culture of fear brewing, and not even ruling by strength—or by blood—can break it. I have no choice but to go back to address the internal threats in Waterfell before we take on Cano.

"Earth to Nerissa," Jenna says, poking me in the ribs.

"What, sorry?"

"I said, how long are you going to be gone for? Back to Waterfell?"

"A few days," I answer distractedly.

Jenna purses her lips, frowning. "So, can this other king, Kyle or whatever, do what he's doing? Destabilize your rule, I mean? I thought you told me that only the true heir can claim the High Court throne, and if there isn't one, then you can have a challenge from the royals of any of the lower courts. Is that right?"

"Yes," I say. "That's correct. And technically, Keil can't challenge me according to our succession laws."

"So he's undermining you to get what he wants."

"Pretty much." Keil is a mastermind, no doubt about that. I'm positive he manipulated Castia into somehow taking the fall for him, so it's no surprise that he is the one at the heart of the insurrection. I shrug and fall back into a Papasan chair tucked in a corner of my room, staring at my replica Waterfell ceiling. "Maybe he's right. I mean, look at me. I've been a queen for six months, and every decision I've made has been wrong. None of them trust me."

"Being a leader isn't about being popular. It's about leading, even if that makes you unpopular," Jenna says. "Martin Luther King once said that a genuine leader doesn't search for consensus. He shapes consensus." She pauses, staring at me. "You were born to lead, Nerissa. It's in your blood. It's in everything you do—down there, up here, out on the hockey field, at the Marine Center, everywhere. You're a leader. You're a *queen*. You've come too far to doubt yourself now."

"How did I get so lucky to have a friend like you?" I say with a wry smile.

To which Jenna shakes her head firmly. "You say that's about luck. It isn't. You draw people to you. You always have, Riss. We're the lucky ones."

Flushing at her quiet praise, I duck my head. "I don't know what I'm doing half the time."

"You don't have to know where you're going every step of the way, or even your destination. Trust in yourself to do what's right and what's needed. You did that last year, didn't you? You fought off a rival queen. You defended your throne. You safeguarded your father's legacy. You made sure *humans* were safe. You did all of that."

I swallow hard. "I had a lot of help."

Jenna crouches down beside me. "That's because we all believe in you, Riss. *I* believe in you. Don't let a bunch of power-hungry idiots make you think otherwise. That's the thing with power, right? Someone less worthy always wants it or thinks they can wield it better."

"This is impossible." Frustrated, I fling myself back into the soft cushion of the chair. "A part of me wants to defend my birthright with everything I have and force them to accept Lo, and the other just wants to let someone more worthy lead the people of Waterfell."

"You'll figure it out." Jenna squeezes my hand sympathetically. "Wish I could come with you."

"Me, too."

Jenna glances at her watch. "Well, call me as soon as you get back. I'm going to go meet Rian at the center to finalize some details for next week. You'll be back in time for that, right? I mean, it'll be moot without you."

"You mean as the bait?" I joke.

"No, dummy," she says. "This is your event. It wouldn't have happened without you, and even if Cano shows up, it's not going to stop something amazing from happening... namely the kind of awareness you're raising for the ocean. The support has been incredible," she says, eyes brightening. "We've raised nearly three hundred and fifty thousand dollars in less than a week, and we're not even done yet. It's as if people were all just waiting to do something. Isn't this what you told me part of your charter here is? To make sure we humans do our part to protect the oceans?"

"Yes."

"See? This is your doing. Even when you don't mean to, you make amazing things happen." She leans over and pulls me in for a heartfelt hug. "Go take care of your business and come back. Whatever you do will be the right choice."

"What if I'm wrong?" I whisper over her shoulder, hugging her back.

She pulls away to look at me, grasping my shoulders and staring me straight in the eye. "There's no right and wrong here, Riss. Don't you get it? It's about choices—meaning one choice determines a specific path, and the other, something different. Neither of them is wrong or right. Just choose, and believe in your choice. Whatever you choose will be worthy."

I force a grin, overwhelmed by Jenna's complete trust in me. "You know, just because I'm a superior alien species doesn't mean I enjoy trippy existential discussions."

"Superior, schmooperior," she snorts, chucking me on the shoulder. "Okay, I really have to go, and so do you. Love you. Be safe, promise?"

"Promise. Love you, too, Jenna."

The courts of Waterfell are wild and uncontained, a violent cacophony of voices echoing along the walls of the gigantic throne room combined with a tornado of impassioned color. We've been here less than a day and already more than half the courts are divided in their allegiance.

All the courts along with the High Council have been convened at my command. It is my duty as queen to hear what the insurgents have to say, and to see that they are given a fair chance to represent their concerns. Fueled largely by venom from the Emerald Court, especially after Queen Castia's imprisonment, those who oppose my rule are vehement in their defiance, and their animosity. They eye me with barely veiled distaste, and Lo with unconcealed rancor. How could I have ever thought they'd accept him just because I do? I flinch at the ugly accusations being thrown my way, and even with Lo standing strong at my side, I'm still vulnerable to their hostile words.

"She brings dishonor to her father's legacy... She will lead us all to nothing but death... Her friendship with the humans is a disgrace... She's bonded to an abomination... She is not fit to lead. She never was..."

The unending vitriol makes me feel like running for cover. Echlios steps forward, his voice booming above all the others. "Enough!" he roars. "You may say your piece, but any such remarks will be considered an act of treason against your queen."

"She is not *my* queen," an old Ruby Court noble says, sneering.

"Then you are free to leave Waterfell," I say, finding a shaky voice and noticing that Keil does nothing to curb the tongues of his court. "The arms of the Pacific Ocean are far-reaching. Exile is a choice open to all."

"You should be the one to be exiled," someone says from the middle of the throng. Silence descends as quickly as death in the room.

"Who dares speak?" Echlios growls in a rage, but I don't have to ask to know. I already know who has spoken, and my heart sinks. The crowd parts as a single Aquarathi steps forward, his face defiant with ferocious scarlet color rippling down his ebony torso.

Nova.

"What are you doing, son?" Echlios says in disbelief. "You are a Queen's Guard."

"First of all, I'm not your son." He sneers, walking forward to join the others at the front. "*Your* son is a weak, spineless, sorry excuse for an Aquarathi."

I spare a glance to Speio, who has gone rigid, his face devoid of any emotion.

"Second, I resign from my post as Queen's Guard. So does my sister."

Nell steps forward to stand at her brother's side with icy black eyes filled with contempt. "We refuse to serve a queen who defiles herself with half-breeds, allows traitors to the crown to go free and fraternizes with humans, flaunting *our* secrets."

The silence in the room erupts into thunder as everyone shouts at once at Nell's stunning admission. I close my eyes with a sigh—my people won't understand what Jenna means to me. I can't glimmer them all as I'd done with my guard to show what she has done for all of us, nor why I chose to disclose the truth of what we are to her. To them, I've broken one of our most stringent laws. Others have been punished for less.

"Tell them, my queen," Nova scoffs, nearly spitting the last word. "Tell them that you showed a feeble human what you are. Tell them that you transformed in front of her. Tell them that you repeatedly break our laws to protect the humans you so love instead of your own people!"

"You're out of line, Nova," Lo says in a deadly voice.

"Ah, look, the half-breed speaks," Nova jeers. "You have no voice here. You are not oceanborn."

"But *I* am," I say. My voice shakes the rock surrounding us. "This was my father's throne." I gesture to Lo. "He is the regent by my choice, and you will bow to him."

"I will not."

"Bow." My voice is terrible, as is the furious power tearing through me like a tsunami. I wrench him down with a flick of my mind, my glimmer twisting into him like a pronged spear. Everyone watches as Nova's neck touches the floor, a keening sound bursting from his lips as I hold him

there with lethal force. Just a little more, and his bones will shatter. My rage is all-consuming, daring me to do just that.

"Nerissa." The word is barely a whisper against the back of my neck from the prince at my side. *Stop this, my love. You're doing what he wants. He wants you to show that you're not in control, especially with me. Release him. It doesn't matter to me what any of them think about me. It only matters what you think. Don't do this in anger—it's something you will regret, and you'll lose the trust of those who still believe you to be the rightful queen. Let him go, Riss.*

With a shattered breath, I dissipate the glimmer and release my iron hold on Nova, who struggles to his feet with the help of his sister. His smile is provoking, and all I want to do is lash out, but I understand that it's emotion—the *human* emotion that Echlios predicted would be my new weakness. I survey the grim faces of my court with Lo's support swirling at my back. There's too much negativity now for me to say anything to defend myself. I have to show them. I have to show them everything.

But I choose to start with words. I raise my voice, reaching every corner. "You believe I'm unfit to lead, when everything I have done has been to protect you. My father was murdered, and I served you his murderer, a queen of the Ruby Court. I battled her on the sands of Waterfell, and I won. She built an army of hybrids to find me on land, and to take Waterfell by force through its sole heir with a hybrid prince of her own. But in the end, he, too, chose me…and chose to defend you and Waterfell against his own mother. You saw this, and that alone deserves your loyalty. Yet the minute you discovered what he is, you turned your backs on him. You deemed him an outcast. Not *oceanborn.*"

I swallow hard. "He may not have been born here, but his heart and allegiance are here, and that should be enough.

"As for the human to whom I've entrusted the secret of our existence without your sanction, it is true. She has seen everything there is to see about who we are." I flick my tail at the sudden twittering, fiery greenish-gold lights illuminating across my brow in warning. "That was my choice, and I stand by it. Without this *feeble* human, you would not have a queen. Or likely a home."

"Lies," someone yells out.

"I have no reason to deceive you," I say. "But if you don't trust my words, then trust what you see. Decide for yourselves."

With a deep breath, I absorb Lo's gently given strength, amassing all of the energy at my core. It may not be enough, but it'll have to do. I close my eyes, only to feel the glimmers of Echlios, Soren and Speio join me, and then the combined strength of the few remaining faithful Queen's Guards who already know the truth. The power rushes out of me like shimmery golden dust, connecting each of the Aquarathi standing before me. As I'd done before with the guards, I show my people exactly what happened and the part Jenna played in all of it.

While connected, I also feel the truth in what Speio said to me about my people's collective fear and insecurity. They're afraid for the future. They're afraid of Lo, and what he means to our existence. Most of all, they fear the humans and what it would mean for them to discover who we are. It'll be Sana—our old, dead planet—once again. Our people coexisted with humanlike creatures once, and they betrayed us and poisoned our planet. Earth has become our home. They can't afford to lose this one, too.

Before I let go of the glimmer, I separate my energy from
Lo and the others behind me and offer it to my people. I fill
it with calm and peace and acceptance. I fill it with forgiveness and hope. I fill it with love, an emotion that many of
them will never know. Sanctum is my gift to them. Afterward, I sag backward, my body nearly colliding with Lo's.
The silence in the great hall is thick and heavy.

"Now you know the truth. Decide if you think my action was unforgivable."

"You value a human more than your own kind." Nova
is the first to speak, his eyes flashing angry black fire at the
lack of response from the rest of the Aquarathi. His rage
makes him immune to reason. "You must pay the price."

"I value her more than most," I agree. "Human or
Aquarathi."

"She is not one of us," he seethes.

"One of *us?*" I ask. "What does that even mean? We live
on this planet together. We *share* it with the humans. At
least one of them is fighting for us—fighting to keep our
waters clean and our home safe. She accepts me for everything that I am without expecting anything in return. Is it
so hard for us to do the same?"

"We can't trust them."

"I can't trust anyone," I say softly. "Not even my own
guard. Not even one bound by a blood oath to defend his
queen. What do you say to that, Nova? What is the price
of such a betrayal?"

"Execution," Verren, the Sapphire Court king, rumbles.

Nova's eyes narrow as if he didn't expect this turn of
events. I can feel his fear rippling through the water. Before anyone can guess what he's about to do, he snarls and
darts toward me with outstretched claws. I prepare to de-

fend myself, but a white-gold shape speeds past me like a bullet to collide head-on with Nova. They both go skidding into the crowd. The silvery Aquarathi is a beastly blur of tail, claws and teeth.

"Is that—" Lo breathes.

"Speio," I say, watching in stupefied silence as Speio nearly rips off half of Nova's jaw. Echlios moves to intervene, but I stop him with a barely audible click. This is Speio's fight to finish.

"I'm not weak, you piece of shit," Speio growls, sitting astride Nova's recoiling body. "The difference between us is that I understand respect, I understand my place and I trust my queen. The truth is, I'd rather be spineless than anything like you. You're a disgrace to the Aquarathi."

Nova bares his teeth in a bloody grin. "If that's so, why do so many of them agree with me? The queen is a fraud who pretends she's human and cares naught for her people. That's why she's with a filthy hybrid."

"Shut up," Speio says, crushing a taloned forearm into Nova's windpipe. "You know nothing."

A blooming wave of chatter makes its way around the room, once more rising to deafening proportions. Jenna's words fill my head, and suddenly I realize what she has been trying to tell me about choices all along. It's not about doing one or the other for the sake of the choice.... It's about doing what's right. And I know what I have to do.

"I am your queen by right and by birth," I begin. "The true heir cannot be challenged for the crown—this is our law, and it is beyond contestation."

I survey my people, sadness swelling inside me at what I'm about to do. My father once told me that part of being a leader is knowing when to withdraw. Perhaps this is what he meant. I address all of the Aquarathi in the room. "However, if you truly cannot accept me as your queen and if it will put all of your fears at rest, I will abdicate my rule to Queen Miral, next in line from the Gold Court."

"My lady," Echlios says swiftly. "No, you cannot. Your father—"

"Told me to be a worthy queen," I say. "If someone else can lead the Aquarathi people better, then I am all for it. This is the right thing to do, Echlios. I told you before. I won't give up Lo, and if the Aquarathi cannot accept me because of it, then so be it. I felt their fear of him. Of me… of what I've become."

"Nerissa," Lo says softly. "I cannot let you do this for me."

I brush his face with mine, wanting to lose myself in him for a moment. "This choice was made the second we bonded. It cannot be undone, nor would I want it to be."

"Then the Aquarathi are fools," Echlios says. "My queen, still, you cannot give up the throne. It is your legacy."

"Echlios, if this is what the people want, I will step aside." I smile a little sadly. "A throne is a thing. My father's legacy is in here." I tap my heart. "Now come, we have worse things to worry about than this." I remember Ehmora's words from my dream several nights ago, and I suppress a shudder. "War is coming."

"But this is our home."

"This will always be your home, Echlios." I meet Lo's melting eyes, the jeweled color of the ocean around us, and smile. "I'd choose a life of exile with Lo over one without him."

"But Waterfell…"

"Will survive. We've survived millennia of change. Whether I am its queen will make little difference. Someone else will rule, and hopefully well. In the end, one cannot fight for something that doesn't want to be won." I stare at my family and my Queen's Guard. "You may all stay here, should you so choose. I release you from your oaths."

But instead of leaving, one by one—Speio, Soren, Echlios, Doras, Mae, Su and Erathion—they each bow to me in front of all the courts of Waterfell, baring their necks to me in undying fealty. "Then we are exiles, too."

"Wait!" someone yells.

I turn as a young male Aquarathi with fiery orange skin and green fins approaches us. Electric green lights shimmer along his body. *Carden. Emerald Court.* Recognition tingles in my mind as he makes himself known to me—the Emerald Court boy who had questioned my rule.

"Weren't you one of the ones who didn't want a queen bonded to a hybrid because he wasn't oceanborn?" I ask mildly.

He bows and I nod for him to speak. "I felt what you made us feel before. Sanctum. I want to come with you."

"You realize you will be considered an exile?"

Carden nods thoughtfully. "I think we should believe in the humans, too. I think without them we have no future. I want to help. I don't want to stay here with my head buried in the sand and do nothing."

"Very well," I say to Doras. "Your replacement for Nova."

My eyes fall on Nova and Nell, still watching me from the sidelines. Jenna was right—there are always those who covet power because they believe that they are more fit to wield it. But power is corrosive, and in the wrong hands, it can only corrupt. I feel sorry for Nova now—sorry for where his choices have taken him.

"Come on," I say with a grim smile. "We're ten Aquarathi strong. Let's go. We have a hybrid army to take down."

21

Catch and No Release

The Marine Center looks like a different place. Multicolored party lights are strung up in the parking lot over various booths with different groups offering contests and games to raise money as well as petitions for safer conservation zones, plastics regulation, world oceans day, seismic testing, oil-spill cleanup, marine pollution and the like. It's amazing and humbling to see all these groups uniting with one common goal—ocean health. Despite the looming threat of Cano, everything has come together without a hitch.

The tanks and pools on the inside are all spotlighted with colored lighting, and the seals and sea lions are shameless, showing off for the public. Even the injured ones are coming out for a peep to see all the people who've come to support them. Dozens of smaller tanks housing rescued or hurt animals have name tags and explanations as to how they came to be at the center. Luca, a shy leatherback turtle, peeks out from his shell. His card reads that he was found with a cracked shell and a broken flipper. With clamps in place helping his bone to heal, Luca is due to be released next spring.

"This is Shaman," one of our guides is explaining to a group of middle school kids on a tour around the glass-enclosed working areas. "He's a six-month-old sea lion. The lacerations on his nose and neck are because he got tangled up in some discarded fishing line, which is why it's so important to keep plastics out of our oceans." The guided tour takes guests through the hospital, research and education wings, as well as to the rehabilitation and release annex.

In the outer section of the center where the saltwater tanks are, the dolphins are the main attraction. Viewable from a platform, another tour guide is telling the story of Sadie and Eragon, two bottle-nosed dolphins who are temporarily living with us. Sadie was attacked by a shark and lost part of her dorsal fin, and Eragon—named by Kevin—was found nearly half-dead with skull damage after a fishing boat collision. Both are well on their way to recovery.

Stooping at the side of a cordoned-off area, I put my hand in the water and pulse softly. Within seconds, the slippery nose of our third resident dolphin butts up against my palm. Margo doesn't like people too much and gets skittish with crowds. Sure enough, she's trembling. I run my hands across her slick rubbery skin around the blowhole, letting my water soothe hers. She, like Shaman, was caught in abandoned fishing debris and had been beached. She was manhandled by a bunch of tourists who were more interested in snapping pictures than helping, and as a result, has a healthy fear of people. I'm the only one she lets close—but then again, I'm not really people.

"Hang in there, Margo," I tell her. "This is all for your benefit. It'll be over soon."

The crowning glory of the event is a massive stage on the neighboring beachside Ellen Browning Scripps Park for later tonight. I have no idea how Cara was able to pull it off, but she managed to get a bunch of popular record- ing artists to do a pro bono concert on crazy short notice, including a British boy band that is apparently an inter- national sensation. Tickets sold out in a matter of minutes once they were posted online. I have to hand it to her—she made this all happen.

"What do you think?" she asks me, putting the finish- ing touches on the some raffle baskets near the entrance.

I shake my head, awed. "How'd you manage to get an event permit application in and approved so quickly from the Parks and Rec Department? And how did you get all these guys to come and perform for free?"

"I have my ways."

"Well, however you did it, it's amazing," I say honestly. "I never expected it to become such a big deal." If it'd been up to me, we'd be having a bake sale along with a few guided tours before having a bonfire on the beach. It wouldn't be an event on this kind of scale with so much media attention.

"Bigger is better," Cara says, tying a bow with a flour- ish. "Especially when it comes to animals. They don't have a voice. I like to give them one. When many people join in, those voices get heard by the people in power who can make things happen."

Suddenly it's like I'm seeing Cara in a new light. I hadn't really given her a chance because of our shaky history after our freshman year, or gotten to know what makes her tick. "That's really cool, Cara. I mean it."

"Thanks." She turns to me, hesitant at first but then more confident at my encouraging look. "You know, that's how Lo and I first met. He was volunteering for a pet-adoption drive for a charity I work with at the cancer hospital. We ended up doing a lot of things like this to raise awareness for abandoned or injured animals," she says with a smile. "I do a lot for the SPCA. Lo leans toward the ocean-conservancy side of things, like you."

Despite the twinge in my stomach at the mention of cancer, I smile back. Cara's mother died from the disease, which put her into foster care—and Cano's hands—for most of her life. "Well, I couldn't have done any of this without you," I say. "So thank you." An odd silence falls between us—not an awkward one, a comfortable one. I reach for one of the unfinished raffle baskets, taking the proverbial olive branch that she extended. "So, do you volunteer a lot?"

"Mostly at the children's cancer hospital. After my mom died, it helped keep me centered. I've always loved animals, but my involvement with that came after the…episode with my uncle that I told you about, especially anything against animal testing. Did you know that ninety percent of testing done on animals fails in humans?" She eyes me, grinning. "I even protested once—it was crazy exhilarating, like we were breaking all these rules. It felt good."

"Better than the time we almost got expelled for going to that rave our freshman year?"

A startled laugh bursts from her mouth. "I totally forgot about that. We were so lucky they didn't kick both of us to the curb. My uncle was so angry that I was tarnishing his pristine reputation, I was grounded for weeks." She stares at me, a smile in her eyes. "But it was worth it, wasn't it?"

"Totally," I snort, giggling.

"What are you two grinning about?" Jenna says, jogging over. "Kevin told me he saw you head over here." Her face is normal, but now that I'm sensitive to how she feels about

Cara, I know it's probably for show. Jenna does a great job of hiding her true feelings when she wants to.

"Grab a basket," I tell her. "Cara and I were talking about a really stupid thing we did freshman year, you know, before you were here to talk some sense into me."

"Oh yeah?" Jenna says, fiddling with one of the baskets. She smiles at Cara. "Everything looks awesome, by the way, Cara. You've really outdone yourself, and made us all look good in the process."

"Thanks," Cara says. "It's kind of my thing. I love charity-event planning. Anyway, that thing we were laughing about? We snuck out to go to a rave. Downtown L.A. By ourselves."

"Not technically by ourselves," I add. "We went with two juniors who got expelled for underage drinking. It was a mess. We were both grounded for ages."

"Wow," Jenna says.

Cara shakes her head at the memory. "In hindsight, we never were really good for each other—we were far too combustible and always trying to outdo the other. Probably better that things worked out the way they did. Otherwise we'd have set the school on fire or something just as idiotic."

"You're probably right," I agree.

She shrugs, looking for me to Jenna. "Not like you two. You guys are like yin and yang."

"Not all the time," I joke, and make a face. "She can be a real beyotch."

"Says queen beyotch herself," Jenna shoots back.

"That's right, minion, and don't you forget it."

Laughing, we finish up the baskets with an interesting dynamic blooming between the three of us—if I have to guess, I'd say it was trust, but I'm way too gun-shy to jump to conclusions after one seemingly normal conversation. Still, I enjoy the easy camaraderie for what it's worth.

"You think he'll come?" Cara asks after a while. "My uncle?"

"I don't know. If his spies are any good, they'll make sure he knows about this."

She frowns. "But why would he want to expose himself if what you're saying is true—about the self-experimentation, I mean?"

"Maybe you're right," I say gently. "He probably won't show."

I exchange a look with Jenna over the top of Cara's head. Cano wouldn't miss this for the world—an event in a public park with lots of people would be the perfect place to make a stand. Unless of course he finds out that I'm no longer the queen of Waterfell. Then again, Cano's vendetta against me is personal. Lo and I cut off his funding by killing Ehmora. We foiled their plans to lead a new generation of hybrids into the world. We hunted him into hiding. Of course he's going to come. Cano has something to prove and an ax to grind.

"Hey, guys!" Sawyer yells out. "Show's about to start, come on!"

Turning around, we wave at him where he's standing with Lo, Speio and Rian. My eyes widen at the packed park grounds, which are literally covered with people waiting for the show to begin. "Seriously, when did they all get here?"

"Some of them have been camped out for hours," Cara says. "I saw these guys at the Garden in New York last summer. They're amazing. It's a global phenomenon."

"Who are they, anyway?" I ask, peering at one of the promotional posters taped to the side of the entry tent. "They look like they're ten."

"Are you serious?" Cara asks. "Do you live under a rock?"

"Kind of," I say with a deadpan expression, and Jenna snorts out loud.

"Am I missing something?"

"Nope, she's just not kidding." Jenna shakes her head, grinning at me. "She totally lives under a rock. You have no idea. This girl knows nothing of pop culture whatsoever. Swimming and hockey, that about sums her up."

"Never heard of the *X-Factor?*" Cara asks in disbelief.

"Don't watch TV." We have one TV in our house that's probably still wrapped up in its box from the store. It's just not part of our world. No electronics are, which is probably why I misplaced my phone. I still haven't found it, come to think of it.

"Wow, that's just wrong," she says as we walk over to join the boys.

"What's wrong?" Lo asks, grabbing me about the waist in a hug.

Something like envy flashes across Cara's eyes, but it's replaced with an overbright smile. "That Nerissa doesn't watch TV."

"I don't, either," Lo says.

Cara shakes her head. "Says the boy who was addicted to *So You Think You Can Dance* all summer." Lo flushes, and we all jump on that bandwagon, poking fun at his expense.

"Show us some of your moves, Lo," Speio teases.

"I'll show you mine if you show me yours," Lo shoots back.

"Dance-off, dance-off, dance-off," Jenna, Cara and I start

chanting, just as the first act comes on the stage and a loud whooping makes its way across the grounds.

"I'll catch you later," Cara whispers to me. "I'll keep my eye out for my uncle, but I really think it's a long shot."

"Where are you going?" I ask, surprised.

"Nowhere, I just thought…" She trails off lamely, and I realize that she's referring to the pairing up of all our friends—me with Lo, Speio and Rian, and Jenna and Sawyer. She's the odd man out.

"Hang on one sec." I disengage myself from Lo and glance over to the beach. I shape a barely audible pulse toward Echlios, who is keeping an eye on me from afar. Despite my recent abdication, he's still taking his royal protection duties very seriously. He eyes me, frowning, and I nod, repeating the request.

"What are you doing?" Cara asks.

I cough loudly. "Nothing, something was in my throat. I was just trying to see if I could see a friend of mine. He's here from out of town."

"Nerissa," Cara says sharply. "You know I'm a big girl, right? And I have a lot of friends of my own. So you don't have to play matchmaker—" Her voice cuts off rapidly as she follows my stare, settling on the tall boy walking briskly in our direction. "Who is *that?*"

I grin at her jaw-dropped expression. The closer he gets, the more her mouth falls open. Stifling a laugh, I have to admit it—Carden looks good in human form. More than good. He's tall and lanky, taller than Lo even, and literally glowing with good health. Jade-green eyes sparkle in his tanned face, and his hair is a deep bronze color. I tried to convince him to leave the orange, but he didn't go for it. Add that to the fact that he's wearing a pair of low-slung jeans, flip-flops and a plain white tee, and he's about as wholesome as you can get. Fresh meat, as they say.

"That's my friend," I say tongue-in-cheek. "The one you don't want to meet. His name is Carden. Want to know more?"

"Is he from here?"

"Nope. He's just visiting. First time to the big city. Feel like showing him around?" I can't resist teasing her just a little. "I mean, unless you have other more important things to do. I thought I saw Lila walk by a few minutes ago."

She glares me into silence just as Carden reaches us and she sticks out her palm with an ear-to-ear smile. He's so tall that she has to arch almost all the way backward to see his face. "Hi, I'm Cara. Nerissa's friend. She's told me so much about you."

"Has she?" Carden says with a smile that could melt the polar icecaps, far less a formerly icy high-school princess. "I'm Carden."

"I know. Our names are really alike," she stammers, at a loss for words, and stares at the ground, blushing furiously.

I can empathize. When Carden first transformed to human form, I honestly could not stop staring for a full minute. Speio had to nudge me and tell me to wipe the drool from my face before Lo saw me, which of course he did. I stood there like a deer in headlights until Echlios of all people cleared his throat. The thing about Aquarathi transformations is that we manipulate our bodies to mimic human form, but our level of physical strength inherently affects human muscle tone. Let's just say that Carden is *incredibly* fit...like chiseled-from-rock fit.

Suffocating a grin at poor Cara's misery, I intervene.

"Cara's the one who organized all this," I say to Carden. "She's the genius mastermind behind it all."

"Well, I wouldn't say that," Cara says with a grateful smile in my direction. "But I am happy with how it all turned out."

"I've never seen anything like it," Carden says.

"Let me show you around."

"Sure."

Watching as Cara takes him under her wing—literally—given how many looks he's getting from guys and girls alike, Jenna nudges me in the ribs. "You need to keep that in the ocean next time, okay? Just fair warning."

"No kidding," I whisper back.

"You know I can hear you," Lo says drily. "Just as long as he keeps his hands off you, I won't have to pulverize him."

I tiptoe to kiss him on the mouth. "You have nothing to worry about. All you have to do is seven thousand crunches a day and you'll be in his league."

"Isn't he supposed to be fourteen?" he grumbles.

"Actually, he just turned seventeen—right in his prime," I tease.

"I used to be seventeen," Speio says, his arm around Rian, who's watching the byplay with curious, if aloof, amusement. "But yeah, not like that. Kid's got forearms bigger than my thighs."

"If you like that kind of thing," Lo says sourly.

"We do," both Jenna and I chorus, before collapsing into hopeless giggles on the grass. Sawyer and Lo shake their heads at each other and leave us to our antics to watch the show. I grab Jenna's hand and squeeze. Despite everything going on beyond the event with Cano and the hybrids, lying there on the soft grass with her, I feel a sense of peace. These are my friends—my family—and this is where I belong.

The show is everything and more than it'd promised to be, with the astounding final act bringing the house down. Who would have thought that five teenage boys could create such a frenzy of frazzled teenagers? Out of the corner of my eye, I notice Madame Dumois—my AP French teacher—also enjoying the performance. I grin to myself and poke Lo in the ribs, jerking my head in her direction. Maybe not just for teenagers, then. I have to admit that the band isn't bad. Their songs are catchy, and they are adorable.

"Next time we get Calvin Harris," I say to Lo. "Or M83."

He gives me an enthusiastic thumbs-up. "Sounds good to me. Want a bottle of water? I'm going to get us a couple. Don't move," he says, taking my mouth in a hard kiss that leaves me breathless.

At the closing of the final act, Rian walks over to where Jenna and I are prancing around together, her glossy auburn hair falling like a curtain across her face. Her green eyes are intense, observing us for a long moment before she says anything.

I clear my throat, slightly discomfited. "So, did you like the show? You did a great job with the posters, Rian."

"I did, and thank you. It was a lot of fun. Thanks for letting me be a part of this," she says. "It's been interesting."

"What has?" I ask, struck by her odd choice of words.

"This." She waves a hand, encompassing all of us. "Your social dynamic…watching Speio with his friends, and you with yours. I've never had many friends, so thank you for including me."

"You're with Speio, right?" I ask her. "I mean, you guys are together, so of course you're going to be included."

Rian smiles a small, tight smile that makes a weird knot form in my belly. "You could say that. We're having fun. I have plans, and college, and he may not be on the same page as I am."

"Same page?"

"Future things," she says.

"Oh."

"Hey, babe," Speio says, whirling Rian into a slow spin. "Come over here."

I watch them, frowning, as they dance together. I never noticed it before, but Rian carries herself very rigidly. There's no slouch in her spine whatsoever. Every step she makes is precise and calculated, even when she's supposed to be dancing. I never noticed that about her before.

"What's wrong?" Jenna says, following my gaze.

"Ever notice anything weird about her?"

"Who? Rian?" Jenna says. I nod. "Like what?"

"Just how she moves. It's all very perfect. Everything about her is just so, like she thinks about it half a second before she does it. Soren's been trying for years to get me to walk like I have a rod up my butt."

"Nice mental image," Jenna snorts. Studying the object of our discussion, she tilts her head to the side and purses her lips, before leaning in to whisper in my ear. "I see what you mean. She checked out, right? Pure human?"

"Yes." But we've been wrong before. Still, she doesn't smell like a hybrid. She doesn't smell like anything. Maybe I'm just overreacting because she's about to break up with Speio, and because I'm paranoid about Cano.

"Maybe she did ballet," Jenna suggests. "Ballerinas all

walk like that, as if there are invisible strings holding them up."

"Maybe," I say. "I think she's going to dump Speio."

Jenna shrugs as if she's not surprised. "I didn't see it from the beginning. They just didn't mesh to me—I mean, she's driven and superaggressive. She just didn't seem like Speio's type, but I figured after he dated Cara last year that maybe he liked those kinds of girls." As if she could feel us staring, Rian turns her green gaze in our direction—an odd, assessing look—before Speio twirls her off in the opposite direction. Jenna and I blink at each other. "Maybe it's a culture thing?" Jenna offers.

"Could be," I say. "I hope Speio'll be okay. He really likes her."

"He's a big boy, Riss. I'm sure he can take care of himself, especially when it comes to girls."

"You're probably right."

"Now, if you'll excuse me..." She grins. "It appears I have a date with destiny." Jenna shrieks as Sawyer picks her up, spinning her around in the air. She slides down his shoulders and throws her arms around him. A fond smile flutters over my lips. When those two dance, it's natural and effortless. There's no pretense, just love.

"What's that smile for?" Lo says, returning to hand me a bottle of water and nuzzle my neck.

"Just watching them," I say, nodding at Sawyer and Jenna, swaying to the music. "Did you have a good time? What'd you think?"

"This event was amazing, Riss."

"I had help. It was mostly all Cara." I glance around. "Where is she, anyway? Have you seen her?"

"Not since she took off with Adonis at the end of the third act."

"I hope she's gentle." I giggle at the thought.

"Speaking of…want to take a walk down to the beach?" Lo says against my neck. The look in his eyes makes my knees feel like rubber. I can only nod and thread my fingers into his.

We walk past Echlios and Soren, who both nod when I explain where we're going. There's been no sign of Cano, so maybe Cara was right after all, but that doesn't mean that either of them will let their guards down. With Doras and Echlios on watch, we'll have plenty of warning if Cano does make an appearance. They've glimmered the perimeter of the Marine Center and the park—there's no way any hybrid can cross it without us knowing.

Down on the sand, it looks like a lot of couples have the same idea we do, and the beach is crowded with people strolling around or sitting on blankets. Lo and I walk until we find a fairly quiet spot, and I kick off my sandals and dig my feet into the crumbly sand. I lean back against him and sigh. The moon is almost full and rising into a brilliantly starred sky. Waves break gently in the distance, their foamy silvery peaks like glittering snowcaps in the darkness.

"What are you thinking?" Lo says, his husky voice making my pulse leap.

"About Waterfell."

"It's normal to miss it, Riss."

I twist my head against his chest so that I'm looking up at him. "That's just it. I don't miss it at all. It's like I'm meant to be here…with you."

I trace the curve of his cheek with a finger, down to his mouth, letting it linger on his lips before tugging his face down to mine. The kiss is tentative, our mouths barely touching, as if it's made of something so fragile neither of us wants to break it.

"I love you," Lo's lips whisper against mine.

It's a human expression, but the underlying tenor of his words makes my heart race and my bones feel liquid. My hands slide into the softness of his hair and down the nape of his neck as I slide my mouth across his cheek to his temple and press a kiss there. In turn, his lips and tongue trace the column of my exposed neck, making my skin tingle and a slow burn ignite in my chest. If he keeps going, I'm not going to be able to control myself. The last thing anyone needs is another light show—and one that defies explanation.

I groan and disentangle myself. "We are so not making out on a public beach. I can't think when you're doing that."

"When I'm doing what?" he says, sliding his hands up my rib cage.

I swat his hand away with a shiver. "You know exactly what."

"Sorry, can't help myself. You're irresistible."

Despite my wanting to fling myself back into his embrace at his words, we sit in quiet silence for a while, staring out at the ocean. I close my eyes for a second when something delicate and wet flutters against my neck.

"Stop that," I tell him. "I'm serious, Lo. Glimmering is the same as touching, probably worse."

"Stop what? I didn't do anything," he protests. I sit up straight, my senses going into sudden overdrive as the feathery sensation envelops my entire body before evolving into something unrecognizable. Shivers—not the good kind—race over every inch of my skin and my blood crawls with the foul force of it. "What's the matter, Riss?" Lo says in alarm.

"Get it off!"

"Get what off?" Lo says, looking at me wildly.

"Can't you sense it?" I say, my entire body shuddering as Soren and Echlios race down the beach toward us. I stand, dragging Lo with me and clawing at my arms. "It's all over me, scuttling under my skin like a thousand spiders. Can't you feel it?"

"What is? Riss, you're scaring the hell out of me."

"*Them*. They're everywhere!"

22
Second Chances

"Get these people off the beach," Echlios commands in a brusque voice to a police officer, who snaps to immediate attention. "Doras, shield. Now."

Within seconds, Doras and the other guards join us, folding Lo and me into a protective circle. Miraculously, the cop and the beach patrol take charge of the situation and manage to disperse the remaining stragglers trying to get a glimpse of the crazy girl scratching at herself. I huddle down, my skin pulling tight.

"Riss!" Jenna shouts, plowing through. "Is she all right?"

"She's okay," I hear Lo say.

"What happened?"

"She said they're here," he says. "The hybrids. But I didn't feel anything. I think it was only her."

"Why would they single her out?" Jenna blurts out. Her eyes widen. "Oh."

"It's a message," Soren says quietly. I can feel her kneeling next to me, running her fingers tenderly along the foot-long claw marks on my arms before wrapping them in gauze. "He wanted her to know that they were watching all along. That we aren't alone." She pauses with a grim look to Echlios. "That we can't protect her."

"What did he do, exactly?" Jenna asks, staring nervously out into the expansive ocean as she's expecting Cano himself to emerge like a giant beast.

"A glimmer."

I find my voice, shaky and uneven, to answer her. "No, it wasn't a full glimmer. It was something else. I sensed the essence of the hybrids, and the minute I reacted to them, it was like he swooped in. It felt like a million spiders crawling along my veins with knives for legs piercing into me."

Jenna shivers, clutching her arms. "That sounds horrible."

"But that's impossible," Soren says, frowning. "Humans can't...they don't..."

"He synthesized my DNA," Lo offers. "Nerissa and I are bonded. We don't know what he can do now." He glances at me. "Obviously he can get to her and hurt her without any of us the wiser for it."

Echlios kneels down. "Did he communicate anything to you?"

"Nothing," I say. "It was gone before I could even reach back out. I mean, it caught me by surprise. It was nothing like I've ever felt and by the time I realized that it was all in my head, it was gone."

"Hey, Nerissa!" someone shouts. It's Cara running down the beach with Carden in tow, followed closely by Speio and Rian. They'd both been warned to keep the girls away the minute the attack happened, but when Cara gets something in her head, nothing but a tornado will stop her.

"Fell on some broken glass," I improvise as she reaches us, gasping for breath. I force a weak grin. "What's a party without a little blood, right?"

"That's only a little morbid," she says. Her eyes rove around the faces surrounding us. "Glad to see your parents are here. They should probably get you home. Don't worry about wrapping up here. I'll take care of it."

"Carden," I say. "Make sure she gets home safely."

He starts to bow and then checks himself at a warning glare from Echlios. "It would be my pleasure."

We hobble to the car and Speio announces that he and Rian are going to help Carden and Cara before he takes her home. "Hang in there," he says to me with forced cheer and a quick hug.

"Hope you feel better," Rian says.

Without thinking, I hug her, too. It's the first time we've ever touched. I don't know if I'm still sensitive from what happened with Cano's hybrid glimmer on the beach, but a shudder of something formidable ripples through me at the brief contact of skin on skin. I meet her eyes for a brief second, and what I see there makes the breath hitch in my chest—she *knows*. She knows that there's something different about us, that we aren't quite who we say we are. Someone who studies human relationships that closely would notice little things that would separate us, mark us apart.

Great, this is all I need on top of everything. We'd be the perfect study to an overzealous student looking to make a splash in the anthropology world. I make a mental note to speak to Speio about it, and see if he's inadvertently revealed anything about himself to her. Maybe that's why she seemed different tonight—more detached. Living on land brought with it so many prying eyes and unnecessary complications. I sigh and rub my temples.

"What's wrong?" Lo says, climbing into the car beside me.

"Nothing. Inventing things."

"Like what?" he says. "Tell me."

"I get the feeling Rian knows more than she's letting on. About us," I add, and then shrug tiredly at his skeptical expression. "Just the way she looked at me before. I know it sounds weird."

"A little," Lo says, replacing my fingers with his and gently massaging the aching areas near my temple. "You've had a bit of a shock. I mean, think about it—nothing she could ever imagine in her wildest dreams would be close to the truth. She studies human patterns, and we are so far outside that it's not even funny. I wouldn't worry about what you think you saw. There's no way that Rian could even suspect what we are, unless she was shown, and we both know that Speio would never go against you." Lo brushes some loose strands of hair out of my eyes, his voice soothing and nearly lulling me to sleep. "Plus, what's the worst that could happen? She tells everyone her boyfriend is an alien? Yeah, that'd go over well."

"Good point," I say, and lean against his warm shoulder, closing my eyes. "Maybe she thinks we're a modern cult or something."

By the time we arrive back at my house, I've drooled all over Lo's shirt. I blink as strong arms lift my body and carry me around the side of the house to the pool. Soft lips kiss me awake. "Wake up," Lo's mouth murmurs against mine. "Time for a dip." He removes my clothing, like a parent would a child, and lowers me into the warm salt water, before undressing and joining me there.

"Where are the others?" I ask.

"Soren's inside. Speio and Carden are still at the Marine Center. Echlios and the rest of the guards are securing the perimeter." He smiles at me, stroking the side of my face.

"Good, you're less pale. Let's have a look at your arms." Gently unwrapping the layers of gauze, he smiles and lifts my palm to his mouth. "Already healing. You really did a number on yourself back there."

"It was awful," I confess. "That feeling. I wanted to peel my skin off my own bones."

"I'm sorry," Lo says with a kiss to my bare shoulder that makes me shiver. "The silver lining is that you'll be able to brace against it, know what to look for if he tries it again."

"He won't try it again."

"How do you know?"

"I just do." I stare at him. "It was a onetime thing."

I don't tell Lo how much the sensation had initially felt like his own glimmer—the feartherlight intimate sensation of him—just before it'd became warped into something dark and ugly. Cano knew exactly how to distort and taint it—how to twist what I feel for Lo into something monstrous. A tremor rips through me at the visceral memory.

"You're safe now," Lo says, correctly reading my expression and slipping his hands about my waist. "You're home, and Echlios has got it covered. Just try to forget it. The more power you give it, the more it'll have over you, and that's what he wants."

I wrap my arms around Lo's shoulders, ignoring the immediate wave of revulsion at the feel of his glimmer swirling around me. "I know exactly what he wants." I kiss Lo's warm, salty lips, feeling his waters surge against my body. "He wants me to hate your touch...to revile it."

"How?" Lo's eyes widen with horror as understanding dawns when I release my glimmer to him, letting him experience what I feel. "Oh."

"Help me forget," I tell him, pulling his head to mine in

a frantic openmouthed kiss and submerging us both beneath the surface. Despite what Cano tried to do, I open myself to Lo completely, our glimmers merging via the bond between us. *Help me forget what it felt like. Bring me back to you.*

Several hours later, something jolts me awake in my bed, but the house is quiet. It must have been a dream. I turn on my side to stare at the boy lying beside me, the blue sheet tangled between his lean limbs. Lo's face is peaceful in sleep, the sandy winged eyebrows relaxed and his mouth slightly open. His silvery-blond hair falls over his brow. He'd done exactly as I'd asked—made me forget Cano's filthy touch— and had completely eviscerated even the memory of it.

Cano wanted to punish me…show me that he could take something from me, just as I'd taken something from him. But it was just like him to make his payback so insidious. I hope the false glimmer took its toll on him—wreaked havoc on his pitiful human body. It would have, too. Human bodies aren't meant to withstand what we Aquarathi can do, which is why our glimmers are always stronger in our true form. I can only hope that the cost to him was great.

Lying on my back, I stare at the ceiling, unable to sleep. Something tugs at me again—nonthreatening. It's more of a plea than a summons. Slightly apprehensive, I pull on a T-shirt and a pair of shorts before walking out onto the patio. The moon is high in the dark, cloudy sky, and the air, balmy. The ocean is whispering to me on the breeze. Pushing out a brief glimmer, I confirm that the beach is clear before walking down to the water's edge. The sea is choppy, waves splashing against my feet in an angry staccato. I sit in the shallows, enjoying the rise and fall of the tide.

"You shouldn't have come alone."

I don't look up. "I knew you would be here."

Neriah emerges from the darkness of the waves, her body transforming with each step. She sits beside me on the sand, smelling of salt and seaweed. A slight sour odor wafts past my nostrils, but I can't pinpoint what it is. She doesn't say anything, but I can feel the power swirling around her in waves. Her face is serene and calm, her eyes glittering in the shadowy light.

"Why do you serve him?" I ask quietly.

She laughs. "Is that what you think? That I serve Cano? A human?"

The way she says it surprises me, almost as if I've disappointed her with the question. "Don't you?"

"Hardly," she says. "He's a scientist with a larger-than-normal ego who has access to all of my research. If I were to challenge him, he'd disappear with everything we've shared with him, and who knows what he'd do then? Wasn't it you who said that you like to keep your enemies close?"

"So kill him," I say bluntly. "It's not like you haven't killed anyone before."

"Contrary to what you may have been led to believe about me, I have never killed another Aquarathi," she says. "Is that who you really think I am?"

"I don't know what to think."

"Have a little faith."

"In you?" I scoff. "That's a little too much to ask, don't you think?"

"Nerissa," she says, her voice even. "Look beyond what you see. I've always taught you that, even as a child. Look past what is right in front of you, and trust yourself. Where do you think you get that? That ability to see into someone—to see the potential in them? Not from your father…you get that from me."

"You tried to kill me."

"I tried to save you," she counters.

"You were with *her*. Ehmora."

I can feel the weight of her stare in the gloomy darkness. "That doesn't mean I wasn't with you. I've always been with you."

This time, I meet her eyes in incredulous silence. "You gave up on me. You left me alone in a kingdom of strangers. You bonded me to the hybrid son of your lover."

"Ehmora wanted to kill you. What would you have had me do? Serve you up on a platter?"

"You kind of did," I argue.

"Nerissa, I tried to release you from her son's bond," she says gently. "And you didn't want to let him go, and with full knowledge of who he is, you accepted him as your regent."

I dig my toes into the sand. "Well, it's a moot point now. I'm no longer queen. But I'm sure you know that already."

My mother doesn't immediately respond to my bombshell. Instead she just sits quietly beside me, staring at the breaking waves. "You can't just stop being who you are—you should know that by now."

"Someone else will be king or queen now," I say. "The Aquarathi will be better off without me."

"Do you really believe that?"

"Yes." I stare at her perfectly carved profile. "Say it," I tell her. "Say what you're thinking…that I am a fool for giving up my crown."

A smile curves the end of her mouth. "I wasn't going to say that at all. In fact, I was going to say that walking away must have taken a lot of courage. Not everyone is willing to give up that much power."

I exhale slowly. "They couldn't accept Lo as I did. He was too different. In their world, he was the alien."

"So you gave it all up for him."

"I told you," I say. "I love him...as the humans do. It's not just about the bond for us. There is no part of the earth that is deep enough to match the depths of my feeling for him. And maybe you think that I'm foolish or that human emotions are weak..." I trail off. "But the truth is, when I'm with him, I feel far from weak. I feel...invincible."

I don't know why I'm telling her all this, but it feels good to talk to someone. Even if it's her. Or maybe I'm talking to her because I want to know why she's really here, and why she's pretending to care after so many years. "Why'd you do it?" I ask her. "Why did you let me save Lo back at Cano's house? Why did you let me...hurt you?"

"You didn't hurt me, my darling. It is more than I deserve."

I turn to face her, my frustration evident. "Seriously, what is with you and all of your cryptic comments? Can't you just say what you mean for once? If I ask you a straight question, can you give me a straight answer?"

"Ask what you will," she says with another of those annoyingly knowing half smiles, as if she can see right through me and all my bravado. The smile is erased by a slight grimace as she readjusts her position on the sand. "The reason I let you fight, encouraged you even, is that the attack had to look real for Cano. I couldn't exactly let you have the prince without so much as a scratch for your efforts."

Her revelation makes something strange flutter in my chest. "Why did you help Ehmora develop the hybrids?"

"They are the future," she says simply. "We have to evolve to survive. Sooner or later the day will come when the humans discover our home, and what will we do then?"

"So you don't want to take over the human race?"

"No," she says. "My research was meant to provide alternative survival options to our people." She takes a breath as if she's unsure of whether to continue. "Once her son was born, Ehmora became consumed with a quest for power. Lotharius was the perfect hybrid, and she wanted him to become king of Waterfell. She murdered your father and claimed the throne in his stead. He was meant to challenge you—and kill you—for the crown when he came of age. I was the one who suggested you be paired together to avoid all-out war." She smiles. "Then Lotharius ended up being prey to those very emotions you speak about and, as the humans say, fell in love with you. It was not what we'd planned." She trails off again, staring out to sea. "I didn't expect Lo to do what he did. He must hold you in high regard."

"Don't expect me to feel sorry for her," I snap. "She was insane. She tried to kill me. I offered her leniency and she refused."

"Thank you for that," she says, a spasm of something— discomfort—shimmering over her face before she breathes it away.

"Do you miss her?" I don't know where the question comes from or why I ask it. Or why I should care whether she misses her or not, but the minute it's out of my mouth, I wish I could take it back. The moon disappears behind a batch of clouds, shrouding the beach in darkness. I flip the human covering off my eyes and lean back on my elbows, watching her. She doesn't answer, not at first.

"Yes," she says. "And no. In the end, Lo did her a favor, really. She had changed, morphed into someone I could hardly recognize." Her voice grows nostalgic. "We were so young and idealistic when we met. We wanted to shape the world—*be* something. Our research would bring us into a new age. But of course, those were dreams. The reality became something far different."

"Because of Cano?"

"Because of many things. People make choices for the greater good, not really knowing what that entails…the sacrifice involved. You, especially."

"Me?" I ask, not connecting the dots.

"Your father did well with you." She smiles fondly. "Despite the terror that you were." I glance at her sharply and her smile widens. "Oh, I kept tabs on you and all your antics over the years. Soren," she adds at my frown.

"Soren," I gasp. "You hate Soren."

"So it would seem."

I ask the question that has been burning a hole in my chest through all the years, through all the loss, through all of it. "Why…did you leave me behind?"

"I could have taken you with me," she says. "But a child on the run, in exile? It wasn't a life I wanted for you. You would have become twisted, as I am."

I frown. "Twisted?"

"The humans. Their energies leach into us, no matter how much we try to stay disconnected. Their desires are so all-consuming that they start to consume you, too." Her voice fades to next to nothing. "Before you know it, you're on a path you don't really want to be on, and you've lost everything that ever meant something."

"Is that why you're helping me now?" I ask.

"No," she says. "It's not the only reason."

"Then, why?"

"I once told you we don't know how to love," she says, turning to me and grimacing. She clutches her side and groans. The same sour smell from earlier rises on the night air.

"What's wrong?"

"I'm fine." She holds up a hand in midair. "Let me finish what I started to say. I don't have much time. We Aquarathi do know love. Only for us, there's no name for it," she says. I frown again, confused. She lets her hand flutter downward, toward the side of my face where she tucks my hair behind my ear. I hold my breath at her gentle touch, her fingers lingering on my cheek for half a second. "When you have your own child one day, you will know what it is to *love* someone with every single drop of water in you. You will learn what it's like the moment that your heart starts living and beating outside your body." She closes her eyes and swallows, obviously in some kind of pain. "*You* are my heart."

My mother doesn't open her eyes after she murmurs those last words, and I am frozen, mute. Her head slumps forward and I scramble to my knees. "Mom?" I say, clutching her shoulders. "What's going on?"

Her eyes flutter open, brilliant like mine, her chest heaving with the effort. "Biotoxin. Lethal dose."

"Lethal?" I repeat in a disbelieving whisper. "But it can't hurt us."

"Reengineered with sea-snake venom." She inhales a labored breath. "Prototype. Effective to paralyze in small doses, lethal in larger ones, especially to…Aquarathi."

"*What?* How?"

"Cano," she breathes. "Smarter than I thought."

"We can get the serum."

Her smile is sad. "It's far too late for that. I destroyed the whole lab and everything in it." She pauses, swallowing painfully. "I hid some extra vials of serum in my house, but it's too far."

"But you swam here. You managed to get away from him. Why didn't you get it before you came here?"

"Didn't want to risk it. I wanted to get here before..." She heaves a breath into her lungs. "I had a choice—you or...the serum. Couldn't do both in time."

I am reeling. "Let's go now. We can get there and back." I jump to my feet, still holding on to her arms.

"Too...late." My mother slumps against me, forcing us both back to the sand, the foul smell of the poison rotting her body from the inside out curling around us. "I destroyed the lab, but he will create more. You will be defenseless against it. Go..." A bubble of saliva foams at the corner of her mouth. "To my house...Ehmora's house. Look for a case...bed wall panel...silver *BT9*...use it."

I form a desperate glimmer and engage Sanctum, forcing my strength into her. "Wait. You can't go. Not now," I whisper.

"Already dying," she says, her voice a shade stronger, but not much. "Sanctum won't work, but thank you." She leans her forehead onto mine, opening herself so that we are connected. Though her body is degenerating faster than she or I can repair it, her glimmer is as powerful as ever. "You are a far worthier queen than I ever was. I am so proud of you, so proud of the leader you have become. There's so much I want to say to you...so much you need to know...but not enough time." My mother places her hand against my chest over my heart. She meets my eyes with fierce spirit, a shimmer of what she once was. "This is what I came here for... Aivana, my gift to you."

A rush of raw power fills my body as it leaves hers. It's the only thing that is sustaining her dying body. I gasp against the sheer force of it, filling me like light.

"What are you doing?" I cry, trying to push her hands away. "No!"

"My water is yours," she murmurs, restraining me gently with the last of her fading strength. "You will need it for what's coming. Keep the hybrid prince near. You need him, too, more than you know."

"Wait? What's coming? Cano?"

"Worse," she whispers. "Much worse."

"What?" I say, terrified. "Mom, what's coming?"

In her final breath, my mother exhales a single word that makes my blood run cold. "Others...."

23
Vendetta

"I'm so sorry, Riss," Lo is saying. I've just finished telling them what had happened on the beach. Lo's voice comes to me like an echo from somewhere far away, as if he isn't sitting right in front of me and holding my numb fingers. I nod automatically, my eyes wandering from face to face, the ache in my chest growing deeper by the minute. I'd held my dead mother in my arms, only releasing her back to the ocean when first light crept across the sky. That was where Echlios found me in the earlier hours of the dawn, tortured and weeping, ankle-deep in a thrashing ocean beneath storm-tossed skies.

I raise burning eyes to Soren. "She said she didn't hate you."

"No, she didn't," she agrees softly. "She entrusted you to me."

"So what was that all about, that time when I summoned her back on the beach? You were nearly at each other's throats. I didn't imagine that."

"You didn't. Your mother changed over the years. When she made me swear a blood oath to protect you with my life, I took—and still take—that oath very seriously. Even if it meant protecting you from her. She didn't like that."

"She respected you for doing it," I say.

"Thank you, my queen."

"Soren," I remind her, rubbing my eyes of any remaining sleep. "I'm not a queen anymore, remember?"

"As you say."

I lean back in my chair and cross my arms, watching each of them in turn—my only remaining Aquarathi family. "There's something else. At the end, before she died, she performed Aivana."

Dead silence descends—no one even breathes. Some Aquarathi kings and queens prefer to die with their power. To others, it is lost before it can be given, as had happened with my father. However, it is a power that can never be taken by force—it must be willed to the recipient.

Just as Neriah willed hers to me.

I clear my throat. "I have to go to Ehmora's house to get something that my mother left," I say into the void of speechless stares. "In Rancho Santa Fe."

"What are the 'others' she said are coming?" Carden ventures.

"We have to assume an army of hybrids that Cano has created in his own image. Meaning tens if not hundreds like him. With Lo's blood."

"Oh."

"And he's concocted a prototype biotoxin that can kill us, which means we have to find him before he can mass-produce it, and kill him first."

"How?" Carden stammers, shaken by the unveiled anger in my tone.

"I summon him."

"But he's a hybrid," Speio interjects.

"No," I clarify. "He's a human playing God with Aquarathi DNA. Lo's DNA, to be specific. And I'm hoping that because Lo is bound to me, he will be, as well. And then I'll kill him."

I can see the concerned looks on Soren's and Echlios's faces, but I don't care. I've never wanted anyone dead more. Killing Cano will be getting rid of scum that no one will miss. And since I'm no longer a queen, I don't have to answer to anyone—far less a group of Aquarathi who willingly exiled me.

I stand. "Are you coming?" I growl to Lo.

"Yes."

"Nerissa—" Echlios begins, and breaks off at the icy glare I turn on him. He sighs. He's been down this road with me too many times. "Be careful. Take Speio with you."

"I think they should go alone," he mutters. "Less conspicuous." My eyes flick to his. Since when does Speio *not* want to jump on the bandwagon? I shrug because he's right. It will be less noticeable with Lo and me.

"You okay?" I ask Speio as I walk past him on the way to get my car keys.

"Yes," he says, and then opens and shuts his mouth as if he wants to say more and doesn't.

I remain mostly silent on the drive up to Rancho Santa Fe, even though I can feel Lo's occasional glances. When we get to the gated security entrance, Lo shows them his ID and they let us through. Luckily the house is still in his last name and hasn't yet been sold, though it's been on the market for months.

"You know what you're looking for?" Lo asks me.

"Where's the bedroom? Your mother's?" *My mother's.*

"Up here," he says.

I follow Lo up a wide staircase covered in plush carpeting to the master bedroom at the top of the stairs. Everything in the house has been repainted and staged to sell, but I can still feel the remnants of them here in this room. Looking around the elegantly decorated room, I suspect that a lot of the furniture belonged to his mother. And mine.

I take a shaky breath. "She mentioned a bed panel."

Lo nods at the intricate paneling of the bed's headboard. "That's the only paneling in this room. There's got to be a secret alcove behind one of them. Come on, you take that side, and I'll take this one."

Together we press against each of the panels and meet in the middle. There's one more right at the top of the center of the headboard. That has to be it. I press the smooth wood and it slides inward, revealing a tiny alcove. In it are four cylindrical tubes filled with different-colored liquids as well as a thumb drive on a lanyard.

"Are those...?" Lo breathes.

"Biotoxin serums," I say. "One human, one Aquarathi, and the cure for each. She was clever, stowing these away. She probably guessed that Cano was going to turn on her. Too bad she didn't have it close by when he did." I grab hold of the lanyard. "What's on this do you think?"

"No idea, but my laptop's in my car."

We leave the house as quietly as we entered it and head back to Lo's car. With bated breath, we plug in the device and wait as a folder opens up on the laptop. There are two internal folders within the main drive—one marked *Cano* and the other marked *Nerissa*. Lo shoots me a questioning look, his fingers hovering over the touchpad on the laptop.

"Click on the Cano one," I say, swallowing past the

burgeoning lump in my throat. He does, and a list of files pops up.

Lo scrolls through them, his eyes widening. "Are you seeing this?" he asks incredulously. "Names, addresses, labs, plane tickets, hotels, meetings, you name it, it's here. About five years' worth."

"She's been tracking him," I say slowly as the magnitude of what she's given us starts to sink in. "Open that one," I say, pointing to a file marked *San Diego*. "It's a map of all his properties. See the *X*'s?" I jab at the screen. "There's the Sierra house, the apartment in La Jolla and the ones in Imperial Beach. Two of those are marked in red—I'll bet anything they're the ones with the labs."

"You know what this means, right?" Lo meets my heated gaze. "With this, we can destroy all of them."

"Yeah." Placing my hand over his on the touchpad, I move the cursor to the file marked *Travel* and click on it. "He's been all over the world with a lot of recent trips to New York. Wonder what's there."

"Any maps on New York?"

I look through the list. "No."

"Then it's probably nothing," Lo says. I want to say that with Cano there's always something, but it's not like I have much else but a gut feeling to go on. Lo glances at me. "You want to see what's in the other file?"

The one marked with my name.

"Sure," I say, but my voice breaks a bit. Lo opens the file and all I can do is stare, my jaw hanging open. Dated folders going back almost six years are filled with photographs—me here in California, my first day at Dover, pictures with Jenna, playing hockey, sitting on the grass studying, surfing, pictures with Speio and Soren and Lo. I look so happy in all of them, nearly always smiling. One with Lo catches my eye and I blush. I'm sitting in the courtyard at Dover, an open book in my lap, and I'm staring at a boy you can just see at the corner of the photo. The picture is in profile and the look on my face is wistful and filled with longing. The camera somehow managed to catch the faint shimmer of something golden and bioluminescent on my cheek. Of course she knew how I felt about him—she captured it right here in shades of vibrant color.

"She must have been keeping tabs on you, too," Lo says, making me jump. I close the file and exit out of the drive in a hurry.

"Yeah," I say, but I can hardly get the word out, my throat is so choked. I put the lanyard around my neck and tuck it into my shirt. "Let's go back to your place. I want to do the summons on the beach, where it'll be the most powerful."

Lo shoots me a look as if he isn't too sure about the summons, but he just nods. "All right."

The drive to Lo's house in La Jolla seems endless, with the disk drive and all its contents burning a hole in my chest. I can't stop thinking about the fact that Neriah had watched me for so long. It didn't even bother me that she'd had someone following me to take the photos. I'm sure that she'd probably gotten some of them, like the ones of me at the pool in our house, from Soren herself. It makes me feel sorry that she'd had a relationship with me through the detached lenses of a camera for so long. If only she had come to me earlier…maybe things could have been different. Or maybe, they'd be the same. I sigh. Martyrizing her won't make her choices with Ehmora any less real or horrible. Still, I can't believe how much it hurts.

"Are you okay?"

"Fine," I say, and then take a breath. It's Lo after all. "It's hard to have something that you've always wanted last for five minutes before it's taken from you. Or to realize that you may have been wrong about someone all along."

Lo smile is sympathetic as he pulls into his driveway. "At least you know she was thinking about you."

"I guess."

We don't go inside, although we both wave at Grayer and Bertha, Lo's solemn staff, before walking down to the quiet, semiprivate stretch of beach that's in front of the house. "You sure you want to do this?" Lo asks.

"I've never been more sure of anything in my life." I can feel my mother's energy swirling inside me, merging with mine as I form the summons. I tie it in to the glimmer I felt from Cano the day before and release it over the ocean. I have no idea if it's going to work—whether he'll be bound to obey via Lo's blood—but at least it's something.

"What now?" Lo says, watching me.

"We wait."

We sit on the sand, facing the ocean. Lo slips his hand into mine, rubbing his thumb in slow circles on my palm. He can tell that I'm on edge but knows me enough to leave well alone. I'll talk when I'm ready. And there's no way I'm ready right now. It's as if I'm holding myself together by the thinnest thread, and the minute I release it, I'll break. I'd rather save that for Cano. I remain silent.

"Can you do me a favor?" I ask Lo after a while.

"Anything."

I remove the lanyard from my neck. "Can you email the file on Cano to Echlios? Just in case Cano doesn't show? At least, we'll have a backup plan. He'll be able to send his men to scout these locations and we can find him that way."

"You'll be all right?" he says, taking the thumb drive from me. His back is to the sun and his face is shaded, but I can feel his worry.

"Yes."

"What if Cano shows up?"

I stare at him with a wry smile. "Trust me, you'll know it."

"I'll be right back," Lo says, dropping a quick kiss on my head.

I watch him over my shoulder as he jogs back to the house and disappears inside. The truth is, I don't know if Cano will come—it's a long shot at best to think that the summons will work.

But I want him to come.

I want him to show up and face me one-on-one. I want to feel his bones shattering beneath my claws, feel the final push of his heart as he draws his last dying breaths. I want him to pay for what he did to my mother...for what he did to Lo, and to me. The sky turns brittle and dark, thick clouds rolling in from the sheer visceral force of my thoughts.

Breathe.

I bury my hands into the wet sand beside me, willing my tumultuous emotions to fade. Facing Cano angry is a sure way to lose, but I can't help myself. My rage builds with every breath, rising like storm tide to suffocate me. Echlios was right—controlling the emotional side of things is going to be far harder than I anticipated. As if in confirmation, forked ice-blue lightning arcs across the sky.

Focus.

I take a deep breath and try once more to release the charged emotion. And then another, and another. Eventually I feel myself becoming calmer, and if the clearing sky is any indication, I'm doing a decent—if painfully slow—job of it. I've got to get this thing under control, because there's no way I'll have the luxury of this kind of time if I'm fin-deep in an actual battle.

I sigh, wrapping my arms around my knees, and stare at a now cloudless sky merging into the darker blue of the sea. Meteorological analysts must love all this unpredictable atmospheric activity—storm-tossed clouds followed in seconds by a perfect blue sky. They probably think the world is going to end. If I can't stop Cano, it just might.

I feel a tug deep in my center at the same time that an indistinct shape on the horizon catches my attention. The shape looms closer. My heart beats a shade faster before I realize that the essence isn't Cano's. It's Aquarathi, although for some reason, I can't identify it. It's fuzzy…tainted. Squinting against the sunlight, I hold my right hand over my brow as the shape condenses into a half-recognizable human form with pale white skin and jet-black hair.

"Hello, Nerissa."

"Nell?" I say, blinking.

"You're probably wondering why you couldn't see who I was," she says conversationally. "Oh, wait, you're not the queen anymore. But still, that wouldn't have helped, either."

"Why are you here?" I rise to my feet.

"You summoned, did you not?"

I frown. "I didn't call you."

"Right, right. You summoned Cano." She wrings the water out of her dark hair, pulling it over one shoulder and staring at me with venom in her eyes. "You think you're so important, all high and mighty…and even now, when you're nothing, you think you can control people. Cano sent me with a message for you."

"You're the spy," I say quietly. "From school. And the traitor—the one who led the hybrids to Waterfell."

"Look who's been paying attention," she says, grinning. "And not just me, Nova, too. Anyway, Cano wants you to come to North Coronado Island in one hour. Alone."

"Or what?"

"Or he takes out your entire family with his new toy." She smirks, her eyes glinting with malice. "You saw what it can do? With your mother? I hope every second was agonizing. She deserved it and more."

I restrain my immediate surge of rage. "You are nothing but a filthy traitor. You and your brother both. Where is Nova, by the way? Skulking?"

"We're hardly traitors if we're with the winning side. It's not our fault that your mother got soft in the end and had to be put down like the dog she was." Nell eyes me, running her hands along her bare rib cage. "I have to tell you I got used to being on land instead of down there in the dark, lifeless depths of Waterfell. And being human without being beholden to you is so much more fun. Cano made that happen."

I sneer, despite the hot wave of pain at her words about my mother. "Let me guess, he promised to give you a pair of legs…let you live on land with the hybrids…happily ever after. You aren't the smart twin, are you, Nell?"

Nell's eyes narrow, her fingers clenching at her side. "North Coronado. One hour. Bring anyone and your family dies."

"Right," I say, and walk toward her. It's gratifying to see her take a couple steps back, fear shimmering across her face for a second. "How much of that toxin was he able to make up after my mother destroyed it all? I'm guessing not much. He's bluffing about my family."

"Bluff or not, Nerissa, he's got enough to put down that slut handler of yours, just like he did your mother. Nova was the one who told Cano what she did, you know. What a stupid bitch, she totally forgot about the video feed—"

I cut off the last word from Nell's mouth as I lunge forward to grab a handful of her hair, yanking with all the force I can muster. I twist it around my fist so hard that tears snap to her eyes. "Stop. Talking. About. My. Mother."

"Cano said I'm not to be harmed," she gasps.

"I'm not harming you, sweetie. I'm just making things easier to understand. Cano lied to you. See, you're in way over your head. There's no way you can become human. Or hybrid. You have to be born that way. This isn't *The Little Mermaid,* and Cano isn't King Triton with a magic trident. Open your eyes—this is reality."

"You don't know what you're talking about," she says.

Something sharp and cold pricks into the soft flesh at the back of my neck. "Let her go," a pissed-off male voice threatens.

"Nova," I guess, releasing my hold so quickly that Nell tumbles to the sand. I turn to face Nova, who is holding a spear in one hand. I hadn't sensed him approach, but I'm not in the slightest bit afraid of him or the weapon pointed at my heart. I'm pretty sure Cano wants the joy of killing me for himself. Plus, I can move twice as fast as Nova on my worst day. I grin. "I was wondering when you were going to turn up."

"I can't kill you," he says. "I'm sure you already know that, but you need to be taught a little lesson."

"And you're going to teach me?" I scoff with as much sarcasm as I can manage. I fold my hands over my chest with a brief glance to the house. Lo is nowhere in sight, which suits me just fine.

"No. We're going to teach you."

Nell rushes me from behind while her brother comes in slashing with the spear. To my overheated senses, it seems like they're both moving in slow motion. I kick out backward, catching Nell in the chest, before swinging back around to bat Nova's spear out of the way. The underside of my palm comes up to connect with his chin and he stumbles back, the end of the spear propelled by my heel to crack him in the face.

Nell vaults to her feet, snarling, and charges me again. This time, I let the rage build and slam her with two closed fists right in the center of her sternum. The crack is loud and unforgiving, echoing down the beach like thunder. She falls to the sand with a gurgle and clutches her chest. I may not be her queen, but I can still hear her heart failing, crushed under the weight of unbreakable Aquarathi bones.

"No!" Nova screams. "I'll kill you."

I eye him calmly. "Who's learning the lesson now?"

"You psycho bitch!"

"You brought the psycho to this party, not me," I say. "You picked a fight with the wrong Aquarathi."

Power is churning around me in massive waves, making me feel light-headed. I hadn't considered how strong my mother's energy would make me…how unbelievably powerful she'd been. A power that she gave to me, every last drop, even though she could have saved herself. She *chose* me. Nova was the one to rat her out to Cano. Her death is on him.

Nova stares at his sister's shuddering body and flexes his fingers. His lips curl back from his teeth. Scarlet lights race along his arms in violent ripples, his Aquarathi eyes burning crimson. "I'm going to take you to Cano alive, but before I do, I'm going to shred you into so many pieces, you're going to wish you were dead."

"I'm so afraid," I mock.

"You should be."

With a demonic shriek, Nova flies toward me, the spear raised. I deflect it easily, and sharpen my fingers into claws as his body continues its course straight into me. He tries to pull back, but it's too late. Momentum drives him forward, his eyes widening just before he impales his stomach on the jagged points of my outstretched hand.

I hold him close, grimacing at the oily sensation of blood pooling over my fingers, my lips against his ear. "That's for my mother, you asshole."

24
Leap Before You Look

Shuddering into Aquarathi form, I swim the fifteen miles to North Coronado in seconds. If Cano wants me alone, that's what he's going to get. I'm going to give him exactly what he's asked for. Fighting Nova and Nell had been child's play. I can handle Cano. I'm going to rip his throat out. I'm so blinded by fury and the violent flood of my mother's strength that I don't consider anything but getting to that island. Not even Lo, whom I left at his house without a word, or Echlios, or anyone. They'll be safer this way.

Fish and other underwater creatures dart out of the way as if they can sense my brewing rage. I don't blame them—I can feel the energy crackling through my veins like wildfire. As I get closer to the Coronado Islands lying to the west of Mexico, a group of playful sea lions approach me—the same ones Lo and I met—but I scatter them with a growl. Their chirps of fear and sorrow along with the mournful expression in their eyes do nothing to weaken my single-minded resolve.

Cano.

Breaking the surface, I scan the horizon to see a boat—

Scylla—bobbing in the waves on the far side of the island. Aldon's boat. Of course he was the one to kill Aldon. I tread water for a few seconds, feeling the salt slide into my mouth and out through my gills. Everything inside me knows it's a trap, but the only way I can get on that boat is to transform into human form.

"Come, now, Nerissa," a jovial voice calls out. "You're not going to float to Catalina, are you? I just want to talk."

Talk, my ass.

It's not like I have much choice, especially if Nell was right about him not bluffing. I shift into human form, tugging on the clothing that Cano has so thoughtfully left near the gunwale. Not that I want to take anything from him at all, but the thought of standing nude anywhere near him creeps me out.

He's sitting in the captain's chair—cigar in hand—looking as if he doesn't have a care in the world. I'd be deceived by the pacifying smile on his face if it weren't for his eyes, which are watching me with calculating, deadly precision. He may look normal on the outside, but I can sense the tainted essence of Lo beneath the surface. This isn't Cano, I remind myself.

"Nova and Nell are dead," I tell him.

Surprise flashes across his face before it's concealed by that conciliatory smile. "Didn't expect that," he says. "Then again, you guys were…what's the word again? Oh yes, frenemies." Cano takes a long drag on the cigar, and leans back in the chair. "I tell you, I don't miss dealing with teenage issues on a daily basis. It's too dramatic," he says with an exaggerated flourish. His voice lowers a cadence. "But drama aside, the twins were loyal. I'll have to make you pay for that, you know. An eye for an eye, as they say."

"You'd know about that, wouldn't you?" I shoot back. "All the innocent lives you've taken?"

"All in the name of science, my dear," he says, leaning forward as if he's about to tell me a secret. "So, tell me, how did Neriah look when she died?"

Energy thrums in my fingertips, pushing against the boundaries of my tight human skin. Greenish-gold lights race along my arms and I can feel the bones pushing against my cheek and brow. Teeth crowd my jutting jaw as my spine arches, fins tearing through the soft cotton of the T-shirt.

Cano raises an eyebrow. "*That* bad?"

"I'm going to tear you apart," I seethe through a mouthful of fangs.

"Really?" he says, a maniacal look coming over him, his eyes darting to something behind me. "And how, pray tell, are you going to do that?"

I sense the presence of the hybrids a hair too late, but it's no matter. They're all going to die just the same. "Enjoy the show," I tell Cano. "Because when it's done, you're next."

Turning in slow motion, I face the six misshapen creatures standing on the wooden diving platform and eyeing me with varying degrees of hunger. One I recognize—the hulking creature on the surf beach and on the pier at Scripps. I *knew* I didn't imagine him! The others are equally hideous—half human, half Aquarathi—with blunt snouts and bulging eyes. Two of them have taloned limbs, while the one on the far right looks the most human but is covered in electric-blue scales. Intelligence shimmers in his eyes. He's the leader, I decide. Him first.

But I don't get the chance to reach him before the ugliest hybrid charges me with surprising agility. Shifting my fingers into pincers, I swipe at his body, leaving bloody red claw marks and gushing entrails in its wake. One down. Five to go. Whirling with furious speed, I duck and dart and kick my way through three more of the hybrids. With my new strength, they're hardly a challenge. Brimming with confidence, I grab the fifth one by the throat and squeeze, snapping his spine in a snap. I'm desperate to get to the last of Cano's hybrids—the blue one. I toss the dead hybrid into the water.

Before Blue Scales can move, I dive toward him with incredible speed. He darts out of my way, and we circle each other. I'm sure I must look as monstrous as he does with finned bones protruding from my head and back, and lit up like a Christmas tree. Blue doesn't attack—he dances out of the way of each of my strikes, almost like he's toying with me. I snarl. Enough of this. Dashing forward, I watch his eyes and veer right to duck behind him, rising and grabbing his neck in a headlock.

"Too predictable," I whisper into his ear. A line of razor-sharp fins emerge from my human flesh along the forearm that's just beneath his neck. Holding my prize, I look triumphantly to the captain's chair to find Cano, only to discover that the chair is empty.

A wet cloak descends upon my shoulders like a noxious cloud. Cano's behind me. "That was indeed a nice show, but sadly, you are the predictable one. Foolish girl, you haven't learned a thing, have you?"

Fear slithers through my veins for the first time since I've stepped onto that boat. Predictable. Reckless. Foolish. Arrogant. Idiotic. I'm all those things, and more. In a desperate move, I try to shift into Aquarathi form to protect myself from whatever's coming, but it's too late.

Something icy pierces the vulnerable side of my still-

human neck, and as my senses go fuzzy, all I can think is
that maybe Cano wasn't bluffing after all.

I'm floating in the ever-reaching arms of the ocean—
cocooned and safe. Dolphins gambol around me, sea lions,
too. Their happy chirps and barks make me smile, until
something scatters them and I am alone. I frown, shivering as the ocean grows cold, the warmth leached out of
it with their absence, but then Lo materializes in the distance, his handsome face beaming. Relieved, I reach out
to him until I remember that we are hundreds of feet deep
and he's in human form. Something isn't quite right. As he
swims closer, he clutches at his belly, his mouth opening in a
soundless scream. Blood pools in the water as a gaping hole
appears beneath his hands. A head emerges from where his
stomach used to be, and then a leering face. Cano, covered
in blood. Lo's blood.

I scream, and try to bolt upright, but my body refuses to
cooperate. Cano's face—unbloodied and normal—looms
over me. The last few minutes before I passed out come
back to me in a rush. He poisoned me...with the same biotoxin that had killed my mother.

"Am I dying?"

"Not quite yet," he says, checking my eyes with some
kind of metal instrument.

I try to move away from him, but once more, my body
remains unresponsive. I glance around, details still somewhat fuzzy. I'm tethered to a metal table. The delayed
thought hits me that we're no longer on Aldon's boat—
we're in some kind of facility on land. I can still sense the
ocean, so maybe we're not that far away from somewhere

familiar. I blink, trying to focus. How long have I been out? I stare at my arm and try to move my fingers. Nothing.

"What'd you do to me?"

"This biotoxin is my greatest work," he says conversationally. "We developed it to inhibit the hybrids, just in case, you know, they went berserk. And we had a few, I'll tell you. Scared the pants off me." Cano holds a scanner in front of my face and peers over it. "Then I…became one, and well, plans change, don't they? Part of one of the great things of being human is our adaptability. We go with the flow." He chuckles at his own joke. "The hybrid version of the toxin worked so well that I started playing around with its Aquarathi counterpart. You see, I needed a contingency plan for you." Cano walks away, stepping out of my sight for a second. "And especially after Neriah started losing focus, I knew I'd have to contain her at some point. Without Ehmora in the picture, I think she started to become sentimental."

"So you killed her," I say. "Just like that."

"Oh, trust me, it was painful. After all, I wouldn't be here without her research. She was quite brilliant, your mother. I will miss her greatly."

"You're a monster."

Cano laughs so hard that tears leak from the corner of his eyes. "Isn't it ironic that you are this fearsome creature with no natural enemies, but you act like a weak human instead of the predator that you should be. And yet here you are, calling me the monster."

"What do you want?"

"Power." His grin is crazed. "They called my research substandard. Fools! Now who is the one in charge? Who is the one with the superior intelligence? They'll rue the day they crossed me."

Ignoring his tirade, I arch my neck forward, trying to see my body. "Why can't I move?"

"Ah, that's the beauty of this toxin," he says, picking up and empty syringe. "Sea snakes...vicious little things. Did you know one drop of their toxin can kill a normal human? Learned about them from Ehmora." He glances at me with a knowing smile. "As I recall, she had a special fondness for them. In small doses, their toxin can cause paralysis and hallucinations. In larger doses, it can lead to unconsciousness. But I wanted it to be lethal, so I started combining different strains of the red-tide toxin we'd developed with it. After many failed experiments, I discovered a workable compound." Cano leans against the table and runs an icy finger down my cheek in an almost gentle—if revolting—caress. He stares idly at a shiny scalpel in his other hand. "Your mother was its first subject. It worked quite well, did it not?"

"I'm going to kill you."

"So you keep saying." He runs the point of the scalpel down the center of my chest. If I could shiver, I would. "But you can't move, lovely. And you're going to stay here so I can use as many testing samples as I need to create the perfect specimen." He taps my breastbone. "And the beauty of my toxin is that you can't transform, keeping you nice and malleable for my needs."

"Lo will come looking for me," I say through my fear.

"Lo," Cano says. "Of course he will, and I am going to drain every drop of blood from his body. He is perfect, you know. The perfect hybrid, master of land and sea."

"He'll die before helping you," I snap. Bravado is all I have left.

"I know. But you're wrong—he won't die," he says with a melodramatic sigh. "Young love is so predictable. He'll offer to trade himself for you, and then I will lock him up, promising your release. Of course, I won't keep my word because I need you, too, for my research. But he won't know that."

"Sounds like you've got it all worked out."

"I do."

I meet his eyes with a fierce glare. "There's only one problem. I know you don't have any more of the toxin prototype left—you used the last on me. Neriah made sure of that, didn't she?" I'm not entirely sure that Cano doesn't have any more of the toxin when I say it—after all, he obviously has enough to incapacitate me—but from the furious look on his face, my guess is right.

"Engineering a new batch as we speak," he says. "But don't worry, my sweet, my hybrids are more than capable of dispatching the remnants of your pitiful group." His smile is evil. "Now that you are no longer queen, no one will come running to your defense. To them, you are nothing but an exile. Now, don't move while I check on the serum, okay?" Chuckling once more at his own joke, he waltzes, whistling loudly, to the other side of the room.

Closing my eyes, I focus on the one thing I have left—the fact that my mind is fully functioning. The water in my body is weak, debilitated by the effects of the toxin, but it's still responsive. With a quiet breath, I try to extract water from the air around me, but it's as dry as a bone.

"That's why it's so cold in here," Cano calls out. "I've installed special watertight walls and floors, meaning that

that's not going to help you. Plus, we are in the middle of the desert. You can't glimmer me, Nerissa."

This is the moment when the fear becomes almost too much to bear, and I lose faith. If I can't use the water around me to form a glimmer, then I can't call Lo or warn anyone. I'm a sitting duck. Soren's words about being a better live sitting duck than a dead one come back to haunt me, and a hysterical laugh bursts from my lips. Why didn't I think twice about telling Lo where I was going, or asking Echlios for help, or bringing the vials my mother had hidden? Why didn't I do something smart, instead of the old jump-first-think-later Nerissa M.O.? I played myself right into Cano's hands.

Stop feeling sorry for yourself and think! I have to come up with something that will rattle Cano, something that will throw him off his game so maybe I'll have a window to use the little energy I have left.

"What about Cara?" I ask.

Cano stays silent for so long that I don't think he has heard me, but then he answers in an unemotional voice, "My niece will learn to understand what I'm doing here. Research is for the greater good of mankind."

"The greater good? Is that what you really care about? Let's be realistic. You only care about yourself. You don't care if anyone dies, far less your own niece." Despite Cano's mounting tension, I keep going, reckless. "You'd murder her in cold blood, wouldn't you? Good thing her father is back—at least he's a better father figure than you could ever be. He's a better principal, too." When I broke into Cano's office, I found an article tucked away in a file in the corner of his office. The journalist had called Cano a two-bit hack and described his findings on DNA as pedestrian. "Too bad you're just mediocre...*pedestrian*."

Cano moves swiftly for a man of his size, slamming his fist down on the side of my metal table so hard that my immobilized body is nearly jerked off. "There are ways to silence you, Nerissa," he snarls, saliva dripping into my face. "Like cutting out your tongue. Don't provoke me."

"I'm just saying what's already been said. You're a hack. You already know it. You said as much just before."

Cano grabs me by the hair, scalpel in hand, his face contorted with rage. I take a breath and summon the last bit of energy in my body, slamming a glimmer into him with everything I have left, straight to the center of his brain. He stumbles back, clutching his head with blood pouring out of his nose and ears. For a second, I think I've gotten him, but then he stops moving and opens blood-rimmed eyes to stare at me. He's too strong. With an unblinking stare, he reaches into his lab coat pocket and pulls out a second syringe. This one has liquid in it.

"Something tells me you're not worth the trouble," he says, advancing toward me.

I close my eyes and picture Lo's face—those navy eyes, the sharp cheekbones and gracefully winged eyebrows, his wide lips, his smile.

Lo, I'm so sorry.

The explosion catches us both by surprise, ripping through the foundation of the building, the smell of smoke acrid in the small room. Cano is thrown to the floor as newfound strength rushes through me. The blast allows air and water from the surrounding ocean to fill my nostrils. We aren't in the desert. We're on an island...surrounded by water.

Water! I inhale a deep, fortifying breath and call the ocean to me. The response is a ferocious surge from the cracked ground beneath us as salt water seeps through cracks, forming rivulets through the air to connect with my body. Desperately, I try to flush out the toxins, feeling the power spread and dissolve into my core as a tingling sensation starts in my toes, rushing up to my knees and my stomach.

But even in its mild form, the toxin is too potent. My cells fire and deaden within seconds. Cano stands, weaving, and grabs the fallen syringe. He rushes toward me, weapon raised. In a second, I command my skin to harden into Aquarathi scales, watching as the sheen of burnished gold flicker down my body. The needle bends and the tip snaps off. But as with the feeling in my legs, as quickly as the scales appear, they disappear. I can't fully transform for any useful period of time. My heart stops.

"More than two ways to skin a cat," Cano screeches. I gasp as Cano's thumb and forefinger pry my left eyelid apart, pushing past the protective human covering. Jerking upward in agony, I'm still shackled to the table. I yank so hard on my bonds that I can feel the warm fluid from my body pooling on the table beneath me. With crazed eyes, he throws himself on top of me and grabs hold of the broken syringe in his other hand. "An eye for an eye," he says, laughing manically.

The heavy metal door crashes inward off its hinges.

"Get the hell off her," Lo shouts. His face is the last thing I see before the syringe sinks into my eye.

25
Girlfriends, Grenades and Goodbye

The pain is excruciating. The sensation of the biotoxin slithering through my skull is nothing like the gentle paralysis I had before. This one makes every single part of me feel like it's being electrocuted cell by agonizing cell. My back arches, my wrists ripping free of the shackles, and I scream. Golden lights ignite like crazy explosions all over my body, leaving blackened spots along my skin in their wake.

Someone grabs Cano off me and tosses him into the wall. Out of the corner of my eye, I see him slump down to a motionless pile on the floor. The satisfaction is brief, eclipsed by another wave of blistering pain as my body incinerates from the inside out. The same rotting, burnt odor I smelled from my mother invades my nostrils. Is this what my mother felt the whole time she'd been sitting with me? She'd seemed so composed through the pain.

"Nerissa."

Lo's face swims into view. Oh God, he's so beautiful. I try to capture every part of him in my head, devouring every curve, every line, every hollow. But as fast as I try to hold on to any part of him, it slips away.

"I—"

"Hold on." Lo's voice comes as if it's far away, and I want to listen to him, but I can't.

He's fading. I'm fading. I close my eyes as a sharp pinch followed by a cool feeling moving through my veins makes me flinch. But then the sting is gone, and there's nothing but emptiness. I feel nothing. The arms of the ocean beckon.

"No," an indistinct voice says. "Stay with me. Nerissa, wake up. Wake up."

Strong arms lift me, cradling me against a warm chest. Hands flutter at my temple, brushing hair away and stroking my cheek. The soft whispers entreating me to stay continue, and then a boy's mouth is on mine, pressing into my lips, kissing me so sweetly one moment and so demanding the next that I can't help responding. I moan against his mouth.

"Kiss me back," the voice entreats. "Come back to me."

Images of a girl and a boy walking on a beach shimmer into two Aquarathi swimming in the darkest, jeweled depths of Waterfell. The boy's face comes into view, piece by piece, with a shock of silvery-gold blond hair and a pair of intense navy eyes. He's so familiar, but I can't quite figure out who he is. My brain won't cooperate. The boy's lips curve into a smile that makes a swarm of butterflies take flight in my stomach. My failing mind may not know him, but my body does.

I know him. I know this boy.

The boy's lips descend to mine, and this time I kiss him back, opening my mouth to his and feeling the memories flooding me with each second. My arms lift to wrap around his shoulders, and he crushes me to him, slanting his mouth against mine. Something glowing and glittery extends out of me to sink into him, our essences weaving together as one, and I gasp against his lips. Awakening, I stare into the most beautiful pair of eyes I have ever seen.

"Welcome back," Lo says.

"Whoa," I whisper. "Now I know how Snow White must have felt when Prince Charming kissed her awake."

"Charming has nothing on me," Lo quips, before dipping his forehead down to meet mine. "You really scared me for a minute," he says after a beat. "I didn't know if the serum your mother had hidden was going to work or not."

"How'd…you find me?"

"Group effort," he says with a nod over his shoulder. "Speio figured it out with the maps you had me send to Echlios, and we tracked you from my beach. Then we spread out and found remnants of the hybrids." He smiles, kissing me again. "That's how I knew you were close."

"This room…" I say, gesturing to the fractured space. "It was watertight. I tried to call to you, but it wouldn't work."

"I know. I couldn't even sense you, even when I was on the other side of that door."

I frown. "How did you know?"

"Jenna."

"Jenna?" I repeat in disbelief.

"Call it a sixth sense, call it what you want," Lo says. "We must have circled the Coronados six times before she insisted that we search on land despite it being illegal to set foot here. Sure enough, we found an abandoned military bunker that once again Jenna insisted we search. She blew up the door, and there you were."

"Wait, what? She blew up a door?" A vague memory of an explosion comes to mind.

"Grenades," Jenna says as she walks into the room and hugs me so hard that I wince. "Found them in a crate down in the back. You should see some of the heavy artillery down there—missile launchers, automatic weapons, the works."

"And you just used them?" I ask wide-eyed. "You could have blown yourself up or something."

"Got the door open, didn't it?" She throws her hands on her hips. "Hey, we are dealing with some seriously ugly business here, like hybrids who can't be killed with guns, Taser guns or any normal weapon. I didn't know what was behind this door, so I had to get creative. And it saved you, so I wouldn't be complaining."

"Not complaining," I say, shaking my head. "Just kind of freaked out right now that you literally just used a grenade that could have been a hundred years old. You could have taken your hand off!"

Jenna rolls her eyes. "It's a Mexican military base that Cano somehow got permission to use. I'm pretty sure that it's not that old. Anyway, I was careful. I watched a video on YouTube on my phone before I pulled the pin."

"You watched a *video?*" I splutter and turn to Lo. "You let her watch a video and use a grenade?"

He shrugs. "It's Jenna," he says, as if that magically explains it all, and then adds, "She had a grenade in her hand. You think I'm going to tell her what she can or can't do? No, thanks."

"I cannot believe the two of you."

"You are seriously going to give yourself a heart attack, undermining all our efforts to save you," Jenna says with a grin. "Now let's get out of here. Echlios is waiting outside with the boat in case you don't feel like swimming."

With Lo's help, I hook my legs over the side of the table, and then loop my arms around his shoulders. He scoops me up like I weigh nothing.

"What about him?" Jenna says with a glance at Cano's still motionless body. "Is he dead?"

"Hang on a sec," Lo says, helping me stand on woozy feet before crouching down over Cano. "I'll check." He places two fingers against Cano's neck, looking for a pulse, and nods to Jenna. "He's alive but out cold. What do we do with him?"

"Turn him in to the FBI," Jenna suggests. "He's still on their most wanted list."

"Sounds like a plan to me," Lo says, walking back to pick me up. "Let's get the hell out of here. This place gives me the creeps."

An enraged yell pierces the room, and suddenly it's like everything is moving in slow motion. Cano is no longer on the floor, but has managed to grab Jenna in a reverse head-lock. His eyes are clear and lucid, as if he's been biding his time all along and waiting for the right moment to attack.

"I knew I should have brought a second grenade," Jenna mutters, gasping against Cano's beefy arm jammed up against her throat.

"Don't worry," I say, sliding down Lo's body until I'm in a standing position. I squash a wave of nausea at the sudden vertigo. "He won't hurt you. Right, Cano? You told me you needed me. So let's trade—me for her."

"Nerissa, no," Lo says swiftly. I glare him into silence.

"And him?" Cano asks.

"You'll have to get Lo another time. Right now you have one thing to trade and I'm offering up myself. Release her and Lo takes her to safety. Take it or leave it."

"What about your people outside?" he says, having clearly eavesdropped on our conversation.

"They leave, too."

"Why should I trust you?"

I swallow, fighting the urge to close my eyes and lean against Lo. I don't want to appear weak to Cano. "Because you really have no other option to walk out of here alive, and you know it. Me for Jenna, and that's the last time I'll ask you."

I can see the wheels ticking over in his head, weighing the possibilities. It almost looks like he's about to give in when an ugly wide grin spreads across his face. He nods to someone at the broken entryway, and a person steps through it—no, not a person—a hybrid with electric-blue scales.

"Thanks for the offer," Cano says. "But I'll just take you both now."

Shouts from outside the bunker make my blood run cold. "Holy shit! Where're they coming from? There's too many of them." I recognize Carden's voice and then I hear Echlios bellow a series of commands to get in defensive formation.

Cano laughs. "Their odds of survival are slim. It's ten-to-one out there. They can't win against my hybrids, and neither will you. You should have killed me when you had the chance, and now you'll pay the price." He glances down at Jenna. "I think I'll kill this one first." But before he can do anything, Jenna flings her head back to connect with the bridge of his nose and jams her elbow into his side. Cano howls in pain, releasing his hold. Jenna skids to the floor and scrambles to where Lo and I are standing.

I raise my chin, glaring at Cano. "Sounds like great odds to me. I killed five of your hybrids single-handedly. What do you think trained Aquarathi guards are going to do to them?"

He snarls and rushes me just as Blue Scales darts toward Lo. Pushing Jenna out of the way under the metal table

I'd been lying on, I face Cano head-on, taking the hit on my shoulder. The collision makes me see stars. I haven't yet fully recovered and my reflexes aren't quite what they should be. Cano gets in a second hit to my stomach that thumps the breath out of me. He comes at me again and I brace for impact. But the blow doesn't fall. Instead Cano backs away as six surgical instruments come flying across the room like darts, impaling him in the arm and clipping his ear. Jenna winks, a tray following the route of the scalpels, which hits Cano square in the head, and he goes down like a sack of potatoes.

Meanwhile, Lo and Blue are locked in a fierce wrestling match, and moving so quickly I can hardly figure out who is who. Lo seems to have the upper hand, though, so I turn my attention back to a maddened Cano. We circle each other cautiously just as Lo and Blue go flying through a wall of glass to crash through to the other side. I watch triumphantly as Lo pummels Blue's face until blood makes his blue scales turn black, and when Lo hits him for the last time, Blue doesn't get up.

"Let me guess," Lo says to a dazed Cano, who is struggling to stand, and wipes his hands on his pants before stepping over the glass window. "He was your best guy?"

Cano stares from me to Lo, his eyes widening. He throws his hands into the air in a gesture of surrender as Lo moves to stand by my side. "I accept your offer."

"My offer was rescinded when you tried to kill me," I say coldly.

Cano grins, cocking his head to the side. "You know nothing about anything, do you, foolish child. About what's coming. You need me."

"That's where you're wrong, Cano. No one needs you.

Finish what you started. Finish your battles or run like the coward you are."

His mouth curls at the insult and the challenge. If looks could kill, I'd be a pile of smoldering ash, but I hold my ground.

"If there's one thing I know how to do, it's to survive," he screams. Cano's eyes narrow to slits and he charges me.

With a deep breath, I let him get close, so close that I can smell his fetid breath, before easing the two silver syringes out of Lo's back pocket. Time slows as I gather my strength to duck and roll beneath Cano, twisting to plunge the two syringes simultaneously into the back of his neck.

"Survive that, douche bag," I say, crouching on the floor and watching as his body crumples and starts convulsing.

"What'd you do?" Cano mumbles.

"Gave you a taste of your own medicine. You did say it was your best work, so I wanted to make sure you sampled both—one for the human side of you and one for anything that thinks it's Aquarathi." I lean down with a whisper. "My mother sends her regards."

Cano's body goes rigid as the toxins make their way simultaneously to his heart. He stares at me. His mouth opens as if he wants to say something more but can't, and then he falls backward, grabbing at his chest.

"Now he's dead," I say to Jenna.

She just looks at me and shakes her head. "And you worry about me with one grenade."

Outside, the scene is just as bloody as the one inside the room, with half-strewn hybrid bodies littering the grass and the nearby rocks. Echlios, Speio and Doras are standing like victorious gladiators in the middle of an arena, with triumphant grins plastered on their faces. Ten-to-one odds are nothing to them. Cano would have been better off sending three hundred hybrids instead of thirty.

"Good workout?" I call out.

Echlios grins and embraces me in a fierce one-armed hug. "Good to see you, my lady. Everything okay in there?" He nods toward the bunker.

"All good. Let's go home."

Echlios nods to Doras before helping me onto the docked boat. Doras, Erathion and Mae will stay behind to clean up and make sure that all evidence of any alien remains has been removed and destroyed. Despite technically being in Mexican territory, we encounter no issues, but that could be due to the rain and thick fog that has come out of nowhere… a manifestation of my panic, perhaps. Nonetheless, the trip back to La Jolla on the Marine Center's boat is quick. We dock it on the pier near our house. One of the men will return it in the morning—Kevin won't mind.

Soren is waiting as we walk up to the house, her eyes flooding with tears as I fall into her arms. "What am I going to do with you?" she murmurs against my hair. "Running off by yourself like that again. Are you hurt?"

"I'm fine," I assure her. "A little worse for wear. The boys and Jenna saved the day."

"Cano?"

"Gone, for good this time. Let's just say he got his just deserts."

"So it's over?"

I smile. "I think so." I glance at Jenna with a smirk. "Although someone needs to have a chat to Jenna about teenagers using grenades."

"She did *what?*" Soren yells.

Echlios and Speio both back out of the room, leaving

poor Lo to stand defenseless to brave Soren's wrath. I start laughing at the bewildered expression on his face, so hard that my stomach hurts, and then I'm crying, the tears falling out of me like a waterfall. It must be post-traumatic stress or something. I sink to my knees, my face in my hands, sobbing. Soren gathers me into her body, rocking me as if I'm a small child.

"It's over, my darling," she soothes me. "Just let it out."

"I don't understand," I sob. "I feel so out of control, like everything inside me is bursting into a million pieces."

"You've been through a lot in the last few days. It's natural."

"Not for me. I'm Aquarathi."

Soren brushes my hair gently. "One who is bonded to a hybrid prince. Human emotion isn't weakness, it's a gift. Treat it as such. To know love, you must know pain, and vice versa."

"It hurts too much."

"Tomorrow, things will be easier."

I raised drenched eyes to hers. "Will they?"

"Yes, I promise. Now, come on. Let's get you out of these clothes and into the shower. You'll feel better."

Soren's right. A shower will help. I feel as if I still have Cano's grime all over me, with the phantom remnants of his biotoxin crawling under my skin. In my bathroom, I turn the water on to as hot a setting as I can manage and scrub my human skin until it's pink and raw. I stay in the water so long that the pads on my fingers turn wrinkled and pruney, but I can't bring myself to get out.

My mind is racing. Everything is still so surreal—the fact that Cano is dead and the fact that there's no army of hybrids trying to kill me—that I can't quite get my mind around it. A part of me feels like I'll blink and wake up from a dream. But then I feel Neriah's power inside me and I know it's not a dream because she's dead, too. Sitting on the floor of my tub, I rock back and forth, letting the scalding hot water fall on top of my shoulders, and I cry for all the ones we lost or left behind. Most of all, I cry for the mother I've never known and for the mother she tried to be, right there at the end.

A knock on the door startles me. It's Lo. As I meet his liquid gaze, something in me settles. A calm floods my entire body as I feel his energy—and his love—flowing into me, and my sorrow recedes like an outgoing tide. I'm still sad but no longer hopeless. In that moment, I know that no matter what—no matter how broken I may feel—Lo will always be there to help piece me back together and to bring me back to him.

26
The Art of War

After the past few weeks, school is unexciting, which is fine by me. I'll take seven scintillating periods of structured teenage education, where lunch is the epitome of excitement, over rogue hybrids on the loose any day. We're back to pretending that we are regular kids who go to high school. Now that we don't have to return to Waterfell, we're going to stick around in La Jolla for Speio and me to finish our senior year.

Lo is recovering, albeit slowly. Although the serum stopped the effects of the biotoxin Cano engineered, it did too much damage for all the effects to be reversed. Although Echlios assures me that Lo's Aquarathi side will repair the damaged cells, there's no guarantee that Lo will ever be able to regain all of his memories. He still has gaps—areas that are shades of gray for him. But we're working on it together…work that he assures me is necessary to his complete recovery. I fail to see how extended make-out sessions help repair broken neurons, but I'm not complaining.

There's also been talk of starting another colony—a colony of exiles—somewhere in the South Pacific, maybe the

Tonga Trench north of New Zealand. I'm pretty sure that if we decide to do that, no one in Waterfell will care. It wouldn't be home, but it'd be something.

Speio pointed out that he'd be surprised if other exiles hadn't done that already. "You could be the Exile Queen," he said.

"Awesome, every girl's dream," I said. "Queen of the outcasts."

"Well, it's like the alpha wolves. If there are two of them, you make another pack. It's werewolf law."

I stared at him in disbelief, torn between giggling and wondering if he was being serious. "Where'd you learn that?"

"Sawyer told me," he said. "It's from *Teen Wolf.*"

Grinning, I shook my head. "Great, now we're taking living advice from Sawyer *and* an MTV show."

Jenna nearly died laughing when I told her what Speio had said. In his defense though, it isn't that far off from what we're probably going to do. I stash my books in my locker and head to the parking lot, instead of the cafeteria, where I'm meeting the others. We're going to try to get in one more surf session before finals. Oh, and we're totally ditching school to do it. Epic surf, Sawyer was saying.

I jam into the front seat of Lo's truck between Cara and Carden on one side and Lo on the other. They seem to have hit it off, despite the one-year age difference. Carden's technically enrolled as a transferring junior, but Cara doesn't care. She's already the envy of every female with a pulse at Dover.

"Seriously, why does every boy I'm ever interested in love to surf?"

I bite my tongue to keep from telling her that maybe she

should try falling for human boys instead. "Um, 'cause we live in Southern California?" I say instead. "Anyway, we've got a foam board for you and Carden's an excellent teacher."

Carden grins. "She gets a kiss every time she pops up."

"Eww, TMI," I yell just as Cara throws her arms around him and kisses him right there. I elbow Lo. "Let's go already before I start puking."

"Aw, they're cute as buttons," Lo says.

"Just drive," I tell him. I twist around to see that Sawyer and Jenna in his Jeep are right behind us, but I notice there's no sign of Speio. "Isn't Speio supposed to be riding with those guys? Did anyone tell him what time we were leaving? I haven't seen him since English first period."

Technically, I haven't seen Speio all day *and* night. Come to think of it, I haven't seen him for a couple of days at home, even though I've seen his face in school. He must have spent the last couple nights at Rian's.

"I talked to him," Lo says, pulling out of the lot. "He said he can't make it."

Surprised, I stare at Lo. "Since when is Speio not up for ditching school to surf?"

"I don't know. He was with Rian, and she looked pissed." Lo frowns. "They must have been having an argument, because Speio looked miserable, come to think of it. So when he said no, I kind of backed off, even though I was totally thinking it wasn't like him to slack off his warden duties." He shrugs. "I mean, where you go, he goes."

"Maybe it's different now, with everything being—" I glance over at Cara, but she's not even on this planet right now "—resolved." I pull out my brand-new cell phone. "I'll text him."

I try texting and calling Speio, but both calls go to voicemail and he doesn't answer my texts. He's probably with Rian, and the last thing I want to do is get caught in the middle of the two of them. I'll try again later.

The waves at Trestles are indeed everything and more that Sawyer predicted they would be—beautifully shaped, overhead perfect sets coming in in groups of four. With ecstatic shrieks, we pull on our wet suits and run down to the beach, boards in hand.

"See you later, suckers!" Sawyer yells, hopping over the white water and paddling out.

"That's my boyfriend." Jenna sighs. "Waits for no one, not even me. Surfing will always be the other woman in our relationship."

"What do you need a boy for?" I ask her. "To hold your hand? Come on, let's show these boys what we girls are made of!" Jenna's a capable surfer, although nowhere near Sawyer's league, but that doesn't mean she can't hold her own out there. She grins and follows me into the water.

When we reach the lineup, both Sawyer and Lo have already caught waves. Jenna and I sit on our boards for a minute. I trail my hands in the water, and stare at Cara and Carden on the beach. He's trying to teach her how to pop up on the board while it's still on the sand, but they seem like they're enjoying fooling around more than mastering surfing technique.

"They make a cute couple," Jenna says, following my stare. "Although she's more of an alien than he is."

I laugh at her droll expression. "Cara's okay."

"Yeah, she is," Jenna says quietly. "Out of everything that has happened this year, I think that's the craziest. Who would ever have thought that you two could be friends again?" She grins at me. "I guess what they say is true."

"What's that?"

"That hot boys and kissing can fix almost everything."

"Who says that?" I ask, giggling.

"Sawyer. He's a master of the haiku, that one." Jenna and I exchange a look and crack up.

"So, you ready to take on these monster waves?" I ask.

"You bet."

We paddle for the same wave together, but I let Jenna take it. I'll get the next one. Lying back on my board with the sun on my back and salt on my lips, I have to admit that getting back into the ocean feels great. And now that everyone's safe, it's even better. Watching my friends surf, I feel a sense of peace. As much as I miss Waterfell, spending today on the beach with them is the best feeling in the world, and worth so much more than any crown.

"Hey, babe," Lo says, padding alongside me and placing a wet kiss on my mouth. "Mmm, you taste like French fries. So, you going to float out here all day or what? Or you need me to school you some?" Grinning mischievously, he knows exactly what to say to get a rise out of me.

"The only person who'll need schooling is you, surfer boy," I say, paddling furiously past him. "Last one in is a rotten egg."

"You didn't say go. That's cheating!" I hear him say behind me, but I laugh and paddle hard.

I catch the wave easily, feeling the wind in my hair and the spray of water on my face. As I twist my hips, the board rips backward in a sharp cutback before gliding down the clear face of the wave. I trail my hands along the face and smile. A few cutbacks later, I see Lo hot on my heels, angling his board to dart past me. I have no idea how he managed to catch my wave. With a wicked grin, I summon my power and swell the wave beneath my board, gaining enough momentum for it to push me into shore.

"I win!" I yell as I streak past him.

Lo jumps off his board and tackles me so that we both fall into the knee-high surf. "Cheater," he says before kissing me senseless. Good thing we can both breathe underwater or else we'd have a situation.

"Stop," I tell him. "People are going to think we're drowning or something."

"Which people?" he says, trailing wet kisses down my neck. "All the others are halfway down the beach."

"Those people," I say, nodding to a group walking down the sand toward us. I blink. "Wait a second, that's Speio." I squint through the water in my eyes. "Who's he with?"

"Looks like Rian." Lo's eyes narrow. "Wait a sec, is that Madame Dumois? From *French* class?"

Speio looks miserable as he approaches us. "Can I talk to you?"

"Sure." Unleashing my board, I lay it on the sand and follow him a few steps away. "What's up?" I toss an eye over my shoulder. "And what's with Dumois? You're not getting expelled or anything, are you?"

"No." He looks at me, his eyes beseeching. "Nerissa, I want you to know that I didn't mean for this to happen. I didn't know, I swear to you."

"Swear what, Speio?" I say. Instead of answering, he stares at the sand as if he can't quite meet my eyes. "Spey, what's going on?"

"I've bonded with someone," he blurts out.

That's what he's getting all bent out of shape about? "That's awesome! Who is it?" I shriek, grinning. "When?

Why didn't you say anything? I'm so happy for you. That's great news!"

"No. No, it's not."

The deadness in his voice makes me pause, the rest of his words sinking in along with a feeling that something doesn't make sense. Why would he be here with Rian and Dumois of all people to tell me that he's finally bonded? And why would he tell me here of all places? My eyes fall on Rian and Dumois, who are studying us from a few feet away, and my stomach free-falls to the ground. Are they hybrids?

"Who did you bond with Speio?" I ask slowly.

"Rian."

Despite almost expecting the answer, I still feel a sense of suspended disbelief. "Is she a hybrid?"

"No," he says.

"What? That makes no sense, Speio. You can't bond with a human, and I'd know if she were Aquarathi."

He swallows. "She's no ordinary Aquarathi. She's an Aquarathi queen."

"Either I just heard you wrong or I'm imagining things. Did you just say she's an Aquarathi *queen?*"

"Yes." He grabs my hand and then drops it as if it's on fire. "I didn't know, Riss. I swear."

Staring at where he touched my fingers, I realize that I can no longer sense him. I was so surprised to see him before that I didn't realize that he didn't make himself known to me...because he's no longer bound to me. He's bound to someone else. Rian—a girl who's been on the edge of our circle at Dover all year, a girl who has been watching us, a girl who has secrets of her own—a girl who is the new Aquarathi queen of Waterfell.

But that doesn't make sense—I still would have been able

to sense her before relinquishing my crown. And Echlios would have known if a new regent was selected. None of this makes any sense.

"Are you with me, Speio?" I ask softly, praying that I've somehow imagined the horror of the last five minutes. I can't lose him, too. Not Speio...not my brother. "Spey?"

"No, Riss. I'm with her now."

As if on cue, Rian walks down to where we're standing. "Nerissa," she says in her soft musical voice as Lo joins us to stand beside me. She does not acknowledge him, keeping her eyes fixed on me. Golden lights flicker along my skin in response to the vibrant violet lights along hers.

"I don't understand. You're the new queen of Waterfell?"

She smiles. "No, not Waterfell. I am a very old queen. Older than you, in fact. My home is on the other side of the world in the Atlantic Ocean."

"The Atlantic? But there's nothing there."

"We did not choose to be seen."

Everything snaps together with swift succession—the images I felt on Aldon's boat after tasting the smear of Aquarathi blood...the unrecognizable alien tug I felt on the hockey field. That was Rian, *not* the hybrids. My mother's last words come back to haunt me. She knew about them— these *other* Aquarathi—and she tried to warn me that they were coming. So had Cano there at the end. And somehow, Lo had found out, too, which is why Cano had poisoned him in the first place—to conceal it from me. The world tilts slightly, making me grab Lo's arm for support. Rian's eyes flick to him, something shadowed flickering in their brilliant jade depths. She knows exactly what he is—who we all are.

"I don't get it," I say, more coldly than I'd intended. "Why are you here? What do you want?"

Her smile disappears. "You'll figure it out. You've proven yourself more than capable of working things out. Did you think your Waterfell was the only colony of Aquarathi?"

Despite my reeling senses, I keep my voice calm. "I guess I did. What does any of this have to do with me?"

"Everything. My people were banished, sent into exile by your great-great-grandfather. My family ruled the High Court, and we were betrayed, forced to leave Waterfell. Living in exile, we made a home, built our own colony and bided our time. I was sent here to study you, learn your weaknesses, and now I'm here to challenge you," she says. "For my throne."

"I hate to inform you of this, but I'm no longer a queen," I say, bristling. "If you'd done your research, you'd know that. And neither are you, queen of the exiles. So you've wasted your time. Go find someone else to fight, because I'm done fighting."

"You see, *Riss,* that's where you're wrong." Her tone is mocking as she steps forward to place a glossy coffee-colored scale in my hand. I close my fist around it without thinking. "Despite what your people may think of you for bonding with a…hybrid—" her contemptuous gaze flicks to Lo "—you are still their queen. Your throne can never be abdicated, your power never given away. You can lose it through death or bequeath it to an heir who is of age. Since you've done neither, you are still the true queen of Waterfell, Nerissa Marin. Therefore, I challenge you to a battle to the death. As the true heir, I challenge you for claim to the Waterfell throne."

"Claim, what claim?" I repeat, stunned, staring at the scale searing a hole in my palm. "Why?"

"The oceans of this earth aren't deep enough for the two of us. You are a disgrace to our ancestors. As is our custom, as a queen, I challenge your rule, and as your friend, I shall offer you six months."

"We were never friends, Rian, and you and I both know you are no queen."

She inclines her head. "Then why is my scale burning a hole in your hand? I am of royal blood, as are you. A lower-court challenge allows for three months of training before battle. I'll give you six."

"Six months for what?"

"To prepare your kingdom," she says. "Because when you see me again, it won't be for fun." She glances at Speio as if he's little more than a dog. "Come, Speio."

And I know then that she's only bonded with him to get to me. She's taken my brother. She's broken my family. She's threatened my people. A grim smile curls the edges of my lip into a half snarl, and I crush the proffered scale to dust in my fingers. "I accept your challenge," I say. "I hope you know what you've signed up for."

The thing is, I've fought queens before and I've won. If it's a fight she wants, it's a fight she'll get.

★ ★ ★ ★ ★

Acknowledgments

And now for the people who deserve ALL the thanks!

First, this book wouldn't be a book without the fabulous guidance of my tremendous editor, Natashya Wilson, who pushed me to take this sequel to the next level. Seriously, Tashya, thank you. You are officially inducted into the honorary Aquarathi Hall of Fame!

Huge thanks to the entire Harlequin TEEN team for all their support through this series.

I wouldn't be enjoying this crazy journey in publishing without my superfierce agents, Liza Fleissig and Ginger Harris-Dontzin. Thank you for rocking out with me.

To my critique partner and friend, Kristi Cook, you know I couldn't have written this book without you! Thanks for all the brainstorming sessions and your mad-awesome critiquing skills.

Thanks to my mom, Nan, who reads everything I send her no matter what, and to my brothers, Kyle and Kris, who always get the word out about my books.

To my ladies, Cindy Chok, Angie Frazier, Danielle Bunner, Kate Kaynak, Kim Purcell and Damaris Cardinali—

you are the real deal. Thanks for keeping a girl sane in the midst of all the madness.

To all the fans, readers, bloggers, librarians and book-sellers (especially The Voracious Reader and Anderson's Book Shop)—a heartfelt thank-you! An extra-special shout-out to Melissa Marie, Wanda, Trini, Brooke, Amy, Maura, Kayla and Meredith for all their awesome Tweets, Instagram and Facebook love—I have two words for you: TACKLE HUGS!

Last but not least, to my amazing family—my husband, Cameron, my kids, Connor, Noah, Olivia, and one forever cat that will always be in my heart, Alley—thanks for putting up with my crazy schedule. I promise things will go back to normal someday, but in the meantime, I will bake you all the cookies to make up for it. I love you to the ends of Waterfell and back.

Playlist

Oblivion (feat. Susanne Sundfør)—M83, *Oblivion (Original Motion Picture Sound Track)*

Meant—Elizaveta, *Elizaveta*

Words—Skylar Grey, *The Buried Sessions of Skylar Grey*

The Lion the Beast the Beat—Grace Potter & The Nocturnals, *The Lion the Beast the Beat*

Sweet Nothing (feat. Florence Welch)—Calvin Harris, *18 Months*

Walls—Stars, *The North*

Steve McQueen—M83, *Hurry Up, We're Dreaming.*

Rain—Blackmill, *Reach for Glory*

As the Rush Comes (Gabriel & Dresden Chillout Mix)—Motorcycle, *As the Rush Comes*

The Longest Road (Deadmau5 Remix Radio Edit)—
Morgan Page, *The Longest Road*

Between the Raindrops (feat. Natasha Bedingfield)—
Lifehouse, *Almeria*

Hold On When You Get Love and Let Go When You
Give It—Stars, *The North*

My Tears Are Becoming a Sea—M83, *Hurry Up, We're
Dreaming.*

Concrete Angel—Gareth Emery, *Concrete Angel (Remixes)
[feat. Christina Novelli]*

State of Grace—Taylor Swift, *Red*

Midnight City—M83, *Hurry Up, We're Dreaming.*

In the Air (feat. Angela McCluskey)—Morgan Page,
Sultan & Ned Shepard & BT, *In the Air*

Tiptoe—Imagine Dragons, *Night Visions*

The Last Time (feat. Gary Lightbody)—Taylor Swift, *Red*

Turn to Stone—Ingrid Michaelson, *Turn to Stone*

Questions for Discussion

1. Discuss the novel's title—*Oceanborn*. Why do you think the author selected this title, and do you think it was relevant to the book?

2. Discuss the warring themes of love and duty in this series— do you think Nerissa made good choices as a queen? Has she become more "queenly" from *Waterfell* to *Oceanborn*?

3. What do you think is motivating Nerissa's actions in the story? Do you think her motives are selfish or reasonable?

4. In *Oceanborn*, Jenna tells Nerissa that "being a leader isn't about being popular. It's about leading, even if that makes you unpopular." Do you agree or disagree with this? Why?

5. Do you think that the play in the novel, *The Importance of Being Earnest*, provided a good parallel to the lives of the Aquarathi? Did you see similar themes? If so, which?

6. In *Oceanborn*, how does the way Nerissa sees herself differ from the way others see her—for example, Jenna or Lo or Soren?

7. Do you think the Aquarathi should continue living in secret or reveal themselves to the humans? Why or why not?

8. Which secondary character do you think had the most pivotal role in the story and why?

9. Do you think that Nerissa did the right thing by abdicating her throne and choosing a life of exile? If not, what would you have done differently if you were in her shoes?

10. Discuss the setting in *Oceanborn*. How do you think it enhanced your experience of the story and your appreciation of the Aquarathi?

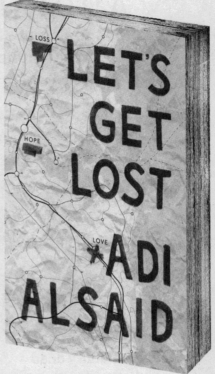